BASALT REGIONAL LIBRARY

99 Midland Avenue
Basalt CO 81621
927-4311

DATE DUE

NR 11 02		
AP 03 02		
AP 12 02		
AP 24 02		
MY -8 02		
MY 30 02		
JY 02 02		
JUN 25 2004		
GAYLORD		PRINTED IN U.S.A.

THE
DREAM
OF THE
BROKEN HORSES

THE

DREAM

OF THE

BROKEN HORSES

WILLIAM BAYER

POCKET BOOKS
NEW YORK LONDON TORONTO SYDNEY SINGAPORE

This is a work of fiction. The events described here are imaginary. The settings and characters are fictitious, even when a real name is used. They are not intended to represent specific places or persons or, even when a real name is used, to suggest that the events described actually occurred.

 POCKET BOOKS, a division of Simon & Schuster, Inc.
1230 Avenue of the Americas, New York, NY 10020

Copyright © 2002 by William Bayer

Library of Congress Cataloging-in-Publication Data

Bayer, William.
    The dream of the broken horses / William Bayer.
      p. cm.
    ISBN 0-7434-0336-3
    1. Suicide victims—Family relationships—Fiction. 2. Women
television journalists—Fiction. 3. Psychotherapist and patient—
Fiction. 4. Fathers and sons—Fiction. 5. Trials (Murder)—
Fiction. 6. Middle West—Fiction. 7. Artists—Fiction. I. Title.

PS3552.A8588 D7 2002
813'.54—dc21

                                              2001036627

First Pocket Books hardcover printing February 2002

10 9 8 7 6 5 4 3 2 1

POCKET and colophon are registered trademarks of
Simon & Schuster, Inc.

For information regarding special discounts for bulk purchases,
please contact Simon & Schuster Special Sales at 1-800-456-6798
or business@simonandschuster.com

Designed by Jaime Putorti

Printed in the U.S.A.

FOR DAD

"We know from our experiences in interpreting dreams that this sense of reality carries a particular significance . . . that is, that the dream relates to an occurrence that really took place and was not merely imagined."

—SIGMUND FREUD,
THE CASE OF THE WOLFMAN

The

Dream

of the

Broken Horses

PROLOGUE

As the boy approached the bathroom door, he heard voices coming from within. He was about to leave, seek out another bathroom, but then, when he detected a certain tone in the voices, a tone people use when they quarrel, he was drawn to stay and try to overhear.

A woman was speaking impatiently to a little girl. Her voice was difficult to make out; she had a strange accent, and the thick door muted some of her words. But he heard enough to understand that she wanted the child to go out with her and that the child was refusing to comply. The quarrel continued. As the woman's tone became more harsh, the little girl's resistance became more adamant.

Suddenly, he heard a quick sharp sound, followed immediately by a cry. He was appalled, frightened, fascinated too by the drama taking place within. The woman, he knew, had slapped the little girl. After that he heard the little girl's sobs interspersed with the voice of the woman trying to calm her, the soothing voice of an adult trying to calm an hysterical child.

Hearing movement behind the door, he backed away. Then, fearing he would be caught eavesdropping, he fled to another room and hid. A few moments later, he heard the woman and the girl pass by. The woman was speaking. "Come along now," she was saying, still impatient, "stop that whimpering. Hurry along or we'll be late." And although he could not see them, he imagined the woman impatiently pulling the little girl along by the hand.

Years later, when he grew up, he realized that though he had actually seen nothing, had only heard a few words and sounds, he had been a witness to a crime.

Yes, he thought, *I was a witness.*

O N E

A man and a woman are making love . . .

A hot August afternoon. A man and a woman are making love in a motel room. The humidity is high, the sheets damp. Venetian blinds cut the light, coating the glistening naked bodies of the lovers with stripes.

A fan spins on the dresser. A ribbon attached to its shield streams out. The room resounds with the noises of the lovers, their short, hard breaths and gasps. Outside the sounds of traffic and the faint din of the amusement park across the road.

The motel room is generic — dresser with TV set, queen-size bed, easy chair, worn beige rug. On the wall above the bed, a framed print of ice skaters, bundled in coats and scarves, gliding gracefully across a frozen pond before a steepled church.

On the wall parallel to the bed there's a large mirror in which the lovers occasionally glance at themselves as they move.

The man is lying on his back. The woman sits upon him. They move slowly, sensually, eyes locked, faint smiles upon their lips.

The woman is in her mid-thirties, the man younger, perhaps twenty-seven or twenty-eight. His hair is sandy, his lean body smooth. The woman's hair is dark and wavy. She is tall, tanned, with well-turned legs, the legs of an athlete, a tennis player.

Their wristwatches lie together beside the phone; their clothing is heaped upon the chair.

Afterwards they cling to one another, unwilling to break the seal of sweat. The man closes his eyes, dozes off while the woman turns to the mirror and stares at herself, seeking to discover whether their lovemaking has changed her appearance in any way.

The sky outside quickly darkens. Then a sudden summer shower. A bolt of lightning followed by a crack of thunder jars them from their reverie.

"That was close. Sounded like it hit the lake," the man mutters.

The woman's nervous. "It's getting dangerous now," she whispers. "I know he suspects. He's violent, too. At first I liked that about him. It made him interesting. My husband was just the opposite." She tightens her lips to show her contempt. "I'm afraid now of what he'll do when he finds out. And he will find out. I'm sure of it. Soon. Very soon, I think."

The man nods. He's heard this kind of talk before and doesn't know what to make of it. The woman lying beside him, this woman whom he adores—she's wealthy, divorced, free, can do whatever she likes. And if she's been involved with some kind of gangster, then, it seems to him, all she has to do is cut it off. He doesn't understand all this talk about "what he'll do when he finds out." But she seems to like talking about it. This "danger" she speaks of—it seems to make her hot.

Feeling her heat now, he kisses her, strokes her thighs, whispers: "Yes, I know . . . it's getting dangerous."

She responds with soft moans of pleasure.

Again they make love, this time even more slowly than before, with him quivering beneath, responding to her every subtle move.

They carry on like this for a long while. He loses track of time. The rain stops. The sky brightens. The strong afternoon light, entering the room through the blinds, again coats their bare bodies with stripes.

"Look! We're zebras!" he says, pointing at their image in the mirror.

She smiles. "Yes, love-making zebras," she whispers. "How do you like being humped by a zebra?" She touches one of the stripes on his neck. "Or would you rather be taken by a lioness?" She makes a catlike sound, then rakes her nails across his chest. She wags her tongue. "Or a slurpy puppy? You'd like that, wouldn't you? I know you would. I know how much you like being licked. . . ."

He revels in her antics. He can't believe that this is happening to him, that he's with this extraordinary woman, that they meet like this, make love like this, that she, with her beauty and wealth and social position, seems truly to love him despite the fact he's just a schoolmaster, new in town and virtually penniless. And she *does* love him. He's certain of it. And still he can't believe it.

She bends to lie down upon him, then whispers directly into his ear. "I love it that we meet here. This slovenly place, so anonymous. Just think of all the couples who've shagged themselves to heaven in here. I love leaving here reeking of you. That's why I don't shower afterwards. I like driving off with the smell of you on me. Then back home, stripping off my clothes, sniffing your essence again before I shower. Then maybe going off to a cocktail party where my friends ask me what I'm up to these days, why the glow upon my face, why I no longer spend afternoons playing tennis at the club. Then back home, lying in bed, thinking of you again as I fall off to sleep. Your hands on my flanks. My head between your legs. Licking you. Tasting you. Feeling you grow hard and throb and come inside my mouth. . . ."

Just hearing her whisper dirty to him like this as she pumps herself against him spins him into a whirlpool of desire. He's on the edge of climax. He can barely restrain himself . . . and yet he does.

They stop moving, become still, close their eyes, then begin to move again, this time even more tormentingly slow. Together they enter a state of heightened bliss wherein even the slightest movement sends powerful currents of yearning through their bodies, waves of longing and lust.

Suddenly the door is thrust open. A cone of blinding light slashes across the room. They turn together, see a dark figure dressed in a black coat and fedora silhouetted in the doorway against the powerful blast of the summer sun.

A moment of utter stillness as the three of them freeze—man and woman naked on the bed, poised figure in the doorway devouring the couple with his eyes.

Time expands. The moment is prolonged. The woman, feeling danger, recoils. The man grasps hold of her in an effort to protect. The figure in the doorway, empowered by their fear, raises something dark and long from beneath his coat. Then the double detonation, the explosions as two quick, loud reports fill the room, then, after a moment, two more. The walls recoil at the shock as the lovers, their faultless young flesh suddenly penetrated by hundreds of tiny steel balls, are hurled back against the headboard of their bed.

Their bodies spasm without control. Dark ruby-red blood sprays like geysers from their wounds.

The echo fades. The lovers, bodies tangled, cease writhing and lie still. The figure in the doorway lowers his gun, sniffs at the room, which smells now of gunpowder, bowels, and blood. His eyes take in what he has wrought. For a moment they feast upon the carnage, illuminated as if by a spotlight by the rays of sunlight breaking through the door. There is, he recognizes, a terrible beauty before him, the beauty of young bodies freshly torn by death. After a moment, he pulls his hat down to his eyes, gathers his dark coat about his frame, turns, and leaves.

T W O

O r so I imagine it happening . . .

I've been sketching this imagined motel room slaughter for several hours, dividing it into scenes, depicting it from various angles. Even now I'm sketching it while seated at the bar in Waldo's, working on the final close-up of the woman. I want to get her face just right—the questioning look in her eyes.

The bar's busy tonight, all the tables taken. Media people, print and network journalists, are gabbing away, exchanging rumors and gossip, as they have every night since the Foster trial began, which we have all come to town to cover.

I finish my drawing, turn the page of my sketchbook, then look around. The Townsend is the media hotel in town; Waldo's, just off the lobby, is the media bar and assembly point. It's a good bar, posh and dark, with mahogany paneling, soft leather seats, art deco sconces, and an excellent barman named Tony who wears a white jacket and an ironic smile.

Tony, his manner announces, has seen it all. Nothing about us or the trial surprises him. Sophisticated journalists from New York, some with famous faces seen often on TV, do not impress him. He has assured me (for he and I have lately become friends) that they would not impress Waldo Channing either, the man whose portrait hangs on the far wall, for whom the bar is named.

"Wasn't he something?"

Tony stands opposite me across the bar. He's stopped to chat, as he often does when he has a free moment. "Noticed you gazing at his picture. Mr. C. knew everybody, you know—all the big stars and personalities. Hemingway and Dietrich, Bogart and Bacall. He wrote about them. They were his friends. He could have lived anywhere—New York, London, the French Riviera—but he chose to stay here. Gotta respect the guy for that. He never gave up on this burg even when most everyone else did. . . ."

Tony moves away to take an order from a slinky black female reporter at the other end of the bar. I make a quick sketch of him shaking a drink. He has sleek silver hair that nicely reflects the light and a complexion so deathly pale I doubt he ever goes out in daytime.

When he returns, he glances at my drawing.

"Not bad," he says. "The guy who painted Mr. C. never knew him." He gestures again at the portrait. "Did it all from photographs. Shows too. Made him look stiff, which Mr. C. wasn't. He was smooth, suave— could turn a mean phrase, too, when he had a mind. Some didn't like him for that, when he made fun of them in his column. But most respected him. He could charm your pants off. First time I saw him I was tending bar at the opera. Came the intermission, all these folks stream toward me, pushing and shoving to get their orders filled. Then I notice this handsome fellow standing among them, smiling at me, waiting his turn. I fill his order first, dry vodka martini with a twist. He thanks me, tips me double. Later I learned he was the columnist, Waldo Channing. So, see, now it's an honor for me to tend bar here."

An honor. Sure, I can see that. For even if the oil portrait of Channing makes him look a little stiff, as Tony says, it also displays his sleek good looks, savoir faire, sense of entitlement, and self-assurance. The brittle quality is there, too, the studied artificiality. And there's a gleam in the painted eyes, the barest trace of his malevolence. I know why Waldo Channing didn't move to London or New York, why he stayed in Calista, where he was born. Because here he could preside not just as society columnist but as social arbiter, a person to whom others revealed their confidences, which he could then preserve or betray as he saw fit.

"Lady wants to meet you," Tony says. He subtly gestures toward a blond sitting alone at a table near the wall. I recognize her at once: Pam Wells, reporting the trial for CNN.

"Interested?" Tony asks.

"Sure."

Tony raises his right eyebrow, slips away. I pick up my drink, pencil, and sketchbook. Ms. Wells observes me closely as I approach.

"Well, hi!" she says, brilliant blue eyes glowing, voice full of good cheer. "Thanks for stopping by."

"Thanks for asking me."

"What a scene!" She indicates the room. "I feel lots of fear and loathing swirling about. I've been sitting here asking myself, 'Pam, what's a nice girl like you doing in a snake pit like this?'"

In person she's looser than on the air. Also she doesn't punch up her words the way they train TV reporters to do. She looks softer, too, blond shoulder-length hair hanging loose, lips unpainted, a good quantity of fun in her lively eyes. Her bust is fine, her scoop neck reveals attractive freckles, and her bare arms show well-tended muscles. I won't have much trouble falling for her if she lets me, I think.

I offer my hand. "David Weiss."

"I know," she says, giving it a nice shake. "I'm Pam—"

"Yeah, isn't it great—we both know who we are."

Her laughter's silver. "I've seen your sketches on the air, David. You're really kicking our butt."

"Henderson's good."

"He's all right, but his stuff doesn't stand up to yours. My producer's looking for someone else."

"Poor Henderson."

"Guy can't cut it . . . what're you going to do?"

Like everyone else in the room, we're talking shop. Two tables away, beneath the portrait, a quartet from NBC are paying rapt attention to Waldo Channing's successor, local society columnist and social guru

Spencer Deval. Deval, who wears an ascot and affects a British accent, is short, stout, bald, has a slack mouth, a smirky grin, and yellowish bags of flesh beneath his eyes. A habitual name-dropper, he's also a compelling storyteller. Last night he held forth at the same table to a spellbound trio from CBS.

"I hear Westin's flying in for a one-on-one with Kit Foster," Pam says.

I shrug. "I'm just the sketch artist. I don't know anything about network stuff."

"A lot more than 'just the sketch artist.' I've seen your ID drawings, David. They're fabulous."

I make a demure gesture to show modesty.

"Oh, they are!" she says. "The Zigzag Killer—you had him cold. Also the Saturn Killer and that guy out in Kansas City who kidnapped those little girls. When they finally catch the monsters, they look just the way you drew them. Yet you never saw them. Or did you?"

"I saw them in my mind," I tell her.

She peers at me, interested. "How'd you do that?"

"The way everyone else does. Eyewitness interviews."

"But your drawings aren't like everyone else's. They're uncanny dead-on accurate."

I shrug.

"What's your secret?"

"It's not like it's a magic trick."

"I'm just wondering how you pull the memories out. You must identify strongly with your witnesses to get inside their heads so deep."

"Yeah," I agree, "that's pretty much it."

She orders another round. As we talk more about the trial, I notice the way her breasts strain against the cotton of her blouse and the firm, bare, tanned flesh of her arms.

She doesn't have much use for Judge Winterson. "Old battle-ax," she calls her. I tell her if Winterson hadn't been tough and refused to allow cameras in her courtroom, I wouldn't have gotten the gig.

"Courtroom sketching's not really your thing, is it?"

"Basically I'm a forensic artist."

"Ever do fine art drawing?"

"Gave that up years ago."

"You're from here, right?"

I nod. "How'd you know?"

"Heard it around. Go to the local art school?"

I shake my head. "They've got a pretty good one, but I went to Pratt."

"Ah!" she smiles. "Midwest boy goes off to the Big City."

"Yeah, that was me, the kid from Calista, desperate to get to New York, seek my fortune. Not like Waldo Channing." I gesture toward the painting. "Tony the barman says old Waldo could've lived anywhere in the world, but he liked it best here. Tony finds that admirable."

Pam Wells gazes at the painting. "Something funny about his eyes." She squints. "Like maybe he wasn't 'nice people.'"

She's got that right, I think.

AN HOUR AND TWO ROUNDS later, we're feeling mellow, interested in one another, flirting. Since she's the one with higher status, I feel it's her place to make the first move.

Finally she glances at her watch. "Almost midnight." She leans forward, smiles, drills me with her sparkling eyes. "Want to come up to my room?"

"That's a very pretty proposition," I tell her.

As we exit, I catch a look from Tony. Again he raises his right eyebrow, his trademark comment on matters of the heart.

MAKING LOVE TO PAM WELLS, I find, is like driving a luxury racing car, say a Ferrari or Lamborghini—not that I've had much experience with either. The engine purrs. You feel its power. There's a perfect fit between driver and machine. You hug the road even as you take dangerous curves. The ride's oil-smooth, faultless, elegant. Even the sound of the meshing gears is beautiful.

Which is not to suggest that Pam makes love like a machine. On the contrary, I find her tender. Nor does she give off an aroma of fine leather and wood; I smell wildflowers on her skin. She's a gifted lover who makes me feel like the expert lover I've longed to be but never had the courage to believe I am. In short, she makes me feel like a great driver, even though I suspect it's she who's doing the driving and me who is the car.

"You're fun," she whispers as we rest. "I had a hunch you'd be good at this."

We share a laugh, then she eases me out, telling me she has to get her "beauty sleep."

"I'd ask you to stay but I know if I do we'll end up playing through the night," she says. "Then I'll look a mess when I do my early stand-up at the courthouse door."

Riding the hotel elevator down to my floor, I realize I've been blown off . . . but in the nicest, coolest, most flattering way.

THE FOSTER CASE: Another one of those sordid celebrity cases that grip the country from time to time. The kind that, just when you think you've had enough of it, along comes a new twist and then, stirred by the media frenzy, you're back in thrall.

I'm here in Calista as part of the pack covering the event. On the very day Judge Stella Winterson banned cameras from her courtroom, I was hired by ABC on an urgent contract basis to make sketches of moments of high drama and conflict during the trial. This entitles me to a reserved seat in the courtroom behind the defendant's table, from which position I have an excellent view of the cast of characters:

The Judge—big, bosomy black woman with white hair, stern demeanor, occasional maternal smile;

The Jurors—usual mix: men and women, blacks and whites, maintenance and postal workers, with a couple of college grads thrown in;

The Defendant, Kit Foster—waiflike with off-center eyes, heartbreaking smile, punked-out auburn hair;

The Prosecutor—young, earnest, articulate, organized;

The Defense Attorney—mellifluous voice, expensive cream linen suit, flowing gray hair that curls over the collars of his beautiful made-to-measure pink shirts.

In the most banal terms, the case comes down to this: super rock star Caleb Meadows (he of the whiny attenuated voice) was alone one afternoon this past winter with his girlfriend, performance artist Kit Foster (she of the scrawny, multi-pierced body), in the Dinosaur Room of the new architecturally brutal Calista Museum Of Natural History.

Moments later Meadows was dead. Hearing screams, a museum security man arrived on the scene to find Foster covered with Meadows's blood and an old hunting knife buried in Meadows's chest. Later examination of silent videotape from a surveillance camera showed the couple apparently quarrelling fiercely in the moments just before the knifing.

According to Foster's statement, made just afterwards to police, Meadows pulled out the knife, thrust it at her, and, in the ensuing struggle, stabbed himself. She was vague about the details, couldn't explain how she, at a mere one hundred two pounds, managed to deflect his attack and turn it around. "I've blocked it all out," she said. Ironically or by design, depending on one's point of view, these final contested moments were, on account of the odd place where the parties were standing at the time, invisible to the surveillance camera and thus not recorded on tape.

Friends of the victim subsequently informed police that Ms. Foster was a heroin addict who had threatened Mr. Meadows with violent bodily harm should he break up with her as he'd been threatening to do for several weeks.

Friends of Ms. Foster counterclaimed that Mr. Meadows was a degenerate who'd threatened to carve up Ms. Foster if she ever left him, which, that very afternoon, she'd informed him she was about to do.

Complicating these contesting claims was the fact that Mr. Meadows and Ms. Foster had each named the other sole beneficiary in reciprocal wills executed several months before. It has been estimated that at the time of his demise, Mr. Meadows was worth approximately sixty million dollars.

So there it is, a tawdry case involving selfish, tacky people with too much money and fame. Yet, the commentators keep reminding us, it has all the ingredients of a great crime story: the essential trio of sex (kinky), lies (stupendous), and videotape (incompetent), not to mention drugs (hard), money (huge), and murder (most foul).

Depending on one's point of view, the killing was either accidental as the defendant claims, or calculated and committed for profit as the prosecution wants desperately to prove. In short, a case of no particular consequence that carries no moral lesson or tragic overtone that may illuminate our fragile human condition. A case that would inspire no interest at all except for the celebrity status of the principals and the odd venue of the scene of blood.

Frankly, I don't care a damn about it and am totally neutral as to its outcome.

CALISTA IN SUMMER: The air hangs heavy here, fraught with high humidity and heat, while the river gives off pungent fumes. I love this kind of weather. It reminds me of the summers of my youth—sweating on baseball diamonds beneath relentless sunshine broken only by occasional fierce summer thunderstorms.

We had one last night. Thunder boomed. Great sheets of rain lashed the streets. Calista's landmark mid-century twin towers, hometown architect Eric Lindstrom's heroic Tower of the Great Plains and Tower of the Great Lakes, stood stark and lonely against the lightning-torn sky.

The residue is still upon the city this hot, damp Tuesday morning, as I make my way along rain-slick sidewalks to the welter of video units and trucks parked at the rear of the ornate beaux-arts Calista County Courthouse.

I've come in search of Pam Wells, hoping to discern whether she regards me as but a one-night stand. Also to see if, indeed, she slept well last night, or, like me, tossed and turned during the storm, unable to expel the memory of our coupling from my mind.

I find her in the CNN Winnebago being worked over by a frizzy-haired hairdresser.

"Well, hi!" she says, with a cheerful smile. "How're you?"

"Sleep well?"

"I did, yes. Thanks for asking."

Since the hair gal ignores us, I figure it's okay to behave as if we're alone.

"Any chance of a get-together after work?"

"How 'bout Waldo's, seven o'clock?"

"Sounds good." I turn to leave.

"Oh, David—" I turn back to her. "What I said last night about you being fun—I meant it."

I search her eyes seeking some trace of irony. Finding none, I still can't bring myself to believe her.

"You're a flatterer, Pam!"

The hair-dresser snorts a laugh.

"Millie here knows better. Don't you, Millie?"

"Go away, Mister," Millie instructs. "Pam's having a bad hair day and I got just two minutes to fix her up."

WINDING MY WAY BACK through the labyrinth of cables, past RVs where other star commentators are being groomed, I feel a certain compassion for on-camera reporters. Not, certainly, on account of their salaries, which are scandalously huge, but for the requirements that they always look great and that their clothing always appear fresh and pressed. Unless, of course, they're covering a hurricane or a war, in which case they carefully ruffle their gorgeous manes of hair and sport tailored bush jackets to resemble dashing correspondents of old.

Having no particular desire for fame or fortune, I prefer my sketch-artist's role behind the scenes. All I have to do is make drawings that, when broadcast, speak for themselves. And if a certain point of view should happen to intrude, it will not be my excitement over this or that twist in the tale, rather my fascination with humans in conflict and their grace or lack of same when under stress.

I enter the courthouse, hang my press ID necklace about my neck, get in a line for the metal detector, hand over my sketchpack, endure a frisking, pick up my pack, then head for the elevators and the fourth floor.

The first two weeks of trial have been hard as I've labored to create an image-bank—portraits of the principals as well as a selection of their facial expressions at moments of excitement, amusement, confrontation, or that great criminal trial standby, the stare of righteous indignation. Now, with these images in hand, I've got the job down to a manageable level, able to quickly build composite drawings that can illustrate most every courtroom situation likely to arise.

Whenever a new piece of physical evidence is introduced or a new witness appears, I immediately sketch it, him, or her, adding same to my store. At which point, unless I sense a fine moment is in the offing, I feel free to go about my business, confident that I can create strong drawings that will please my producer so long as she receives them in time for broadcast on the early evening news.

Courtroom work is not my specialty; forensic ID portraiture is. I've made perhaps a thousand drawings of wanted felons, with an accuracy that has propelled me to the top rank of my profession.

These days, what with Identi-Kits and computer programs that the average cop can operate, we forensic artists are often viewed as relics. But composites generated by systems are never as accurate as freehand drawings made by an artist working closely with an eyewitness. We can introduce emotion, depict characteristic expressions, even create the aura of a subject, his menace, craftiness, joviality, or, if appropriate, that distinctive strange, almost bland, vacant stare so typical of the socio- pathic killer.

I enjoy forensic work, the unhurried pace of it, long eyewitness inter- views, evoking the original trauma of the crime, breaking through screen memories to uncover real ones, then the drawing itself, the slow accre- tion of detail that can bring a portrait of a criminal to life.

So why now courtroom sketching, a business requiring the speedy production of cartoons? For a change of pace, perhaps, a chance to make a few extra bucks, but most especially for the opportunity to revisit my hometown where another homicide, one that took place more than a quarter century ago, grips my interest and fills my dreams with an inten- sity the Foster trial cannot even begin to touch.

I have come back, you see, to try and resolve my past. Also, hopefully, to complete my father's great unfinished case.

THIS MORNING THE COURTHOUSE seems especially tense. Perhaps it's last night's thunderstorm. Exasperated reporters, having bad hair days, lope morosely along the corridors. Even the bailiffs, normally an even-tempered bunch, appear unduly stressed.

I nod to acquaintances, catching, in the process, a dour glance from Jim Henderson, the CNN courtroom sketch artist whom Pam Wells's producer wants to replace. Just as I'm about to show him a friendly smile, my own producer, Harriet Mills, sidles up.

"Hear about the overnights? We beat the competition again thanks to you." Harriet's a tough go-get-'em type. She grins at me. "Hear you were seen leaving Waldo's with Pam Wells. What's she like?"

I shrug.

"Well, I hear she's a real bitch," Harriet says.

There's more media baiting and back-biting at this trial than any I've attended, perhaps because the pickings are so slim and the competition so intense. I feel bad for Henderson. He's a nice guy and his drawings are decent enough, but he lacks a feeling for trial-as-theater. I'm pretty sure he dislikes me because he thinks I think I'm slumming. Probably he also finds it disgraceful I don't stay in my seat, but instead wander out of the courtroom on my own business for hours at a time.

Judge Winterson's bailiff appears at the door.

"Okay, folks—you can enter now. Keep it orderly. No shoving like yesterday. Judge was plenty pissed when she heard." Dramatic pause. "Believe me, it's not fun for us when Judge gets pissed."

And with that in mind, we of the media herd file solemnly in to take our seats.

COURT LETS OUT EARLY. There are evidentiary issues that require thrashing out. I speedily finish up my drawings, drop them off with Harriet at the ABC suite, plant a kiss on her less-than-tender cheek, then call down for my rental car in the hotel garage.

*   *   *

3:00 P.M. I'M DRIVING EAST along Dawson Drive entering the narrow portion where it passes through elegant, shady Delamere.

The old suburb has changed since my day. High-rise condominium buildings have sprung up. But many of the old mansions still stand far back from the road behind walls and gates with enormous well-groomed lawns in front. Long, straight driveways lined with evenly spaced trees lead to these stately homes, contrived to remind the visitor of the approach to a French chateau or English country manor.

The architecture here is European revival: mansard-roofed Normans, brick Georgians, timber-in-stucco Tudors, even a couple of Gothic-style castles with arched windows and crenellated parapets. All were constructed with lovingly lavish detail between the end of World War I and the start of the Great Depression.

I slow as I approach the Fulraine house. Built in the manner of a Palladian villa, it is perhaps the finest residence in Delamere. I pull over opposite the gate, then peer in, able to catch a glimpse of the entryway at the far end of the gravel drive.

Here, I know, there's a turnabout where, in the days when the Fulraines gave parties, limousines would pull up and leave off guests. I also know that on the far side of the house, facing Delamere Lake, lies the tennis court where Barbara Fulraine played steamy matches against her young lover, Tom Jessup, while her sons, my classmates, whom Jessup tutored, frolicked in the vast swimming pool further down the slope.

But it's the gate itself that's burned into my memory. As I look at it now the old television images flood back: Barbara and Andrew Fulraine begging for the return of their kidnapped daughter, Belle, as microphones are thrust toward them and cameras mercilessly strobe their tear-streaked cheeks.

I feel my own eyes grow wet as I recall those impromptu press conferences. I will never forget something my father said to my mother as we watched.

"People love this kind of thing. It shows them even the rich and powerful feel pain."

Oh, yes, I think, Dad was right . . . for what happened before this gate was the very substance of tragedy—the anguished bellowings of great lords rolling in the dust.

ONCE PAST THE FULRAINE PLACE, I pick up speed, arriving a few minutes later at a cluster of apartment towers where Tremont Park once stood.

It was one of the great amusement parks of its era, a complex embracing dance halls, lovers' lanes, penny arcades, cotton candy stands, and numerous marvelous rides: Flying Ponies, Flying Scooters, Mill Chute, Roller Coaster, Over the Falls, and the inimitable Laf-in-the-Dark, where, alone in a boat in total blackness on a murky canal, between the barrel of stars and the enormous sliding spider, I imagine Barbara Fulraine and Tom Jessup kissing for the first time.

My destination today is the Flamingo Court Motel situated on the other side of Dawson. It was shabby then and still is today, but not by any means repulsive—a decent enough place for a family to spend the night or a pair of lovers to while away a hot summer afternoon.

The two-story powder-blue facade sports a fading mural of pink flamingos caught in mid-flutter between the trunks of lime-green palms. Looming above is a neon sign depicting a flamingo and, beneath that, another informing weary travelers and/or randy lovers that vacant rooms are still available within.

I pull into the lot across the street between Moe's Burgers and the Shanghai Sapphire Restaurant, then cross the street on foot and enter the motel courtyard. There's a rectangular pool here, its aquamarine interior fading, rust stains on the surrounding concrete, and water that appears less than perfectly clean. Two small boys splash happily at the shallow end. Nearby a woman in the skimpiest possible yellow bikini reads a magazine while taking the sun on an angry orange plastic-strap chaise longue.

Not many clients at this hour. Perhaps a slew will appear at dusk. I note the configuration of the court—a two-story U-shaped building with exterior staircases and covered open porticos providing access to room doors running along the courtyard sides.

The office is to the right of the entrance. I'm about to turn toward it when I notice the woman on the chaise observing me over the top of her magazine.

"Hi," I greet her.

"Hi, yourself. Help you?"

"I'm looking for Johnny."

"You'll find him in the office," she says, then turns back to her magazine.

I find Johnny Powell leaning on the reception counter gazing at the TV set across the room. A Calista Forgers-Boston Red Sox game's in progress, the score 5-2 in favor of the Sox.

I introduce myself.

"Oh, sure," he says, "been expecting you. You picked a good time. Nothing going on now 'cept the baseball. Forgers playing like fools today."

If I've ever seen a person to whom one could apply the moniker "geezer" it would be the old man grinning at me now. He's stooped, thin, gaunt, unshaven, a pair of bright blue eyes in a tanned, cracked-leather face. His voice is cracked too, with a nasal twang. He looks the type who play wily old prospectors in westerns, spouting cracker-barrel philosophy about the lure of gold and how it's akin to the lust stirred by a wicked woman.

He mutes the TV with a remote.

"So you're here to see old two-oh-one?" he says. "Been a couple of years since anyone asked. First year after the killings they came in all the time, curiosity seekers wanting to take pictures and snatch up souvenirs. Mr. Evans—he's dead now, that's his daughter sunning herself outside—he decided not to let the room out or even paint it up. 'Just leave it be, Johnny,' he told me. Didn't even want me to scrub the bloodstains off the walls, though of course I did. We charged 'em five dollars for a five-minute look. Made a bushel of money that way.

When stuff started getting swiped—ashtrays, lamps, even one of the pictures on the wall—he had me screw everything down. For a couple years old two-oh-one was our top-producing room. Biggest thing ever happened here at the Flamingo. Biggest thing ever will happen, I betcha."

I ask Johnny if he was here the day of the murders.

"Sure was," he says. "Was afternoon man then, same as now. Knew the couple too, since they were regulars. Knew Mr. Jessup actually. Not the lady. Never exchanged two words with her. He'd come in, register, then wait for her up in the room. Or, if Mrs. Fulraine got here first, she'd wait out in her car till he registered, then follow him up. He always asked for an end room near the parking. That meant one-oh-one or two-oh-one depending which was occupied.

"He was a nice fella. Soft spoken. Private schoolteacher, you know. Taught out at the Hayes School. Later I heard that's where they met. Seems she sent her boys there. One day she goes out to meet the teachers. Then—pop! Wow! Flyin' sparks! That whole summer they met here three, four times a week. They say she's the one actually paid since she was rolling in moolah and he barely had a pot to piss in. . . ."

After a brief negotiation, I hand him fifty bucks for a one-hour rental, plus an extra ten for himself.

"Hour's kinda odd length of time," he says, handing over the key. "Won't take you but a couple of minutes to get the feel. 'Less you're planning on takin' a snooze. . . ."

No napping, I tell him, I'm going to be sketching and that's a slow process, a lot slower than taking photographs.

"You'll find it pretty much the way it was. Furniture and bed frames still original. New mattress, of course. New carpeting. New TV. Maybe nine or ten paint jobs and seventy or eighty changes of shower curtains, but otherwise just the same."

The woman in the yellow bikini watches me as I ascend the exterior stairs. When I pause on the balcony, she raises herself from the chaise and marches authoritatively to the end of the diving board. As she does, I notice endearing pink marks on her back from lying against the plastic straps. After another quick glance at me, she makes a beautiful swan dive into the water. If I were an Olympic judge I'd give her a 9.5.

Two-oh-one is a decent-sized room, not a confining shoe box the way they build them today. The moment I enter I feel like an intruder. Since I know sketching will calm me, I go to the bed, sit on it, set the pillows behind my back, then prop my sketchpad against my knees. I check my watch. 3:30 P.M. It was a little before four in the afternoon when the killings took place, just this time of year.

I gaze around, look carefully at everything, then close my eyes trying to imagine how it happened that day, what it was like.

I'VE BEEN SKETCHING for an hour. I finish up my drawing: the open doorway filled with light, the broken figures on the bed lost in shadow. I set down my sketchpad, lie back, my heart beating wildly in my chest.

I'm exhausted. Perhaps, I think, this project will prove to be a mistake. Then I tell myself: It's no mistake. Difficult at times, sure; fraught with the pain that often accompanies necessity, but that's the point, it *is* necessary if I'm ever to obtain peace of mind.

I get up from the bed, go to the open door, and peer down over the balcony at the pool. The two boys are now playing in the shade, while their mother, once again on the chaise, bikini top untied, bare back to the sun, turns her head slightly to engage my eyes.

I quickly shut the door, cutting off the light, then return to the bed to rest a while in the gloom. This room, I think, was the Scene of Blood, and thus it is well that I have come here to breathe the air, take it all in with my eyes, understand how sounds reverberate in the space and the particular way the light cuts across the floor. I scan the walls knowing there is impacted in them echoes of the death throes of Tom Jessup and Barbara Fulraine, whose agony, in some deep sense I cannot understand, seems still present in the room.

WALDO'S, 7:00 P.M. I sit at the bar, sipping from a margarita beautifully made by Tony, awaiting the arrival of Pam Wells.

The usual suspects are out in force. The CBS group. The NBC

group. Spencer Deval, at his regular table beneath the portrait, holding forth to a different media contingent tonight. The slinky black female reporter from Chicago, who, Tony has told me, has a contract from a New York publisher to do a book on the trial, regards me curiously from the far end of the bar.

I hear there are two other reporters' books under contract, but I doubt it'll matter much whose book comes out first. The way I see it, this time next year the Foster trial will be deader than dust.

"There you are." It's Pam.

"Hi. Want a drink?"

"Sure." She grins. "Then let's go upstairs. I've been thinking about you all day. There're all sorts of nasty things I want us to do."

She takes a sip from my margarita while waiting for Tony to make one for her. "What'd you do this afternoon anyway?"

"Went out sketching."

"In this heat?"

"I found a cool place."

"You like to keep busy, don't you? Keep your hand moving. Now why do you feel you have to do that, David?"

"I think it keeps me sane."

She thinks that one over. "You're a pretty interesting guy." She smiles. "I have a hunch about you."

"What's that?"

"That you've got a story."

"Everyone's got a story."

"Sure. But yours is special. You're up to something here. That's what I think. I trust my hunches too."

Tony presents her with her drink. She clicks her glass against mine, then sips.

So she thinks she's got me psyched-out after one session in the sack. *Well, two can play that game,* I think.

"If I tell you my story you might lose interest."

"Try me and find out," she challenges.

"I'll think about it. You know what they say about you, Pam?"

"What?"

" 'She's a real bitch.' "

She stares at me a moment, then laughs. "Well, maybe I am," she says. "And maybe I've met my match."

Having nicely cleared the air, we finish our drinks, then ascend to her room where we nearly tear off one another's clothes.

AN HOUR LATER, showered and refreshed, we step out the front door of the Townsend, stroll along the night streets of downtown to Riverwalk, then on to a neighborhood of bars and restaurants along the Calista River, an area locals call Irontown.

Calista, in fact, is a very interesting city, as special and atmospheric in its way as Boston or Miami. It's a true river town with all the trappings that description implies—bridges, docks, barges, boats. It has a sultry river town charm and the play of light can be spectacular. There's ethnic richness, a plenitude of trees, and a locally much-spoken-of "Athenian" aspect, Calista's self-image as an oasis of culture in the culturally barren Midwest. Beyond all that, it's the kind of city that, long after you've left it because you thought it wasn't your rightful place, continues to haunt your dreams.

There was enormous wealth here as there was in all the great rust-belt cities of the American plain, wealth on a scale that people from the East rarely understand. People here formed fabulous art collections. Growing up, I played with kids whose parents had Rembrandts in their houses, in one case an El Greco hanging in the dining room. The rich here built distinguished cultural institutions: churches, temples, a magnificent art museum, fine symphony orchestra, world-class university and medical center, ballet company, repertory theater company, champion sports teams, elegant, gracious suburbs.

They also built great factories and mills that were among the most hellish places on earth, polluting the river to the extent that at one point it literally turned red from the iron precipitate runoff from the smelters.

As befits a city of great wealth and power, Calista too became a city of great crimes and, sometimes, punishments: the Wandering Strangler killings, the Heller-Hinton murders, the Barton Paint Factory explosion . . . and a good fifty notorious murders and disasters more. Some were solved, others not, some still haunt the populace, while others obsess only those whose lives they touched. In the latter category, I would place the double murder at the Flamingo Court of Tom Jessup and Barbara Fulraine, which the local press dubbed simply "Fulraine," because in this city Fulraine was a name to be reckoned with, while poor Tom Jessup was pretty much a nonentity.

Pam Wells and I are standing in one of the semicircular overlooks on Riverwalk. The snaking Calista River glows below us, its surface, reflecting the night sky, smooth like slick, black oil, broken only by the girder bridges and jackknife drawbridges that cross it at odd and varying angles.

"So this is the famous river that turned red?" Pam shakes her blond hair free, sniffs the air. "Doesn't smell bad at all."

"The redness was a warning call. They knew they had to clean it up. See that?" I point south toward a cluster of slag heaps and the ruins of a steel plant.

"Looks like a bunch of old dinosaur bones."

"That's what's left of Fulraine Steel, once one of the great mills here. Last twenty years the steel business has gone to hell. Most steel's imported now or made in energy-efficient plants. But there was a time when those ruins were alive with smelters, when black smoke and cinders poured out of the stacks. The smell pervaded the city. You couldn't walk the route we just took without getting cinders in your eyes. It was dirty here, also rich, a place where wealth was created beyond men's dreams. Iron ore and coal came downriver on barges. Steel was forged, then shipped back out to the world. Steel is what made this town . . . and for a while ruined it too."

The restaurant we choose is a noisy yuppie hangout, filled with affluent young people talking and laughing—stockbrokers, attorneys, ad execs. As we walk in, a few people, recognizing Pam, follow us with their eyes. Passing a table, I pick up a snatch of conversation about the Foster trial:

"It's the money. Jury'll see she did it for the money," a young man tells his date.

"She'll walk. Reasonable doubt," his companion replies.

We find a secluded booth in back, order pasta, salad, and a bottle of wine, then gaze into one another's eyes.

"Funny how I keep wanting to flatter you, David," she says. "You bring out the nice girl in me, I guess."

She asks me about past relationships. I describe my brief failed marriage, aimless dalliances, numerous ruptured love affairs. When I ask about hers, she tells me she lived with a guy the last four years, a news producer for another network whom she met when she first moved to New York.

"We broke up this winter. It was pretty traumatic. Lots of quarreling about who owned what and who'd get to keep our great apartment on Riverside Drive. After torturous negotiations, I bought him out, then decided I didn't want to live there anymore. Too many memories. So I took the CNN job in D.C. and put the apartment up for sale. Now he says I only wanted it out of spite."

She asks about my life in San Francisco. I describe my loft on Telegraph Hill, the view over the Bay, and how in the early morning the sun seems to rise in slow motion before my bay windows, radiating light so blinding I'm forced to turn away. I tell her about my pair of big World War II-vintage tripod-mounted binoculars installed beside my drafting table in the bay, which I use to watch ships come and go during the day and to scan the city for interesting dramas at night. I tell her I'm something of a voyeur and that she's right, I do have a busy hand. I tell her about my hundreds of sketchbooks, how together they constitute an enormous incoherent diary of my life—places I've visited, people I've met, situations I've observed. It's as if, I tell her, I'm seeking to draw some kind of definitive scene, which, when sketched, will solve a mystery I seem to have spent the better part of my life puzzling out. I tell her I don't know what this mystery is, nor why I feel compelled to solve it, but that I believe its source is here in this city where I was born.

She goes quiet after that, making me think I've spoken with too much candor. Then suddenly her face breaks into the warm smile that makes her so effective on TV.

"I wish like you I'd come here on a quest," she says, "instead of to cover some scummy trial." She locks eyes with mine. "Like I said, David, you're a pretty interesting guy."

We grin at one another, slurp up our spaghetti, devour our salads, work our way methodically through our bottle of wine. Then, like lovers, we slowly make our way back to the Townsend along lonely Riverwalk lit by gracefully turned streetlamp candelabra, breathing air that smells of iron and dead flowers, arms loosely embracing one another's waists.

THREE

A man and a woman are making love . . .

The phrase haunts me, seems to follow me around like a shadow. I want to put faces to these people. All I'm drawing now are their heads lost in shadow. I want to see them clearly, hear their voices, the rhythm of their breathing, the thumping of their hearts. Most of all, I want to see their *eyes.*

This morning I ask Townsend Hotel management to move me to a lower floor. The desk is happy to oblige as most guests prefer the upper floors with views. But I want the sound of the streets and the strange play of light that comes from passing traffic in the night.

I'm delighted when they offer me a room on the second floor. It takes me but fifteen minutes to move. After stowing my clothing, I post several of my drawings of the lovers on the wall facing the window.

Tonight, with the room lamps turned off, I study them as cars come and go, casting headlight beams into the room. These beams hit the eyes on my drawings filled in with graphite pencil. The graphite reflects the light, the eyes glow, and then, as the cars pass and the headlight beams cross the space, the eyes move, *they come alive!*

THE FULRAINE KIDNAPPING: I'm sitting in the local archives room of the Calista Public Library across from Danzig Park, going through old file folders containing yellowed clippings culled from *The Calista Times-Dispatch*.

An odd aspect, one I'd forgotten, was that the Fulraine infant was not kidnapped in the traditional sense. There was never a demand for ransom. Rather Belle Fulraine disappeared at the age of three, along with a recently hired au pair, never to be seen again.

This au pair, one Becky Hallworth from Dorset in England, turned up dead a week later, her nude torso (missing head and hands) washed onto the eastern shore of Delamere Lake. For several days her torso remained unidentified, causing the police to dub her the "Lady of the Lake." When, finally, an ID was made, based on freckles and birthmarks viewed in a pornographic film in which Becky, unbeknownst to her agency and employers, had recently performed, the implications of the kidnapping grew grave.

Could little Belle have been rented or sold by Becky to purveyors of child smut and Becky killed because, due to the prominence of the Fulraine family, her collaborators in the crime were frightened by the unexpected heat? If so, where was little Belle now? Had she too been killed? Would films or photographs turn up on the underground pedophile market in which the innocent child would be shown abused?

I read all the clippings, then carefully study the accompanying photographs.

The Fulraines were quite a pair. In one picture of the couple, Barbara, though in grief, exudes extraordinary glamour. Her haunting, almond-shaped eyes and well-modeled mouth, pale skin, and luxurious wavy, dark hair make her appear more like a movie star than an aggrieved local socialite. Standing beside her, Andrew Fulraine exhibits matinee idol looks. Steady eyes, squared-off jaw, hair meticulously combed back, his physiognomy speaks of willfulness and power, a refusal to be broken no matter the depth of his pain.

Little Belle is appropriately cute and vulnerable, while the older Fulraine sons, my schoolmates, six-year-old Robin and seven-year-old Mark, combine the manly demeanor of their father and the soft, exotic beauty of their mom.

In another photo of Barbara alone, she's handsomely dressed in a light cashmere crewneck sweater with single strand of pearls about her graceful neck—so different from her garb in a photograph in my possession that shows her in quite a different frame of mind.

Finally, there's Becky Hallworth in whose lightly freckled countenance I detect the seeds of the Fulraines' misfortune. There's definitely something "off" about the girl, a glint of craziness in the eyes, of slutty fiendishness in the mouth, of come-hither-and-be-damned in the grin. I ask myself how closely the Fulraines interviewed her and whether they were so dazzled by her schooled British accent and peaches-and-cream complexion that they neglected the most elementary of precautions—checking the girl's references.

Strangely Waldo Channing's column on the subject is the most poignant in the folder. I say "strangely" because Waldo's columns tended to be pretty superficial stuff. Yet every so often, particularly when people he cared about were involved, he managed to rise to the occasion:

> It's been a year since my dear friends, Andy and Barb, lost their child. When I write that word "lost" I feel a great throb in my chest, for of course little Belle Fulraine wasn't lost at all. She was *taken*. And therein lies the tragedy.
>
> "Tragedy" is a term I don't use lightly. Those of you who regularly drop in on This Department know I generally concern myself with the lighter side of life. Who's who, who's been seen with whom, who's been doing what. I write about theater, film, and cabaret, love gained and lost, weddings and divorces, tales of our Fair City, its bars and clubs, fun and froth, and, occasionally, its underbelly too. But rarely tragedy. Tragedy, you see, is really not my beat. But today is different. Today is an anniversary no one wants to celebrate, an anniversary that brings tears to my eyes.

A greatly adored girl child just three years old is taken by the caregiver in whom her parents placed a sacred trust. No note is left behind, no ransom demand is made. The little girl seems literally to disappear off the face of the earth. Later the body of the cruel betrayer is found, horribly mutilated as if to conceal her identity. Numerous theories are spun, but in the end neither the police, the FBI, nor private detectives hired by the Fulraine family can come up with an explanation.

A child disappears, a year passes, and there is no explanation. Think about that. Think, most particularly, about what that would mean to *you,* were you the parent of the stolen child.

It would surely mean indescribable grief. Despair, terror, also anger, blind fury, and yet more grief.

Someone once wrote: "That which does not kill me can only make me stronger." I think the person who wrote that was a fool. For to be a victim in a situation like this is to face what is perhaps even worse than death.

Andy and Barb live separately now. Their friends, though hopeful, do not believe their marriage can be saved. I have recently spoken to them both. There is only one thing, they assure me, in their hearts: a prayerful wish that their stolen daughter will one day be returned home safe. Experts in these matters do not hold out much hope, but hope is all the Fulraines have. So they cling to it. And we must too. For at this point, a year later, hope is all there is.

I didn't set out today to write a sappy column about how brave my friends have been. But they *are* brave, braver than I can

conceive. One purpose of this column is to
let them know that we stand with them and
always shall.

Another purpose is to appeal to anyone,
anywhere, with any knowledge that may
illuminate this matter, to come forward
now and tell the authorities what you
know. . . .

Yeah, Waldo could really lay it on when he had a mind to. Reading
his piece, I sense he genuinely cared about the handsome young
Fulraines, truly did grieve with them, was appalled by the crime committed against them . . . not only because it was so terribly cruel, but also
because it contradicted his world view.

Waldo Channing, you see, saw the world in terms of social events—
beautifully assembled parties, exquisitely hosted dinners, lavish weddings, luxurious homes, chic resorts. He savored urbane gatherings,
suave displays of wit, most of all that odd symbiosis between people of
wealth and people of achievement, society and celebrity, money and
fame, summed up in his favorite phrase (purloined, perhaps unknowingly, from Stendhal): "The Happy Few."

It's a phrase that turns up again and again in his columns through the
years in numerous and varying contexts:

" 'The Happy Few' were out in full-dress force last night, at the opening of Symphony . . ."

"After the party, the Charles Dunphys, Brownie Dillers, Babe
Keniston, her veddy good friend, Timmy Knowlton-Smith, and others of
'The Happy Few' assembled in the back room at Rob's for nightcaps,
laughter and lotsa giggles . . ."

"The fun masquerade party over at Andy and Barb Fulraine's was
well attended by members in good standing of our 'Happy Few.' Dot
Bartlett took first prize for 'best headdress' with her amusing . . ."

Ad nauseam.

But still I must concede this to Waldo—when he really cared (a rare event), he was capable of setting aside such drivel and writing from the heart.

THE OTHER PHOTO OF BARBARA: I am studying it again as I sit in my rental car parked across from the Doubleton Building at the corner of Harp and Spencer Avenues—the very building where I believe it was taken more than twenty-six years ago in a back-room photographer's studio on the seventh floor.

Despite the numerous times I've looked at it, this photo always amazes me. Time, I think, to confess that it is this picture that has brought me back to Calista, that it is the driving force behind my quest.

Please imagine: a black and white posed studio photograph of a beautiful woman, glamorously lit as if by Horst or some other skilled Hollywood photographer of the 1940s.

Imagine her dressed in lustrous black leather riding boots, dark fitted jodhpurs, and, except for a pair of long, laced pigskin gloves, otherwise totally bare above the waist.

Imagine her leaning forward in this amazing state of dishabille, one raised foot resting on a bench, engaging the camera with beguiling eyes.

Imagine precisely rouged lips (the lipstick showing black in the photo), loose, dark hair cascading in waves across pale shoulders, perfectly proportioned breasts surmounted by taut upraised nipples, while long, multistory black pearl earrings dangle seductively from her finely modeled ears.

And if all this is insufficient to hold your attention, imagine The Lady holding a long, narrow riding crop, bowing it slightly as if to test for stiffness and strength, while she gazes at you-the-viewer—the voyeur!— with an expression combining amusement, desire, hauteur, and, perhaps too, the barest modicum of scorn.

The picture is compelling not only on account of the beauty of its subject and the fetishistic manner in which she's been attired and posed, but also because of the exquisite photographic technique with which the image has been rendered. The lighting has been designed to highlight each engaging detail—sparkling eyes, glossy lips, delicate areolas, the very texture of the lady's skin. And the illumination of the background wall has been contrived so that vectors of light and shadow converge to make delicious contrast with her luminous naked upper body as well as the dark riding attire she wears below.

I'm certain this picture was taken with a large-view camera under studio conditions, perhaps with the photographer hiding his head beneath a cloth. A signature stamp graces the bottom of the print, raised in fine silver script: *Studio Fessé*. A pseudonym, of course, one he used on this particular brand of work. His actual name, I happen to know, was Max Rakoubian, still listed on the register in the Doubleton Building lobby.

A BLACK ATTENDANT with jaundiced eyes takes me up to seven in a very old, silent cage elevator. After I step out, the elevator descends like a waterlogged raft sinking slowly in a lake.

I make my way down a hushed corridor lined with pebbled glass doors bearing the names of firms: FESTIVE FOLLIES; HYDE INSURANCE; MARITZ INVESTIGATIONS . . . PHOTOS BY MAX.

I knock on MAX. No response so I turn the knob and walk in. There's an odd aroma in the reception area, not the photochemical smell I expect. I hear hissing on the other side of an inner door. I move toward it, call out:

"Anyone here?"

"Yeah," a male voice responds.

"Okay if I come in?"

"Suit yourself."

I push the door open, and the smell hits me at once, a foundry smell, hot metal and gas.

A sweaty, muscular man in his thirties, stripped to the waist, face covered with a visor, is applying a welding torch to a sculpture in which a number of skeletal figures, men, women, and children, are entwined with one another in an agonized group embrace.

"Sorry, can't shake hands," he tells me. "Hope you don't mind pigeons. They fly in on hot days. One comes at you, my advice is duck. 'Less you like pigeon shit on your face."

The windows are wide open, the sound of the city—street noise, car horns, distant sirens—makes a din against the hissing of the torch. Two pigeons flap about near the ceiling, while another stands attentive on the windowsill as if deciding whether to depart or stick around.

"I'm looking for Max Rakoubian."

The sculptor grins. "Max's been in the ground eight years. I'm Chip, his son . . . one of them anyway. I took over his lease, never bothered to change the name on the door."

"Or downstairs."

He grins again. "Kind of a tip of the hat to the old man, you might say. Me being the only one of his bastards ever gave a shit."

He finishes his weld, closes the valve of his gas tank, puts down his torch, and pulls up his visor.

"Bet I know why you've come," he says, wiping his face with a rag. A good-looking guy despite a couple days beard growth, he reminds me of one of those underwear models, the brawny kind with surly mouth and soulful eyes.

"Wanna know whether I got some of Pop's old 'art studies' sitting around. Willing to pay top dollar for them, too."

"Not exactly."

He gazes at me. "Well, I doubt you dropped by to see *my* work."

I turn to the sculpture. "Interesting piece."

"It's for a Holocaust Memorial. Commissioned by a synagogue in Van Buren Heights."

"The one on Dover?"

Chip nods.

I introduce myself. "I'm interested in your father's work, Chip, but I didn't come looking to buy more of it. Just want to ask a couple questions about a photograph I've got." I hold up my eight-by-ten envelope.

"Woman with a whip?"

"How'd you know?"

Chip peels off his gloves, wipes his face again and then his chest, pulls on a black T-shirt, and extends his hand. We shake.

"Don't know which one you have there, but they're all pretty much alike. Different models, different poses, sometimes with some poor naked slob down on his knees groveling or licking the lady's boots. But the idea's always the same. Women rule. Dominatrixes. I know a lot about that, see, 'cause my mom was one of 'em. Which was why Pop adored her." He gestures toward my envelope. "Let's see which you got."

We adjourn to the reception room to inspect my photo. Chip nods the moment I bring it out.

"Sure, I recognize her. Mint condition print, too." He turns it over, points to some numbers scrawled in pencil on the back. "Pop's darkroom notes, enlarger lens opening, print timing and such." He turns the picture again, appraises it like a connoisseur. "Mint condition vintage print. I've had collectors offer me two, three thousand bucks for one like this. Seems vintage prints of Pop's 'Fessé' line are highly desirable these days. Too bad they didn't discover him before he died. He could've used the cash."

"Do you have more like this?"

Chip raises his eyebrows. "So you *are* a collector?"

"No, but I'm curious about this woman. Do you know anything about her?"

Chip scratches his neck. "Hot day. What say we go down to the pub across the street? Buy me a couple of brewskies, I'll tell you what I know."

THE RATHSKELLER'S one of those Teutonic places you find throughout the Midwest: imbedded exterior timbers, dark paneling within, wooden booths, gemütlichkeit stuff on the walls—oversize meerschaum pipes, fancy old beer steins, photos of stout guys in lederhosen, the occasional cuckoo clock, and friendly buxom waitresses wearing dirndls. In short, the opposite of Waldo's.

Chip Rakoubian is greeted warmly as we saunter in: "Hey, Chipo!" "Hot 'nuf for ya, Chipper?"

We take a booth, he orders two mugs of the local brew, and, when they come, he takes a long, slow sip, then settles back.

"Pop was a fine all-around photographer," he tells me. "Weddings, portraits, catalogue work. Also corporate annual reports—beaming workers on plant floors and finely lit pictures of whatever they made: gleaming metal widgets, glossy machine tools, shiny objects radiating abstract beauty. The old man was a master of the lustrous inanimate object." Chip takes another long sip. "But there was another side, what he called his 'personal work.' Artistic nudes for one. For these he'd light the women the same careful way he lit the widgets, sparkle here, highlight there, making them look more like sculptures than living people."

Chip shrugs. "That was how he saw them, I guess. But then, later, with his Fessé series he followed a different route—fetish photographs of gorgeous dominant women holding whips. 'Fessé' means something like 'spanked' in French. I think the French word for spanking is *fessée*. Anyway, *Studio Fessé* was the marque he put on them. People into that kind of stuff saw that and knew what to expect."

I find Chip remarkably forthcoming about his father. He seems to enjoy discussing his old man's "personal work." Max, as Chip describes him, was not an especially impressive-looking man—stooped, of medium height, with the bushy eyebrows and beak characteristic of his Armenian heritage, excessively hairy ears, chest hair showing at his throat, with two wild patches of gray head hair flanking a shiny pate. But there was a quality about him, a gentle intensity that drew people in. It was this, Chip tells me, that made it possible for him to convince women to pose for him in postures that, had the suggestions been made by anybody else, they would have been taken as the gravest of insults.

"He'd approach a woman, tell her he found her extremely beautiful, then hand her his card saying he hoped she'd consider calling him to arrange for a portrait sitting. Approximately half would accept, an extraordinarily good batting average when you think about it. With these women, in the course of the session, he'd create a bond. He adored women, you see—put them on a pedestal, and some women found they liked that very much.

"Say a week or so after the session, he'd invite the subject back to the studio to look at prints. The portraits would be good, often the best photos the woman ever had taken. Then, if he felt there were possibilities, he'd show her some of his personal work, first the nudes, and then, after considerable coaxing, perhaps several of the whip photographs as well. Then, depending on the woman's reaction, he'd let it be known he'd be thrilled to take a few shots of her in a similar vein. Or, more often than you might expect, she might broach the notion herself."

They'd have great fun then picking out an appropriate wardrobe from his studio closet filled with fetish gear—riding apparel, glossy black boots, black leather bustiers, a huge selection of gloves and crops, plus all sorts of provocative underthings, lacy black bras, black silk stockings, stiletto-heel shoes in sizes ranging down to petite.

Provocative as the Fessé photographs were, there was no nudity in them. Cleavage—yes! Sexuality—the pictures radiated it. They were choked with implication, innuendo. But there was never anything vulgar or brazen, nothing that smacked of a pornographic magazine. Their brilliance lay in their restraint. That was the art of them. In his Fessé pictures, Max showed himself to be an artist. Which was why his Fessé series has become so collectible.

"The print you've got, the one of Mrs. Fulraine—the fact that she's bare breasted makes it a real rarity. Pop didn't distribute shots like that, never sold them to clients. But sometimes near the end of a session he'd ask a model whether she'd let him take a few of her stripped down just for fun. And if she did, they'd put in an extra hour, and, if he liked the negatives, he'd make just two prints, one for her, the other for himself."

Chip meets my eyes. "I have Pop's album. There's a print in it identical to yours. So the print you have must have once belonged to Mrs. Fulraine." He pauses. "How'd you get it?"

"It came to me by a circuitous route."

Before he can pursue the issue, I ask how his father met Barbara Fulraine.

Chip shrugs. Perhaps Max saw her, he says, when he was working on an annual report for Fulraine Steel. Chip knows the lady was murdered the following year. It was a famous Calista scandal—she and her lover gunned down in a sleazy motel room near Tremont Park. But he doesn't think his father would have made more prints of the bare-breast shot simply because his sitter was no longer alive. That wasn't Max's style, he was an honorable guy, and the *Studio Fessé* pictures weren't made for profit.

I ask Chip if he has other shots of Mrs. Fulraine.

He nods. "Yeah, a few, but the one you've got is the best. Pop really caught something there, something perhaps the lady didn't recognize herself till Pop brought it out. You get the feeling from that picture she was truly relishing her role. I don't know much about her beyond that she was a society woman and that she was killed. I doubt she ever thought of herself as a dominatrix, not until Max posed her that way. Then, in that split second, she became one. Not a society lady pretending to be one, but a dominatrix pure and true. Again, there's the art . . . which is why I won't sell any of Pop's Fessé prints or allow new prints to be struck from his negatives. The nude studies are another matter. I've sold off most of those. But not the Fessé shots." He looks into my eyes. "You're lucky to possess one so fine."

TONIGHT THE MOOD in Waldo's is not exuberant. It's been a long, dull day at the Foster trial, filled with boring technical testimony and tedious arguments. I sensed that early, knew there would be nothing worth drawing, said as much to Harriet, then left the courthouse to pursue my own interests.

Judging from the tenor of the room, those who stayed in court wish they hadn't.

Pam Wells is not in a pretty mood.

"I would've left too," she says, "if there was anything else for me to do." She studies me. "Where do you go off to anyway?"

"Oh . . . Memory Lane," I tell her casually.

"Uh huh." She gives me her cynical reporter's look. "My ass! You're on a story, David. I can smell it. So clue me in, Lover Boy. Unless you're afraid I'll crowd your turf."

She shows me a tight little smile, her way of warning me I'd be a fool to think she wouldn't.

"It's an old story, Pam. You like new stories."

"Sometimes old *is* new."

"True enough. . . ."

I'm rescued by the strutting entrance of Spencer Deval, who joins a group two tables away. Pam squints as she studies him.

"I don't get it about that guy," she whispers. "He's such a self-important little shit. And that accent! It's so phony. Who *is* he anyway?"

I gesture at the portrait of Waldo on the wall.

"He used to report stories for Waldo Channing. When Waldo died, he took over the column. The two of them were lovers, at least started out that way. Spencer, it's alleged, was quite lovely in his youth."

"You'd never know."

"Waldo left him his house and furniture. There're also rumors about something shady in Spencer's past. They say Waldo, who was to the manner born, cleaned him up, taught him manners, even sent him to England for a year to learn how to speak."

Pam grins. "That explains the accent. I get it now. Pygmalion," she says.

I TAKE HER TO DINNER at Enrico's on Torrance Hill, a quiet, family-owned Sicilian place. It's a weekday night, and there aren't many customers, certainly no out-of-town reporters. Pam is charmed.

"Candles stuck in old Chianti bottles, red and white checked table-cloths—I love it, David. Right out of the fifties."

The owner doesn't stand beside our table like a waiter; rather he pulls up a chair, turns it around, then sits leaning over the back in spectator-sporting-event position to take our order.

When he moves away, Pam gives me a serious look.

"Please tell me what you're working on, David. And, please, no bullshit about how it wouldn't interest me. Everything interests me. Especially if it interests you."

"I'm not ready to talk about it yet."

"Must have to do with those weird drawings taped to your walls."

I'm stunned. "You've been in my room?" She shrugs. "Aren't you the little sneak?"

"Curious little bitch is what you mean. You're just too polite to say it."

"How'd you get in?"

"Told the chambermaid I might have left a bra in there. Please don't get mad at her, David. She watched my every move."

"What were you looking for?"

"David Weiss. Like who *are* you, David?" She widens her eyes. "What're you up to? What's your game?"

"What's yours, Pam?"

"Investigative reporter." She smiles. "And you know what? I think that's your game, too."

I stare at her more annoyed than angry, but I know I can't let her get away with what she did. "Talking your way into my room," I eye her sternly, "you've got a fucking nerve."

She shrinks back as if taking a blow across the face. "I did it because you intrigue me so much. I know that's no excuse. Please forgive me," she pleads. "I'm sorry. I really am."

Nothing hypocritical about her apology; I read sincerity in her eyes. "I like you, Pam. I really do. But don't ever do anything like that to me again."

FOUR

I'm standing by the once grand entrance to the grounds of The Elms, a morose sight this sultry summer afternoon. The skeletal gate frames hang loose from rusted hinges. With most of the ornamental ironwork missing, they resemble an assembly of bare bones. The stone pillars on either side are also in decay—mortar crumbling, moss attacking the rock. Only one of the two statues of griffins that once perched upon them remains and that one's now headless. This deteriorated entrance would make a fine drawing, I think.

In the old days, of course, these gates were well attended. Members arriving at night would find the griffins illuminated by lights concealed in the surrounding foliage. A guard would stop cars, then relay names by intercom to the reception desk up at the club. People in the cars, the men in tuxedos, the women swathed in furs, would wait with mock joviality for admittance.

A night at The Elms was exciting; visitors felt they were entering forbidden terrain. Often too there would be anxiety in the car when the clearance procedure took longer than expected. Then laughter and relief when approval came and the guard waved them through. Then the slow journey down the long lit drive between magnificent evenly spaced English elms; the arrival at the great house, its banks of leaded windows lit from within; a cheerful greeting from the parking valet; the sweet aroma of burning wood in the air on winter nights as guests strode up the broad flagstone steps to the main door.

The walls of the entrance hall were adorned with third-tier old master paintings in heavy gilded frames. In winter, fires crackled in the hearths, for the club was installed in what had once been a great private home. The sound of a singer would drift out to the hall, one of those torch-song specialists Jack Cody, club owner and host, brought in from Chicago or New York. Then Jack himself would appear, ultra-suave in his trademark white double-breasted dinner jacket and Errol Flynn pencil-line mustache.

Everyone was fascinated by Jack, a handsome, craggy-faced man of medium height and compact build, with a year-round tan, sharp eyes, crocodile smile, precision-cut salt and pepper hair, and a voice so husky and soft it came out in a fierce whisper. Men were charmed by his two-handed shake, women by his gallant kisses. Often he would honor arriving guests with a few choice words, perhaps notification that a famous ballplayer was in the house or a certain out-of-state high roller was at the craps table in back playing like there was no tomorrow.

Then Jack would smoothly turn his clients over to Jürgen, the opaque maitre d'hotel, who, rumor had it, had killed a man in Mexico, then served in the French Foreign Legion. Jürgen would escort them to their tables in the Cub Room, the air lightly permeated by a sumptuous aroma composed of the smoke of fine Havanas, a touch of Channel Number Five, and the lusty smell of fabulous thick, rare, juicy, broiled steaks.

Elms staff members were expertly cast: short-skirted cigarette girl with dazzling smile; stoic barman with slicked-down black hair; hovering European waiters; cool black backup musicians; cooks in immaculate starched white jackets and high white hats; bearded sommelier with accent, tasting spoon, and cellar key. Steaks, lobsters, wine, and liquor were always superb, service attentive, chairs soft, flowers fresh, tablecloths damask. Everything was luxurious, expensive, "best of class."

The Elms, sometimes called a "roadhouse" in the downtown papers, was the closest thing Calista had to a fantasy nightclub-casino. Its glamorous Manhattan atmosphere was borrowed from The Stork Club and El Morocco, and some of its particulars, alluring singers and back-room gaming parlor, from such Hollywood noir classics as *Dead Reckoning* and *Casablanca.*

Jack Cody, imitating the ironic manner of Humphrey Bogart, always referred to the club as "my joint." Wealthy locals called it simply The Elms and were thrilled to dine and gamble there, not least because gaming was illegal throughout the state. The Elms was entirely Jack's creation. Everything that happened inside, every nuance, was choreographed by him for maximum effect.

A sure sign that one had become a friend of the house would be a whispered confidence from Jack, a tip, say, on a horse running at a Florida track, or a choice piece of gossip about some sordid event of which even columnist Waldo Channing would be unaware — an adultery or financial scandal, a dope and sex party, a fistfight between gentlemen who'd stepped outside to settle a dispute, or an exchange of slaps in the lady's restroom.

Such privileged information was not easily shared. Jack kept his distance until one became a regular or lost a minimum of twenty thousand dollars in his gaming room. After that anything was possible: a complimentary bottle of rare French wine sent to one's table; a speeding ticket efficiently fixed; a high-end call-girl introduction discreetly made. People said that due to his wide acquaintanceship there was nothing Jack could not arrange, and, in truth, he did seem to know everyone in town — athletes and entertainers, socialites and judges, politicians, cops and mobsters. It was this last category, Jack Cody's rumored underworld connections, that originally brought Barbara Fulraine within his ken.

"AT FIRST WE COULDN'T figure out what she was doing with the guy. Put him in a jail jumpsuit and he was just another cheap crook."

Mace Bartel, chief investigator for the Calista County Sheriff's

Department, is talking as we walk together down the long driveway toward The Elms. At my request, we've met at the ruined gates so that Mace can show me the remnants of the club. Twenty-six years ago when Barbara Fulraine and Tom Jessup were murdered at the Flamingo Court, Mace, then a young detective working County Homicide, was primary investigator on the case.

"She was such an elegant lady and Cody was such a low-rent creep, we couldn't figure the relationship out. Then we learned she was steered to him because someone told her he could help her find her missing girl."

As we approach the house, I'm struck by its facade: fine stonework, magnificent arrays of windows and eight turned brick chimneys rising symmetrically out of a complex of intersecting pitched slate roofs.

"Cody strung her along," Mace continues. "Uncovered all these 'rumors' and 'sightings,' a tale about a pretty little white girl spotted with blacks in the bowels of the Gunktown ghetto. He told her he had 'operatives' working on it, 'informants' who'd been well paid and would sooner or later come up with solid info. It was bullshit, but she was vulnerable so she believed him. After that it wasn't long before he got into her pants."

Mace sighs. "She must have liked that too, the way she kept coming back for more. Maybe she found Cody attractive because he seemed so dangerous. You know, the old hood glamour bit. And of course he liked her because she was unlike any woman he'd ever had: rich, classy, educated, superbly groomed, even—what's the word?"

"Demure?"

Mace shrugs. "Whatever. Point is she wasn't a floozy. Barbara Fulraine was the real thing. Sure, The Elms was a gold mine, Cody was raking in money, but he recognized class when he saw it. Class was what he lacked and what he craved."

Mace is rail thin. With his granny glasses and carefully tended goatee, he looks more like a professor than a cop. He's also, I'm discovering, a shrewd street-smart psychologist. That he'd struggled to reason out the attraction between this unlikely pair tells me he's probably good at his job.

We're at the end of the drive, the turnabout area, heading toward the broad steps that lead to the front door.

"We were sure Cody did it," Mace tells me. "He was vicious and he was jealous. Two years before the Flamingo killings, he found out his girlfriend, a singer, was two-timing him. He used the broken end of a gin bottle to rip her face, and, though there wasn't any proof, we were pretty sure he also had her lover whacked. His body turned up in a ravine in Lucinda Heights. No family. Nobody cared. Cody's lawyers settled with the girl. She refused to press charges and left the state. It was common knowledge he was capable of whacking people who crossed him or people he thought had done so. So why not Mrs. Fulraine and Jessup? She was his mistress after all, then he found out she was spending dirty afternoons with this nothing schoolteacher. That made him murderously furious so he killed them. Least that's how we had it figured."

The Elms house, unlike the gates, appears to be in good repair. When I mention this, Mace tells me a syndicate acquired the property last year with a plan to divide it into high-end condos.

When Mace opens the front door, we're hit by a blast of over-heated air.

"Closed up this time of year, it gets like a furnace. Of course Cody had it air-conditioned. They'll redo that, heating, wiring, plumbing. Some snazzy downtown firm's got it figured out. The top unit'll be a duplex enclosing the old gaming room, an upstairs suite, and the terrace and garden area off the back. I hear they'll be asking a million four for that one." Mace mops his brow. "Come on, I'll show you around. . . ."

He takes me first into the Cub Room where the torch singers performed. Even though it's daytime and the room's been stripped of furniture, I can sense what it must have been like. Thick, plush carpeting, tufted white leather banquettes, tables arranged on tiers, and a sweeping, curving staircase like the one in the fabulous Buenos Aires nightclub in

Gilda that Rita Hayworth descends while singing "Put the Blame on Mame."

"The singers made their entrances down those steps," Mace tells me. "The musicians worked against the back wall. The dining banquettes were on the upper level, the smaller tables for drinkers below. There was a small dance floor for customer dancing between sets."

He leads me into an adjoining room. "Quieter dining in here." He points toward the glassed-in kitchen. "The partition's triple glazed so you could watch the chefs but not hear the noise."

He shows me a small private dining room reserved for Cody's mob pals.

"They'd start all-night poker games in here after the swells went home."

" 'Swells'?"

Mace laughs. "Don't you love it? Right out of the twenties. Even back twenty-six years, this scene was from another era. I tell you, this was one swanky joint."

We retrace our steps to the entrance hall, pass through a small room with an intimate curved bar where people waited for friends or gamblers retired to take a break, then enter the long gaming room in the back, which extends the length of the building. It's a magnificent space with three sets of French doors leading to a terrace overlooking a garden, now gone to seed.

Mace gestures. "This was the heart of The Elms. The Cub Room, bar and entertainers—they were just bait to lure the suckers. I'll say this for Cody, he ran an honest club. No fixed roulette wheel or loaded dice. Wasn't necessary. This room was a money machine. 'Course he had his costs including payoffs to local law enforcement. Every so often the complaints would pile up, forcing the sheriff to stage a raid. They never found anything. No craps tables, roulette wheels, or blackjack stands. Cody was always tipped with enough time to truck his stuff out. All they'd find when they got here would be a couple of old geezers shooting pool."

Mace leans against the wall, lights a cigarette, and smokes it while I start a quick sketch of the gaming room. Later, I'll insert Jack Cody, Barbara Fulraine, and perhaps Jürgen the maitre d', if I can find a photo of him.

"They used each other," Mace says. "She slept with him so he'd keep looking for her daughter, and he told her he was getting closer to finding the kid so she'd continue to sleep with him. The part I could never figure was her stealing off to sleep with Jessup. Was she turned on by the notion of crossing Cody or did it just turn her on to sleep with different guys?

"Oh, there'd been plenty of lovers over the years—we found that out soon enough. Even when she was married to Fulraine, she had lovers on the side. She may have been classy, but she liked sex, so there was a carload of secondary suspects. Including Fulraine, who had a private investigator tailing her butt. He wanted custody of his boys and was looking for evidence to have her ruled unfit."

I tell him about the Fessé photograph.

"Doesn't surprise me," he says, stroking his goatee. "She was a complicated woman.

He suggests we go upstairs to look at Cody's office. It turns out to be a handsome room paneled in fine mahogany. Mace feels around, then slides open a panel to reveal a concealed wall safe.

"He kept the gaming receipts in here along with his private files. By the time we got a search warrant, he'd cleaned everything out."

Cody, as prime suspect, had what amounted to a perfect alibi: At the exact time of the Flamingo shootings, he was lunching at the Downtown Athletic Club with a municipal judge. Mace wasn't surprised. In his view the alibi only served to confirmed Cody's involvement.

"It was too pat, like he went to a lot of trouble to make sure his actions were accounted for that afternoon. That told me he'd ordered the hit, which from an investigative point of view was happy news. When whoever killed those people was picked up, he'd have something valuable to trade. And hitmen eventually are picked up, or else they boast to a pal or girlfriend. Then when the pal develops a grievance or the girlfriend gets dumped, he/she's got a way to get payback."

Cody's old living quarters are down the hall, with a one-way glass viewing window set into the floor so he could observe the action in the gaming room.

"This is where they fucked," Mace tells me. "The bed was over there."

He gazes almost wistfully at the empty space as if imagining Jack and Barbara making love. Watching him, I wonder if he fell a little in love with her back when he was actively working the case.

"Did she spend nights here?" I ask, wondering too whether I'm starting to fall a little in love with her myself.

Mace shakes his head. "She always went home. She had live-in help, but even years after the kidnapping she was afraid for her sons. Two or three times a week she'd drop in here for lunch, then she and Cody'd come up here and screw. But she'd always leave in time to meet her boys when they got home from school.

"That final summer, when the boys were away at camp, she started meeting Cody here at night. That gave her free time in the afternoons to hook up with Jessup. Everyone knew she was sleeping with Cody, but no one knew about Jessup. To keep it that way, keep Cody and her ex from finding out, they'd meet secretly at that crummy motel. Except *she* wasn't so secretive. She drove a Jag. People spotted her turning into the motel lot. Still boggles my mind—she had such a tremendous amount to lose and still she risked it."

We descend the main stairs, exit the house, then circle round back to look at the gardens. Mace tells me that all the trees near the house were strung with lights, creating a magical effect outside the club windows at night.

"I've been waiting years for someone to come forward, say he knew who did the Flamingo hit on Cody's orders. But no one has. Maybe they figured once Jack was dead there was nothing to be gained."

Mace describes how less than a year after the Flamingo killings, Cody was ambushed.

"He was in his Cadillac, sitting beside his driver the way he liked to do, when they stopped at the traffic light at the corner of Joslin and

Tremaine. Suddenly two gloved and helmeted motorcyclists pulled up on either side, drew pistols, and blasted the driver and Cody at the same time. Then the shooter nearest Cody pulled open the door and shot him twice in the head. It was all over in a couple of seconds. Both shooters dropped their weapons, then peeled off in opposite directions."

"Did this have anything to do with Flamingo?"

"Not as far as we know. Cody was connected with the Torrance Hill mob, then there was a falling out. We thought it had to do with the big stickup happened out here. Quite an event. One Saturday night, just after the midnight floor show, eight guys with submachine guns, wearing fatigues and stocking masks, came in through the kitchen door, rounded up the staff, pushed them into the Cub Room, shot up the ceiling to get attention, announced a stickup, and demanded jewelry and wallets. Three of them went around collecting valuables while two escorted Cody upstairs, where they forced him to open his safe and hand over the weekend receipts. It was scary and also exciting. A couple of the more clever ladies had the presence of mind to hide their rings by dropping them into their coffees. One guy dumped his watch into a pitcher of cream. Later everyone spoke with admiration of how well Cody handled himself. Even though he was cleaned out, he never lost control. Next morning it was all over the papers: GAMING CLUB HEIST. Everyone was talking about it: 'D'you hear what happened out at The Elms?' 'Wow, isn't that wild!' Contrary to what you'd expect, it added another layer of glamour to the place. Among Cody's regulars, it was prestigious to have been here. People who were nowhere near at the time went around claiming they were among the robbed. Meantime, Cody told some of his friends he knew who'd done the job and promised he'd get even."

We mount the terrace that runs along the length of the gaming room.

"The robbers came in through there," Mace says, gesturing toward a field below the gardens. "They avoided Cody's security guys by crossing the adjacent property, then approaching from the rear. It was a slick operation, showed intimate knowledge of The Elms, which is why some, me included, thought Cody staged it.

"Later when he was assassinated, I changed my mind. Then it looked more and more like a chill off, a bunch of out-of-town guys, maybe the Purple Gang from Detroit acting for the Torrance Hill mob, brought in to send Cody a message. They wanted a bigger slice of the action, Cody refused, so they sent in some muscle to show what they could do. A classic move, what they used to call 'dressing down the joint,' 'giving the joint a shake.' Afterwards Cody confronted them, there were hard feelings, and a few months later they had him killed."

As we walk back up the drive, I tell him what bothers me about his theory that Cody ordered the Flamingo killings.

"Seems like there's a big difference," I tell him, "between ripping up your girlfriend's face with a broken bottle and ordering your mistress and her lover killed. One's a hot, angry act that has to do with punishment. The other's totally cold-blooded."

Mace shrugs. "Depends on how you size the guy up. I saw him as a sociopath subject to flashes of rage but also cold and cruel. So, see, for me it can work either way. Also, who else had a motive?"

"Andrew Fulraine?"

"He wanted his kids back and was looking for evidence to get custody, but he was in New York at the time and wouldn't have had the slightest idea how to hire a hitman. Bottom line—he didn't have the heart. He was too fancy and wimpy. When he heard what happened, he burst into tears."

"What about her other lovers?"

"We checked them out. Cody and Jessup were the only current ones. Far as we could tell all the old ones had cooled off."

"What about someone you didn't know about?"

"You mean like someone who'd been spurned. Look, we did a thorough investigation. Since we suspected Cody from the start, we made a point of looking deep to eliminate everybody else. When a couple's killed like that, shot to pieces in their love nest, the motive's almost certain to be sexual jealousy. Jessup wasn't involved with anybody. He was new in town, been here less than a year, barely knew anyone outside his colleagues at the Hayes School. Barbara Fulraine had had a string of lovers, but she was a classy lady who ended her affairs in a classy way. Several were visibly upset when they heard the news. All seemed genuinely sad. We looked at Cody's old flames but couldn't find one who cared. Couple of them made it clear they weren't even sorry. Cody was the only one who refused to talk with us. He referred us to his lawyer, who told us to arrest him or buzz off. So if there was someone else, we didn't find him. And, God knows, we looked."

Back at the ruined gates, there's a quiet moment as Mace and I get ready to part. He looks me in the eye in the manner of a seasoned cop. ·

"Those drawings you did of the Zigzag Killer," he says, "they were knockouts. Law enforcement folks give you great references. After you called I checked you out, wanted to know who you were before I agreed to meet."

"Guess I passed the test."

"You did. But I'm curious about something, David. Why so much interest in a twenty-six-year-old crime that's been mostly forgotten by everyone else?"

"You haven't forgotten it."

"That's for sure. I doubt a day goes by I don't think about it."

"Then you of all people should understand."

The way he continues to stare tells me he needs a better answer.

"Put it like this," I tell him. "I was a kid when Flamingo happened. All of twelve years old. I was a student at the Hayes School. Mr. Jessup was my French teacher. I played soccer, and he was assistant coach of the lower-school soccer squad. I also knew the Fulraine boys. Mark Fulraine was in my class. Me and all my friends read about the case. The following autumn, we could talk of nothing else. It was morbid and romantic, and I guess you could say some of us got obsessed. In a weird way, considering the career I've had, I think for me those killings were a defining event. They haunted me. So now, twenty-six years later, I find myself back in Calista. With that in the background, how can I *not* make time to give the case my best professional look?"

Mace nods casually as if to say he's willing to accept my explanation, though he's still not completely satisfied.

We shake hands.

"If you come up with more questions, give me a call." He smiles. "Flamingo's one case I'm always happy to talk about."

F I V E

*T*he *Hayes School*: Standing now before its gracious Georgian facade, I'm suffused with melancholy. It was here that I, like all children at their schools, learned some of the awful lessons of life: that human beings compete; that competition can be ruthless; that those we love best may turn upon us and betray us; that those we respect most may show themselves to be flawed.

It's summer now. School is out of session. But the campus is open for two summer programs, a day camp for soccer players, and a high school theater workshop. When I arrive, the soccer players are practicing on the school's lush green athletic fields, while the theater students are in the midst of a dress rehearsal. I stop by the school auditorium, watch a couple of scenes from Shakespeare's *As You Like It*, then wander off.

The smells here bring back memories: polished stone, freshly waxed wood floors, the lingering odor of bad school food. "Fish eyes and glue" and "mystery meat" were among our gleeful descriptions of Hayes specialties.

Off the main foyer, lined by glass cases filled with sports trophies, is the corridor that leads in one direction to the Headmaster's Office, in the other to the school Common Room. I walk through, then enter the gym, immediately noticing several unfamiliar features—new Plexiglas basketball backboards and differently colored markings on the floor. Most of all, I'm impressed by the volume of the space. It used to seem so vast. Now it strikes me as small, almost intimate.

I've come to revisit the site of a boxing match I fought here under Athletic Department auspices. In fact, it was a mean, ferocious battle waged to settle a bitter personal feud.

Tom Jessup, acting that day as coach and referee, appeared to view it as simply another fair if particularly combative bout. Perhaps, as I and my opponent were being bloodied as we flailed away, he was daydreaming about his new socially prominent paramour. Or perhaps, as I believed at the time, he unfairly refereed the bout so I would lose, my opponent, after all, being Mark Fulraine, scion of a founder of the school.

I walk to the end of the gym where the boxing ring was set up. Mats, perhaps the very ones we trod upon that day, are piled neatly in a corner. The vaulting horses are in their niche; the climbing ropes are hoisted to the ceiling. Taking a seat on the bench in front of the radiators, I feel the grid against my back, the same grid I leaned so hard against that day while my friend, Jerry Glickman, laced up my gloves.

Funny how many things come back when you revisit the scene of a traumatic event, details I would not remember were I not now at the site. As the memories flood in, I set my sketchbook on my knees and begin to draw, working to recapture the awful drama of that day.

There'd been much anticipation surrounding our fight. People knew we hated one another, that Mark, president of the Lower School Student Council, had deeply offended me, calling me "Jewboy" because he didn't like a caricature I'd drawn of him for the school paper. After he spat out the epithet, we stared at one another, me incredulous, he, perhaps, equally shocked that he'd uttered such a vicious affront. Then I swore I'd knock his fucking block off.

Just as we were about to come to blows, a teacher intervened, which led to our being called separately into the Head of Lower School's office. Mr. Leonard, who owned that kingly title, decided that since our rancor was high and we were approximately the same weight, we should settle our differences in the ring.

An idiotic solution. Had I been Head of Lower School, I'd have sus-
pended Mark till he issued a public apology. But the Fulraine family was
a major benefactor of Hayes, people felt sorry for Mark because his sister
had been kidnapped, and, anyway, in those days, genteel anti-Semitic
remarks were not uncommon in the homes of Calista's social and financial elite.

Since our feud erupted on a Monday morning, Mark and I had five
full days to look forward to our bout, scheduled to follow regular optional
boxing practice on Friday afternoon. In that time, we carefully kept our
distance so as to avoid exchanging further words.

My friends, all two of them, Tim Hawthorn and Jerry Glickman,
assured me I'd win if I kept my head.

"Make him fight your fight," Jerry coached me.

"Sucker punch the creep, then sock him," Tim advised, smacking
his fist into his palm.

Both pieces of advice seemed valid enough, though I had no clear
idea what they meant. All I knew was that I was facing the fight of my
life, and, unlike other student fights, it was being sanctioned by the
school. Though participation in a grudge match was a fearful
prospect, at least I could count on it being fairly refereed. Mr. Jessup,
who had boxed as an undergraduate at State, was, I knew, not only an
honorable guy but was also a favorite teacher, and, I then believed, my
friend.

Friday, 2 P.M., the day of the match: I enter the Lower School locker
room. Mark's already there wearing nothing but a pair of gym shorts, one
foot on the bench tying up his sneakers. We glare at one another as we
suit up side by side.

"It's going to be fun whipping your ass," he taunts.

"There's an ambulance outside waiting for you," I respond.

Every student, upon admittance to Hayes, is assigned to one of two
teams, Eagles or Mustangs. Thereafter, no matter the sport, all intra-
mural teams are demarcated this way. Mark Fulraine was a Mustang,
thus the tanktop he pulled over his head was a vivid fighting scarlet.
Since I was an Eagle, mine was but a muted blue.

Together we strode into the gym to receive our gloves, headguards, and mouthpieces. Another match was in progress with at least a hundred boys seated about the ring. Normally less than twenty spectators attended Friday practice, but that afternoon interest was high as word of our impending battle had spread through Lower School.

Mark was popular; I was not. He was a star athlete, a football player, graceful and handsome with manly features and a head of unruly golden locks. I, dark-haired, skinny, sometimes gawky, was not particularly good at sports. Moreover, I was disliked on account of my sarcastic manner and for being among the smartest kids in sixth grade.

As we walked forward, I could sense the waves of approval washing over him and feel the disdain directed at me.

"Give it to him, Mark!"

"Beat the crap out of him!" yelled Mark's brother, Robin, who would be acting as Mark's second.

I think I might have choked out of sheer loneliness if Jerry Glickman hadn't come forward then to encourage me and help me with my gloves. Since psychology is half of any battle, choking up would have doomed me for sure. But thanks to Jerry, despite the favoritism of the crowd, I managed to keep my head.

"He's too cocky," Jerry whispered. "He's riding for a fall."

Filled with gratitude, I looked around for Tim, my other friend. Appalled to find him in Mark's corner whispering encouragement, I heard mumbling in the audience: "Hawthorn's turned. Hawthorn's rooting for Fulraine!"

You will be betrayed.

That was the first lesson I learned that Friday afternoon. But strangely instead of eroding my confidence, Tim's betrayal gave me strength. *I'll show him!* I remember thinking. And at that I focused my anger on my betrayer, glaring at him so hard I forced him to lower his eyes.

The Hayes School, now coed but in those days exclusively for boys, prided itself on its instruction in manly sporting arts and values. Hayes boys, we were taught, played fair and true. Hayes football players never shirked a tackle, Hayes basketball players always leapt for heaven, and, in the boxing ring, Hayes boys gave all with honor and heart.

Mr. Jessup came over to check my mouthpiece and gloves.

"Everything okay?" he asked. I nodded. "Best now you do like Mark, shadowbox a little to warm up," he advised.

I nodded again, then stood and joined Mark, flamboyantly shadowboxing around the ring. Then Mr. Jessup beckoned us to the center to instruct us in the rules.

"Three two-minute rounds. Compulsory ten count on a knockdown. Break when I tell you. If either of you wants to stop, say so and it's over."

Mark and I nodded.

"Good! Now come out swinging. May the best man win!"

Mark and I briefly touch gloved hands, Jessup stood back, then Mark and I began to fight.

I don't remember much about the bout, have no memory of particular blows. But I do remember they came fast and hard, and that after a slow start, to my surprise, I began to give as good as I got. There was ebb and flow; at times I became the aggressor, pursuing Mark across the ring. Other times he backed me against the ropes with a flurry of hooks and jabs. I remember Jerry encouraging me while offering me water during the breaks. I also recall Robin Fulraine yelling taunts from the opposing corner. At one point, I remember connecting a right and feeling great satisfaction as Mark's eyes clouded and blood spurted from his nose. I wasn't aware how bloodied up I was myself till the second rest period when I looked with shock at the red towel in Jerry's hand.

"You're a mess, but you're doing great," Jerry assured me.

Mr. Jessup came over.

"You okay?"

I nodded.

"Good! Terrific fight," he said, then moved away.

If I had managed to hold my own in the first two rounds, things fell apart for me in the third. Perhaps it was exhaustion, also Mark's superior athletic ability. Whatever the cause, I realized I was getting beaten. Then suddenly, I remember, I felt my legs give out from under me as I was rocked by a terrific blow to the chin. I fell to the mat. I remember Mr. Jessup giving me a ten count as I struggled to stand up, then shaking my gloves and staring deeply into my eyes while motioning Mark back. I remember standing there stunned, barely able to raise my gloves, as Mark attacked, hitting me in the stomach, then letting loose with a vicious blow to my lower belly that sent me down again.

I remember writhing on the mat in pain and blood, feeling I was going to throw up. It was so obviously an illegal low blow, Mr. Jessup should have stopped the bout right there. Instead he methodically counted me out, yanked me up, then raised Mark's arm in victory. Then amidst cheers from the crowd, he instructed us to shake hands . . . which we did.

Later in the locker room, Jerry beside me while I bent over a sink trying to stanch a cut on my lip, several kids came up to say I'd gotten a rotten deal, that after the low blow Jessup should have stopped the fight and called a draw. Better still, Mark Fulraine came over to apologize.

"The low blow was an accident. I don't fight dirty," he said solemnly. "I still don't like that picture you drew," he added before going off with his friends.

Still later, showered and dressed, crossing the empty gym, I remember watching as a school janitor mopped our blood off the white rubber cover they used to protect the mats.

Contrary to schoolboy mythology, Mark Fulraine and I did not become friends. But after our fight he showed me decent respect, his way, I guess, of saying he was sorry for what he'd said. Suddenly more kids seemed to like me, too. On Graduation Day, there was an exhibition of my sketches in one of the hallways of Lower School. Several boys made a point of introducing me as "class artist" to their parents.

I'VE BEEN DRAWING here in the gym for nearly an hour. Now, hearing the sounds of kids returning from soccer practice, I put down my pencil and examine my work. I've got the fight down pretty well, I think. Rather than depicting myself as victim, a role I dislike, I've drawn Mark and me as equally fierce competitors. I also have Mr. Jessup as he appeared to me that day, aloof and out of touch; Jerry, my friend, rooting for me in my corner; and Tim, my betrayer, half turned away, treason in his eyes. But it's my depiction of the audience I like best, their faces filled with those particular pleasureful expressions boys assume while watching other boys fight—identification with aggression, intense interest in the outcome, enjoying too the suffering and debasement of the loser.

As for Mr. Jessup, though he never acknowledged that he'd refereed unfairly, in class he continued to praise my work. Still I soured on him. I assumed he'd favored Mark because of the Fulraine family connection to the school. It was only later that I found out that Mrs. Fulraine had hired him that spring to give private tennis and boxing lessons to Mark and Robin, and that, in the early days of their romance, those coaching sessions served as the pretext for Tom to visit the Fulraine estate, where, afterwards, while the boys frolicked in the family pool, he and Barbara Fulraine retreated to her bedroom to make frantic, illicit love.

TOM JESSUP HAD A SECRET. I was convinced of it. There was something different about him that spring, the way he spoke and moved, which, perhaps because of my hurt over his betrayal, I was eager to understand. The sincere and boyish young schoolmaster, previously so generous and kind, seemed somehow to have changed.

Almost immediately upon his arrival the previous autumn, our new French teacher had become one of the most popular instructors at Hayes. Young, eager, not jaded like the older masters, he had that rare teacher's gift of making a foreign language come alive. Though a conscientious objector, he hadn't fled the country but had served heroically as an army medic in Vietnam. After discharge, he'd worked his way through State, majoring in romance languages. In short, a man I could admire.

But in the spring, his teaching went flat. It was clear that whatever was going on in his interior life was not concern over the education and coaching of pubescent boys. Until the Flamingo shootings the following

August, I had no idea why he'd changed. Then it was all over the newspapers, his affair with Barbara Fulraine. The most surprising part of their
story, at least to Jerry Glickman and me, was the news that they'd met at
Hayes the preceding April on Parents Day.

In September following the shootings, when school resumed for the
new term, that meeting became a subject of endless speculation. Jerry
and I, then new seventh graders, spent hours going over the events of
that day, trying to imagine how it had occurred. We remembered Mrs.
Fulraine. Even if nothing dramatic had followed, it would have been
impossible to forget her, she was so beautiful, gracious, and glamorously
dressed.

Fortunately for Hayes it had been a beautiful spring day; the previous year Parents Day had been rained out. Flower beds were in full
bloom; playing fields shimmered green beneath the afternoon sun. The
curving drive that wound up to the front of Hayes was lined with parents'
cars—shiny station wagons, splendid Jaguars, Mercedes, BMWs, a Rolls
or two. Parents wandered the campus, fathers in tweed jackets, mothers
in gaily colored frocks. Mrs. Fulraine, we recalled, wore a sleeveless off-
white linen dress that glistened in the light.

The purpose of Parents Day was to give parents an opportunity to see
the school in action, visit classes, view scheduled sporting events, and
most particularly meet with those in whose tender care they had
entrusted the education of their sons. Teachers were primed not only to
discuss schoolwork but also their students' moral progress, the true and
underlying purpose, our headmaster often proclaimed, of a Hayes education.

I recall standing to the side that day as my parents discussed me with
my favorite teacher, Miss Hilda Tucker, who had guided and encouraged my interest in art throughout my Hayes career.

Mark's younger brother Robin was in fifth grade. His homeroom
teacher was Mr. Jessup. Thus it was natural that Mrs. Fulraine seek an
audience to find out how Robin was doing. Replaying the swirl of events
that afternoon, Jerry Glickman and I recalled seeing the two of them
speaking quietly somewhat apart from the crowd of parents, teachers,

and boys, with a greater intensity and for a longer span of time than normal between a mother and teacher.

As seventh graders, our fantasies about their conversation were naive.

"Maybe he told her she had great tits," Jerry offered.

My response: "Maybe she stared down at his crotch."

We agreed it couldn't have happened that way.

"Then how did it happen?" Jerry asked.

I scratched my head. "They talked about Robin and Mark, what great little guys they were. Maybe she told him she was worried how, with the divorce and all, they weren't getting the kind of fathering boys need."

"So then—?"

I improvised. "He told her they were doing great, but he was available if they needed extra help . . . like coaching, tutoring, and such."

"What about sex?"

"They didn't get to that. They were attracted, but they were smooth about it. By offering extra help, Mr. Jessup signaled he was interested in coming out to the house."

"Right! So if she took him up on it, he'd figure she was interested too."

"Yeah!"

Now standing where Tom and Barbara stood that day, by the fountain in the paved school courtyard bounded by the Common Room and classroom wings, I imagine the play of their eyes, their searching looks, the unspoken yearning each sensed and felt.

Perhaps Barbara, being a vibrant, sensual woman, felt a sudden, unaccountable animal hunger for this attractive young man standing so straight and attentive before her—fresh, lean, clean-cut, the very opposite of the stout, lined, jaded quasi-gangster with whom she'd had slimy sex earlier that afternoon.

Tom, I think, would have been shattered by her beauty and entranced by her sultry gaze. No other mother that day had looked at him like this. No other mother exuded such pure and forceful sexual energy. Since starting at Hayes, his life had been consumed by boys.

He'd had no time to date, no opportunity to meet young women. Now, suddenly, here was a person in whose eyes he could read desire.

Whatever they said to one another—and it was probably fairly close to what Jerry and I imagined once we got over our first crude fantasies—it was the silent dance of their eyes that pierced those secret places in human hearts where attraction and love are suddenly born. This eye-ballet would have been further enhanced by their surroundings—spring air scented by flowers and freshly mowed grass, a special slant of golden afternoon light, most of all the warm air bath that raised an attractive gloss from their sun-washed skin while releasing those aromatic attractors Mr. Butterfield, our science teacher, told us were called pheromones.

I'd like to draw them as they stood together that day, two gorgeous, silent, poised about-to-become lovers facing one another just outside the jabbering crowd. But it's getting late, the light is failing, I may not have the skill . . . and, also, I have an appointment I must keep.

HILDA TUCKER TAUGHT ART at Hayes for thirty years. She was already in her forties when I entered the school in the first grade, a patient, nurturing buxom woman, who, from the first day, recognizing a slim talent, took me under her gentle wing.

"Work hard on your drawing, David," she would tell me. "Drawing is the basis of art."

I believed her, worked hard on my drawing, ending up not the painter she'd hoped, but a glib draftsman specializing in eyewitness portraits and, my latest incarnation, rapidly drawn courtroom caricatures.

She still lives in the small tract house just two miles down the road from Hayes, from which she would bicycle to and from school every day, except during snowstorms when she walked. Driving up to the house, I distill an image of her from my schooldays, not crouched over the handlebars of her bike the way people ride today, but sitting upright in the traditional manner, pedaling proudly, cheerfully oblivious to passing cars.

"David . . . !" She embraces me at her door with the same warm, welcoming expression she always displayed when greeting me at school. "I've been looking forward to this all week!"

She ushers me into a small living room dominated by a baby grand piano covered with framed photographs of former students. The paintings clustered on the walls are not at all conventional—brilliant color-filled landscapes reminiscent of the French Fauves. I gaze at them and then at Miss Tucker and then at her canvasses again, executed on her annual summer trips to France where she'd set up her easel in a field or by the side of a road, then proceed, as she used to put it, to "paint the light."

"Your paintings still move me."

"So kind of you to say that, David."

"The large one over the mantle—didn't it used to hang in your classroom beside the door?" She nods. "Now seeing so many together, I understand what you were doing. Why, I wonder, didn't I see it before?"

"Simple, David. You were a child. Now you're an adult, an artist, too."

She leaves me with her pictures while she retreats to her backyard garden to fetch her companion, Helen Slater. Miss Slater, also retired, taught music for years at Ashley-Burnett, the private school for girls in Van Buren Heights attended by my sister, Rachel.

A couple minutes later Miss Tucker returns.

"Helen'll be in soon. Still got some weeding to do. I do miss our summers in France, but the garden's a great joy. Not quite so glorious as our bicycle trips through Provence . . . ," she smiles, "but nearly so." She pauses. "You know, David, back when you were in school, people called our relationship, Helen's and mine, a 'Boston marriage.' Times have changed. Now we're just 'those two old dykes across the road.' "

She shakes her head when I protest. "We really *are* old," she says. "But I don't regret a thing. Not even giving the better part of my life to the art education of little boys. Students like you, who took up art as a career, made it all worthwhile."

"I'm not really an artist," I remind her gently. "Just an illustrator."

"I wouldn't care if you drew comic books. You've chosen to live in the realm of art." Her gentle brown eyes settle upon me. "It pleases me to think I had something to do with that."

She had much to do with it. She also instilled in me standards according to which I came to understand, my second year at Pratt, that I was never going to be a serious painter. For one thing, I wasn't interested in conceptual art or in using artwork to explore theory. For another, I was fascinated with character as revealed in portraits. Yet the prospect of painting flattering commissioned portraits of social and corporate types filled me with despair. Better, I thought, to use whatever skill I had to explore the dark side, to draw kidnappers, murderers, and rapists.

"I've been recalling Tom Jessup ever since you phoned," Miss Tucker tells me. "It's been years since I've thought of him. I was probably his closest friend on the faculty. Those old Hayes teachers didn't take kindly to new blood. You had to put in ten years of drudgery before they'd accept you as a peer. Tom was sweet, innocent, almost naive. He didn't understand their coldness. 'What's their problem, Hildy?' He always called me that. 'Why won't they help me out?' Tom wanted to be a great teacher. He thought of teaching as a calling. He couldn't understand why those old farts wouldn't mentor him a bit."

"Was he really so innocent?" I ask. "After all, he went into that affair."

"Yes . . . of course . . . but for me that's the proof. A more sophisticated man would have had the good sense to stay away from a woman like that. She was too rich, too beautiful, much too high above his station, plus she was older and the mother of two of his students. You don't come new into a school like Hayes and start sleeping around with your students' parents. Barbara Fulraine, as we all later found out, had been around the block a few times. Just the sort of woman who could bring ruin upon a young man. Once she tired of Tom, and sooner or later she would, she'd have left him miserable if not destroyed. So, you see, I think it *was* innocent of him to get involved with her. I'm sure it was loneliness that drove him to it. And her guile."

Guile: You don't hear a word like that too often these days, but Hilda

Tucker employs it straight-faced. It's clear she still feels distaste for Barbara Fulraine and blames her for everything that happened.

"No one hated Tom," she says. "No one wanted *him* dead. It was *her* they were after. And since he was *with* her, they killed him too."

I don't tell her that for a while I actually did hate Tom Jessup, that, even after he was dead, when I found out that he'd been privately coaching the Fulraine boys, I remained angry at him for his favoritism.

"You describe him as sweet and naive," I tell her, "but for me that's much too vague. What was he *really* like? What were his passions? Surely he'd had girlfriends before."

"That's true," she says. "There was a girl, Susan something—I can't remember her name. They met in college, lived together. He didn't talk much about her, just mentioned that it hadn't worked out. She moved to New York, became a stockbroker. They stayed friends, kept in touch by phone. I don't think you know, David, how lonely the man was. He lived in a rooming house on Ohio Street down near the university. Had virtually no social life, barely knew anyone in town. As Lower School French teacher and coach, he was surrounded all day by little boys. Every so often Helen and I would have him for dinner. He was an excellent guest—bright, charming, full of life. The three of us would speak French, his, of course, a lot better than ours. We loved those evenings. It was good practice for our summers. I remember too he'd always bring a bouquet and a bottle of wine."

I'm not buying it.

"Wasn't there anything wrong with the guy?"

She gazes at me.

"Actually, there was," she says finally. "Not wrong exactly. In fact not wrong at all. But he was so innocent he *thought* it was wrong. We talked about it. I was touched he chose me as his confidante. Later Helen, too. We both tried to help."

"What?"

"Seems there was a young woman in his rooming house, a high-strung grad student who occupied the room next door. Somehow she became smitten with him to the extent she'd wait by her door until she heard him leaving, then step into the hallway, acting as if these meetings were just amusing coincidences. When that didn't get her anywhere, she became more aggressive, once actually bursting in on him when he was showering in the shared bathroom down the hall. Tom took a kind tack with her, but that only increased her interest. Finally, to put an end to it, he fibbed and told her he was gay. Once it was clear there was no possibility of romance, she was content just to be his friend."

"Seems a good solution. I don't see why he was upset about it."

"Tom was so honest it pained him to tell a lie. And now the big lie he'd told her led to a whole series of little lies, which became a terrible burden on his conscience and his time."

"Why didn't he just move out?"

"That's what we advised. But he had the guilts over this girl, was afraid if he left suddenly she'd be hurt. They did a lot of things together—went to movies, took hikes, stuff like that. His plan was to leave at the end of spring term, go off for the summer, maybe take a camp counseling job, then find a new place to live come fall. But I had my own theory."

"Which was—?"

"That because he was so lonely he became attached to her, and, more interesting, that there was a side of him that enjoyed the deceit. Tom's whole life had been devoted to virtue. At one point, he told us, he seriously considered attending divinity school. He'd been a Boy Scout as a kid, then an Eagle Scout, then a conscientious objector who'd volunteered to be a field medic, one of the most dangerous jobs in the Vietnam War. He'd always been a straight-shooter—kind, generous, the sort who'd always tried to do the right thing. Now he was deep into deception with this girl, and the thicker the web of lies the more rotten he felt about it. And yet in some weird way he didn't understand and to which he couldn't admit, I believe he reveled in his deception."

"That *is* weird!"

"It was all those lies, I think, that set him up for the affair with Mrs. Fulraine. We didn't know who she was, of course. Not at the time. All we knew was she was someone in society. That worried us. Helen and I talked about it that summer in France. Then when we heard what happened and who she was—well, we just felt awful, felt that we'd failed him, hadn't helped him understand where he was going with his life."

Miss Tucker shakes her head. "I think what happened to Tom is that his rectitude burned out. He'd come to a point where he needed to go down a different path, and that woman showed him just how to do it."

I stare at her, surprised at the revelation. That Tom Jessup, in his affair with Barbara, was exploring the dark side of his nature had never occurred to me. But now, thinking about it, a new set of ideas starts taking shape. All the passion of that summer, the obsessive lovemaking— was that but a means for Tom to discover the kind of person he really was?

"Do you think there was love between them?"

Miss Tucker scoffs. "He may have deluded himself. I'm sure she didn't. I'm certain that when he stopped satisfying and amusing her, she'd have dumped him, harshly too. As for Tom, all the sneaking around probably added to his excitement. Plus the novelty of being with such an experienced woman. Poor boy! He was blinded—by her position, money, beauty, and guile. My God! she was sleeping with a gangster! She wasn't the sort of person you could be tender with. She was exploiting him, using him to make the other man jealous."

Helen Slater enters the room. A handsome, gray-haired woman in tanktop and shorts, she greets me with a warm smile.

"I remember you well," she says. "Hildy spoke about you often. 'There's this one kid over there who can really draw!' I also remember teaching your sister at Ashley-Burnett. We've followed your career, David. All those killers! Who'd have thought you'd end up drawing people like that!"

We talk about the Foster trial. Because both victim and accused were musicians, Helen's fascinated and wants to hear all the gossip. While I fill her in, Miss Tucker retires to prepare tea. When she appears again, with a tray holding a teapot, cups, and a platter of sweets, I turn the conversation back to Tom Jessup.

Helen's view is similar to Hilda's, but they differ in their appraisal.

"He was morally immature," Helen says. "I think he could have gone either way, stuck to virtue, become a professional do-gooder, or gone over the edge exploring his selfish side. But I think if he hadn't been killed and his affair with that woman had fizzled, he'd have fallen into a depression, then pulled himself out pretty quickly. Hildy, of course, thinks he would have been shattered." She puts her arm lovingly around her companion. "Anyhow, I like to think Tom found some happiness those last steamy months of his life."

At the door I remind Miss Tucker of something she whispered to me my last day at Hayes.

" 'Don't think you can snatch a leaf from the laurel tree of art without paying for it with your life.' "

"Yes, of course," she says, beaming. "From *Tonio Kröger* by Thomas Mann. It's still one of my favorite quotes." She turns to Helen. "It's true too, don't you think?"

Helen nods. "Oh, so true," she agrees.

A different feeling in Waldo's tonight. People seem to be in a rotten mood. I learn that an hour ago a CNN cameraman and a local sound-man got into a fistfight.

Tony the barman fills me in. Seems that while competing for position to pick up the day's crucial sound bite, the local stepped on the network guy's foot.

"It wasn't about his foot."

Tony and I look up. This offering comes from Sylvie Browne, the black reporter from Chicago under contract to write a book. She's perched on her usual stool at the end of the bar.

"What was it about, Sylvie?" Tony asks.

"A woman," she says.

Tony rolls his eyes. "Isn't it always?"

"What woman?" I ask.

"Actually your girlfriend."

"Pam?"

Sylvie grins. "More than one girlfriend, David?"

"What'd it have to do with Pam?"

"This afternoon she elbowed the local station's girl reporter aside. The foot stamping was retaliation."

"How do you know this?"

Sylvie beams. "I observe. What's interesting here isn't the trial, it's the media battles surrounding it. It's all going into my book. By the way, David—you better watch out. This morning CNN fired Henderson. I hear they're bringing in Washburn. He's *good.*" She giggles, then turns away.

I step out to the lobby to call Pam on my cell phone.

"Where are you?" I ask when she picks up.

"Production suite."

"Hear about the fight?"

"Yeah. Boys'll be boys."

"Is it true Henderson's out and Washburn's in?"

"You've got good sources, David. I'm with Wash now."

"You really call him that?"

"Hey, Wash!" she says. "It's David Weiss. He doesn't like your nickname."

I hear a male voice mutter something in the background.

Pam conveys the message: "Starret says Wash'll cream your ass."

So . . . Pam, her producer, Jim Starret, and their new courtroom artist hire, Lee Washburn, are in a strategy meeting upstairs plotting my professional demise. Chastened, I return to Waldo's for a second margarita.

Washburn, I know, could be a serious competitor. One of the two or three top courtroom artists in the country, he's known for his powerful compositions and incredible speed. Well, he may draw faster than me, but I'm confident I'm better at characterization. Since this'll be the first time we've covered the same trial, I also know I can expect a battle. And no mercy from Pam, though she's been especially sweet and ingratiating since I dressed her down for snooping in my room.

I'M FAIRLY WELL LUBRICATED by the time they come downstairs— Pam, Starret, and the famous Wash whom I recognize from photographs that accompanied a profile in *TV Guide.* He's got himself up like an artist—long, black hair, drooping black mustache, black pants, and black silk shirt billowing around his cadaverous arms.

Pam gives me a quick peck on the cheek.

"Hi," Wash says, extending his hand. "Really love your work."

I nod. We shake. His eyes, I note, are soft and liquid, sensitive artist's eyes.

As Starret pulls him toward a table across the room, Pam perches beside me and orders a margarita.

"Nice guy," I tell her. "All he lacks is a beret."

She grins. "You're not worried, are you?"

"I wish you'd told me you were bringing him in."

"Starret's decision. Anyhow I try to keep my private life separate."

"Yeah, I understand. I do that myself. Which is why I haven't told you my secrets yet."

"I know something's going on with you," she says. "I even think you enjoy cutting me out. You've got that smug, cut-out look."

I flip open my sketch pad, press a pencil to the paper. "Describe it."

"What?"

"That look."

"Oh . . . you know." She shrugs. "The knowing little twinkle in the eye. The secretive little curl to the lip."

I quickly draw pairs of eyes and lips. "Like this?"

"No, worse," she says. "The tight I'm-going-to-scoop-you grin."

This girl's not only smart, she's got me psyched.

"What's the matter, David? Can't draw it?"

"Show it to me."

She makes a couple of awful faces, then sticks out her tongue. "Nya-nya-nya!" She drains off half her margarita. "If you really want to know what I'm talking about, take a look in the mirror."

At that she lightly pats my shoulder, picks up her glass, and saunters off toward the CNN table across the room, giving me just the flimsiest little wave before sitting down with Starret and Wash, my new rival in the courtroom drawing wars.

FOUR HOURS LATER, after dinner at a seafood restaurant in Irontown and a bout of lovemaking that leaves us sweaty and spent, I turn to her, ask if she's ready to hear my story.

She perks up immediately, props her head on her elbow, and tells me, yes, she's ready.

I lie back, stare up at the blank ceiling of her hotel room, and spill.

"There was a double murder here when I was a kid. I went to a private day school out in the country. Turned out one of my teachers was having an affair with the mother of a classmate. One hot summer afternoon, when they were making love at a sleazy motel, someone burst in with a shotgun and blasted them both to bits. Huge local scandal. The woman was a socialite and a great beauty, divorced in-law of one of the richest families in town. The prime suspect was another man she'd been having an affair with, a guy who owned a nightclub and illegal casino across the county line. No arrests, nothing was proven, and the nightclub guy himself was gunned down within the year. That was more or less the end of it. Interest wound down. But me and my best friend at school were fascinated by the crime. For one thing, we'd been particularly fond of the teacher. He was a gentle guy—or so we thought. Also because his death was so shocking to us, we spent a huge amount of time talking the murders through, thinking we could solve them like you can solve a puzzle in a mystery novel.

"There was other stuff. Everyone at school was upset by what happened . . . as was everyone in Calista society. But the murders seemed to affect my parents to an unusual degree. It was about that time that my family came apart. My mom and dad were at dagger points. Dad was a doctor, a shrink. Turned out he was treating the victim, Mrs. Fulraine. Turned out he'd met her the same day she met the teacher, spring Parents Day at our school. There's the coincidence—this incredibly glamorous woman appears at Parents Day and, within a couple hours, meets a shrink with whom, shortly thereafter, she begins a course of psychoanalysis, and a young teacher with whom, shortly thereafter, she starts a tumultuous and ultimately tragic affair."

I turn from the ceiling to look at Pam. Fascinated, she peers into my eyes.

"What happened?"

"I told you—they were killed."

"I mean with your folks?"

"They separated. A few months after the murders, Mom decided she wanted to move back to California where she'd been brought up. I didn't want to leave my school and friends, but Mom was determined. We—Mom, my sister Rachel, and me—left Calista that January in the middle of a blizzard. The following week, I started at a new school in L.A. Six weeks later, Dad committed suicide.

"They say he lingered in his office after his last appointment of the day, then, a couple hours later when it was dark, leapt out his office window. It was a medical building on Gale Avenue. The window faced the back so no one saw him fall. He landed in the doctors' parking lot. They didn't find him till the next morning. He didn't die immediately, might have been saved if there'd been someone around to call for an ambulance. Instead he lay there all night, body broken, bleeding to death in the snow.

"My mother brought us back for the funeral, held, coincidentally, in a synagogue in Van Buren Heights for which the son of a man who took a haunting, erotic photo of Mrs. Fulraine is now creating a sculpture for a Holocaust memorial. A couple years later, Mom married another doctor, an internist. My father's last name was Rubin; Mom's second husband's name was Weiss. When he adopted me, I took his name. David Rubin became David Weiss."

Pam seems moved. "Thank you for telling me this, David."

"You've been so good lately about not asking me to spill my guts, I figured it was finally time for me to spill them. You see, for years I believed, and still do, that everything that happened—my parents' breakup, Dad's suicide, the fact I now have a name different from the one I started out with—had something to do, tenuously or directly, with the strange woman whose life and death I want to understand, the murder victim, Barbara Fulraine."

Pam nods, lies back, again exposing her wondrously freckled chest. She's glad, she tells me, that I finally opened up to her.

"I know it's hurtful to talk about these things. I'm touched you've shared them with me."

"So you see I'm not working on something newsworthy behind your back. It's a private inquiry. Time-consuming too. I guess now that Washburn's in town, I'm going to have to spend more time at the trial."

"You can always quit, do your own thing."

"And pay for my own hotel room and car."

"Is that the only reason you stick with the trial?"

I admit it isn't, that the real reason I don't quit and spend full time on the Flamingo killings is that then I'd have to face the fact that I'd given myself over to a ruling passion, that I'm not just conducting a hobby investigation but am on an obsessive personal quest.

"Why did you wait so long?" she asks. "You could have looked into this years ago . . . before the trail went cold."

"I wasn't ready. But this spring, when my mom died, some new material came my way. Then a couple months later the Foster trial and the offer from ABC. Everything seemed to gel. The message was clear. It was time to go home and face my demons." I glance at her. "Such as they are."

"Oh, they definitely sound like demons," she says.

No mention from her this evening about having to get her "beauty sleep." Rather, I'm invited for the first time to spend the night.

Later she says, "Let me help you, David. I've got free time. We could backtrack your story together."

"Boy-girl investigative team. Nice idea. But I work best on my own." I look at her. "You wouldn't be trying to distract me now, so Wash can put out better drawings?"

She laughs. "Life isn't always a media war." She places her hands on my cheeks, stares into my eyes. "I like you, David. Don't you get it? I really do."

THERE'S A HEALTH CLUB on the top floor of the Townsend Hotel. If you're coming or going from there in workout clothes, you're supposed to take a special elevator lest guests in business attire be offended by the exposure.

Pam and I head up there at 6:00 A.M. to join other lean-mean media folk into physical fitness and self-torture. Gym workouts aren't my thing, but when Pam asks me to join her, I tag along lest she take me for a wimp. The exercise room is spacious, with plate-glass windows facing the city skyline and several rows of equipment—treadmills, StairMasters, Nautilus machines—all gleaming chrome and sleek black leatherette, shiny and welcoming in the brilliant early morning light.

Pam starts on a Nautilus circuit. I mount an exercise bike. An NBC reporter, Cynthia Liu, is pedaling furiously on an adjacent machine. I give her the once-over. She's already slick with sweat. She wears black Lycra tights and a sports bra, the kind with a little porthole in back. She's a skinny girl, her spine protrudes, and her frail shoulder blades stick out. She stares straight ahead at a TV monitor set to the daybreak program on the local NBC affiliate.

News of the early morning commute: expressway jam-up due to an accident. Promise of another sweltering day: one hundred percent humidity with a projected high of ninety-one degrees. No end in sight to the Forgers' losing streak; team in the cellar for the third straight week. As the attractive, youthful, blow-dried anchors slip into casual morning happy-talk, I catch myself panting, slow my pedaling, then wipe myself down with the towel hanging from my handlebars.

"Kinda out of shape, aren't you?" Cynthia Liu comments, pedaling away, still looking straight ahead.

"Excuse me?"

She glances at me. "Whatsamatta? Girlfriend wear you out?"

Annoyed, I shake my head. "I thought you were supposed to be nice."

She smirks. Our eyes lock. Suddenly I feel like putting her down.

"Tell me," I ask, "are you bulimic?"

For a moment she holds the smirk, then her face squeezes up as if she's sucking on a lemon. She stops pedaling, shows me a hard gaze of hatred, dismounts, and stalks out of the gym.

Pam mounts the StairMaster on my other side. "What was that about?"

"Little Miss Perfect made a personal remark. I chose to respond in kind."

"Good for you, David! Now pedal up. Want an aerobic effect, you gotta work for it."

She spends the next twenty minutes sweetly putting me through my paces, enjoying her new self-assigned role as my personal trainer: "Faster, David! Faster!" "Go for the burn!" "Give me another, David. *Another!*" And, most sweetly of all: "Hey! Don't pussy out on me . . . please!"

At 6:30 we step into the gym elevator. She snuggles with me on the descent. Her body, warm and moist, turns me on. Alas, she informs me sadly, she doesn't have time now to make love. Too much to do, a meeting with Starret and Wash, then over to the county courthouse for her early stand-up. She smooches me as the doors open, steps out of the elevator, turns to face me, and grins. The doors close, the elevator descends. Still excited, I head down to my room for a shower.

WASH AND I EXCHANGE polite nods in the courtroom corridor. Inside he takes a seat four down from mine. Then, lest he think he's got me outgunned, I make a point of sketching furiously.

It's a good day for courtroom drawing. The prosecutor and defense counsel get into a snit, the judge becomes impatient, and soon the three are glaring at one another with anger and disgust. Meantime, defendant Foster shows the jury a beatific smile. Out of this conflict I create a stunning four-face portrait, which Harriet loves, and which, when broadcast on the early evening news, puts Wash's first-day efforts to shame.

Slam-dunk for the good guy . . . which is not to say that Wash won't soon snag a few baskets himself. Still I've out-psyched him his first day and can count on holding my lead a while. He'll start becoming dangerous when he gets the players' physiognomies clear. Until then I'll rule the court.

DURING ONE OF THE AFTERNOON breaks, I phone Mace Bartel and ask if I can have a photocopy of the Flamingo file.

"The whole thing? There're thousands of pages."

"I'll gladly pay copying charges."

"It's not the money, David. It's the time and effort. I can't spare any-one for the job."

"I'll do the scutwork." Long pause. "I don't see myself as a rival inves-tigator on this, Mace. After all, it's been twenty-six years."

"It's not that."

"What is it then?"

When he goes silent, I start feeling guilty.

"Listen, Mace, I wasn't a hundred percent straight with you out at The Elms the other day when you asked why I was so interested in the case."

"I figured."

"I have a very personal reason for being interested."

"Which is?"

"My father was Mrs. Fulraine's shrink."

"Well," he says, "that's very interesting. I appreciate your telling me."

"I should have told you the other day, but I didn't feel like discussing it. Dad committed suicide, and. . . ."

"I know. One of my guys interviewed him. Couple months later I wanted to do a follow-up, but then . . . well, it was too late. I spoke to his secretary. She couldn't find his file on Mrs. Fulraine. For a while I won-dered if maybe there was a connection. You'll find our notes on the inter-views when you come over."

"You're saying—?"

"Sure, you can look at everything we got, make copies too if you like." A pause. "See, David, long as you're straight with me, I'll be straight with you."

PAM WANTS TO VISIT the scene of the crime, so tonight after dinner I drive her out to Tremont Park. As we pass through Delamere, she oohs and ahs.

"Seems people here are very rich."

"The Fulraines were." I slow as I pass their house. "It's an institution now. Old folks home or something."

"I'd like to take a look."

I tell her I'll try and set it up.

"What I don't get," she says, as we approach the motel, "is why they chose to meet out here."

"It was convenient for her. Less than ten minutes from her house. And it was a place they weren't likely to be seen. They started meeting secretly in the amusement park. She liked the idea of their meeting in a place so scummy and low class."

"How do you know what she liked?"

"Just a guess," I lie. "When I draw, I try to get inside peoples' heads. How did the actors get from here to there? How did the fateful intersections take place?"

She asks me to describe the old Tremont Park. It's a pleasure to do so. I tell her about the sounds—hubbub, hurdy-gurdy music, swish as the toboggans went over the falls, roar of the rollercoasters, pings from the shooting gallery, raucous laughter of the oversize automatons that guarded the Fun House doors. The smells too: horses, taffy, sugared popcorn balls, cotton candy, suntan lotion, perfume on summer-heated skin.

"The Fun House was my favorite," I tell her. "It was a labyrinth filled with tricky corners, weird slanted floors, floors made of moving rollers, holes in the floor through which air sporadically shot up. The air would hiss right up your pants leg or blow up a girl's skirt. There were strange sounds and funny mirrors that made you look fat, thin, or just plain grotesque. There was one point where you turned a corner and this huge black spider came rushing at you from the dark. Everything was set up to make you scream.

"I imagine Barbara and Tom meeting there one hot summer afternoon. Stumbling through the Fun House would have aroused her. She'd grab hold of Tom's arm, squeeze his bicep, scream out in fright. Then they'd double over with laughter, clench, and kiss. It was dark as hell inside. No one would see them. Even if someone did, no one would care. Teenage couples went through there all the time. It was a rite of passage to take a girl in there, get excited, then fool around in the dark. What a thing for Barbara Fulraine—country club tennis champ, symphony box-holder, wearer of Harry Winston jewels and Saint-Laurent gowns — to be groped in the Fun House by her earnest, attractive, secret lover, so adoring of her, so stricken, so madly in her thrall. How could they resist one another after an hour spent like that? They would emerge holding hands, wondering where they could go to be alone. There was only one choice: the Flamingo Court across the road, so convenient and anonymous, with a reputation as a 'hot sheets' motel. She'd have reveled in the humbleness of it, the notion that no matter how privileged, highly placed in the social order, she had her needs, was flesh and blood, carnal and horny as any lubricious teenage girl finally giving in to the panted entreaties of her boyfriend."

"Whew!" Pam says. We're parked now in the Flamingo lot. She turns to me. "Was it really like that?"

"Maybe. I think so. Sure. A wild, passionate adventure. Think about it. She comes out here to make love with Tom Jessup after spending an hour or so at midday in Jack Cody's bed. She's a fastidious woman. She showers in between. Then, again ready for abandon, she drives here telling herself that no matter the elegant mask she shows the world, she's a reckless virago in pursuit of her pleasures. Consider how much fun it would be for her to feel she was leading a secret double life! And remember, too, she had the added luxury of being able to study her excitement with her new, brilliant, respectful psychoanalyst. In effect she becomes the center of her own universe. And so privileged, so very privileged . . . for she is always perfectly groomed, beautifully dressed, driving the finest make of car, living in a luxurious home amidst splendid things where she's waited upon by loyal servants. She's loved, admired, perhaps best of all from her point of view, wildly envied by her rivals. With all that, how could she *not* feel she was living at some rarefied peak level of human experience? And yet . . . still . . . she would tell her devoted analyst how devastatingly miserable she was, riven by guilt for allowing her infant daughter to be kidnapped and believing in her heart of hearts that at best she's a self-indulgent fake, at worst a fancy whore."

We sit still in the car. To break the silence, I point out the window of room 201 where the killings took place.

"If the blinds were open," Pam observes, "someone sitting down here could see inside."

"Only at night. Anyhow, I'm sure they kept the blinds closed while they made love. Or partially closed so the shadows would stripe their bodies."

"Still, from here the shooter could see them arrive, park, go up to the room. Then he could sit here and make his plan, wait for the right moment when no one was coming or going so he wouldn't be seen. Maybe wait till the pool area cleared, then coolly get out, walk across the courtyard, mount the stairs, smash his way into the room."

"He didn't have to smash his way in. They left the door unlocked. All he had to do was fling it open and fire."

"The gun—how did he hide it?"

"Beneath a dark raincoat."

"I thought you said it was a sweltering afternoon."

"It was, yes, but then there was a summer storm. It rained hard earlier. Would you take any notice if you saw a man coming up the stairs wearing a raincoat? You'd just give him a glance then turn away."

Pam scans the motel walls. "Everything must look different here in daylight."

"You don't notice the neon piping on the roof. The pastel colors leap out. Surfaces are bright, shadows deep. The pool area smells of chlorine."

"Seems to me whoever was on duty in the office would have seen him when he came in."

"Unless the desk clerk was waiting on a client or watching a baseball game on the lobby TV."

"He must have heard the shots?"

"He thought he heard a motorcycle backfiring."

"Weren't there witnesses?"

"Several. But they didn't see much. Just a guy in a dark raincoat with a dark hat pulled down to his eyes, rushing down the stairs, crossing the street, then jumping into a dark car and taking off."

"I think you're right about it not feeling like a jealous lover's hit," she says. "From what you tell me about Cody, he sounds like the kind who'd take on something like that himself. To vent his anger, get it out of his system. What would be the point of hiring someone else to take them down?"

"And how would killing her teach her a lesson? Beat her up, throw acid at her, gouge her face—but kill her because she's two-timing you? Doesn't make sense."

"Still his alibi sounds awfully pat."

"Unless he made a practice of lunching with judges. The guy was connected, not just to the mob but also to the local political establishment."

"So if Cody wasn't behind it, who was?"

"Other people might have wanted her dead."

"Or Jessup."

"Or both of them."

"Maybe it was a mistake. The shooter mistook them for another couple."

I tell her I hadn't thought of that.

"I want to see the room," she says.

"We'll come back sometime and have a look."

"Not now?"

"I'd rather not, Pam. I was in there last week. Anyhow, it's getting late."

"You think I want to make love with you up there?"

"Do you?"

"I'm not *that* kinky!" She cuddles against me. "This is so *interesting*. How're you going to develop new information after so many years?"

"I probably won't. Anyway, what I find out doesn't have to be new. I just want to get it right, feel it the way it happened. Otherwise it's just an exercise."

"*Feeling it*—that's how you do your drawings, isn't it? Get into peoples' heads, then draw what they've seen."

ON THE DRIVE BACK downtown, she asks me about the Zigzag Killer. She's familiar with some of the tabloid details: that the press called him that because of the zigzag knifework pattern he left on his victims' torsos.

Also that he attacked men in the gay enclaves of San Francisco, and that unlike most serial killers, who murder at an increased rate of frequency, he struck only rarely and sporadically over a period of years.

"The knifework was curious. Lots of speculation about it, that it carried a cryptic meaning, that he was trying to cut lightning bolts, leaving a calling card, trying to obliterate his victims, sending the police some kind of message. None of that concerned me. My job was to draw his face. Only two people were known to have seen him—a middle-aged female resident apartment house manager, who spotted him briefly as he left her building after killing one of the tenants, and a guy who saw the killer leave a gay bar with another victim two years later. Both had worked with good police artists, yet the resulting pictures had nothing in common. In fact, they were so different they canceled each other out. Other artists were brought in to try and reconcile the descriptions. When they couldn't do it, the cops began to think at least one of their witnesses wasn't reliable."

"So then they brought in the great David Weiss."

"Who hadn't yet been deemed 'great.'"

"But who became 'great' when he managed to reconcile the two irreconcilable witness descriptions."

As we speed up Dawson Drive, the skyline of Calista comes into view. The city shows a strong signature at night—a cluster of variegated buildings dominated by Lindstrom's spectacular twin towers, lights on inside for the night cleaning crews, poised against the moonlit sky. The heart of the city casts a light gray glow that surrounds it like a nimbus. Calista seems almost heroic tonight, with a hard, urban beauty rarely noticeable when walking its streets during the day.

Yes, I tell her, my Zigzag Killer drawing made my name. I spent hours with the two witnesses, trying to extract details each had forgotten, acting always as if I believed everything they told me even while trying to determine whether one or the other had fantasized what each claimed to have seen.

"It had been six years since the woman saw the guy. Four for the man. The sightings were brief, yet each claimed the guy's face was clearly etched. There was just something about him, both said, that made him unforgettable—a look in his eyes, a confidence, possibly even a smirk . . . though neither witness ever used that word.

"My approach is different from most forensic artists. They ask questions about the shape of a suspect's face, hair, eyes, eyebrows, nose, mouth, and ears. I do it another way. I want to know how they *felt* when they saw him, their angle of vision, even the cast of the light. Most important, the set of his face, his expression, because for me that's what best conveys character.

"I took the male witness back to the bar where he made the sighting. We found the very bar stool where he'd sat. We got the positions right, then reenacted the scene.

"Seems he was cruising the victim, then was disconcerted when he realized the victim was interested in someone else. So he viewed this other man as a rival. Right away that told me a lot about his mindset.

"We talked the whole thing through, or rather I let him talk, because what I do best is get a witness going then listen closely to what he says. We narrowed down his viewing time. Turned out he got his only clear look when he checked the guy out in the mirror behind the bar. Then he remembered there was something unattractive about him—an asymmetry in his face. Seems the killer looked quite different in the mirror than when my witness observed him straight on.

"We were getting somewhere. We went back to his place and I started to draw. I had him sit beside me. Together we shaped the picture. Within an hour we came up with three different views.

"Next I went to work with the woman. Again we reenacted the scene. The way the cops reconstructed it, he'd just finished his kill. She got a good look at his profile for about a second and a half and from a very narrow angle of view. She'd been sitting in her apartment with the door partially open. He was sort of 'sliding' his way out, she said, and his face was set into a rather memorable grimace. When he realized someone was watching, he glanced her way. When he did that, she responded the way most people would—she looked away.

"At once I understood what was wrong with the other artists' drawings. They'd taken her description then tried to extrapolate a frontal view. I stayed with the profile. We worked on that, trying to get the grimace and set of the eye on the left side of his face as she'd remembered it. When we were done, I showed her the drawings I'd made with the other witness. 'Yes!' she said. 'That's him, that's the guy.' And the male witness said the same thing when I showed him the drawings I made with her."

We're off Dawson now, driving on city streets. There's a loneliness to downtown Calista at this hour. The business district's deserted, and the night wind, funneled through the valley, is transformed by the spaces between buildings into whirlpools, miniature tornadoes, that lift and whirl scraps of paper and debris.

"So that's how you came to draw that famous triple view."

"Turned out to be my trifecta."

"I remember how when they caught him everyone was so amazed. He had the same weird, lopsided face you'd drawn. When I saw live shots of him as the cops hurried him along, he wore the same gloating expression."

"The best part," I tell her, "was that my drawings led directly to his arrest. That rarely happens. He was arrested twenty-four hours after my sketches appeared on the front page of *The Examiner*. Soon as they were published, people recognized him and started calling in."

I pull up in front of The Townsend, turn my car over to the car valet.

"Have you thought of trying to work with the Flamingo witnesses?"

"I've thought about it. That's why I've asked to see the file. But it's been twenty-six years. I've never heard of a case where an artist worked with witnesses on something so far back."

In the lobby, Pam pauses outside the glass doors to Waldo's. "Nightcap?" she asks.

The bar's half filled. Spencer Deval is mesmerizing Cynthia Liu, my dear friend from the gym, doubtless with one of his well-worn high society sagas. Raucous laughter issues from a corner table where six cameramen trade journalists' war stories. Tony the barman stands straight in his characteristic pose wearing his best world-weary expression.

We take a pair of stools before him, order cognacs.

"You look especially pale tonight, Tony," Pam says.

"Pale as death," Tony agrees.

"What'd you think about as you stand here?"

"This 'n that. Also about him."

Tony nods at the opposite wall. Pam and I turn. The eyes of Waldo Channing gaze back at us out of the portrait.

"He looks very 'period,' " Pam says.

"Oh, he was," Tony agrees.

She's too young to have firsthand memories of columnists like Channing, but I recall the man quite well. He was a type; most big cities possessed one—a local writer celebrated because he wrote about local celebrities. Such men seemed actually to rule the societies about which they wrote. They inhabited their cities' upper crusts but were capable too of writing about the common folk. A sentimental vignette about a humble laundress might be juxtaposed with scathing notes about a nouveau riche couple on the make. Each strove to glamorize his town, waxing poetic about it even when the place was ugly. They were social arbiters, insiders, walkers, party animals, name-droppers, star-fuckers who would gush like schoolgirls over visiting celebrity singers, actors, entertainers. But if the celebrity wouldn't kiss butt, they'd get him/her really good— belittle her singing, mock his performance in order to proclaim that even us 'rubes out here in the sticks' knew the difference between 'class and trash.' And if you inhabited one of the great cities of the American plain, you dared not cross the one who ruled your town lest you earn his enmity and ever after suffer the poisonous bite of his pen.

When Tony leaves us to fill drink orders, I tell Pam I didn't like Waldo Channing much.

"He was small time and a snob. I also think he was anti-Semitic. He wrote some mean things about my dad before and after my parents broke up."

"Anti-Semitic stuff?"

"He couldn't get away with that, though genteel anti-Semitism was an unspoken given in his set. No, he ran a gratuitous item about 'a well-known local shrink' whose marriage was 'on the rocks.' And just weeks before the killings, he ran a blind item implying my dad was having a closer than professional relationship with Barbara Fulraine. He didn't name names, didn't have to. If you were in the know, it was obvious whom he meant. I wish he were still alive. I'd ask him about that item, whether Barbara planted it. They were great pals. I'm sure he knew all about her affairs."

"But why would she plant something mean about your dad?"

"Maybe to divert attention from her affair with Jessup. Jack Cody wasn't stupid. He had to know something was going on."

"Why didn't she just break it off with Cody?"

"She was afraid of him. At least that's what she said."

"Seems to me that if he was that dangerous, it was riskier to have an affair behind his back than to break it off."

"He had some kind of hold over her."

"The kidnapped child? If she was so smart why didn't she see through that game?"

"Maybe it wasn't a game. Maybe he was on to something. If the au pair did turn the kid over to her pornographer friends, Cody had the resources to track those people down."

"But surely the kid was dead."

"Yes, according to the odds. But a grieving mom will hold on to even the slenderest of threads."

SINCE I REVEALED MYSELF to her two nights ago, I've been itching to spill the rest—my strange ambiguous intersection with the Fulraine kidnapping that filled me with guilt throughout my youth.

Back up in her room, Pam turns to me: "If you're obsessed with the Flamingo case, David—and I believe you are—there must be more to it than that you knew the teacher, went to school with the Fulraine kids, caught occasional glimpses of their mom. You told me about your dad's connection, but I still have a feeling you left something out."

She's shrewd, I'll give her that. She's also gotten to me in a way I hadn't expected. But then, I wonder, what *did* I expect? A simple location affair? That we'd each serve the other as bedmate without complications for the duration of the trial?

That kind of shallow relationship usually suits my nature. But I'm really starting to like this girl. She's turned out to be a lot more than a routinely ambitious reporter. I view her now as both generous and compassionate.

"Come on, David. Let me help you.

"I told you, I do better on my own."

"I don't mean as co-investigator. I mean as your friend. Talk to me. You'll feel better if you do."

Which is what I myself often tell eyewitnesses when they start to close down on me during an interview. But confession comes hard for me. Tonight, I decide, will not be the night.

7:00 P.M. I'm sitting in a conference room at the Calista County Sheriff's Department just down the hall from Mace Bartel's office. The setting sun paints the opposite wall, covered by framed photos of former sheriffs, with sumptuous light. The result is a reddening of the images, a bloodying. An appropriate effect, I think, considering the material heaped on the conference table in front of me.

A two foot-high stack of file folders constitutes the entire written record of the Flamingo Court killings investigation. Three additional boxes contain physical evidence taken from the crime scene. An Aladdin's Cave of treasure for the true crime connoisseur; for me, in a way I've yet fully to comprehend, these are "the family jewels."

I spend an hour working to gain an overview. Mace, thorough police professional that he is, has attached a detailed index to the documents. The first one I examine is the write-up of interviews conducted by a Detective Joe Burns with Dad. My heart speeds up as I read:

DR. THOMAS RUBIN

First interview, 8/24, phone:

Witness states he treated victim Fulraine for depression over past five months. Witness, citing doctor-patient confidentiality, states he's reluctant to supply information about therapy sessions. Witness states that much as he would like to assist, he must refer matter to his personal attorney.

Second interview, 8/26, witness' office:

Witness states that having consulted attorney he is now prepared to answer questions about victim's psychotherapy in limited way. Witness states he was shocked by victim's death. Witness states he was 'personally greatly saddened' as he was 'very fond' of victim and felt 'great empathy' for her sons, who will now most likely go to live with their father who has been seeking custody.

Witness states he has no idea who might want to kill victim. Witness states it is common knowledge that victim was involved in long-term love affair with Mr. Jack Cody, and that in therapy she occasionally spoke of her fear Cody might lose control if he discovered she was having 'a fling' with co-victim Jessup. Witness states victim was not specific about this nor was it clear to him what she meant. Witness states victim's greatest fear centered around possibility her ex-husband would find out about her love life and use said information to gain custody of sons. Witness states that victim, having already lost one child to kidnappers, had long been obsessed by fears of losing other children as well.

Witness states he has no specific knowledge of victim's love-life habits and practices. Witness states his sessions with victim dealt with her 'precarious emotional state, occasionally debilitating depression, and fear that bordered on terror aroused by a haunting recurrent dream.' Witness refuses to divulge contents of dream, again citing doctor-patient confidentiality. Witness adds that in any case, dream is not relevant to homicide investigation. Witness states that if he can think of anything helpful he will immediately pass said information on. Meantime he will review all notes on victim's sessions to make certain he has not forgotten anything relevant.

Witness states he wants it understood his refusal to provide details of victim's private thoughts and feelings is not meant to impede investigation but is 'matter of principle that I as a physician am obligated to uphold.'

Third interview, 8/27, phone follow-up:

Witness states he has reviewed all therapy notes and has found nothing 'germane to your investigation.'

Evaluation:

Witness has excellent reputation, seems sincere in his reluctance to breach confidential medical relationship with victim and is otherwise forthcoming in all respects.

Additional notes:

Investigator consulted with supervisor about whether victim's recurrent nightmare was relevant and whether witness's therapy notes should be subpoenaed. Supervisor agreed nightmare was not important and subpoenaing notes would probably result in long legal fight and would not yield useful information.

Respectfully submitted,

Joe Burns, Det.

A perfectly straightforward account of what seems to be a well-conducted police interview. The witness appears sincere and reliable. "Forthcoming in all respects." Yet I'm amazed at the superficiality of the information and the lack of probing follow-up questions. Surely a competent shrink would know a great deal about his patient's love-life practices, let alone her fears. And where are the questions about Jessup? Why did she consider her affair with him merely a "fling"? Just what did she mean about Cody "losing control?" And if the upcoming custody battle with her ex-spouse loomed so fearfully, why did she engage in conduct certain to assist his cause?

I pull out the folder containing interviews with Andrew Fulraine conducted by Mace Bartel. Mace's notes run more than twenty pages. His questioning strikes me as a lot sharper than Detective Burns':

Witness appeared greatly distraught. Witness wept when shown crime-scene photos of ex-spouse. Witness spoke of ex in respectful manner, expressing sorrow over her demise and effect it would have on sons who, he stated, loved their mother very much. Witness stated that if ex-wife had died in automobile accident or other 'normal way,' that would have been bad enough, but that being killed 'like this' will probably 'stigmatize' sons' memories of her forever.

Witness expressed great shock that ex had been having affair with one of sons' teachers. Witness stated: 'That's terrible. She shouldn't have done that.' Witness spoke harshly of Tom Jessup for 'breaking the trust and faith we place in our children's teachers.' Witness stated he had met Jessup and thought well of him for his interest in boys' schooling. Witness stated he had approved victim's hiring of Jessup as tutor, tennis and boxing coach.

Witness stated he knew ex had engaged in love affairs even when they were married and this behavior had been primary factor in their divorce. Witness stated he had loved ex, but could not bear to be cheated on this way. Witness stated that ex began to indulge in affairs shortly after their daughter's abduction. Witness stated he put up with it for a while, but reached point where 'it simply became unbearable.'

Witness stated that though ex was decent enough mother and truly loved sons, he had reluctantly come to conclusion her promiscuity was harmful to sons and for said reason initiated action to gain custody.

Witness stated he was not 'strict moralistic kind of guy or religious nut.' He simply wanted 'very best for my boys.' He has remarried and his new wife, Margaret, loves his kids as if they were her own. Witness stated he had explained to ex that he had no intention of denying her fair visiting rights and vacations with boys. On contrary, he wanted her to play significant parental role. But so far as day-to-day living went, he knew he could provide a more stable home environment.

I put down the document, then pick it up again. There's a major hole in Andrew Fulraine's statement. How could he *not* have known about Barbara's affair with Jessup? According to what Mace told me when we met out at The Elms, Andrew had a private detective watching her, collecting evidence to be used against her in their custody battle.

I read on:

Witness stated he was in New York City on business day of killings. Witness stated he was in his hotel suite when he received emergency call from wife. Witness stated that upon hearing news, he immediately phoned director of summer camp in Maine where sons were enrolled to arrange for sons to be escorted early next day to Logan Airport, Boston, where he would meet them and accompany them back to Calista. Witness stated he instructed camp director to tell sons there was family emergency and their dad would explain it when they all met up following day.

Witness stated he took late evening shuttle to Boston, where he spent sleepless night at airport Hilton, 'trying desperately to figure out some way to break this devastating news without causing my boys undue pain.' Witness stated he decided sons were of sufficient maturity that it would be impossible to hide facts surrounding their mother's demise. Witness stated: 'That morning, telling them what happened was the hardest thing I've ever had to do.' Witness stated that 'at first sons took news like brave little guys, but then they both broke down.' Witness stated that older son, Mark, mentioned that over spring and early summer his mom had become 'good friends' with Mr. Jessup and that the four of them had gone out several times to restaurants and twice to Tremont Park.

Witness stated that sons said nothing indicating knowledge of amorous relationship between victims, and that subject has not since come up. When asked how, considering continuing media reports of 'lovers' and 'love nest' he has kept such information from boys, witness stated that though he assumed they saw news stories and heard details from friends, in his family this was not the sort of matter that gets discussed. Witness stated that when he proposed professional counseling to boys, both declined. Witness stated that his greatest concern is short-term effects on boys as they ease back into school life.

Witness again broke down, stating that over last few days he has wondered if his family is somehow 'cursed.' Witness, sobbing, stated: 'Five years ago our darling little girl was snatched. Now this. These nights I lie awake wondering what will happen to us next.'

At this point, due to witness's emotional state, investigator postponed conclusion of interview until following day.

Though I'm impressed by Mace's sensitivity, I'm underwhelmed by Andrew Fulraine's WASPy approach to life, his notion that in *his* family certain intimate matters were best left unbroached. Of course Mark and Robin immediately found out their mother and Tom Jessup had been shotgunned to death while lying naked together in a motel room bed. And of course they found this greatly disturbing. How could they not? Jessup had befriended them, been their trusted teacher, tutor, and coach. Now it turned out he'd also been their mother's lover and possibly the cause of her murder.

The humiliation must have been terrible for them. I remember how we watched them when school reopened that fall, surreptitiously tried to read their faces. Both Fulraine boys put up brave fronts, showing the stiff upper lip that was their heritage. But we, needing to see their pain, found it in their eyes—a glistening up, a turning away when our gazes became too bluff. They knew what we were looking for and expended much effort not to show it to us. But we saw it anyway, for in their hiding of it we discovered its revelation.

The next day, in his continuation of the interview, Mace attempted to corner Andrew Fulraine about his professed ignorance of his ex-wife's affairs:

Witness showed anger when asked why he had not previously revealed that he had solicited and received reports from a private detective on ex-wife's love affairs. Witness responded that now that ex was dead 'the matter of our sons' custody is moot.' When told this was an inadequate response, witness stated he wished to consult attorney. He left room, returned fifteen minutes later, told investigator attorney was en route and he would decline to answer further questions until he arrived.

When witness's attorney, Howard Breckenridge, appeared, he and witness consulted privately. When interview resumed, witness stated he had engaged a private detective, Walter M. Maritz, to collect evidence regarding activities of ex in preparation for custody battle. Witness stated he was seeking evidence that would prove embarrassing to ex so she would yield on custody question rather than have said evidence introduced in open court.

Witness stated he had met Maritz, a former Calista Police Department detective, five years before when he and ex retained Jenkins Investigations to find his daughter's abductors. Maritz had been sympathetic and witness had been impressed by his competence. Maritz had since left Jenkins and opened his own agency.

Witness stated that since hiring Maritz he had received three reports, none of which named Jessup as ex's lover. At this point, attorney Breckenridge handed over copies of reports.

When asked how this was possible since, within hours of killings, Sheriff's Department investigators documented a five-month affair between victims including more than forty meetings at the Flamingo Court, witness responded with disgust that he could only conclude that Maritz had goofed off on the job. When asked why he retained a man to tail his former wife whom she would recognize from the earlier investigation, witness stated that Maritz had satisfied him on that point by bringing in a second operative for close surveillance.

I put the interview down. Andrew Fulraine, it seems, was an odd combination of sensitive father, old-style WASP, and not-too-bright litigant. As for Walter M. Maritz, I search out his interview, eager to discover how *he* explained his investigatory incompetence.

Here too the interview was conducted by Mace:

Witness states that in late June he was retained by Mr. Andrew Fulraine to collect evidence of victim Fulraine's promiscuity and bad parenting. Witness states that, since he remembered liking Mrs. Fulraine, he had reservations about taking job, but agreed to do so because he needed the work and the fee offered, $12,500, was 'exceptionally good.' Witness added 'it's no secret I haven't been doing too well of late.' In response to direct queries about career, witness admitted he'd been asked to resign from the Calista P.D. eight years previous for drinking on the job and this past January had been 'fired for cause' from operative position at Jenkins Investigations.

Witness stated he had taken special care when trailing victim because 'target knew me from before, and, in fact, we'd gotten on very well.' Witness stated he hired retired detective Jerry O'Neill as operative to assist in investigation, since 'target did not know O'Neill and he's a good tracker with many years experience.' In response to direct query, witness admitted he knew O'Neill had been forced to retire from force due to alcoholism. Witness stated: 'So both of us like a drink or two? So what? We both know how to do the job.'

Witness stated he and O'Neill kept a log of victim's activities and submitted full accounts in their reports to client. Witness stated he couldn't legally turn over copies of these reports without client's permission.

Witness stated he and O'Neill trailed victim numerous times to Elms Club where she went two or three times a week to meet Jack Cody. Witness stated he and O'Neill interviewed several Elms Club employees, all of whom reported victim and Cody 'always eat a quick lunch together then go upstairs and fuck.' Witness stated he had compiled file on Cody so his client, Mr. Fulraine, would know the sort of man his ex was involved with.

Witness stated that client's other activities included afternoons spent at Delamere Country Club lunching with girlfriends and playing tennis, and twice a week visits to Maple Hills Hunt Club where she rode her horse. Witness reported that victim was regarded as excellent tennis player and equestrienne, and over the years had won numerous club trophies in both sports.

Witness stated on several occasions he and operative O'Neill observed victim Jessup arriving and departing target residence. Witness stated it was his understanding, based on interviews with target's servants, that Jessup went there to tutor and coach target's sons. Witness stated he was greatly surprised to learn victims were having affair and that they'd rendezvoused numerous times at Flamingo Court. In response to query as to how it was possible, since he was surveilling victim, he hadn't observed these meetings, witness admitted he'd slacked off on job.

Witness stated: 'It never occurred to me she was involved with two different men. Once I got a fix on her routine, I assumed she spent afternoons at one of her clubs, doing errands, or seeing her shrink.' Witness stated he spent most afternoons drinking and watching baseball games on TV in one of several Irontown bars.

Confronted by fact that if he'd been doing his job properly he would have been surveilling Flamingo Court day of killings and would most likely have observed killer's arrival and departure, witness stated he wished to terminate interview in order to consult attorney.

Four hours later, Mace resumed his interview with Maritz, this time in an interrogation room at the Calista County Sheriff's Department:

Witness's attorney, Justin Slotnik, stated that his client, Walter M. Maritz, was now prepared to make a statement in regard to his surveillance of Mrs. Barbara Fulraine, which statement might cost him his private investigator's license. Nonetheless, in view of the gravity of the circumstances, Mr. Maritz wished to go on record with his information.

Witness Maritz then stated the following: He had always liked and admired Mrs. Fulraine, who had treated him in a friendly, respectful manner when he had investigated the Fulraine infant abduction. Mr. Fulraine, on the other hand, had been high-handed and

arrogant. Witness stated: 'Far as I was concerned, she was a lady and
he was a prick.' Witness stated he only agreed to accept surveillance
assignment from Mr. Fulraine because he needed the money, and that
shortly after he commenced surveillance, he phoned Mrs. Fulraine
and set up meeting with her at Rusty's Pub in Joslin/Pitt shopping
center. At this meeting, he informed victim he'd been hired by her ex
to conduct surveillance in order to collect evidence that would prove
her an unfit mother.

Witness stated he told victim that as much as he needed money
he didn't wish to do anything that would harm her. Witness further
informed victim he'd invited her to meeting to warn her of what was
going on and to advise her not to do anything contrary to her
interests because if she did and he observed said behavior, he would
be obligated to report it to her ex.

Witness stated that victim thanked him for warning and offered
to compensate him for his trouble. Witness stated he was reluctant to
accept money from victim since this would create conflict of interest.
Witness stated that as he and victim continued discussion it was
clear to both that if witness withdrew from assignment, victim's ex
would simply hire someone else to carry it out because he was intent
on collecting negative information on victim's lifestyle.

Witness stated that at end of discussion, he and victim reached
an understanding: Witness would only report personal information
that was already common knowledge, namely that victim and Jack
Cody were having an affair. According to witness, victim told him: 'I'm
not married and neither is he, and I'm not a nun and he's not a priest.
I'm entitled to have a love affair same as anybody else. So don't
worry about reporting it. It won't harm me a bit.'

Witness stated that victim went on to say there were matters in
her life that were none of anybody's business and she'd prefer to keep
them that way. Witness stated victim offered to pay him an amount
equal to fee he was receiving from her ex, in return for which he
could be a little careless in his investigation. Witness recalled
victim's exact words. 'She said I should, you know, "fudge it a bit,

since, after all, if you don't see me doing something you can't very well report it then, can you?" '

Witness stated out of respect and admiration for victim, he agreed to consider her proposition. Witness stated that he met victim at same location two days later at which time he proposed that victim hire him to look further into abduction case. Victim agreed and paid him $12,500 in cash.

Witness stated: 'To cover my ass, I brought in Jerry O'Neill who's an even bigger drunk than I am.' Witness cleared hiring of O'Neill with client who agreed to pay an additional $5,000 to cover O'Neill's wages. Witness stated: 'I knew O'Neill would fuck up good, and that's just what I wanted. Meantime, I was going to clear twenty-five grand on the deal.'

Witness stated there were several important things he wished to add. First he wanted it understood he felt terrible about what happened to Mrs. Fulraine, 'as I liked her and respected her very much.' Witness stated that even if he'd been surveilling her day of killings, he doubted he could have prevented murders. Witness stated: 'At best I might have seen something and been able to give you some leads on who did it, license plate numbers, stuff like that. But who knows? I could just as easily have been asleep. Nothing more boring than sitting in your car in a motel parking lot with nothing but a goddamn bag of stale potato chips while folks are making whoopee upstairs.'

Witness stated he wanted it on the record that he did not meet with victim in order to extort money, that payment was entirely her idea. Witness stated: 'I never solicited a bribe.' Witness stated that of course he was happy to accept money since 'I live pretty close to the edge these days,' but that money was not his primary motivation. Witness stated: 'All I wanted to do was help the lady who'd been through a hell of a lot and didn't deserve to lose her kids.' Witness stated that when he accepted cash at second meeting, he told victim: 'I owe you plenty for this, and I intend to work my ass off going back over ground we covered when we tried to find out what happened to your little girl. Who knows? Maybe

something will turn up after all these years.' Witness stated that
when he said this, tears formed in victim's eyes. Witness stated:
'She took my hand and squeezed it and said, "I thank you with all
my heart." '

Witness stated it was always his intention to honor pledge to
victim and he still intends to do so. Witness stated: 'Soon as the
custody case was finished I was going to go back to work on the
Fulraine infant abduction. That's what she paid me for. That was
our deal. So, see, I didn't take her money to screw Mr. Fulraine. I
took it to do an additional job for her. Meantime, I gave her a
warning and offered to do my best to see she wasn't screwed by her
ex along the way.' Witness stated he still intends to carry out
assignment on his own time, 'because she paid me to do it and when
something terrible happens like this, no one should be allowed to get
away with it.'

Amazing! I put the papers down. The web of interlocking agendas is
growing dense and I've only just started reading through the documents.

Time to take a break. I step out into the corridor, refresh myself at the
water cooler. The Sheriff's Department is quiet this time of night. Down
the hall the pebbled glass panel in Mace's office door is still lit up.

Returning to the conference room, I decide to examine some of the
physical evidence. I pull on a pair of latex gloves, open the first big carton . . . and am horrified! It contains the bedding from room 201—blanket, sheets, pillow slips—discolored, bullet-rent, encrusted with rust-col-
ored stains, which I take for residue of the victims' spilled blood and guts,
even possibly of their sex.

I reel back from the table. One thing to imagine the scene, quite
another to be confronted by its effluvia.

I close the first carton, open the second. This one contains the victims' clothing and personal possessions recovered from the crime scene:
a woman's white tennis shirt, long khaki shorts, underwear, and sandals;
a pair of men's jeans and blue denim work shirt, underwear, socks and
sneakers; assorted men's and women's rings, watches, wallets, and keys.

Just seeing this stuff makes me feel strange. Suddenly the victims are all too close. In my imagination, I realize, I've endowed them with mythic stature. Now, looking at these humble garments, they seem smaller and ever so vulnerable.

I open a third box, find it filled with numerous glassine envelopes identified by neat handwritten labels. Some contain fingerprints lifted from room 201: exterior and interior doorknobs, phone receiver and dial, water glasses, faucets, bureau drawer handles, even the handle of the toilet. Others contain samples of hairs, fibers, various sweepings, scrapings and swabs, four red, ejected empty shotgun shells, and, most distressing, numerous shotgun pellets recovered from the room. There is a treasure trove of forensic evidence here—DNA samples, possible identifiers such as shoe and weapon material—all carefully preserved for presentation in a court of law, still available for analysis by forensic technologies that at the time of the murders did not exist.

I examine the crime scene photographs. Like everything else in the case file, I find them meticulously keyed in Mace's hand to numbers inscribed on the lower right corners: (1) VICTIMS VIEWED FROM FOOT OF BED; (2) VICTIMS VIEWED FROM NORTH WALL; (3) VICTIMS VIEWED FROM BATHROOM DOORWAY . . . the list goes on.

The pictures are brutal. It's the harsh colors that makes them so, and their total lack of artistry. It's clear no effort was expended on lighting or composition. These are straight-on, flash-lit police photographs that rob the victims of anything heroic. I barely recognize the neat and undistinguished motel room where I executed my moody drawings. The room, depicted in these photographs, appears smaller, more confining, and totally befouled. I sense the photographer's distaste, his wish to quickly do his job and get out. In one shot I note a reflection in the mirror above the bureau of young, eager Mace Bartel holding a handkerchief to his nose, wincing with disgust.

Enough! I prefer my own drawings, my imagined romantic renderings of the scene. When I drew the slain lovers, I wrapped them in gloom; in these pictures, their bodies are etched by a pitiless strobe.

I turn back to the file folders, start reading through eyewitness statements. There isn't much of substance.

Motel office clerk Johnny Powell thought the shots were backfire noises. By the time he turned to look, all he saw was the back of a man in a black raincoat running toward the street.

A Mr. Jeff Slade, vendor of kewpie dolls and other amusement park prizes and giveaways, was returning to his room on foot after a taxing negotiation with the managers at Tremont Park, when he saw a man rush from the Flamingo Court into the adjoining parking lot. He didn't think much about it until a few seconds later when, entering the courtyard, he saw a number of people wearing dazed expressions standing on the motel balconies. Perhaps, Mr. Slade surmised, it was on account of his military training that he turned just as a dark car pulled rapidly out of the lot. He identified the car as a late-model Olds and caught a quick glimpse of the driver. The product of this sighting accompanies the interview report, a crude Identi-Kit portrait that resembles a classic square-faced cartoon thug. At the bottom, the interviewing officer notes that he doubts the reliability of Slade's account as two other persons independently identified the suspect car as a four-year-old Chevrolet.

A Mr. and Mrs. Albert Cranston from Buffalo reported a fleeing black-hatted, black-raincoated man, as did a Miss Bonnie Lanette, known to local police as a prostitute who worked the grounds of the amusement park and frequently brought her johns to the Flamingo for fun and games.

Two small children were interviewed, a boy and girl who'd been frolicking in the pool at the time. Neither could offer anything beyond the fact that a man had run down the exterior stairs then out toward the parking area just after the shots.

All four of the ejected shotgun shells had been wiped clean of fingerprints, suggesting a well-thought out professional hit. It was also conjectured that since the shooter had worn a long coat and wide brim hat, he was also probably wearing gloves.

Mr. Andrew Fulraine, through his attorneys, offered a $50,000 reward for information leading to the arrest of the shooter. Later this offer was raised to $75,000 and still later to $100,000. Investigators passed on word of this offer, huge for the time, in the hope of prying information from snitches. In fact, according to an advisory from the FBI, only two men in the entire Midwest were suspected of specializing in hitman work, neither of whom had recently been sighted in the Calista area.

A search of public trash barrels, private garbage cans, and construction debris Dumpsters within a quarter-mile radius of the Flamingo yielded no sign of weapon, hat, coat, or gloves. A thorough but fruitless search was made of trash-collection points within Tremont Park on the theory that the car seen leaving the motel parking lot might not have been an escape vehicle driven by the shooter. Rather, according to this alternative theory, the shooter had left the scene on foot, then merged into the crowds that thronged the amusement park that hot, humid afternoon.

Fliers were printed up and placed beneath the doors of all rooms at the Flamingo, also posted on telephone poles and lampposts surrounding the motel, soliciting information about anyone seen hovering suspiciously in the vicinity of the motel as far back as a week before the killings.

Six people responded to this solicitation. None was able to provide any information beyond the fact that they'd seen a man (described by some as "tall and thin," by others as "medium height and stocky") either gazing at the motel from a booth in Moe's Burgers across the street or strolling by the motel at a suspiciously slow speed.

A thirty-two-year-old black man named Ralph "Snooky" Vaughan, former employee of the Flamingo fired three months before for petty pilfering of soap, toilet tissue, and other room disposables, was interviewed by Detective Joe Burns for six hours. Vaughan had a criminal record for minor crimes going back to his early teenage years. A search of his room in a Gunktown rooming house produced a black raincoat and black fedora-style hat. Vaughan swore he'd been nowhere near the Flamingo Court since the day he was fired and had been engaged in a game of pick-up basketball on a housing project court the afternoon of the shootings. Nine witnesses verified his alibi. When his coat proved negative for powder burns, he was released.

Seven of Barbara Fulraine's former lovers were interviewed, culled from a list provided by her ex. Of the seven, five were married. All begged investigators not to leak their names.

Charles Maw was associate director of the Calista Repertory Theater Company. He stated that he had been a longtime friend of Barbara Fulraine, that they'd been lovers prior to her marriage, and had resumed their affair approximately six months after the Fulraine child was snatched.

Maw stated he had acted as intermediary in a bizarre encounter in connection with the earlier crime. According to his account, about a year and a half after the snatching, Mrs. Fulraine, desperate to find her daughter, was actively consulting gypsy fortune-tellers around town. One, a card reader who worked out of a storefront at Danvers and 36th, told her that her child was dead and promised to provide information on the whereabouts of the body in return for $15,000 cash, $5,000 to be paid up front, the balance on delivery of the girl's corpse.

A late night meeting was arranged. Charles Maw, acting for Mrs. Fulraine, placed the $10,000 final payment in a locker at the Central Bus Terminal, then followed a chain of complicated instructions that led him, in the style of a treasure hunt, from a public phone booth to a message secreted in the men's room of a Gunktown bar to another message hidden beneath a rock on the east bank of the Calista River. Finally, he was picked up by a van with blacked-out windows, driven around town for a while, then into a garage at an unknown location.

Here a man and two women, faces encased in stockings, pointed to a cardboard carton that, they said, contained the preserved remains of the Fulraine child. When Maw opened the carton, he found what he took to be the body of an infant, but the lighting was so dim, the odor so horrific, the corpse so wrinkled and distorted, he could not possibly identify it as Belle Fulraine. Nevertheless, intimidated by the people surrounding him, he handed over the key to the locker, at which point the three jumped into the van and sped off, leaving him alone with the pungent leathery remains.

When Maw picked up the carton and stumbled out of the garage, he found himself not two hundred yards from smelters with smokestacks bearing the words FULRAINE STEEL.

It had been a swindle, of course. The little body was that of a black male infant, preserved, according to experts, in a manner employed by Haitian voodoo practitioners. By the time police were brought in, the $10,000 was gone and the storefront card reader had disappeared. The incident marked the end of Charles Maw's affair with Barbara Fulraine and left him with badly shattered nerves.

It's a strange story and it fills me with pity. It hurts to think of Barbara stooping so low, then being taken in by such a transparent scam. That she was running around consulting with scummy fortune-tellers tells me how very desperate she must have been. As for Maw, he strikes me as a fool. What kind of a friend was he not to have warned her off these con artists?

The six other interviewed former lovers were a junior executive at Fulraine Steel; a star third baseman with the Calista Forgers, a cellist who played with the Calista Symphony; an orthopedic surgeon from the Lucinda Taft Medical Center; a professor of theology at Calista State University; and a mechanic who worked at British Motors in Van Buren Heights where he took care of Mrs. Fulraine's Jaguar coupe.

All spoke of her with affection and respect, not one expressing the slightest degree of ill will. The mechanic described her as "a gracious person" whom it had been his "great privilege" to know. The theologian said, "She was quite the finest woman I've ever known." The cellist said that making love with her was "akin to reveling in the music of the spheres." Charles Maw, the only one to make negative comments, described her as "a user who left many husks behind . . . and I count myself among them." But even he claimed he harbored no animus toward her. "With Barbara I had some of the most memorable and plea-sureful experiences of my life."

Gossip columnist Waldo Channing was interviewed by Mace Bartel.

His comments, unlike those of the former lovers, were not respectful at all:

> Witness stated he was close friend and confidant of victim for many years. Witness stated victim was 'splendid, exciting person of great passion and sensuality' and 'I was privy to all her secrets. There was nothing that happened in her life she did not reveal to me, knowing I would always hold her confidences.'
>
> Witness stated that contrary to opinion commonly held in victim's circle, victim was not promiscuous. Witness stated, 'She did not engage in serial affairs. She was a one-guy-at-a-time-type gal.' Witness stated he and victim were in love, but 'a physical affair between us was not to be. Our affair was far more sublime than that, what the French call "une affaire de coeur." '
>
> Witness stated he is certain victim Fulraine was not romantically involved with victim Jessup. Witness stated, 'If she were she would certainly have told me about it. So, you see, it's simply impossible. There has to be another explanation.' When told that investigators had proof that victims met numerous times at the Flamingo Court, witness became angry. 'Impossible! Can't be true!' When assured that it was, witness broke out in a sweat. Witness then asked for a glass of water and time-out 'to collect my thoughts.'
>
> When interview resumed, witness stated, 'If you ask me, there was something fishy going on between Barbara and that shrink she was seeing.' Asked to explain what he meant, witness stated, 'That's my impression. I just don't trust the man. I think he's a total opportunist. Anyhow, I very much doubt she revealed to him the same intimate details of her life she shared with me. I'm sure she never shared those secrets with anyone else.'
>
> Witness stated that now that victim is deceased, he feels free to reveal some of her confidences. Witness stated victim despised Jack Cody. Witness stated, 'She thought him common, which of course he was. She told me the only reason she continued to see him was that they were into the same kind of sexual kinks and that made sex with

him a lot of fun. She never believed for one instant that he could turn up her missing daughter, but still she pretended she did. She told me, "He thinks he's using me, Waldo, but really I'm using him." She told me she was not afraid of Cody, that "he puts on a tough front, but he's just a big pussy underneath." '

Witness stated victim believed her ex-husband had homosexual inclinations and that she'd had him followed by a private detective in hope she could turn up sufficient proof to embarrass him so he'd back down on his custody claim. Witness stated victim told him the private eye she hired never came up with anything. Witness stated victim told him, 'I think Andrew's just too uptight to indulge himself like that around here.'

Witness stated, 'Barbara had all sorts of evil schemes up her sleeve. She could be pretty malicious at times, which is why we got along so famously. She had no use for the hypocrites who run Calista society, especially her former in-laws. In fact, she held the Fulraines in utter contempt.'

Witness stated that victim told him her shrink was secretly in love with her. Witness stated victim told him, 'I can tell by the way he looks at me, he wants to get into my pants.' Witness stated victim told him she often tried to arouse shrink with tales about her sexual depravity. Witness stated victim was contemptuous of shrink and only continued to see him 'because it amused her to see how crazy and lovesick she could make him.'

Witness stated, 'Barbara was a great actress. She could convince anyone of anything. If she'd gone on the stage, she'd have been a tremendous star.' Witness stated, 'People thought she was this self-confident, cool beauty. In fact she was terribly insecure about herself, didn't even think she was particularly attractive. One time when I was with her, she looked at herself in a mirror then ran her hands down the sides of her face. "Soon it'll be all over for me, Waldo," she told me. "I'll become an old bag and no one will lust after me anymore." '

Witness stated victim feared old age. ' "It's like a shipwreck," she told me. "You get bashed and battered against the rocks, pieces of you break off, then finally you slip into the drink." '

Witness stated victim was a manipulator who played up to other women she viewed as her rivals. Witness stated victim actually loathed these women but 'she beguiled them with her false concern and friendly smile.' Witness stated victim 'was the sort of woman who, if she discovered one of her rivals was in love with a man, she'd go after that man, seduce him, just to hurt and vanquish the rival.' Witness stated victim told him tales about her affairs and then mocked the way her former lovers acted when she broke off with them. Witness stated victim enjoyed 'sending them scurrying back to their wives knowing that having been with her, tasted her delights, they'd never be content with their little "wifie-poos" again.'

Witness stated that if it were true that victim Fulraine had been carrying on an affair with victim Jessup, 'it must have been one of those inconsequential ventures with which she amused herself, and I'm certain the only reason she didn't tell me about it was she was saving up the story till she'd engineered an amusing denouement.'

Witness stated he had no idea who might have wanted to harm victim or have her killed. Witness stated, 'She probably had a zillion enemies, so your guess is as good as mine.'

Evaluation:

Witness started out praising victim. However, once witness was assured victim had been involved with Jessup, he became so angry she hadn't confided in him about affair that he attempted to use remainder of the interview to destroy her character and reputation. There is absolutely no evidence that victim's psychiatrist had anything but a professional relationship with her, nor that victim hired a private investigator to find proof that her husband was homosexual. For these reasons, and because witness's remarks contradict information conveyed by other interviewees, investigator deems this witness unreliable.

Whew! Impossible not to concur with Mace's evaluation. Waldo Channing's portrait of Barbara is at odds with everything I know of her, the ravings of a man consumed by spite.

What upsets me most, of course, are his comments about Dad—that he was an opportunist and that there was "something fishy going on" between him and Barbara. Here again I feel the sharp edge of Waldo's malice, a nearly insane jealousy of anyone beside himself who had access to Barbara's confidences. Unable to make love to her yet spellbound by her glamour, he had to believe he was her only confidant. That a mere psychiatrist, not even a member of their "Happy Few," might have access to secrets she denied to him seems to have sent Waldo into paroxysms of rage.

It's also difficult for me to believe Barbara spent three hours a week on Dad's analytic couch merely because it "amused her to see how crazy and lovesick she could make him." Between her two affairs she had sufficient diversions in her life . . . and as anyone who's been in analysis knows, the process is a good deal more painful than amusing.

Continuing to read through the case file, I come upon a folder devoted to Jack Cody: interviews with his friends and Elms Club staff and those who supported his alibi—the judge who was his luncheon companion at the Downtown Athletic Club the day of the killings, as well as the waiters and barman who served them as they ate and drank.

Mace interviewed Jürgen Hoff, maitre d'hotel at The Elms:

Witness states he's been employed by Cody since the opening of The Elms eleven years ago. Witness states before that he worked for two years as maitre d' at a restaurant in Cuernavaca, Mexico, and before that held enlisted rank in French Foreign Legion, serving in Algerian war, where he was wounded and awarded several medals. Witness states he was born in Germany, obtained French citizenship due to military service, and is now a naturalized U.S. citizen. Witness states he considers Cody a friend, adding 'I'm extremely loyal to my friends.' Witness states that despite this friendship he will answer all questions truthfully.

Witness states Cody was devoted to victim and would never do anything to harm her. Witness states Cody always looked forward to victim's visits and 'he was almost like a little boy when she was around he was so excited by her.' Witness states of victim, 'I found Madame Fulraine charming. She was also cool and haughty, not my type. But Mr. Cody liked women like that so they got along just fine.'

Witness states, 'In my eleven years with Mr. Cody, I never once saw him lose control. He can get very angry, certainly, and you will feel his anger when he turns it upon you, not a boiling rage that makes you sweat, but an ice-cold anger that chills you to the bone.'

Witness states he is familiar with story that Cody disfigured Marcéline Forestière, an entertainer he was going with, when he discovered Miss Forestière was sleeping with club backup musician, Randy Wayne. Witness states this story is totally false. Witness states he knew Miss Forestière, a Canadian citizen, very well, that they always spoke French together, and that after she was disfigured she told him Randy Wayne was the one who'd cut her face. Witness states Cody was so incensed by what Wayne did to her he asked some gangster friends to 'punish' Wayne for his transgression. Witness states he doesn't know what happened, but he heard Cody's friends got carried away and since Wayne's body was recovered a little later 'maybe they went too far.'

Witness states that even though Cody was betrayed by Forestière, he sent her to Los Angeles to be treated by a famous plastic surgeon and ended up paying thousands of dollars for operations so she could sing in public once again. Witness states, 'I tell you this so you know the kind of man we are talking about, a man who, yes, shows a hard face to the world, but who has a big, soft heart beneath.'

Asked by interviewer if Cody, discovering he was being two-timed by victim, might have asked these same friends to 'punish' his girlfriend's lover and maybe the friends again 'went too far,' witness states, 'I do not believe that could have happened.'

Witness states Cody is a very smart man who always learns from

his mistakes and that after what his friends did to Randy Wayne he
would never again have entrusted them with such a
mission. Witness states, 'What they did caused Mr. Cody a lot of
trouble, and Mr. Cody doesn't like trouble. Many people still think he
cut up Marci. I happen to know he didn't. But you must understand
Mr. Cody is not the type to go around telling people "I didn't do this"
or "I didn't do that." He is not the type who denies. Rather he's the
kind who demonstrates his character to the world by his actions and
demeanor. People can think what they like. Mr. Cody doesn't care. He
knows who he is and who he is not, and those, such as myself, who
know him well know he would never have allowed anyone to hurt
Madame Fulraine, a woman he loved, no matter whether she fucked
every busboy, guard, and gardener at The Elms.'

    Evaluation: Witness, by his own admission, is extremely loyal to
Cody, who was primary sponsor of his U.S. citizenship. Witness's
statements about Marcéline Forestière are strictly hearsay.
Witness's statements about Cody's character and what he is and is
not capable of are simply impressions of a loyal employee and for this
reason cannot be viewed as credible.

No wonder Mace dismisses Jürgen Hoff's impressions: In his interview, Jürgen, with great fervor, knocks down Mace's theory of the crime.
If the Flamingo Court killings were in fact a hit ordered by Cody, a hit
against Tom Jessup that went terribly wrong when the shooter, finding
Jessup in bed with Barbara, executed them both, then it's clear the only
hope Mace has of making such a case is to identify, arrest, and then
"flip" the shooter.

The folder on Tom Jessup is pitifully thin, commensurate with his
lowly status. To the media, the Flamingo Court killings were about
Barbara Fulraine: SOCIALITE GUNNED TO DEATH IN LOVE NEST. Although
the cops viewed the victims equally, Barbara became the focus of their
investigation. Still they made a decent effort to learn more about Jessup,
even going so far as to track down his college sweetheart, Susan
Pettibone, in New York. Joe Burns interviewed her by phone:

Witness states she is twenty-eight years old, unmarried, a broker at Merrill Lynch. Witness states she met victim in college, they dated for a year, then lived together for two years in an off-campus apartment. Witness describes victim as 'highly sensitive and one of the sweetest guys I've ever known.' Witness states, 'In the time I knew him, I doubt Tom had an enemy in the world.'

Witness states she and victim kept in close touch even after they decided to go separate ways. Witness states victim phoned her approximately once a week, usually on Sunday afternoons. Witness states victim was 'terribly lonely' in Calista and had not managed to make any close friends since taking job at Hayes School. Witness states victim told her he liked teaching at Hayes and generally liked the kids, though he thought 'some were really spoiled brats.' Witness states victim told her he would probably not stay at Hayes after second year, unless his social life improved.

Witness states victim informed her sometime in May that he'd 'finally met somebody.' Witness states victim sounded happier than he had in over a year. Witness states that when she pressed him, he told her, 'It's an impossible love, there's probably no future in it, but still I'm enjoying every minute.'

Witness states sometime in June, victim told her he no longer felt his love was so 'impossible.' Witness states victim told her, 'We love each other, we're really well suited, and the sex is, well, just great!' Witness states she found this last comment annoying 'because actually the sex between *us* hadn't been all that terrific, at least during the last year or so we were together.'

Witness states that when Hayes broke for summer in late June, victim told her he was seeing his new love nearly every day, and 'it keeps getting better and better. Neither of us can believe how great it is.'

Witness states that when she asked victim to describe the woman, he told her she was gorgeous, divorced, had kids, and was trying to extricate herself from another relationship, 'so we have to be careful, as this other guy is, you know, kind of a hood.' Witness states victim told her his lover 'has problems, but she's seeing a shrink, trying to work them out.' Witness states victim told her he was 'optimistic' about relationship, and that if everything went as he hoped 'my situation will change in ways you can't imagine.'

Witness states she received a call from victim in mid August. 'I was surprised to hear from him since it was a weekday night. He sounded pretty upset.' Witness states victim told her he called 'because I just wanted to hear your voice.' Witness states victim did not offer specific reason for his agitated state, but did say 'problems' had arisen in his love affair and 'I hope we can work them out.' Witness states victim asked her if she'd consider visiting him in Calista for a few days. Witness states victim told her, 'I'd like you to meet Barbara then give me your honest opinion.' Witness states this was first time victim mentioned his lover by name.

Witness states, 'I remember when I put down the phone I felt really disturbed, like something was wrong out there and Tom was too embarrassed to tell me what was happening.' Witness states she brooded over matter, then last Sunday she phoned victim late at night.

Witness states, 'I woke him up. I think for a moment he thought I was Barbara, because he mumbled something weird like, "God! Did you really do it?" or "Did he really do it?" Then when victim realized that it was witness calling, he apologized, told witness 'things are looking better now' and 'of course I'd love to see you, but I don't think you should come out now. It's too hot and humid here in summer.'

Witness states, 'That was our last conversation. Two days ago his cousin called from Michigan and told me he'd been killed.'

Evaluation: Witness is helpful and sincere. Unfortunately, her information on causes of victim's agitation is too sketchy to be of use.

At 6 A.M., having read through the bulk of the case file, I take a few key documents to the photocopy room across the hall. Feeding the pages by rote into the machine, I fall into a kind of daze.

I'm exhausted, I realize, and not just on account of lack of sleep. It's the intensity of my expedition into the past that's worn me out. The fatigue is similar to what I feel after a long eyewitness interview—vague, drained, detached, having not yet reentered my own reality after stepping out of someone else's nightmare.

Mace pops in just as I'm finishing.

"Kinda red-eyed, aren't you?" He grins. "I figured it'd take you the night."

His eyes are clear, his cheeks freshly shaved. "So what'd you think?" he asks, accompanying me downstairs.

"The Identi-Kit composite was pretty amusing. Otherwise I think you guys did a thorough job."

"We hit most every angle. But like any case, there're still hundreds of loose ends. And much as I've studied the file, I still don't have a clear picture of the victims. What they were up to, particularly her. What was she doing with that guy? Was it just physical or was there something else at work?"

"I guess you should have gotten more out of the shrink."

He laughs. "That whip photograph. I've been kicking myself over that, like why I didn't turn it up. Your father had it, didn't he?"

I nod. "My mom died this spring. She had a folder of stuff that belonged to him. The photo was there. It's what got me started on this again."

"Anything else I should know about?"

"Yeah, an unfinished draft of a case study Dad was writing about Mrs. Fulraine."

Mace touches his goatee. "I think doctor-patient confidentiality has pretty much expired by now, don't you?"

"I'll make a copy for you."

"Thanks, David. I appreciate that."

At the main door, he extends his hand. "Let's have dinner this week. You can give me the copy and we can talk the whole thing through."

After we set a date, he claps me on the shoulder. "And please bring along the whip photograph. I'm eager to see that too."

*   *   *

I PULL UP AT THE TOWNSEND a little before 7 A.M. The network TV crews are loading their equipment into vans. Pam, I figure, is probably in the rooftop gym finishing up her workout. Too weary to search her out, I go up to my room, order coffee from room service, then shave and shower.

I'm standing under the hot spray, reveling in the sensual, stingy aquatic drilling of my flesh, when it hits me: Just ten days before the killings Tom Jessup phoned Susan Pettibone and, apparently agitated, told her problems had arisen in his love affair. *What sort of problems?* What could Tom have meant? And what did he mean when, on the Sunday before he was killed, mistaking Susan's voice for Barbara's when she phoned him late at night, he muttered, "Did you really do it?" or "Did he really do it?" or words to that effect?

Something important there, I think—something Mace should have picked up on and probed. For if there was trouble in the affair, perhaps that same trouble was at the root of the killings. If that was the case, then, it seems, Tom Jessup had an inkling of the coming storm.

EIGHT

This morning, Judge Winterson's clerk beckons me aside.

"Judge likes the way you're drawing her," he tells me. "She says you make her look wise."

"She *is* wise."

"On the other hand, she doesn't much like the way this fella Washboard's—"

"Washburn."

"—doing her. Angles her head like she's stuckup. Makes her shadowy like she's a dark presence. The woman's a *judge* for Christ's sake, not some goddamn Aunt Jemima."

Ah! Vanitas Vanitatum!

"Wash is probably just being artistic," I tell him.

WHEN THE TRIAL BREAKS early at 3 P.M., Pam suggests we drive out to the Fulraine mansion for a look. I phone ahead and obtain permission to tour the grounds though not to enter the house.

"Our residents don't like being disturbed," the snooty manager tells me.

The place is now called LAKE VIEW EAST, the words engraved on a brass plate discreetly attached to a stanchion at the driveway gate. Ten years ago, it was converted into a ritzy assisted-living establishment for six wealthy elderly residents, each of whom now occupies a luxury suite.

We drive slowly down the long gravel driveway, park in the turn-about before the graceful beige stone house. It's a perfect copy of a Palladian villa, a tall central section, arched doorway embracing a great room, and two symmetrical wings on either side. There are loggias and arcades, curved windows and columns, with clusters of rhododendra softening the base of the facade. As we stroll around the west side, past the greenhouse and garages, I tell Pam about the last time I was here, twenty-eight years ago, at Mark Fulraine's tenth birthday party to which I and Jerry Glickman were probably invited only because to leave out the two Jewish kids in the class would have been too obvious a slight.

Mark and I were never friends. Our sixth-grade boxing bout was but the culmination of years of mutual dislike. Now, standing out on the main terrace, facing the tennis court, pool, and great lawn that slopes down to Delamere Lake, I recall for Pam my main memory of that party, the reason I had such a lousy time.

"Birthday parties were usually fun," I tell her, "especially when the kid's parents had a place like this. They'd set up tents, bring in ponies, hire a couple of clowns, then we'd go wild, have ourselves a ball. But this time when we arrived, Mrs. Fulraine wasn't here, though she did turn up at the end. Instead we found Mr. Lafferty, Hayes Lower School athletic director, waiting for us in his coach's outfit—faded football pants, red baseball cap, and chrome whistle dangling from his neck. Immediately Lafferty started ordering us around. He organized us into teams, then made us play touch football, not the fun, free-for-all way, but *his* way by school rules. Suddenly the party wasn't a day off, it was like compulsory athletics. I guess Mrs. Fulraine felt she had to bring him in since she didn't have a man in the house."

Pam smiles. "Maybe Mrs. Fulraine was fucking Mr. Lafferty. Maybe Jessup was just one of several lovers she recruited from your fancy school."

I snort out a laugh. "Jessup was young and good looking. Lafferty was a gnarled old guy with a white sidewalls haircut and stick-out ears." I pause. "But there was something else, something we'd all forgotten—that it was three years before at Mark's seventh birthday party when Belle Fulraine and the au pair disappeared. I think that's why Mrs. Fulraine wasn't in the house that day. It was not an anniversary she'd want to recall.

Pam's impressed with the estate. "It's beautiful here," she says, turning back toward the house, scanning the long protected arcade furnished with groupings of tables and wicker chairs. Several times she's described her own background, growing up working class in south Jersey where her father ran a gas station and her mother worked as a practical nurse. Now it occurs to me she may be fascinated by the trappings of wealth.

"That kidnapping—I think it was the key," she says. "It's like everything stemmed from that—the breakup of Barbara's marriage, her affair with Cody, her fear Andrew would get custody of her boys. You told me about watching the Fulraines on TV, begging and weeping at their gate. Think of what it must have been like here then—the terror they must have felt!"

She shakes her head. "After seeing the Flamingo, I had a lot of questions. I thought maybe Tom Jessup was intimidated by the house. After all, with her kids away at camp, Barbara and Tom could have screwed away their afternoons here. So why the Flamingo? You said she liked the scumminess of it. Funny enough, I can relate to that . . . once, twice, three times maybe. But on a regular basis—I don't get it. I think the low-rent appeal would wear pretty thin. Then she'd start longing for the luxury to which she was accustomed. But now, hearing why she wasn't here for Mark's tenth birthday party, I have another theory. I wonder if she thought screwing Jessup here, where her daughter was kidnapped, would somehow, you know, *defile* the place."

An interesting perception, making me glad Pam came along.

We stroll down to the pool. It's a big, old-style turquoise-bottomed rectangle lined up lengthwise with the lake, framed by Moorish tiles. There's a pool house with cupola built in fantasy Arabian style, with a portico that protects a line of bar stools and an exterior bar.

Pam savors the setting. "Those Fulraine boys had it good. Gorgeous house, servants, private tennis court, coach, and pool. For them this must have been a paradise."

She turns to me. "I suppose with the boys away at camp, there was no excuse to have Tom over anymore. The servants might talk. Andrew could use them against her at the custody hearing. So she decided they should meet at the motel and made the best of it, turning it into something romantic and dangerous." Pam pauses. "But still I think if she was into danger, she could have courted it in other ways. The motel was too drab to keep her excited. She needed more. I think they did other things, David. Extraordinary things. She was too stylish to be satisfied with just the tacky, old Flamingo Court."

I like her approach, though I can't imagine what kind of other extraordinary things they might have done.

As we walk back up the slope to my car, I try to remember my departure from Mark's tenth birthday party, whether it was Mom or Dad who picked me up.

If it was Dad, then Barbara may have met him before that Parents Day at Hayes. But then I think it was probably some other kid's parents who took me home.

PAM WANTS TO TAKE another look at the Flamingo, see it in hard daylight, she says. She clocks the drive. As we pull into the motel lot, she tells me it has taken just nine minutes to get here from the Fulraine house.

"This time I want to see the room," she says.

At the pool, I spot the same woman and kids who were hanging around when I visited two weeks ago. The woman's wearing the same yellow bikini and sunning herself on the same orange strap chaise and the kids are splashing around the shallow end as before.

As we walk into the courtyard the woman looks up, pulls off her sunglasses, is about to speak, then apparently recognizes me and settles back.

"She's the owner-manager," I whisper to Pam. "Her dad ran the place at the time of the killings. When I came by before, she gave me the once-over like I was some kind of ghoulish crime buff come to jerk off in the murder room."

"Well, you *are* ghoulish," Pam says.

Johnny Powell's on duty in the office, and, just as before, his geezer's eyes are riveted to a baseball game on the lobby TV.

"Howdy," he says, looking up. "I figured you'd be back."

"Johnny, this is Pam Wells."

"Howdy, Pam. Here to check out old two-oh-one?"

When I nod, he slaps the key down on the counter. Then he looks at me and squints. "Someone's been around asking about you, Mr. Weiss."

Pam and I exchange a look.

"Who?"

"A fella. Didn't give his name. Seemed like a cop, but didn't show me a badge or nothin."

"What did he want?"

"Asked whether I'd seen you. Said your name then showed me your picture. When I shrugged, he flashed the inside of his palm to show me a folded fifty-dollar bill. Being in the motel business, I know better than to talk about other people's business. I told him I didn't know fifty bucks worth of nothin' and to please leave me alone so I could do my work."

"Then what?"

"He smiled like he understood it was going to take more than fifty to open *me* up. Then he irked me, started calling me 'old-timer,' like 'He went to 201, didn't he, old-timer? Asked a lot of questions about the old days? Yeah, I figured that. What I want to know is what kinda questions and how much time did he spend up there in the room?' "

"That's an odd thing to ask."

"I thought so. When I told him to get lost, he winked at me like he was onto me somehow. 'You'll talk to me yet, old-timer,' he said. Then he turned and shuffled out."

I thank Johnny for keeping my confidence, tip him fifty bucks to make up for what he lost on my account, and ask him to please call me if the nosy guy comes around again.

*   *   *

I FEEL MS. EVANS'S EYES on us as we move across the courtyard. When we're up on the balcony, I glance down. She's got her dark glasses back on, but I can tell she's still watching. She smiles slightly and I smile back.

Pam unlocks the door, hesitates, then walks in. I glance back at Ms. Evans. Though I can't read her eyes, I sense the intensity of her gaze by the set of her mouth and the erect position of her head. She sits still as if interested to observe what I'll do next, whether I'll enter swiftly or with trepidation. There's a moment between us as if each is daring the other to look away, broken by the shrill cry of one of her kids.

"Hey, Mom! Watch this!" the smaller boy shouts, taking a running cannonball leap into the middle of the pool.

I find Pam inside seated on the bed.

After a long silence, she ventures an opinion: "It's just so ordinary." She glances at me. "Or is it, David? Do you feel something weird?"

"I did before, probably because I was alone and I'd done a lot of imagining about this room. I think I'll leave you here a while, give you a chance to take in the vibes."

Pam nods, then starts studying her reflection in the big mirror above the dresser. I quietly slip out, close the door, then lean over the exterior balcony. Ms. Evans, sensing my presence again, looks up at me from her chaise. Again I meet her sunglass-shielded eyes.

Obviously something's on her mind. I nod to her, move quickly to the staircase, descend, then stride over to where she's lying. To my surprise, she doesn't react or sit up, rather continues to lie back as if expecting the intrusion.

"Pardon me—I'm David Weiss," I tell her, crouching beside her, extending my hand.

"I know. I'm Kate Evans."

We shake, then she invites me to sit on the adjacent chaise.

"I couldn't help but notice you've been checking me out."

She smiles slightly. "The other day I asked Johnny who you were. It's been years since anyone asked to see the murder room."

She reaches into her pool bag, pulls out a pack of L&Ms and an elegant, thin, gold lighter. She takes her time lighting up, inhales deeply, then exhales in a long, steady plume that hangs like the exhaust trail of a jet in the still, humid air.

"I saw him, you know—the man who did the shooting, saw him clear for a second or two. Then for a long time I saw him in my dreams, not every night or anything like that—maybe two, three times a year for . . . six, seven years. Scary dreams." She exhales again. "Kinda dreams you wish you could forget."

She points to her boys. "Me and another kid were playing here, splashing around like them. Then suddenly—BOOM!BOOM! BOOM!BOOM!" She smiles, takes another long drag from her cigarette, then crushes it out against the concrete beneath her chaise. "He came running down the stairs, then he saw us. That's when our eyes met." She smiles slightly again. "It was like . . . we locked. Then he scooted off under the archway and out into the street. I told the cops I saw him. They were nice, asked me to describe him. I did, but then they never showed me any suspect pictures or anything like that."

I feel a surge of excitement bolting through my body.

She saw the shooter! Even after twenty-six years she remembers his face, saw it in her dreams.

"I'm a forensic artist," I tell her casually, though my mind's racing and my heart's thumping away.

"So Johnny said. He said you've been making drawings at the Foster trial."

"Following the case?"

Kate shrugs. "Doesn't interest me much. But I did watch ABC a couple nights just to see your work. Pretty good. Made me feel like I was there."

"Eyewitness drawings are my specialty," I tell her. "The courtroom work's a sideline."

She nods politely.

"Would you be willing to work with me on a sketch of the Flamingo shooter?"

She shrugs, again shows her restrained half-smile. "It's been such a long while."

Though my heart's still pounding, I try my best to appear cool. Having stumbled into this one-in-a-million opportunity, I warn myself not to blow it.

"Your girlfriend's watching us." She says the words so softly that for a moment I don't react. Then I glance up to find Pam leaning over the balcony gazing down on us, curious.

"Hi!" I wave to her.

Pam hesitates, then unenthusiastically waves back.

I introduce them. "Pam—this is Kate. Pam's a reporter for CNN," I tell Kate. "Kate owns the joint," I call up to Pam.

Kate calls up to her. "Wanna swim? I can loan you guys suits."

Her offer seems to melt Pam's frost. "Great kids," she says, indicating Kate's boys. Then she starts toward the stairs.

Kate turns to me. She speaks very softly but with an intensity she hasn't used before.

"Call me in a couple days. If I decide to work with you, it'd be just the two of us, okay?"

"Sexy little number back there," Pam says. "Blondes like her don't take well to the sun. Couple more years of it she'll start looking like a prune."

We're in my car driving back toward the city, having declined Kate Evans's offer of a swim.

"Are you being catty?"

"She was *flirting* with you, David."

"She says she saw the killer. She was in the pool during the shootings. Their eyes met when he ran out."

"Okay, that's a different story. Will she work with you?"

"She's going to think about it. It's a real longshot. I don't know of a case where a witness recalled a face after twenty-six years. Even Holocaust survivors. Some, who were able to identify their abusers in court years after the fact, couldn't assist with forensic sketches prior to trial."

"If she saw him, I know you'll come up with a face."

Something about the way she touches me then, touches my arm, the smile on her face as she does it, makes me want to open up to her.

I pull over to the side of the road.

"When we were at the Fulraine house, you said something that really hit me," I tell her.

"About Barbara not wanting to defile the house?"

"Yes . . . because, you said, that's where the kidnapping took place. I was there twice actually. I told you about Mark's tenth birthday party, but I was also there for his seventh. That's when I saw Belle with Becky, the English au pair, the one who took her, whose torso later washed up on the beach."

Pam is studying me now, her face creased with interest.

"I didn't take much notice of them. We were whooping around like typical seven-year-olds and they were kinda watching from the fringes. But then I wandered into the house to find a bathroom, and that's when I saw them, heard them actually . . . through an upstairs bathroom door. Becky had one of those British accents that's hard to understand unless you're used to it, so I'm not sure I heard exactly what she said. But her tone was clear. She was balling Belle out. 'You'll do what I say, understand, Missy?'—something like that. And Belle protesting: 'But Mommy says not to do that—it's wrong!' Then a sharp sound like a slap, then Belle crying out in pain. I remember cowering back, upset. Then I heard Becky say something like, 'Now wipe your face, dearie, we're going back outside.' Belle was still whimpering. Then Becky said, 'Come on, dearie. It's not as bad as all that. We'll go out for a drive, meet Ted, have some ice cream—' or maybe she said 'Ed' or 'Ned' or some similar name. To which Belle said something like, 'They're going to serve ice cream here. Cake too.' 'Well, then we'll have ice cream twice, nothing wrong with that, is there? And it'll be better this time with Ted'—or whomever. 'This time you'll like it, Belle, you'll see.' "

"Jesus!"

"Yeah! Still chills me to the bone. Anyway, when I heard them coming out, I ran into a bedroom and hid there till they passed by the door.

Then I went into the bathroom to do my business. I remember there was some Kleenex or something in the toilet, which, of course, I flushed away." I meet Pam's eyes. "That was the day they disappeared, while Mark's seventh birthday party was going on in the garden. I may have been the last person to 'see' them that afternoon."

"Oh, David . . ."

"They never returned from wherever they went and by the next morning it was all over school—Belle Fulraine and the Fulraines' English au pair were missing and there may have been a kidnapping, though that wasn't clear yet and never would be since there never was a ransom note or even a call. They found the car Becky'd used in a shopping center parking lot a mile away. After that, till Becky's torso washed up, it was like they disappeared off the face of the earth.

"I told my parents what I'd overheard, and of course they called the cops. A tough, old Irish detective came out to the house. I went over it again and again with him, my parents sitting beside me on the couch. He kept asking me questions, circling my story, poking around at it for holes: 'You never really saw anything, did you?' 'If you hid, how could you have seen them pass by the door?' Questions like that. I guess I started to cry because at one point my father stepped in and stopped the interview and the detective said something like, 'Well, doctor, I'm sure you can understand we have to make sure the boy's not fibbing to attract attention.' My father said, 'My son doesn't lie!' The detective raised his eyebrows, shrugged, and shortly after that he left.

"That night Dad came to my room. He asked me the same questions the detective asked, in his own gentle, fatherly shrink's way, of course. But no matter how loving he was about it, the subtext was the same— there *were* inconsistencies, maybe I *hadn't* really heard what I thought I'd heard, maybe I'd exaggerated or embellished the story. I was after all a highly imaginative kid prone to visualization. No doubt I heard something, then maybe 'visualized' it into something else. I loved watching cop shows on TV. Wasn't it a little implausible that Becky slapped Belle without Belle running out to her mother to complain? And wasn't the mysterious 'Ted' a standard TV bogeyman and the 'ice cream' right out of a TV movie bogeyman story? And did Belle, who was only three, really talk like that?

I wasn't embellishing or visualizing, at least I didn't think I was, but when I realized people including my own dad thought so, I stopped protesting, bottled it up, admitted maybe they were right, maybe my imagination had gotten the better of me. After that I didn't talk about it anymore. But still I was convinced I'd been a witness—you know, 'a witness before-the-fact'—and that made me feel awful. Like I should have *told* someone what I'd heard right when I heard it, *should* have gone straight to an adult, Mr. or Mrs. Fulraine, then they would have stopped Becky and Belle wouldn't have been taken."

"Oh, David—!" she moans again.

"Thing is, I still don't know whether that's the way it happened or whether I did imagine or embellish it. I do know I visualized it, because I started seeing the scene in my dreams. I dreamt about it for years—seeing all sorts of details, the expression on Becky's face when she slapped Belle, the tears pulsing out of Belle's eyes. And, crazy as it is, there's still a side of me that believes I *could* have saved her. You've accused me of being secretive. Maybe that's the reason. I'm still afraid I won't be believed. That's also the reason I'm so attentive when I work with witnesses. No matter what I feel, I always act as if I believe them, believe totally in everything they tell me. I do that because I never want to undermine a witness's confidence . . . as mine was undermined.

"So, you see, my involvement with the Fulraine family goes beyond the coincidences that Barbara's sons were classmates, Tom Jessup was a favorite teacher, and my dad was Barbara's shrink. Like you said back at the house, looking at it a certain way, everything that happened can be traced back to the kidnapping. Belle's disappearance, to which I was a naive, unwitting, and perhaps even an untrustworthy witness, was the seminal event."

TODAY I MOVE ABOUT in a daze. My confession to Pam, if I can rightly call it that, has served to cleanse my soul. She says she understands me better now—my need to draw, imagine scenes, trust witnesses, relive their experiences, get inside their heads. And now the possibility of producing a drawing of the Flamingo shooter is so exciting I can think of nothing else.

I sit at the bar in Waldo's, oblivious to the swirl, relishing the prospect, fantasizing the result: By an incredible stroke of fortune, I'll fulfill Jerry Glickman's and my childhood dream—solve the Flamingo case, surpassing even my achievement on the Zigzag.

Hold on! I tell myself. *Kate may decide she doesn't want to help. And even if she does, I may not get a decent ID.*

To distract myself I focus on work, turning out a series of sketches that seriously challenge Wash. This effort creates a crisis of loyalty in Pam, who, though my lover, owes a professional allegiance to CNN.

"Why're you suddenly working so hard?" she asks me in the courthouse corridor during afternoon break. "I thought you didn't give a shit about this case."

"Professional pride," I tell her. "I can't let myself be bested by an asshole."

"Wash is a good guy. Everybody likes him."

"Not the Judge," I whisper back.

WHEN MACE PICKS ME UP at the Townsend, he's more relaxed than at earlier encounters, especially when I hand him a copy of Dad's draft case study of Barbara Fulraine.

"Heavy," he says, weighing it in his hand.

"But unfortunately unfinished," I remind him.

As he drives, I make an effort to match his affable manner while trying to force the prospect of working with Kate Evans from my mind. But it keeps intruding. *After all*, I ask myself, *how can I not think about it?*

Mace drives us out to Covington along the Gold Coast, then south a couple of blocks to Indiana Street, a trendy area of boutiques, artisan shops, bars, coffee houses, and little restaurants. I pick up the scent of affluence here, straight and gay young urban professionals. I also observe the same twinkle in Mace's eyes that Pam detected in mine last week—a smug have-I-ever-got-something-in-store-for-you look.

Fine, I decide, *let him play his hand.*

The restaurant's called Spezia. It's a cute storefront place with a three-star review taped to the door. Inside, visible from the street, happy diners are seated at crowded little tables tended by friendly servers.

A tall, lean, erect maitre d' with thick, gray, brush-cut hair greets us at the door with a sad, world-weary smile.

"Well . . . if it isn't our old friend, Inspector Bartel! We've missed you, Inspector. Nice to see you again."

He speaks with a generic continental accent and exhibits an ultra-suave manner that doesn't go with the lack of pretension of the place.

"Our best table, perfect for discreet conversations," he says, showing us to a table in the rear. "You see, Inspector, even after a long absence, we don't forget our clients' special needs."

He whispers something to a waiter, then moves away. Half a minute later, two kirs are delivered. "Compliments of the house," the waiter says.

"Jürgen's the owner," Mace tells me. "You probably ran across his statement in the file."

I glance again at the man, now greeting a group at the door.

"Jürgen Hoff of The Elms?"

Mace nods. "Funny, isn't it, the way he acts? Like he's still running the Cub Room out there. The young crowd here seems to like his style. Makes them feel like they're in Europe . . . or at least New York."

The waiter takes our order. After he moves away, Mace lowers his voice.

"Jürgen's the reason I brought you here. I always thought he was the key. He was close to Jack Cody, a lot closer than people knew. Cody left him some stuff in his will including his watch, an expensive gold job-bie—I saw it on his wrist when we came in. Twenty-five years and he's still wearing the damn thing."

"Isn't he the one supposedly killed a man in Mexico?"

"I think Cody started that rumor. Still I don't doubt Jürgen could've done it. Those Foreign Legion guys played rough. There's something grave about him, isn't there? Something in his eyes like he's seen stuff he doesn't want to talk about. He's a bachelor. Never had a live-in girlfriend far as I know. Dates classy black call girls. Interesting they're always black."

"You seem to know a lot about him. What makes you think he's the key?"

"If Cody ordered the killings, Jürgen knows. Maybe even carried them out."

"If I recall, he had an alibi."

"A call girl, Winnie something. She was probably lying. Actually I don't think Jürgen did it. But he *could* have. I wonder sometimes. With Cody dead and so many years gone by, I can't think why else he won't tell me what he knows."

"You've asked him?"

"I ask him regularly. I'll ask him again tonight before we leave. He always gets a little nervous when I come in because he knows I'm going to ask. It's this game we play. I ask, he smiles and shrugs. What he wants is for me to think he doesn't know anything but that it amuses him to string me along."

Now, studying Mace, I start seeing him in a different light.

"I know what you're thinking," he says. " 'Hey, Mace, get a life!' "

"You do seem a little obsessed."

"I am. I've had other cases that didn't get solved, but this is the only one that still haunts me late at night."

He eats several forkfuls of chicken, wipes his mouth.

"There was this girl back in high school, Stephanie Beer. Great-looking kid, enigmatic, you never knew what she was thinking. I had a crush on her, but every time I asked her out, she'd smile mysteriously and shake her head. I've known a lot of girls since, married a couple too, but the only one I still think about is her . . . and to this day I don't know what she was about." He takes a sip of wine. "It's the same with Flamingo. It's the only case that still drives me nuts."

Well, I think, *we all have our ruling passions.* But what I'm learning tonight is that though Mace and I share an obsession, we do so for entirely different reasons.

"It'd probably be easy for you now to track her down."

He chuckles softly. "Sure . . . and find a bloated-up cow with a hair salon called STEF'S. Tell you, David, far as Stephanie's concerned, it's better for me not to know. I get too much pleasure savoring my regret. That's what's different about Flamingo. I want to keep open the possibility of Stephanie, but I want closure on Flamingo, because the way that stirs me isn't fun. It's like an ache in a back tooth."

We discuss the case through dinner. When I mention how struck I was by Susan Pettibone's account of Tom Jessup's agitation ten days before he was killed, Mace shrugs that off as just the telephone impression of a tangential witness.

Over dessert, Mace asks if I brought along the whip picture. I pull it out of my sketchpack, hand it to him. He adjusts his granny glasses and studies it.

"Yeah, it's her all right. Great tits." He shakes his head. "Amazing! Though I don't know why I think that . . . or what it really means." He looks at me. "Okay if I show this to Jürgen?"

"Go ahead."

Mace turns the picture face down on the envelope, summons the waiter, asks him to send Jürgen over.

A couple minutes later, Jürgen appears. Mace invites him to sit down.

"Just for a minute." Jürgen sits. "Busy night. Lots of clients requiring attention."

Mace introduces me without mentioning my connection to law enforcement. "David's come up with an interesting artifact. I'd like to get your take."

He pushes the picture, still face-down, toward Jürgen. Jürgen smiles slightly, then turns it over. Mace and I watch him as he studies it. If Jürgen feels anything, he doesn't show it.

"Very artistic," he says finally. "Looks like Max Rakoubian's work."

"You knew Max?" I ask.

Jürgen nods. "Max was one of the best." He turns to Mace. "Brings back lots of memories."

"Of Barbara Fulraine?"

"Of Mrs. Fulraine, Jack Cody, The Elms, people and places from another time." He glances at the photo again, smiles solemnly, and pushes it back toward Mace. "We're all getting older, Inspector. The years pass . . . and, well . . . perhaps some things are best left behind."

He smiles again, offers his hand. "Nice to meet you, Mr. Weiss." He stands. "Gentlemen, I hope you enjoyed your dinner. And please, Inspector, don't be a stranger here. We treasure our loyal clients."

WE'RE ON THE INTERSTATE heading downtown.

"Damn!" Mace slaps the steering wheel. "I played a good card and still he trumped me. I'll say this for Jürgen, he's quick on his feet."

Mace is frustrated. He didn't even get a chance to ask Jürgen the usual question—whether Cody ordered the Flamingo killings. When I tell him I think it's interesting Jürgen knew Rakoubian, Mace says maitre d's know thousands of people, that's what the job's about.

He turns to me when we reach the Townsend. "You in a rush?"

I shake my head.

"Let me show you where Barbara Fulraine was brought up. I think you'll find it interesting."

He turns west on Proctor. "Everyone thought she was well-born. In fact, she had a plain background, certainly not Old Money. Her father deserted early. Her mother brought her up alone."

Soon, I realize, we're going to pass the medical building where Dad kept his office, a block that so far I've carefully avoided on my various jaunts around town.

"Barbara's mom's name was Doris Lyman," Mace continues. "Doris made her living as a gambler. A good enough living to give her only child the best of everything—nice clothes, private schools, tennis and riding lessons, fancy summer camps, Vassar College. Doris was a regular at Woodmere Downs. She liked to play the ponies. She also played cards like a demon—poker, bridge, gin, you name it. She had a fantastic memory and a computer-type mind, so she could remember long runs and rapidly calculate odds."

He pulls up in front of a gray concrete apartment building in the

Danvers-Torrington area, one of many in town constructed in the 1920s. This one has the name FAIRVIEW APARTMENTS cut into the stone above the door. Above that there's a molded escutcheon, an empty shield crossed by two long swords.

"Neighborhood's the same," Mace says. "Ordinary, middle class, lots of elderly. In these buildings there's always an old crab who complains about the kids, and a faint smell of cabbage and cat piss in the halls."

I gaze at the building, trying to imagine Barbara's childhood. What must it have been like for her to depart this place every morning for Ashley-Burnett, sister school to Hayes, where the girls all came from big houses in Delamere, Van Buren Heights, and Maple Hills? Her only choice would have been to outdo them, be smarter, prettier, more ath-letic, and display such savoir-faire that her classmates, rather than look-ing down on her, would vie for her favor.

"Barbara's mom knew everybody out at the track," Mace says. "All the owners, trainers, jocks. Early on, she had Barbara up on horses. The kid was a natural. Started winning trophies when she was six. When we went into her house after she was killed, we found a room full of them, hundreds of blue ribbons and silver cups. It was her horsemanship that got her into society. It was at a Maple Hills Hunt Club Christmas dance where she met Fulraine. She was back on holiday from her junior year at Vassar. He was home from his senior year at Yale. He fell for her right away, but she didn't make it easy for him. There were lots of young men interested in Barbara Lyman. Took three years of courtship before she agreed to get engaged."

So it was by her excellent horseback riding that she won her station in life—wealth, social position, her magnificent house. By her charm too, no doubt, also her beauty, intelligence, ambition, and, of course, her smoldering sexuality. Then tragedy! Her infant daughter was abducted. It's from that point, the point of the abduction, that her life started turn-ing strange.

"I met Doris Lyman at the funeral," Mace tells me.

We're heading back up Gale now, passing antique shops, galleries, trendy bars.

"She'd moved down to Florida. Barbara had bought her a little place in Coral Gables. She still looked pretty good. Had a few facelifts, no doubt. She told me she still played the ponies, got herself over to Hialeah two, three times a week. I gave her my typical homicide investigator's speech about how we weren't going to rest till we found her daughter's killer. Then she said, 'I had a feeling it would end for Barb like this.' I was so surprised I forgot to ask her what she meant. When I called her a couple days later, she played hard-ass, said she didn't remember saying that, I must've misheard or misunderstood."

Mace turns to me. "But I hadn't. No mistake. I'd heard her perfectly. I can even remember the expression on her face."

I STOP IN AT WALDO'S. find the usual crowd of journalists and network people. No sign of Pam. I'm about to leave when I notice Tony standing in his usual meditative position behind the bar.

"How's it going, Tony?"

"Same as usual," he says.

I take a stool across from him. "You've been around, Tony. You know this town pretty well."

"Well as any barman, I'd say."

"Over the years ever hear of a guy named Max Rakoubian?"

Tony grins. "Sure, I remember Max. Been a while. He kicked the bucket few years back."

"What'd you know about him?"

Tony strokes his chin. "Max was kinda slimy as I recall. Took pictures, some of 'em nice, some not—know what I mean?"

"He did porn?"

"Not porn exactly. More like bust-in stuff."

" 'Bust-in'?"

"You know, say a gentleman's looking to divorce, he doesn't want to get taken to the cleaners, so he needs proof his spouse is shacking up. Pictures make good proof. To get pictures he needs a bust-in guy, guy who'll bust in on the spouse and lover, take a few shots. That's bust-in stuff."

"Max did that?"

"His specialty. This'll probably surprise you—he and Mr. C were fairly tight. I think they had some deals going. Max'd tip Mr. C off on stuff. There was also talk Max did bust-ins freelance, busted in on folks without being hired to. Then he'd try and sell the pictures back. Those were the rumors anyway."

"Blackmail photographs?"

"You could call them that."

"Jesus!"

"Don't think badly of him, Mr. Weiss. Max was a gent. Knew how to talk to the ladies. Could sweet-talk 'em into taking off their clothes, not for any reason but to let him record their God-given beauty—or so he used to put it."

"Doesn't sound like much of a gent to me, Tony."

"Well, each to his own I always say."

BUST-IN GUY, BUST-IN STUFF—seems to me that's exactly what the shooter did at the Flamingo Court, burst in on Barbara and Tom, not with a camera but with a gun. I'm thinking about that, working myself toward sleep, when I hear knocking at my door. I open up to find Pam looking sexy, swaying in the doorway.

"Hi, loverboy!" she purrs in her sexiest voice. "Mind if I come in?"

THIS MORNING, AFTER PAM goes up to the gym for her workout, I phone Kate Evans, ask if she's made a decision.

"I've given it a lot of thought," she says. "I don't know if I can help, but I'm willing to try."

Great!

We agree to meet at the Flamingo at 2:00 P.M. She'll leave her kids at her mother's for the afternoon. I'm to come directly to her suite above the office.

"I'm a little nervous about this," she tells me, "but I guess it's something that's gotta be done."

*   *   *

FOR ME, AN ID INTERVIEW is an exploration into another person's mind. I don't do so-called cognitive interviews or employ standard forensic techniques. I also don't put such techniques down. They work well for most forensic artists. However, I'm interested in probing deep, uncovering repressed material, stripping away protective layers, plumbing the unconscious of my informants. In this respect, I'm following in the footsteps of my dad. As I often remind myself, plumbing the unconscious is the family trade.

At exactly two o'clock, sketchpack in hand, I climb an exterior staircase on the Dawson side of the Flamingo, then follow a narrow walkway to the owner's apartment. One side of this walkway is demarcated by the back of the large neon Flamingo image that proclaims the name of the motel to passing cars.

It's another hot, humid Calista summer afternoon. Standing before Kate Evans's door, I feel my shirt sticking to my back. I knock, then hear footsteps. The door opens and Kate peers at me out of the gloom. She's wearing sandals, tight shorts, and a skinny, ribbed tanktop. The blinds in the room have been pulled.

Her eyes seem to glow in her face. They're large eyes alive with curiosity, perhaps some trepidation, too. I've been made uneasy by her scrutiny before—on my first visit to room 201 and two days ago when we spoke. I like the fact that she makes strong eye contact; that's usually a lifelong trait. If her vision was as direct when she was a girl, she may have seen the shooter clearly.

She invites me in, offers me a beer. I opt for a Coke. While she fetches it, I check out her living room: basic furniture with tough fabric upholstery, the kind of indestructible stuff one expects to find in a residence inhabited by a couple of rowdy kids. The carpeting's wall-to-wall, the pictures are conventional. The only striking characteristic, the single feature that differentiates the room from American Motel, are the shelves crammed with paperback editions of self-help books—books about how to get along, make money, build self-esteem, find success, analyze your own dreams, become your own best friend. Books too about wicca, tarot, astrology, and the occult.

This tells me that she's a troubled soul in search of easy remedies. It will be my task not to let her stray into the mystical, keep her in the here and now.

"I see you're a New Ager," I tell her, gesturing toward the books.

"Can't seem to get enough of that stuff."

"Are you a witch, Kate?"

"Not quite." She lights a cigarette, perches on her couch, then draws her tanned legs beneath her like a swami. "I'm an aspirant goddess. Not so easy with two boys roughhousing all the time."

She's a single mother. Her sons' father lived with them for a while, left when things didn't work out. "And I think now we're the better for it," she says.

To relax her, I ask about her boys, where they go to school, what their interests are. Then I ask her what's it like being owner-manager of a motel, the joys, pains, special problems of the job. We chat about the old amusement park, the rides and games, especially the Fun House, how weird and spooky it was. We talk about Calista, the changes that've taken place, the new Natural History Museum, and how the old stuff, like Lindstrom's magical twin towers, still look good as ever. As we gab, I realize we're fairly close in age—she was seven the summer of the killings; I was twelve.

I tell her about my work, my ID sketches of the Zigzag Killer, the Kansas City kidnapper, and the serial murderer dubbed the Saturn Killer because he drew wide concentric rings around the bodies of his victims. In each case, I emphasize that I worked *with* my witnesses. Rather than taking personal credit for my portraits, I make it clear I regard them as collaborations. In each case, I give her a little background so she'll understand that the amount of time between a sighting and production of a sketch varies greatly and needn't be an issue.

"In your case," I tell her, "the fact that you were seven at the time probably works in your favor. Often kids engrave their early memories, especially when they're traumatic. Also the fact that afterwards you saw his face in dreams tells me it registered pretty well."

"I don't know," she says, squashing out her cigarette. "I tried to draw him myself last night. Didn't get too far."

Damn! I should have told her not to try that. Now it's too late. I'll have to play along.

"Still have the sketches?"

She nods, uncurls herself from the couch, retreats to another room, returns with a child's sketchpad. I move to the couch, sit beside her so we can look at what she drew together.

She shows me a pair of drawings on facing pages. Soon as I see them, I start feeling better: Her sketches are rudimentary egg-shaped outlines of a man's head with the features schematically portrayed in a childlike hand.

"As you can see, I'm no artist."

"You don't have to be," I assure her. "That's my job."

I suggest we use her sketches as a base from which we'll develop more refined portraits as we go along.

"First," I tell her, "I want you to set the scene. Close your eyes, imagine yourself back then, recall what you were doing before you heard the shots."

She starts by describing the heat. "It was like today . . . ," she says.

A hot, humid summer afternoon, the kind of sweaty, buggy afternoon typical of a Calista August.

The noises around were also typical: the hurdy-gurdy sounds of Tremont Park drifting from across the road; the high pitch of kids whooping it up out on the sidewalk in front.

She spent a lot of afternoons that summer playing in the pool, splashing around, meeting kids whose parents were motel guests, forging quick friendships that would flourish over a couple of hours then dissolve the following morning when the visiting family checked out and drove away.

Even back then Johnny Powell manned the desk weekday afternoons. He was in his cubicle watching a ball game just like he probably is today. She could hear the sounds of the game, the commentary of the announcers, the roar of the crowd when there was a hit. She was also conscious that her father was around, probably doing maintenance and repairs, and that every so often her mother appeared in the window of the owner apartment to check up on her, make sure she was all right.

"This window," she says, pointing at it.

I ask her why she's drawn the blinds.

She tells me she finds the summer light too harsh. "Even with the air-conditioning, it makes the room too hot."

This causes concern about her vision. "Were you wearing glasses, Kate?"

"No. I see very well."

"Sunglasses?"

She shakes her head.

"So the harsh light might have made you squint?"

Yes, she remembers that. She used to squint a lot. "I'd get these sunburnt wrinkle marks from squinting all the time."

Her mother was always after her to use sun lotion. Sometimes she'd come down to the pool area and massage it into Kate's back.

She remembers the swimsuit she wore that summer, one piece, bright yellow, with straps that crisscrossed her back. She still likes yellow swimsuits, she says. She remembers the smell of chlorine from the pool, the sting of the cold water when the little boy she was playing with splashed her to induce her to jump in. She remembers slipping in a few times and the feeling in her arms when she held onto the rungs of the pool ladder to pull herself back out. She remembers the energy she had, the tirelessness, the way her skin tanned, the sun marks left by her swimsuit straps. She remembers sitting on the edge of the pool with just her feet in the water, swishing the water around, kicking at it, kicking it in the face of the little boy.

"That summer the pool was my life." She smiles. "I guess it still is. I'm out there most every afternoon now with my boys, reading, watching them, working on my tan. Also keeping track of whatever's going on, who's coming and going, whether guests look okay or whether they're the type I'd rather not have in-house."

She was always aware of the motel guests, she tells me, even as a little girl. Her father taught her that, to always be on the lookout, keep track because some folks weren't decent. "A lot of people who go to motels are up to no good," he used to say. Guests, she tells me, sometimes do the most amazing things. There's one regular the chambermaids call "Mister-Piss-on-the-Bed." Then there are the people who steal stuff—toilet paper, shower curtains, pillows, mattresses, even the locks on the doors. Often they'll try to steal TVs. They'll check in with a box of tools, unscrew a room set from its stand, then lower it out a back window to a confederate in the middle of the night. Her father's policy was not to confront the crooks, just get their plate numbers and phone them into the cops.

"Of course now we have a security system with round-the-clock videotape surveillance." If they'd had that back then, she tells me, the killings probably wouldn't have taken place . . . at least not at the Flamingo Court.

She remembers people coming and going through the afternoon, though she doesn't recall any of them individually.

I ask her if she was in the pool before the thunderstorm

She shakes her head. "Mom wouldn't let me swim when a storm was coming on. Too dangerous, she said. Lightning could strike and electrocute you right there in the water."

"How would she know a storm was coming?"

"The sky would get dark. It was dark that day and the storm was wild. It came in fast and fierce."

"How long did it last?"

"Ten, fifteen minutes. Pounding rain. Then the sky cleared, fast too. It was right after it cleared I asked Mom if I could go down to the pool. She said sure, go down, enjoy."

"Was the concrete wet?"

"It was slick. But it dried fast. When the sun came back out, it got real hot."

"This was about—?"

"Three, maybe a little past."

"And the little boy—was he there when you went down?"

She thinks a moment. "No, he came down later. Maybe he saw me fooling around in the pool and asked his folks if he could go on down and play."

"So you played a while, then the man came into the courtyard?"

Kate nods. She thinks she remembers seeing the man in the raincoat come in through the arch. It was nearly four o'clock. That's when folks usually start checking in, so there was always some coming and going around that time. She thinks she remembers him, that he seemed to know where he was going—right up to room 201. Maybe because of that she assumed he was a guest. Maybe that's why she didn't pay him much attention. The raincoat didn't register because a lot of people wore raincoats when it rained. But of course it had stopped, was muggy and hot, so maybe the raincoat *did* register. In fact she *does* remember him coming in. In that kind of heat, the raincoat didn't fit and neither did the hat. Most people caught out in the rain would carry their raincoats on their arms in heat like that. And a hat was for autumn, not a steamy August afternoon.

Kate's trying hard to work for me now, putting her story together. And if she's distorting her recollections a bit, imposing adult logic on childhood memories, that's okay too. I've deliberately put off asking her to describe the shooter, wanting first to get her into a proper recollective state.

"I remember the shots," she says. "To me they were loud, a lot louder than people said. Some folks said they sounded like firecrackers, but down there in the pool—I was *in* the water, not on the concrete—they came to me like roars. I even think they made the water shake. So of course we looked up."

"We?"

"Me and the boy, Jimmy. It's coming back now. Jimmy was his name. We were right next to each other in the water, splashing around. That was the game—to splash the other kid, try to make him duck."

She didn't see the man come down. She was probably still turning around. But she remembers him appearing at the bottom of the stairs. That's when their eyes locked and she got a good look at his face.

He didn't look urgent or upset, surprising considering what he'd just done. He seemed calm. She thinks he may even have smiled at her. There was kindness in his eyes, at least that was her impression. He had a kind man's face, the face of a man who listened to you, listened to your troubles, cared about you, cared about how you felt.

My heart sinks. *How is that possible? How could the shooter have presented himself like that just seconds after committing murder?*

She insists on her description, that no matter what he'd done he had a kindly face. A certain amount of insistence can validate a description; too much will tend to impeach it. But if he really looked so kindly, I wonder, what was he doing in her nightmares?

He had large, sensitive eyes. Nice eyes, she says. His eyebrows arched above them. He was clean-shaven, his cheekbones prominent, his cheeks slightly sunken, making him look somewhat gaunt. His chin was sensitive, too. He was probably in his late thirties. She couldn't see his hair—he was wearing that fedora—but she had the impression it was full. . . .

I'm sketching rapidly now, working from her impressions, altering features as she refines her memories.

"The eyes were bigger . . . the nose a little longer, I think . . . lips fuller. No, that's too much. A little less . . . yeah, like that. . . . I don't think you got his eyebrows right. They weren't so heavy. Lighter, nicer. . . . Can't remember anything about his ears. Maybe his hair curled down over them. Which means I saw his hair, doesn't it? So I ought to know what color it was. Brown, I guess. . . ."

I assure her hair color isn't important, only its lightness or darkness since I'm working in a range of grays.

I ask her to show me his smile, imitate it for me. She tries, screws up her face several times before finding the right fit. In the end, she shows me a friendly half-smile. So . . . perhaps his face did show kindness. Perhaps he was the kind of sentimental killer who related well to children, a psychotic hitman who loved his mother, visited her religiously on Sundays, went all teary-eyed over the plight of orphans, broken-winged birds, and mangy, three-legged dogs.

There was nothing furtive about him, she says, no attempt to hide his face. His gaze was penetrating and direct, without challenging her or trying to force her to look away.

His skin was smooth. His teeth were even.

There was nothing mean about him, nothing predatory. His eyes and smile were warm.

"He was almost. . . ."

"What?"

"Pleasant."

"Show me what you mean."

The face she shows me is almost sweet.

She didn't see the gun. Must have been hidden under his raincoat, though she doesn't remember a bulge. Could he have gotten rid of the gun before he came down the stairs? Impossible, of course, since the gun was never found.

"Oh, that's close!" she says. "I think you're onto him now. Maybe loosen the skin a little beneath the eyes. I don't remember him so young, so tight."

Seeing him in my drawing doesn't make her afraid, she says. She was never afraid of him, she says.

If that's true, I ask, why was he so fearful when she saw him in her dreams?

"Because of what he'd done," she says. "He killed that couple, blasted them to bits. It was all the more scary that he didn't look like a man who would do a thing like that. My mom used to warn me about men who seemed nice but weren't. She said never get in a car with one, especially when he acts nice and seems to like kids. He'll trick you, she said, give you candy and stuff, then take you away with him, and you'll never be seen again."

I know what to do now. I start to sketch on a fresh page. No erasures this time, no changes. I work rapidly, drawing him just as she's described him from start to finish. She lights a cigarette, inhales, watches intently as I draw, fascinated as the face emerges out of the whiteness of the paper.

"This is amazing," she says. "You draw so quickly. I can't believe the way you make him come alive."

She nods when I've finished. "Yes!" she says. "That's the man! That's him, that's him!"

And then I know she never saw the man she's been describing so fully to me this afternoon. I have drawn a self-portrait. The face that stares back at me out of the paper is . . . my own.

NINE

*W*ho *can know the human heart?*

We call it "transference," the phenomenon that occurs when a witness believes he or she can recall a face, and then, failing to do so, describes the features of the artist. In such cases, the witness does not intend deceit and rarely recognizes what he/she has done. It's an unconscious process, but when it occurs the witness must be considered unreliable. Even if Kate were now to revise her description of the shooter, her memory has been contaminated. Any drawings made with her must now be held suspect.

AFTER SOME SERIOUS DRINKING in Waldo's, I return to my room, tape the drawing to the mirror above the desk, sit before it, and gaze at the two images of myself.

Not a bad self-portrait, I think. In retrospect, I'm not surprised Kate couldn't recall the shooter. My wish that she could was founded more in hope than in belief.

Except . . . there's another possibility, one so abhorrent and painful I can barely bring myself to consider it.

I step over to the closet and retrieve the locked briefcase I keep hidden at the bottom of my garment bag. It's here I've secreted the folder I came upon last spring in the attic of my mother's house in L.A. when, following her death, my sister and I cleaned it out.

The folder contains various documents concerning my father: a copy of his will; papers having to do with the sale of our old house on Demington Drive; personal letters; family photographs; the incomplete draft of a professional paper he'd been working on at the time of his death; an agenda book showing his professional appointments that final year; and the strange photograph of Barbara Fulraine bearing the signature *Studio Fessé*.

It doesn't take me long to find what I'm looking for, a formal studio photograph of Dad taken but a few months before he leapt to his death. It appeared, along with similar photos of other local shrinks, in a *Fetschrift* published by the Calista Psychoanalytic Institute to honor Dad's mentor and training analyst, the much-loved and admired Dr. Isadore Mendoza, who'd studied with and been analyzed by Dr. V. D. Nadel, who in turn had studied with and been analyzed by Sigmund Freud himself.

I take the photo over to the mirror, tape it beside my drawing, resume my seat, then study the three images together.

Sensitive eyes, prominent cheekbones, slightly sunken cheeks: no question there's a strong resemblance. When Dad took the plunge he was forty-three, five years older than I am now.

A kind man's face, the face of a man who listens to you, cares about you, cares about your feelings—the face of a man who can help you uncover and comprehend your truth.

Yes, Dad and I, father and son, definitely look alike. The resemblance, I've been told, is striking. People have mentioned it to me all my life.

So . . . was Kate's description a classic transference reaction, as I would like to think, or was it, as I would hate to believe, an uncannily accurate description of the man she saw in a black raincoat and fedora departing the Flamingo Court just seconds after Barbara Fulraine and Tom Jessup were shot?

TONIGHT, LYING IN BED, I reread Dad's unfinished draft case history, the same document I copied for Mace:

D R A F T

"THE DREAM OF THE BROKEN HORSES"
by Thomas Rubin, M.D.

INTRODUCTORY NOTE: The following case study is of necessity incomplete due to the death by homicide of the patient while undergoing psycho-analysis. Nevertheless, I believe it to be of special interest on account of the nature of the patient's neurosis, including a debilitating recurrent dream; difficult resistance, transference and countertransference issues; and the possibility that these issues, being still unresolved, contributed to the tragic end of the patient's life.

Although for this reason one might conclude that the analysis was a failure, I hope it will be viewed in a different light: an example of the limitations of traditional therapeutic practice and an inspiration to those in our profession who, out of a desire to alleviate human suffering, are willing to plough new ground even when doing so creates risk.

THE ANALYSAND: Mrs. F, a white divorced female in her mid-thirties of high social and financial standing, well-educated and in excellent physical health, the mother of three children, the youngest of whom was abducted and, it is believed, murdered five years prior to the commencement of treatment. Mrs. F could be fairly described as possessing great beauty and personal allure, qualities for which she was well-known in her community. She came across as extremely poised and self-possessed, yet stated:

"All the people who envy me would pity me if they knew how screwed up I am."

PRESENTING SYMPTOMS: Mrs. F, self-referred, described herself as deeply unhappy ("I see myself as a tragic figure"); suffering from erotomania ("I think I might be a nymphomaniac"); ego disturbed ("sometimes I feel like I don't know who I am"); perverted ("I have these kinky fantasies, which I guess is all right . . . except I try to live them out"); in spiritual pain ("I feel wounded in my sex"); and possessed by a terrifying enigmatic recurring dream ("it haunts my days, ruins my nights"). Mrs. F, summing up: "So, doctor, I'm one sick babe, right?"

FAMILY HISTORY: Mrs. F had unusual parents. She described her father as "drop-dead handsome, a lady-killer. Women would take one look at him then go weak in the knees." Her father, Jack, was a racehorse trainer and self-described racetrack character and tout. People around the track called him "Blackjack" on account of his dark complexion and dashing good looks. Mrs. F described him as charming, easygoing, a philanderer, and "a man's man in that men instantly liked him and usually continued to like him even when they found out he was making it with their wives."

Mrs. F's mother was also a member of the gambling demimonde, an expert poker player and racetrack handicapper. Mrs. F described her as "pale and beautiful, a glacial ice goddess type." According to Mrs. F, her mother, unlike her father, was respected but not well liked.

Mrs. F described her as tough, aloof, and extremely strict. Whenever she caught Mrs. F in a fib, she would slap her hard across the face, telling her "You're acting like your father's child" and/or "You want to know why you're a liar? Because you're from a bad seed."

Mrs. F's parents fought constantly and were divorced when she was seven. After that, she lived with her mother while seeing her father two weekends a month until, two years later, he relocated to another part of the country. Although her parents moved in the same racetrack circle, during that two-year period they rarely spoke and could barely bring themselves to be civil. Mrs. F recalled her mother constantly referring to her father as "that bastard," "that son of a bitch," etc. And although her father did not speak poorly of her mother, he would ask after her in such a way as to suggest barely concealed contempt.

A couple of years after Mrs. F's father left town, he stopped sending child-support payments. Nevertheless, Mrs. F's mother made enormous sacrifices to keep Mrs. F in the exclusive private girls' day school in which she was enrolled. In return, her mother required her to maintain top grades, excel in sports, and participate in extracurricular activities and student government. As Mrs. F put it: "She turned me into a supreme competitor. I was to compete in every possible field with the goal of achieving total victory in each. Nothing less would be tolerated. Even the slightest failure was punished." Beside such punishments as slaps and grounding,

Mrs. F's mother's favorite disciplinary method was to withhold affection. "If she wasn't happy with me, she'd go glacial. Then she'd act like I was this object of revulsion, too disgusting even to be acknowledged."

Mrs. F believes her mother's sole objective those years was to groom her to make what her mother would term "a magnificent marriage." Later, when Mrs. F married into one of the wealthiest, most socially prominent families in her city, her mother changed her tack. The morning of her wedding day, she whispered into Mrs. F's ear: "I know you're marrying for money and position and in my eyes that makes you a whore."

Mrs. F stated that throughout her school years she loathed her mother while adoring the memory of her absent father, spending hours recalling their wonderful times together. Most of these memories centered around horses. Her father had taught her to ride, first putting her on a horse when she was three years old. "He was a wonderful teacher, kind, helpful, always calm. 'You'll be a great horsewoman,' he'd tell me. 'Maybe the first girl jock to win a major derby.' When I was five, he gave me my first horse, a filly with a white-tipped tail whom I named Banjo. He taught me how to groom her, care for her, and love her. He trained us together, me to ride her, she to be ridden by me. Oh, he was so proud!"

After Mrs. F's father left town, her mother wanted her to continue riding but in a different style. She took her out of the racetrack environment, enrolling her in a school of traditional equitation. Here the objective was not to learn how to race but to become a show equestrienne. The instructor, G, a middle-aged Hungarian refugee, taught the demanding art of dressage. G was the opposite of Mrs. F's father, strict, tense, an old-school disciplinarian. Mrs. F longed to ride fast and free again but under G's tutelage was not allowed to do so. And since Banjo had not been trained for dressage, her mother sold the horse, using the money to pay for her riding lessons. Of this betrayal, Mrs. F stated: "I've never forgiven her for that and I never will."

Although her mother insisted Mrs. F's father had abandoned her, Mrs. F always believed her father would reappear one day to rescue her from her mother's strict discipline. Although her father drifted around the country from track to track, he still managed to write occasionally, sending her notes around Christmas and on her birthdays. These communications tended to be brief and increasingly impersonal in tone. He never gave his phone number, and several times, when Mrs. F tried to call him, she discovered he was unlisted or had moved. She harbored the fantasy that one day she would run away from her mother, find her father, and that they would live together happily ever after. When despite numerous written pleas her father did not appear at her high school graduation, Mrs. F finally gave up the fantasy. By that time, having followed her mother's design, she was the second top student in academics in her class, captain of the field hockey and tennis teams, a member of the student council, easily the most honored girl in her school. "I was also the most envied," she said. "Mother always warned me that was the price I'd pay. 'They'll envy you when you beat them,' she told me, 'but still you'll hold the power.' "

Mrs. F recalled early sexual feelings dating from around the time her father moved out of the house. She found the atmosphere around the race-track stables "sexy" and constantly schemed to spend time there with her dad. She liked the smell of the horses and the smell of the leather tack. She was also fascinated by the genitalia of male horses. It was at the stables, she believed, in an atmosphere fraught with talk of mares, stallions, and geldings, that she became conscious of and fascinated by gender differences. Here, too, it was possible to embrace horses without hearing recriminations that such embraces were improper. She believed this was important, as her mother often warned her about touching people and allowing herself to be touched. She remembers over-hearing her mother angrily accuse her father of fondling her too much, and her father replying that he would continue to do so " 'cause I don't want her to end up a frigid hard-ass like you"—or words to that effect.

After her father left, her mother took on a succession of lovers. These relationships rarely lasted more than a year. Just as Mrs. F would grow fond of one of these boyfriends, her mother would break up with him. The breakups were inevitably bitter. Her mother would berate the boyfriend, banish him from her presence, angrily tear up all photos of him, and command Mrs. F never to utter his name again.

Mrs. F's mother warned her about men, their rotten nature and ulterior motives. "Men," she told Mrs. F, "only want one thing. Once you give it to them, you're finished." Cautioning Mrs. F not to engage in premarital sexual activity, she admonished: "Remember, no one buys a used slip!"

Mrs. F's mother was a stickler for cleanliness. Donning rubber gloves, she thoroughly cleaned house every day. She assiduously trained Mrs. F in matters of personal hygiene and inspected her nails each morning before she left for school. On one occasion, when Mrs. F left a ring around the tub, she was forced to scour the entire bathroom again and again. Whenever Mrs. F dared to use foul language or speak of sex, she was instructed to wash out her mouth with soap. Mrs. F was taught that sex was dirty. Her mother told her: "Men are dirty and your father was the dirtiest of them all." She also told her that boys were her enemy and that in dance class, which Mrs. F's school held jointly with a nearby boys' academy, she should not allow boys to hold her too close or else "you'll feel their stupid things poking at you through their trousers." Mrs. F recalled that when her mother broached the subject of menstruation, "she did so with a lot of nose twitching and disgust."

On one occasion, when Mrs. F was twelve, her riding instructor, G, slapped her to punish an error she'd made in dressage. Mrs. F, outraged, fled class. When she reported the slap to her mother, her mother told her she'd already heard from G about the incident. "You weren't paying attention so he slapped you to wake you up," her mother said. "He has my permission to do so again if necessary."

Thereafter Mrs. F was terrified of G, whom, in any case, she had never liked. In retrospect, she believed G colluded with her mother, then took advantage of his authority over her by touching her in intimate ways. Though not overtly abusive, this touching was clearly sexual. Under the guise of correcting her posture, G would lightly grasp her buttocks and graze her budding breasts with his hands. He insisted she ride bareback "so you can feel the horses' withers in your wound."[1] He instructed her to grasp the horse with her knees, then "grind in with your crotch." He also instructed her not to wear underclothing beneath her jodhpurs during these bareback riding sessions "so you can make close contact, really feel the animal, control him with your body." Mrs. F found this latter statement disconcerting since she was riding a filly at the time. When closely questioned about this, she insisted her memory was correct. "G was formal and correct. He always addressed me as 'Miss' and of course riders are always aware of the gender of their horses. So when he spoke of controlling 'him with your body' I took that as a deliberate reference to having sex."

---

[1]When asked whether G really used the word "wound," Mrs. F insisted that he had. When asked whether it were possible G had actually said "womb," Mrs. F vigorously shook her head, replying, "I'm positive he called it my wound." Note the similarity in concept between her belief that G called her genital area her wound and perhaps the most vividly described of her presenting symptoms: "I feel injured in my sex."

Over the next year, she heard similar tales of intimate touching by G from other girls in her riding class. Realizing that with this information she now had power over G, she told him one day after class that she wished to speak to him in private:

"I was nearly fourteen. I had a good figure and knew males found me attractive. G suggested we talk in the tack room. Once inside, he closed the door. I told him all the girls were complaining about his touching and that if he didn't stop sooner or later one would tell her parents and then he'd be in a sea of trouble. He glared at me, told me he didn't know what I was talking about and I'd better be sure of my ground before making accusations. Something about his manner told me he was bluffing, that all I had to do was hold my own and stare him down. So I told him I was sure, that he wasn't to touch me anymore, and that if he did I'd make it my mission in life to see him ruined. He asked me if that was all. No, I told him, there was something else. I told him I still resented that he'd slapped me, and I wanted an apology for that. He looked at me curiously, smiled slightly, told me he could do better. 'You can slap me back,' he said, then paused. 'If you have the nerve.' Well, I don't know where I found the nerve, but somehow I did. I pulled back my arm and slapped him as hard as I could across his face. He took my slap, didn't flinch. 'Not bad,' he said afterwards, smiling, massaging his cheek. 'I like a girl who stands up for herself.' "

Mrs. F confessed that she'd taken great pleasure in delivering that slap, and not just
because she'd had her revenge. "I felt physically warm and slick below. I got a sexual
charge out of it, no question."

From that time until she went off to college
four years later, she continued her riding
lessons with G but on a new basis. Though G continued to instruct her, his manner with her
became almost obsequious. And now that she no
longer feared him, she learned much more from
him than before. "He wasn't at all like Dad. He
wasn't easygoing or fun, but he was a fine
teacher, respectful and full of good advice. And
now there was something between us, the light
slap he'd given me years before and the very
hard one I'd returned. Those two slaps were
always in the background of our relationship."

Over the next few years, G attempted to train
Mrs. F to Olympic standards. She rode well, won
numerous competitions, accumulated numerous
trophies and ribbons. But they both knew there
was no way she could become an Olympic-level
equestrienne without training on a champion-cal-
iber horse. This was not to be. She had other
interests, her mother didn't have the money, and
she didn't want to be beholden to a wealthy
sponsor.

In the spring of her senior year, she went
for her final lesson with G. The lesson went
well. She took all her jumps with great poise.
Afterwards, G invited her into the tack room for
a farewell toast. There he opened a bottle of
champagne and poured them each a glass. "To a

fine rider and magnificent woman," he said,
clicking his glass against hers. They remi-
nisced, laughed, she thanked him for his efforts
with her, and he thanked her for her diligence
and talent. Just as it was getting time to be on
her way, he asked if she remembered the slap
she'd given him in that very room. Over the
years they'd never spoken of it. Now, suddenly,
G brought it up.

Yes, she told him, she remembered. "That was
our turning point," she said. He agreed it had
been and that he was sorry for any sorrow he may
have caused her. He told her that, yes, he did
like young women, found them beautiful, and that
he knew he'd been wrong to touch them the way he
had, and that he was grateful to her for having
warned him off this admittedly unattractive
practice. "I owe you a great deal for that," G
said, "and yet there's something else I'd ask
you to do for me." When she asked him what that
was, he told her he would appreciate it very
much if she would slap him hard once again.

She was astonished by his request, excited by
it, too. "You really want that?" she asked. He
said he did, that he needed it as a reminder to
behave himself. Though she would be gone, he
told her, he would still be instructing young
girls, thus he wanted to carry the sting of her
slap as a memory. She let him plead a while, then
agreed.

"Again," she said, "I pulled back my arm and
hit him as hard as I could. I was bigger then,
stronger, able to hit much harder. In fact, I
hit him so hard that this time he reeled back."

Again she felt the same slick warmth below, but much more powerfully than when she was four- teen. She was eighteen years old then, knew she was a beauty, had confidence, poise, was a fully sexual being. And this time G reacted differ- ently. He fell to his knees before her, lowered his head, and slavishly kissed the uppers of her tall, black riding boots. Studying him as he did, she felt a great surge of power. She reached down, placed her fingers in G's hair, pulled his head toward her crotch. At this, he gently pulled down her jodhpurs, buried his head in her groin, and performed cunnilingus upon her. "I came within seconds," she said. It was the first time she'd ever had oral sex with a man. After her orgasm, she pushed him away, but- toned up her riding pants, and told him she had to go. Her last image of G was of him still on his knees, bent over, head turned toward the tack room floor. She never saw him again.[2]

During the winter term of her first year in college, she received news of her father's death. He was training a horse while drunk, fell off, and suffered a mortal head injury. She was greatly upset by this news and went into what she termed "a deep depression."

Coming out of it that spring, she began a succession of brief sexual affairs with boys. Most were one- or two-night stands, others con- tinued for several weeks. She wanted to learn

---

[2]Various bits in this narrative, not recounted here, strongly suggest the possibility that G and Mrs. F's mother had an affair in the past and that Mrs. F somehow understood this.

about men and male sexuality and felt the best
way to do this was to have sex with as many boys
as possible.

She said she found these sexual explorations
enormously liberating, as she was now for the
first time away from home and out of her
mother's control. And she made an effort, she
said, when breaking up with her lovers, not to
replicate the cruel, dismissive manner of her
mother. Rather, she said, she took pains "to
show compassion, letting them down easy so as
not to bruise their tender egos."

She soon developed a fondness for experienced, affectionate men, culminating in an
affair with a graduate teaching assistant, H, who
was ten years older, and which lasted through the
winter and spring terms of her sophomore year.

When it came time to break off with H, his
reaction was unexpected. Rather than accepting
her decision, as others had, H took to stalking
her, following her about campus, phoning her
then hanging up when she answered, finding her
in the college library when she was studying,
sitting across the table from her then staring
at her until she looked up, etc. Frightened, she
confronted him. H told her he adored her and
couldn't live without her, that he didn't want
to stalk her but felt compelled to do so since
the compulsion was beyond his control. Though
unmoved by his professions of adoration, she
felt thrilled for having inspired them.
Describing the sensation, she said: "I felt
enormously powerful and I believe the feeling
was erotic."

She knew she was seductive and felt moved to test her seductive powers again and again. "I think I was searching for validation. If I could make men fall in love with me, bring them to their knees so to speak, then I would reaffirm my power as a woman. But once I conquered them, I quickly lost interest. For me the seductions were far more interesting than the relation-ships. Actually I found hanging out with these lovesick guys quite tiresome after a while."

Concerned that her sexual behavior was becom-ing obsessive, she sought out therapy at the student health services division of her college. Here, asked whether she had a gender preference in regard to a therapist, she specifically requested a male. Dr. L, the man to whom she was assigned, was a clinical psychologist in his forties, married with three children. Asked how she knew this, she replied that he displayed an array of family photographs on his office desk.

Immediately, she said, she set out to seduce him. All she had to do, she said, was recount her sexual adventures, including detailed descriptions of her lovemaking and the explosive power of her orgasms. "I had him panting for me before the end of our first hour," she said.

After two weeks, Dr. L yielded to her com-pletely. "He was an easy score," she said. She described pulling off her panties, balling them up and throwing them at him, then perching on his desk and pulling up her skirt. Immediately, she said, he performed cunnilingus upon her. "I came so wildly," she said, "thrashing about, I swept all his family photos to the floor."

When asked if this gesture was deliberate, whether in retrospect she thought she was trying to displace Dr. L's loved ones, she answered in the affirmative. "I think I wanted to demolish his crummy little middle-class existence."

Afterwards, Dr. L expressed great remorse, declaring he'd acted unprofessionally and would probably be fired, perhaps even blacklisted, if she ever told anyone what they'd done.

She remembered holding Dr. L in her arms, assuring him she would never tell and assuming all blame for their "indiscretion." At the end of the session, Dr. L told her he could not treat her any longer, that she had "acted out" her problem on him and "I stupidly fell for the bait." He told her that in his opinion she needed intensive psychotherapy and recommended a female colleague. "But please," he begged, "don't tell Dr. D what we did." When she asked how she could *not* tell Dr. D since what they had done was a symptom of the problem she needed to work through, Dr. L placed his head in his arms on his desk and sobbed.[3]

Mrs. F decided not to pursue treatment with Dr. D. "For one thing, I'd lost confidence in the process. These psychologists, it seemed to me, were as weak or weaker than my fellow students. Also I had no desire to work with a woman. That would be too much like trying to get help from my mom."

Instead, Mrs. F threw herself into sports and

---

[3]For further discussion of this incident and its relation to Mrs. F's psychoanalysis, see TRANSFERENCE ISSUES ARISING IN THERAPY below.

extracurricular activities, trying out for and winning a place on the women's varsity tennis squad. She also joined the college drama society and played secondary roles in several school plays.[4]

She met her future husband, A, her junior year at a horse-riding club dance when she was home for Christmas break. He was handsome, rich, smart, charming, and athletic, having all the qualities she felt a suitable husband should possess. He was clearly taken with her and she liked him too. "I don't know that I was actually in love with him, because, you see, I don't know if I'm really capable of love. But he was wonderful to be with. We had a lot of fun and the sex was great. So I decided 'Hey! This one's probably worth holding onto.' "

They became engaged and were married three years later. Meantime, after graduation, she'd moved back to her hometown, taking up a job with a local arts organization. She rented her own apartment far from her mother's and spent several nights a week with her fiance.

During the period of her engagement, Mrs. F tried to work things out with her mother. They had a number of conversations in which each

---

[4]In the course of one of these productions, she began an affair with another student, M, a drama major, who wanted to pursue a professional career in the theater. Some years later, after she was married, she used her position as a board member of the professional theater company in her city to secure M an appointment there as associate director. Then, when M moved to her city to take up his new position, she resumed her affair with him even though she was still married.

pledged to respect the choices of the other. They seemed to reach a modus vivendi, and she was pleased that her mother seemed to like and approve of her fiance. For this reason, she was shocked when on her wedding day her mother accused her of being a whore. "It was as if she was trying to ruin the little happiness I'd managed to eke out."

A year or so into the marriage, her pleasure in having sex with A began to diminish. By the second year, each had discreetly taken on a lover, accepted practice in their circle.[5]

Together she and A had three children, two sons and a daughter. Then, eight years into her marriage, her three-year-old-daughter, Belle, was snatched by her live-in au pair. The au pair turned up dead, and although the little girl was never seen again, Mrs. F was convinced she was still alive.

Mrs. F was frantic. She made immense efforts to find her missing daughter, including, when law-enforcement officials admitted they were stymied, hiring private investigators, fortune-tellers, psychics, anyone she thought could help. She was also racked with guilt, blaming herself for Belle's abduction. "If I'd been home taking care of my children the way a decent

---

[5]"We weren't swingers or wife swappers or anything tacky as that," Mrs. F explained, "but in our crowd we all had covert affairs outside our marriages. This added spice and the sneaking around was fun, all the hushed phone calls and secret meetings in out-of-the-way places. My husband enjoyed it as much as I, and when he and I had sex, it was always in the background. I'm pretty sure it added to his excitement. I know it did to mine."

mother should . . . if I hadn't been so spoiled
by A's money that I entrusted my children to
that horrible woman . . . if I hadn't been
spending so much of my time screwing everything
in trousers. . . ." Resigned, she added: "Well,
I guess I got what was coming to me. You
know . . . punishment for my sins."

When asked whom she thought was punishing her
in this way, she had no ready answer. "I don't
know. God, I suppose." When asked if she genuinely believed that the tragedy of her daughter's disappearance (and presumed death) was
commensurate with the sins she thought she'd committed, she shrugged off the query. "Rationally,
no, of course not." But still, whenever she mentioned the event, which she termed "the central
tragedy of my life," she spoke of it in such a
way as to suggest she believed the crime had been
directed personally against her.[6]

It was approximately six weeks after the
abduction that Mrs. F had a certain vivid
dream for the first time, a dream she
described as "a sex dream" and which she came
to call "The Dream of the Broken Horses." She
dreamt this dream in several variations over a
period of five years. It was the repetition of
the dream, its haunting quality, and her
belief that it contained an encoded message
pertaining to the whereabouts of her abducted
daughter that had, she said, brought on her

---

[6]In one session, Mrs. F related her fantasy that Belle,
still alive, was working as a child sex slave in a
whorehouse catering to sailors. "She could be paying for
my sins even as we speak," she added tearfully.

decision to undergo psychoanalysis. It was her hope, she said, that analysis might lead to the decoding of her dream or at least to an interpretation that would free her from its terrifying power.

THE DREAM: Mrs. F recounted the dream during her first session. Later she would recount it in other versions. In each case, though, the matrix would remain the same but certain particulars (such as genders, locales, colors, times of day) would be changed and even reversed. When asked about these variations, Mrs. F insisted that this was the way she dreamt, i.e., sometimes she would be wearing a red lower garment, at other times would be naked, etc.

This was so odd that the possibility had to be considered that Mrs. F was unconsciously inventing these variations to screen the essential dream and thus render it opaque. It also suggested a great richness of meanings, strata that would have to be explored level by level before the essential underlying meaning would be revealed.

In a footnote to the famous *The Case of the Wolfman*, Freud wrote: "It is always a strict law of dream interpretation that an explanation must be found for every detail." But the founder offered no practical approach to interpretation of a dream such as the one under discussion here, in which the details appear to be in a state of flux. Thus taking both views into account, I determined that Mrs. F's first rendition was the most important, the die or mold, so to speak, from which all the later recounted variations were cast:

"It's dusk. I'm riding a black horse, a stallion. I'm wearing red jodhpurs with nothing underneath, feeling the warmth and muscularity of my horse in my sex. At first I'm riding alone on a prairie with mountains in the background. Then other riders join me from behind, hooded men in black garments whose faces I cannot see. We become a kind of posse, with me in the lead, though soon I notice two of the other riders gaining on my flanks. I try to escape them. All our horses are frothing from the exertion. I want to be the lead rider. Then suddenly I realize we are not a posse; *they* are the posse and I am their quarry. Terrified, I drive my heels into the flanks of my horse, slash at his shoulder with my crop, and surge ahead. Soon I'm flying fast. My horse is foaming at the mouth. When I touch him I can feel his sweat and can also feel my own wetness in my crotch. I turn to see the posse falling behind. Then, suddenly, the horses in the posse began to break up. Legs snap and crumble, heads fall off at the neck, riders are thrown to the ground as the horses, which now no longer appear to be living creatures but rather made of something hard and brittle like clay or bronze, tumble and crash, breaking apart like fallen statues. At last, free of the threat, I feel released and victorious. But then I discover that my own horse is breaking apart too. This is when I always wake up, sexually aroused, panting, heart beating rapidly, nightgown and sheets drenched with sweat."

Variations recounted at other times:

  • Mrs. F, rather than wearing red jodhpurs, wears flesh-colored ones, or rides bottomless, or rides topless while wearing red jodhpurs;
  • Rather than being pursued by a posse, a sole faceless, hooded horseperson is in pursuit, revealed to be a woman when the wind blows the hood back from the pursuer's face, revealing in turn that the hood is lined with flaming red fabric;
  • The pursuit takes place in a Western desert, or along a dangerous narrow winding path up into hills, or on a dangerous steep descent;
  • The dream takes place against a sky blood-red from the setting sun with very long shadows cast upon the sands, or upon a moonlit rocky landscape at night;
  • There is someone riding ahead of her, someone she, in turn, is pursuing, someone frightening whom she cannot see except for occasional glimpses from the rear;
  • She has an orgasm at the moment her own horse breaks apart.

  ANALYSIS: Before discussing Mrs. F's associations to this rich lode of dream material, it might be well, in terms of clarification, to anticipate certain questions.

  In response to my query "Why do you believe this dream has anything to do with your daughter's disappearance and present whereabouts?" Mrs. F repeated that she'd dreamt it for the first time shortly after Belle's abduction.

"Also it's so mysterious I always assumed there was a connection; after all, finding Belle was the only thing that mattered to me then." When asked in a follow-up whether she believed dreams contain hidden messages, she replied with a question of her own: "Isn't that what you analysts believe?"

In the ensuing discussion about the nature of dreams, their relevance as internal messages, windows into the unconscious processes of the dreamer as opposed to coded messages from an external source, Mrs. F showed herself fully aware of the difference. But she stated that although she had never thought of herself as particularly superstitious, the crisis of Belle's disappearance had opened her to such paranormal notions as telepathy. "I guess maybe I'm like a terminal cancer patient holding out for some kind of miracle cure. I so need to find Belle if she's still alive that I'll hang on to anything that offers me the slightest hope."

With this in mind, despite doubts that the actual dream content (as opposed to the emotional crisis state in which the dream was dreamt) had anything to do with Belle, I nevertheless told Mrs. F, in hopes of motivating her to work hard on the interpretation, that her dream, properly interpreted, might convey some message pertaining to Belle, a message from her unconscious that she already knew but hadn't yet been able to face. To this Mrs. F responded with a knowing nod. "If my dream tells me I must give up my search, I'm prepared to accept that. But first I must be convinced."

Mrs. F's numerous associations to the dream material poured out of her over several sessions in what can only be described as a torrent. The dream's central image—the transformation of the horses from creatures of sinew and blood into brittle, breakable horse statues—reminded her, she said, of the broken agonized horse in Picasso's great painting, "Guernica," which had transfixed her when she'd first seen it in the Museum of Modern Art in New York. "Every time I'm in New York, I go to see it again. I don't know why I'm so fascinated by it, because the Spanish Civil War context doesn't interest me much. I think it's just that horse, his pain, you know . . . since I love horses and always have. Yes, that's what kills me—his agony, his pain."

Since even a cursory look at a reproduction of "Guernica" suggests the twisted broken horse is female[7] (no visible external genitalia), this gender confusion, so reminiscent of Mrs. F's distress when her riding instructor, G, referred to the filly she was riding as "him," suggested the possibility that much of the dream might be connected to G, perhaps to relations between them that Mrs. F had repressed.

When asked to free-associate to her vision of red jodhpurs, Mrs. F replied immediately that this was her sex. "That's why I think I'm some-times bottomless in the dream," she said. "For me being bottomless and wearing red jodhpurs

---

[7]Many commentators have interpreted the broken horse in the painting as a symbol of the suffering of the Spanish Republic, a feminine entity.

(and I've never seen jodhpurs that color) amount to the same thing. And of course riding a horse makes me feel sexy, not just in the dream but in real life too. I adore horses and all that, but I think the reason I still ride is the sexy way it makes me feel."

After more discussion, I pointed out that red was the only vivid color in her dream. Everything else—hooded men, horses, the terrain—was either muted or black. But not only were her jodhpurs red; in one of the variations, the pursuing posse consisted of a woman wearing a flaming red lined hood and in another variation the sky was blood red. To this Mrs. F responded: "So red must stand for blood. I wonder . . . ," she said, again associating the dream with something G had said, " . . . might that be blood from my 'wound'?"[8]

Associating to the concept of a woman's sex as a wound, Mrs. F recounted more about how her mother had conveyed revulsion when warning her of the agonies of menstruation. "She always called it 'the curse' and told me it was a punishment for sexual thoughts and acts. Of course, I knew a lot about it already. There was endless talk about it at school. I also remember when I was little and came across her tampons and asked her what they were, she made up some cover story that I knew was phony. That told me there must be something dis-

---

[8]In an earlier session, Mrs. F described a dream in which she saw herself lying on a snow-white sheet covered with hundreds of droplets of blood. Though, in my view not connected to the recurrent dream under discussion, this second dream seemed most curiously to prophesy her own death scene in that she was killed by pellets fired from a shotgun while lying with her lover on a motel room bed.

gusting about those things, and I knew that if Mom thought something was disgusting it either had to do with going to the bathroom or with sex."[9]

Was this why she called her dream "a sex dream"?

"Yes," she replied, "and also because I some- times come just at the climax of it. And even when I don't come and am terrified when I wake up, still after dreaming it I almost always feel aroused. Like I said, riding arouses me. I like to have sex that way too—you know, sitting on the man, riding him. That's always been my favorite way of having sex. And of course in the dream I'm on a stallion."

What about some of the other imagery in the dream, the references to the pursuing men gain- ing on her "flanks" and of her driving her heels into "the flanks" of her horse.

Yes, she agreed, that imagery too was sexual, as was the riding crop.[10] In fact, she said, she'd recently posed for what she called "an art photograph" in riding attire bowing a riding crop between her hands. "I was bare breasted in it, too," she added with a giggle, "just like I am sometimes in the dream."

At this point, she stated that in her opinion the dream was totally about sex and nothing else. "Talking it over with you, I see that. Everything in it is about sex. Everything! The

---

[9]Again, this is reminiscent of Mrs. F's presenting symptom: "I feel injured in my sex."

[10]Mrs. F spoke of having assembled a large collection of riding crops, the most prized of which, she said, was a crop her father had given her when she was a little girl and he first set her on a horse.

faceless men—often when I have sex with a man I don't see his face. I may be looking at him, staring right into his eyes, but while in the act I don't 'see' him at all."

There was also the matter of the men's horses breaking apart. "Those are their orgasms," she said. "They lose their seats, topple over. Once they come they're finished. So am I the horses breaking up beneath them? No, I don't think so. I think *they* are the horses breaking beneath me. I ride them till they break to bits!"

What about the sensation of being part of the posse then the sudden frightening realization that she's the one being pursued?

"Isn't that what sex is like? It is for me. Men pursue me all the time. Sometimes I'm out with people when suddenly someone in the group decides to make me his sexual prey. Or I decide to make prey of him." She laughed. "Actually, more often than not, though they may not know it, it's *me* who's in pursuit."

PATIENT'S SITUATION AT THE TIME OF ANALYSIS: At this point, it might be well to break off from the interpretation of the dream and review Mrs. F's personal situation and the background that led to the start of her analysis.

She approached me at a social gathering held at the school that our sons attended. She and I had met casually on other occasions, but this was the first time we spoke in private.

She told me she was interested in undergoing psychoanalysis and asked if she could call me at my office the following day for some professional advice. When she called, she

stated she'd decided she wanted to undertake
analysis with me "rather than with some 'perfectly competent' shrink you might refer me
to."

An appointment was made to discuss the pros
and cons of her seeking treatment with an analyst
with whom she shared several social acquaintances. At this meeting, she resisted all suggestions that she follow up on my proffered
referrals. "I want you! The truth is we barely
know one another and our circles barely touch.
The only connection is that our sons attend the
same school. Should I be deprived of your analytic skills because of that? Or is there something else? Yes, I think there is! You've heard
gossip about me . . . me and some of my peccadilloes. Well, maybe that's why I need you. Isn't
a person in need entitled to the therapist of her
choice?"[11]

---

[11]What Mrs. F had said was true: I had heard gossip
about her. She was well-known in the community because of
the notoriety surrounding Belle's abduction, her activities
were regularly reported in the social columns of the local
papers, and certain aspects of her behavior, regarded by
some as scandalous, were widely discussed. For this reason,
I deferred a decision until I could consult on ethical and
professional considerations with a colleague, my former
training analyst who was also president of the local
psychoanalytic institute. After a wide-ranging discussion,
this colleague recommended that I accept Mrs. F's
suggestion. "You certainly have my blessing in the matter.
After all, why *should* the lady be deprived? And if problems
do arise, my door is always open for consultation."
    I bring this up for two reasons: to clarify the record
as to all ramifications surrounding treatment, and to put
the transference and countertransference issues that arose
during therapy into better perspective.

The gossip to which Mrs. F referred concerned her relationship with a certain notorious local personality. This man, C, owner of a
high-class restaurant-nightclub that also had a
back room for illegal gambling, was widely
believed to have underworld connections. It was
also widely believed that Mrs. F was C's mistress, a fact Mrs. F confirmed in her second
session. In the same session, she stated that
her relationship with C was "extremely complex"
and that she had thought about breaking it off
but was hesitant because C "has this terrible
temper" and "he's been known to get violent
with women when he thinks they're betraying
him." In response to my query as to whether in
fact she was betraying him, she smiled
demurely, adding "that depends on what you mean
by betrayal."[12]

As these seductive references arose frequently over the weeks during which her key

---

[12]When I remained silent in accordance with standard
therapeutic practice, Mrs. F contiued: "I may not be
betraying him now but I have in the past and I can't
imagine I won't want to again."

From the very start of her analysis, Mrs. F slipped in
numerous references such as this regarding her
self-described "voracious sexuality." She seemed to go to
great pains and to take special pleasure in making it clear
to me just how highly sexed she was. She said of herself "I
guess I'm a, you know—a real nympho . . ." and on many
occasions she referred to herself as "a slut," "a hussy,"
"a real bitch-slut," "a bitch-in-heat," etc. Such usages
made sharp contrast with her otherwise dignified, ladylike,
indeed aristocratic self-presentation. There was no
question that these references were blatant attempts to be
seductive with me.

dream was under interpretation, I made numerous attempts to demonstrate connections between this behavior and the dream content.

ANALYSIS (continued): Having established that "everything in [the dream] is about sex," I reminded Mrs. F of her seduction of her college therapist, Dr. L.

"Do you think I'm doing the same thing with you?" she asked. Then, in the face of my silence, she offered the following extraordinarily perceptive response to her query: "If it's true I am, and I can see why you might think so, then there must be some connection to the dream."

This was the opening I'd been waiting for, an opportunity to explore the dream at a deeper level. "I'd like you to tell me about the horse you're riding, whatever comes to mind."

"Well," she said, "as I've told you, he was a stallion, black, black as night." She broke off her statement and then, after a brief silence, suddenly turned her head around to meet my eyes. "I know just what you're thinking," she said, aggressively. Resuming her normal position on the couch, she continued scornfully: "You're thinking 'black horse' equals 'Blackjack.' You'd have me having sex with my father in the dream. That's what all you analysts think we want—to screw our fathers, right?"

When I reminded Mrs. F that the equation she'd just presented had come from her not me, she stated: "You led me straight to it like a horse to water, didn't you?"

But despite her brief flurry of resistance, Mrs. F quickly showed interest in pursuing this line of interpretation. She offered: "Dad was teaching me to ride fast and free. That was how I always wanted to ride but wasn't allowed to by Mom. All those years studying with G, learning to do that stupid dressage! But riding fast and free is what I do in the dream, once I get going anyway. I break out from the pack. I go so fast I nearly fly. That's what's so wonderful, so liberating, so sexy, I guess—riding my magnificent black horse faster than the wind!"

At the end of the session, Mrs. F said she felt exhilarated. "I think we made real progress today." She apologized for snapping at me. "I think maybe I did that because what you said just cut too close to the bone."

During the next session, resistance showed itself again. "I know what you're thinking— that Dad fondled me too much the way Mom accused him of doing. But I know that isn't true. He was a loving guy, a real hands-on-type guy. That's how he trained horses—talking to them softly, touching them, fondling them if you will. That's just how he was. There wasn't anything sexual about the way he touched me."

However, again her resistance quickly gave way when I explained to her that it wasn't so much a matter of her father's intentions or what he actually did, but how his touching affected her, especially as the overheard quarrel about it between her mother and father planted her mother's notion that it was wrongly sexual in her mind.

Mrs. F readily accepted this interpretation. "If I'm twisted, it must be Mom who made me this way," she said. She then launched into a lengthy list of grievances against her mother, all pertaining to her mother's teachings that sex was dirty and wrong and thus should not and could not be enjoyed. "I sure rebelled against that!" she said. "I adore sex!"

When I pointed out that she used the same word, "adore," in regard to her feelings toward horses, she quickly put the interpretations together: "I 'adore' sex and I 'adore' horses. I feel sexy riding horses and I like to 'ride' my lovers when I have sex. I like to ride their cocks and I like to ride their faces, too. In the dream I ride a big black horse, which could be Blackjack, and it was Blackjack, Dad, who first put me on a horse and taught me how to ride. I know having sex with Blackjack is wrong, so Blackjack breaks apart beneath me as I ride him. And then I come, just the way I do when I have sex with my lovers. I ride them till they come, till they 'break.' Then I come and break too. So there it is, at least the center of it." At which point she turned her head toward me. "That's what you wanted me to see, isn't it?"

At the start of the next session, Mrs. F handed me a large manila envelope. When I asked her what it contained, she responded: "It's something we talked about. I thought you'd be interested in seeing it."

Opening the envelope, I noticed Mrs. F observing me closely. Inside was the "art photograph" she'd previously mentioned, the one of her in riding clothes, naked above the waist, staring seductively at the lens while bowing a taut riding crop between her hands.[13]

TRANSFERENCE ISSUES ARISING IN THERAPY: One Monday morning Mrs. F arrived, flung off her coat, then, beaming, announced: "Seems on Friday

---

[13]At this point I should state that in all my years of practice I never worked with an analysand so intent on my seduction. Though training teaches us how to employ strong transference reactions in furtherance of analytic goals, it cannot fully prepare one for an onslaught of such intensity, epecially when the analysand is extraordinarily attractive, experienced, and well tuned to her effect upon men. Furthermore, in the case under discussion, I was well warned by the analysand via her tale of her seduction of Dr. L. But despite my experience and training and the clear warning issued by the analysand herself, I had no adequate preparation for an offering such as the one described above, in which the analysand presented me with a recent photograph of herself half naked in a highly charged and bizarre erotic posture.

As mentioned, this offering was just one of several such démarches made by Mrs. F, nearly all of which occurred in the context of our probing of the meaning to her "sex dream." It was as if, the closer we came to a deep interpretation of her dream, the more compulsive became her attempts to seduce me.

These maneuvers usually took place at or near the beginning of our sessions. Mrs. F would introduce something provocative as if in an attempt to confuse me and throw the analysis off course. These transparent attempts to derail treatment were easily parried by ignoring the provocation or offering a quick and pointed interpretation. It soon became apparent that Mrs. F prepared these incitements in advance. When swiftly dealt with, she would settle down, ready to do the hard and painful work that is a requirement of a successful analysis.

our sons gave each other bloody noses."[14] To this
I promptly responded: "Does this excite you in
some way?" "Well, yes, actually it does," she
said. "It seems so . . . well, you know . . .
intimate." I suggested we try to analyze why she
found a fistfight between our sons to be sexually stimulating. Mrs. F, intelligent and quick-
witted as ever, immediately made the connection:
"It's the blood, isn't it? The wound. The red
jodhpurs. The flaming hood. Our flesh-and-blood
bloodied each other, and that's like you and me
having sex."

The following week she came in with another
prepared bombshell: "Guess what, Doctor? I've
taken on a new lover. And he has the same first
name as you. Now that *must* mean something, mustn't
it?"

Mrs. F, of course, knew perfectly well what
it meant and seemed highly amused at my concern.
"You think I'm doing a number on you, but it's
really just a coincidence. He's so cute, this
guy, that I decided I couldn't deprive myself
just because your names happen to be the same."

Again we analyzed her statements. She had
used the very same expression ("deprive myself")
when I'd expressed doubts about undertaking her
analysis. And I assured her that my concern was
not over the coincidence of the names[15] but that

---

[14]In fact, authorities at our sons' school had arranged a
boxing match to settle a personal quarrel between them.

[15]In fact, though mine is a fairly common name, I didn't
doubt for a moment that this was far more than mere
coincidence. However, I decided not to dwell on the matter just
then, believing there was something deeper to be uncovered.

by taking on a new lover without having first broken with C, betraying him in effect, she might be unconsciously courting danger.

She then imparted the following unexpected information: She had first met T at the same school reception where she'd approached me about her desire to undergo analysis. In fact, T was a teacher at our sons' school. After meeting him and hearing how much her sons liked him, she'd hired him to give her sons private coaching and tutoring.

In our next session, she described in detail how she'd decided that T, employed in this capacity, would make a good lover and how she'd initiated (i.e., seduced him into) an affair:

"I went out to our tennis court to watch him practice with my boys because they were proud of their progress and wanted me to see it for myself. It was a very hot afternoon. My boys and T, all three in shorts and stripped to the waist, were batting balls back and forth, really working up a sweat. So here's this really good-looking guy with the body of a Greek god! How could I resist? After my boys finished their lesson, they urged the two of us to play. 'Come on, Mom!' 'Yeah, Mom, we know you're club champ, but I bet T can kick your butt!' 'Yeah, let's see who's better, Mom. Come on! Just one set, okay?'

"So I went down to the pool house, changed into tennis gear, then stepped onto the court. T's a terrific player. It was fun to play with him. Soon it was clear we were very much in tune. And with the boys there urging us on, cheering for him, clearly wanting him to win,

all my competitive juices were aroused. I wanted
to win, *needed* to, so I started playing really
hard. And he, responding, quickly raised the
level of his game."

The tennis match, as she described it, was
clearly foreplay for the sex that followed
within the hour. Mrs. F was quick to grasp that
much of her imagery—"in tune," "aroused,"
"juices," "playing hard," "raised the level"—
was highly sexual in nature. And with my assis-
tance, she came to understand that the performance of such an extended act of foreplay in the
presence of her sons was a provocation in
itself.

"So how do you think all this relates to your
dream?" I asked near the end of the session.

"I'm having sex in front of my sons."

"And in the dream?"

Mrs. F shrugged. "I don't see any connection."

I suggested we go back and reexamine the circumstances under which she first met T, at the
same occasion, in fact within the same hour,
that she first broached the possibility of analytic treatment with me.

I offered her the following interpretation:

"There we are, two men, both with the same
first name. And the context in which you meet
us is almost incestuous—my son and yours attend
the same school. Within days you retain me as
your analyst and retain T as your son's coach.
Then, while filling our sessions here three
mornings a week with provocative sexual statements, setting upon my seduction, even going so

far as to present me with an erotic photograph of yourself, you literally seduce this other man, my double so to speak, and in fact do so right in front of your sons. What's more, while this double seduction is going on—my 'psychic seduction' and T's literal seduction—one of your sons fights a boxing match with mine in which each boy bloodies the other's nose. And there's something else you mentioned in only the most peripheral way—T not only coached your sons in tennis, he coached them in boxing too. In fact, I learned from my own boy that he served as referee of their match. So in a sense, we could say you hired T to teach your sons to bloody my son's nose. Next session let's try to pull this all together in the context of your dream, because, you see, I think we're getting close now to its underlying meaning, the meaning that terrifies you even as it excites you."

ANALYSIS (continued): Consistent with past behavior, Mrs. F immediately demonstrated her resistance at the start of the next session by making the following statement:

"I'm having such a busy twenty-four hours! Last night I had The Dream again and got all sexy on account of it. Early this morning I went riding, and that, as usual, got me juiced up. Now I'm here to discuss it . . . and I always find our meetings sexy in a cool sort of way. Then I'm off to meet C for lunch and a hot bout of rough sex. Then after a quick stop home for a shower, I'll meet T at our usual seedy motel for silken loving sex, the kind I've come lately to appre-

ciate more and more. He's so tender with me, so
sweet, loving, and eager to please . . . ," etc.[16]

Feeling that this could be a crucial session,
I decided to postpone further analysis of her
dream till later in the hour. Instead I asked
her to describe the difference between the sex
she was having with her two lovers, whom, she
had just made clear, she was no longer meeting
on separate days but was now seeing, provoca-
tively, back to back.

"Well, Doctor," she smirked, "to satisfy your
prurient interest, C is one hard-ass lover. That,
I think, is originally what attracted me. He's
dark, hairy, charming, glossy, an old-fashioned
'lounge lizard' type. But there isn't a hell of a
lot of heart there if you know what I mean. For
him sex is rough-and-tumble without much tenderness. When we started our affair, I pretty much
let him take over. You know, 'do with me what you
will.' He told me, 'You're a classy lady and that
makes me want to dirty you up.' When I asked him
what he meant, he said he wanted to make me gasp
and scream. 'No polite little orgasms, thank you,
ma'am,' he said. So I told him, 'I love getting
carried away, so please, if you think you can
send me like that, by all means try.' Oh, he
tried all right! I really made him *work* for it!
We'd wrestle and slap and scratch—the whole nine
yards. But, see, being dominated doesn't really

---

[16]In response to my query, "Do you see how you always
start our sessions like this, talking about your sex life and
never failing to add me to the mix?" Mrs. F laughed. "Well,
isn't sex what psychoanalysis is about? Aren't I being a good
patient by building up a strong transference bond with you?"

do it for me. To be satisfied, I need to be in control. So over the course of time, things began to change, with me taking over more and more. The way things are now, we both get 'dirtied' up. Now he loses *his* cool. With me he's no longer the unflappable, slightly malevolent, hail-fellow-well-met nightclub impresario. When I ride him, he turns into just another panting boy screaming for release."

I quote Mrs. F's statement in extenso to illustrate how her neurosis, as exemplified in what I had now come to regard as her "key" or "master" dream, was determining her love relationships. Her descriptions of C were so close to her earlier descriptions of her father, Blackjack, as to be transparent to even the most naive observer. Yet it seemed that Mrs. F still resisted making this connection.[17]

Here now is her description of her lovemaking with my namesake and "love-proxy" T:

"T is a really gorgeous guy, lean, hard, blondish, fair-skinned without much body hair. So physically he and C couldn't be more different. Different in personality too, because T's a sweetheart. With him there's none of the slapping and scratching I do with C. We make love gently and slowly, excruciatingly slowly sometimes. Yeah, C makes me scream, but with T, I can really lose myself, forget who I am. He doesn't want to

---

[17]Strangely she'd also seemingly never made the connection between her father's profession of racehorse trainer and C's ownership of a casino. The fact that both men worked in the gambling industry appeared to have entirely escaped her notice.

'dirty' me up. He only wants to worship me. He adores me for who I am, not what I represent. I find that so refreshing.[18] But if you're wondering why I keep seeing them both, I guess it's because each satisfies a different need. C gives me what I think I crave, while T gives me what I really want." Mrs. F smiled. "Pretty complicated, huh?"

As the hour was now nearly over and since she'd redreamt her key dream the night before, I asked her to relate any new particulars she'd found memorable.

She said that in this latest rendition, the lone pursuing faceless hooded horseman was revealed, when the wind blew back his hood, to be the pursuing horsewoman whose hood was lined with flaming red silk.

When I asked her to describe the features and/or expression on this pursuing horsewoman's face, she said the woman appeared cold and grim, "kind of like my mother watching a race when she had a lot of money riding on a horse."

----

[18]I found this idealization of her relationhip with T suspect in view of other information she imparted. For instance, she told me how she'd arranged to meet him one day at the Municipal Aquarium in front of a large tank containing sharks. Describing their kiss in front of the lit tank while the sharks swirled behind, she said: "That felt so bold. I think I did it to insert some drama into our affair." Later, when I described this encounter to a colleague, he pointed out a strong similarity to a scene in the film *Lady from Shanghai* in which the actors, Orson Welles and Rita Hayworth, kiss in front of an aquarium containing a huge octopus. Unfortunately, I never had the opportunity to ask Mrs. F if she'd seen this film and whether it had inspired her choice of the location of her rendezvous. Still, whether she knew the film or not, the scene suggests she saw herself in a femme fatale role with T.

Considering this a major breakthrough, I urged her to give me her associations to the red-lined hood. Her response was immediate: "It's like the hood of a clitoris."

"So," I said, pursuing the interpretation, "the face of the pursuing horseman turns out to be like your mother's, peering at you out of her clitoris."

Mrs. F, accepting that, urged me to go on.

"And the horseman you're pursuing—did you see him a little better last night?"

She said she did get a couple of good glimpses of him before their horses broke.

And what did she see?

Not much, she said. Just that he was big, broad-shouldered, and was wearing a black, hooded duster that covered him completely from the rear. Also that his horse was black.

"Could he be Blackjack?" she suddenly asked. "Not the horse I'm riding, but the horse and rider ahead?"

I assured her that indeed he could be Blackjack. As it was now the end of the hour, I added that I felt that her being pursued by her mother while in the act of pursuing her father was a key to opening the meaning of her dream, a key I hoped we would turn together next time.

"You think it really happened, the dream?" she asked.

I told her that I felt that the way she reworked the dream material in different ways suggested she was circling some dreaded and real traumatic event that she'd repressed and that she was now attempting to bring to the surface.

A NEW APPROACH TO A TRANSFERENCE CRISIS IN
PSYCHOANALYSIS: "ENTERING IN": Sexual seduction
was Mrs. F's game, her stock-in-trade. It was
also the clearest manifestation of her neurosis.
By attempting to draw me into her web, she was
acting out in accordance with the very compul-
sions that made her so unhappy. The pitiful Dr.
L, whom she'd so quickly seduced in her college
days, was but one of a string of seductees used
and then discarded as she veered ever more
rapidly into a sexual maelstrom that, as it
turned out, would lead to her destruction.[19]

---

[19]At this point, it would be disingenuous not to mention
certain difficult countertransference issues that arose in the
course of this analysis. Mrs. F, it shoud be remembered, was a
woman of stunning attractiveness with well-honed and well-
practiced techniques of seduction at her command. Though I, an
experienced analyst, understood exactly what she was doing and
why she was doing it, I nevertheless felt it incumbent to seek
special counseling from my former training analyst in order to
forestall reactions on my part that could hinder the analysis of
this anguished and highly vulnerable patient.

I recommend such counseling to colleagues who find
themselves facing a similar dilemma. The stresses of such
provocations must not be underestimated. In such
situations, normal analytic techniques may be insufficient
to deflect the patient's fantasies, and the strain upon the
analyst's professional demeanor, not to mention his/her
ego, can be crushingly intense.

For me to have yielded in any fashion to her campaign
(and it truly was a campaign, waged by her the way a
military commander marshals resources while waging war)
would not only have vitiated any gains made during the
analysis, but also would likely have served to hasten the
breakdown toward which this astonishing patient appeared to
be heading. She was spinning her web around me the way the
predatory black widow spider spins a web about its sexual
mate, with the purpose of luring me into an affair or even
a single sexual act that would "break" me just as it had
broken the unfortunate Dr. L. Such breaking, I believed,
was akin to the "breaking" of the horses in her dream.

This analytic dilemma was made all the more acute by the possibility that real harm could come upon Mrs. F on account of her risky engagements—back-to-back affairs with a naive, young man disarmed by her guile, and an insanely jealous lover with underworld connections and a reputation for violence. And I had to take seriously my own role should a tragedy occur: that her provocation (i.e., taking on T as a lover), though clearly directed at me, might also provoke C into a violent response.[20]

For these reasons, I decided to embark upon a new approach[21].

At our next session, anticipating the usual

---

[20]As I put it to my former training analyst: To what extent was I obliged to step out of my role as analyst and directly warn Mrs. F of the danger she was courting?

The answer was not so obvious. By stepping out of my analytic role, I could, by that single stroke, dismantle the entire substructure of the analysis. But by maintaining "analytic distance," I might not only be acquiescing but also contributing toward a posssible tragic denouement.

Left with such a difficult choice, I set upon a course of action (see following) that, though unorthodox in the extreme, I believed was the only course open to me in what I considered to be urgent circumstances. Having received counseling against this course from my most respected colleague, I undertook it nevertheless and take full responsibility for all its consequences, foreseen and unforeseen.

I raise the matter here not as a mea culpa nor to anticipate criticism of my handling of the case, but simply to suggest the complexities that may arise in an analysis in which the transference/countertransference phenomenon reaches proportions beyond the normal range.

[21]My first step was to quickly determine whether Mrs. F was telling the truth, whether, in fact, she really was conducting two simultaneous affairs or whether this was a fantasy or a claim contrived to arouse me. Though I believed her story was real, I needed to know for certain in order to evaluate the hazards inherent in her situation.

sexual provocations, I told Mrs. F, the moment she lay down on the couch, that I'd been thinking of her a great deal lately and not only in an analytic way.

"Perhaps," I told her, "my regard for you is not so cool as you think."

At this, just as I anticipated, she twisted around so she could meet my eyes. "God! What are you telling me?" she asked.

"Look, we've agreed you've been trying to seduce me. I'm telling you you've succeeded. Consider me seduced. Think of me dreaming about you, getting horny thinking of you, masturbating with you in mind. Think about that. How does that make you feel?"

Still staring at me, she started to blink. Clearly I'd taken her by surprise. "Well, I don't know," she said. "I mean . . . how should I feel?"

"Victorious?"

"A little maybe."

"Satisfied?"

"We'd have to make love for me to feel that."

"Ambushed?"

"Yes," she smiled, "a little." She peered at

Using information she'd given me, I staked out the motel where, she'd told me, she and T met for their afternoon rendezvous. (I hope colleagues will forgive my use of a word normally associated with detective fiction; in fact, as Freud himself pointed out numerous times, much of what we do in our profession is akin to detective work.)

While doing this, I was careful not to be seen, well aware of the risks both to my professional reputation and to the analysis itself. Confirming by sight that indeed she was meeting T at the motel, I put my plan into play.

me. "Are you putting me on, or is this for real?"

"Sounds like you're confused?"

"Yes . . . yes I'm confused," she admitted.

At this point, I urged her to assume her normal position on the couch. We were, I reminded her, still in session and our exchanges were part of her therapy.

"Doesn't sound very orthodox to me," she opined.

I told her that even in so rigorous a discipline as psychoanalysis, extraordinary situations may require extraordinary methods. I'd decided, I told her, to depart from normative technique because I felt that was the best way to access the unconscious processes inherent in her dream.

"What I want you to do," I told her, "is to imagine you've been successful, that I've been thoroughly seduced. With that as a given, I'm hopeful you'll dispense with further efforts along those lines and proceed into fresh territory, territory that may be truly fearful but which for your own good we must explore."

"Okay, I get it now," she said. "It's like a game, isn't it?"

"What's your fantasy about us?" I asked.

"Oh, Doctor, we're being prurient again!" she said. But launching into her sex fantasy, she quickly gave up her sarcastic tone as highly charged descriptions of the most lascivious acts spewed from her mouth.

I won't record the whole gamut here. In our practices, many of us have experienced similar onslaughts. Of course what was important was not the particular content of Mrs. F's fantasies but the fact she was finally able to let loose with them in a manner at odds with all her earlier braggadocio. Now, at last, with her feelings out of control, she was involved in true associative work. She was, so to speak, "clearing the air," or, perhaps better put, cleaning the cobwebs from her id. When, finally, she stopped, it was clear this outpouring had been cathartic. Her forehead was moist, her blouse was soaked, her body was trembling on the couch.

"Guess what, Doctor?" she said. "I think I've . . . well, can you believe it? I've been touching myself all this time while I've been talking and . . . I believe I've had . . . an orgasm."

By this latest display, Mrs. F, it seemed, had, at least in her own mind, successfully trumped my new approach to her treatment. But I quickly countered with a ploy of my own, which, I admit, under the duress of her provocation, I improvised on the spot. I told her: "What you've just done is try to sabotage our

At this point, in mid-sentence, Dad's draft case study suddenly breaks off.

T E N

I t's all in the final footnotes, David. His madness is in those footnotes."

Dr. Isadore Mendoza gazes at me intently. We're sitting in the living
room of his house on Taschen Drive, a house he and his late wife built
in the 1950s, one of only a dozen private residences designed by Eric
Lindstrom, Calista's famous mid-century architect.

Izzy, as my father called him, is eighty now. His hair still hangs
across his forehead, but now the bangs are white, giving him the appearance of a Roman senator. His blue eyes sparkle fire no less than on those
evenings when he and Mrs. Mendoza would come to our house for
Sunday dinner. Founder of the Calista Psychoanalytic Institute, he had
been my father's mentor and training analyst.

"Of course Tom had Freud's *The Case of the Wolfman* in mind,"
Izzy continues, "the most famous case study in psychoanalytic literature. He believed that with Mrs. Fulraine he'd latched onto a case of
equal importance that would propel him into the top rank of our profession. Was that grandiose? I think so . . . though the case was certainly interesting. I told him as gently as I could that I thought his
draft was promising, but his enormous countertransference problems
were standing in his way. I loved him as a son. I wanted desperately to
help. But I believe he was beyond any kind of help I could give. After

Mrs. Fulraine was killed, he completely fell apart, fell into a deep depression."

As Izzy peers at me, I detect traces of an old grief. Perplexity too, for even after so many years he still hasn't reconciled himself to Dad's suicide.

I wrote him, as I did to my old art teacher, Hilda Tucker, to say I'd be back in Calista over the summer and hoped he'd find time to meet with me and talk. Izzy answered right away. He remembered me well, he wrote, was sorry to hear of my mother's passing. My father, he wrote, had been his most promising protégé, the man he'd hoped would build upon his legacy.

Izzy's gaze is kindly. "You look so much like him, David. Uncannily so. Even your gestures and the way you hold your head. I understand why you changed your name, but to me you'll always be Tom Rubin's boy."

There's only one piece of art in the room. It hangs above the fireplace: a large black and white etching of six wolves' heads peering out of the branches of a tree, with the words "The Wolfman's Dream" inscribed across the bottom in brilliant red.

As we talk, my eyes keep wandering to this picture. What is it, I wonder, about the Wolfman Case that so intrigued Dad? Izzy notes my interest.

"The etching's by Jim Dine, a gift from colleagues when I gave up directorship of the Institute. Perhaps you know that the patient Freud called The Wolfman made his own sketch of the wolves he saw in his famous dream. Here Dine reinterprets that vision, matching, I think, the artistry one finds in Freud's case study. Freud, of course, wrote many great papers, but in certain ways for us in the profession, *The Case of the Wolfman* is the holy grail." Izzy pauses. "How arrogant of Tom to think his analysis of Mrs. Fulraine could match such a dazzling penetration."

Izzy, I know, is a generous man. And he truly loved Dad as he said. But in this last remark, he shows his ambivalence. Dad, it seemed, had overreached, dared to fly too close to the sun, and so he had fallen—literally, in fact, from the window of his office into a snow-covered doctor's parking lot below.

"Let me tell you about that dream," Izzy says. "Tom thought he had it figured out. You probably saw where he was heading—toward a father/infant daughter seduction interpretation. As a child, Mrs. Fulraine was sexually touched by her father. Her 'Dream of the Broken Horses' was a vision of that trauma triggered by a deep sense of guilt and loss brought on by her own daughter's abduction. Tom felt that a good interpretation along those lines would help her overcome her erotomania. I had my own ideas. I still remember Tom coming to me after their first session. He was so excited. 'Izzy, this is what I've been waiting for my entire professional life, a multilayered dream with rich erotic content that cries out to be solved and written up.' "

Izzy smiles. "Of course, I encouraged him. No question he'd lucked into a glamorous patient. So many of our patients are tiresome. Listening to their drivel three and four hours a week—you can imagine what a drain that is. Now, of course, there aren't enough patients, with psychoanalysis so out of fashion."

Izzy's sharp eyes tear up. His voice, soothing till now, starts to break.

"For all Tom's hopes, things didn't work out. He had this screwy idea he should 'enter in,' step inside her neurosis, work on it from the interior. He wasn't the first to try a move like that. But before you attempt something so extreme, you must closely examine your motives. Are you in love with the patient? In lust with her? Has she so entranced you that you're looking to therapeutically justify an affair? If she hadn't been murdered—God knows how it might have ended!"

He excuses himself, returns with two bottles of German beer, then suggests we sit outside.

His garden is subtly beautiful, a medley of muted greens and grays. A lively creek, winding though the property, creates a soothing sound. We sit on an old wooden bench, stick out our legs, and listen to the water running over smooth stones.

The garden, he tells me, was crucial to Lindstrom's concept for the house.

"I explained how my work involved me in turmoil. 'Give me a safe haven,' I said, 'a place to escape from other peoples' craziness.' Lindstrom liked that. It was a way to create a contrast to the clean, sharp lines of the building."

He turns to me. "Martha loved this place. That final summer, when she knew she was dying, she'd have me wheel her out here, then we'd sit for hours just listening to the water."

I remember Martha Mendoza, a quiet, sad-eyed lady, a talented art weaver who'd had several successful shows in New York. We had one of her strange, dark yarn sculptures hanging in our house.

"Listen, David, you have every right to look into your father's life. But I must advise you that the deeper you delve, the greater the possibility you'll become upset and depressed. So . . . as long as you're aware. . . ."

I assure him I am.

"Well, then, I'll tell you what I know. As I said, Tom was devastated when Mrs. Fulraine was killed. In his paper, he tells us proudly how he parried her seductions. In fact, I believe, he *was* seduced. It was the most severe case of countertransference reaction I'd ever seen."

Izzy shakes his head. "He knew what was happening. At first he tried to convince himself it was just sex. She aroused him—simple as that. But it was so much more. He wanted her, needed her, lived for their sessions. When he came to me for help and I put him back on the couch, he told me his fantasy: that he'd solve her dream, show her how she could be happy, then, after a decent interval, divorce your mother and marry her. They'd become this great romantic couple, the rich girl and the shrink who'd cured her. I told him that was pretty much the story Scott Fitzgerald had written in *Tender Is the Night*, except the marriage in that novel turns out badly and in the end the shrink finds himself used up and destroyed."

Izzy takes a deep breath. "Then something happened, a clue to what she was up to. There was this columnist—"

"Waldo Channing?"

Izzy nods. "Nasty man, but he could turn a phrase. One day that summer Channing ran what they call a blind item. Knowing you were coming today, I dug it out."

He pulls a yellowed clipping from his breast pocket, puts on his glasses, reads the item aloud:

" 'A little birdie tells us a certain well-known divorcée, one of Our Happy Few, has lately been making whoopee-do with her shrink. We know those weird guys use couches and get their patients to yap about sex, but this is the first we've heard of one getting down and dirty in the office. Guess all that sex talk can stir the bodily juices . . . so to speak.' "

Listening, I'm struck again by Channing's viciousness.

Izzy takes a sip of beer. "It hit Tom and your mother very hard. The giveaway was Channing's 'Happy Few.' Since his crowd consisted of a couple dozen people, it was obvious whom he meant. So was Tom making 'whoopee-do' with the lady? I asked him point-blank. That's when he told me she'd masturbated in his office. 'For God's sake,' I told him, 'you've got to get out of this! She's unstable. She'll end up suing you for malpractice!'

"Tom assured me that wouldn't happen, that he and Barbara were on the verge of a breakthrough." Izzy shakes his head. "For me it was clear. The woman was malicious. Her relationship with the gangster was part and parcel of her fantasy that she was some kind of femme fatale in a real-life film noir. Most likely she'd planted the item with Channing. Now she was pulling Tom into her vortex, and he was so besotted he didn't see it. 'She'll destroy you,' I told him. 'That column item's just a taste. Turn her over to someone else. If you like, I'll take her on myself.'

"Tom, I can tell you, was not at all happy to hear that. This was going to be *his* Great Case, and he wasn't turning it over to anybody, least of all me." Izzy looks at me. "You know about the condom?"

I shake my head.

Izzy gives me a quick glance. Over the last weeks of her life, Mrs. Fulraine received a number of envelopes addressed in block capitals. No writing inside, just artifacts, including, in one case, a condom."

I stare at him. "In what condition? I mean, was—?"

"—it used?" Izzy shrugs. "It was filled with some sort of substance, then tied off at the top. Today, of course, with DNA testing, a semen sample, if indeed it was semen, would make powerful forensic evidence.

But it was the sequence of those envelopes that was so disturbing, the ascending expression of rage. To Tom it looked like a cleverly contrived campaign of intimidation and terror."

"That's so vile! Why didn't Mrs. Fulraine go to the cops?"

"Tom urged her to, but she refused. She told him she believed the letters came from someone with whom she'd had a major falling out, that they were some sort of complex message about her daughter, money, and sex. I didn't believe that. I thought it was much too pat. I suggested to Tom that the letters were bogus, that she may have sent them to herself. He insisted that wasn't true, too adamantly, I thought. Then I wondered if Tom had gone off the deep end and sent them to her *himself*."

"*Why?* What could he have gained?"

"Drawn her closer. She brought out strange things in him. Since he was smitten by her, any behavior, even the most improbable, couldn't be ruled out. There's a reason I bring this up. It has to do with Mrs. Fulraine's dream and the possibility that, like the letters, the dream may have been bogus, too."

Bogus! I find this notion disturbing, perhaps because it reminds me of how once I was disbelieved. Following Izzy back into the house, I'm drawn again to the "The Wolfman's Dream."

What if, I ask him, the patient Freud called The Wolfman made up his dream to gain Freud's attention? Or what if Freud made up the entire case to show off his brilliance? Can any dream be trusted? Any story? Don't humans depend on trust as a moral necessity? Isn't that why any breach, such as a shrink who sends crude anonymous letters to a patient or a patient who fabricates an erotic dream to seduce a shrink, strikes us as an outrageous breaking of a compact?

Izzy nods at each of my points.

"You're right to feel outraged," he says. "After all, how dare I question your father's integrity? But these are human failings I'm talking about, not issues of good and evil. No, I don't think Tom sent those letters and I don't really believe Mrs. Fulraine counterfeited her dream. I just raise those possibilities to show you how complicated the case was and the extent to which I'm still confused by it."

He positions himself before his fireplace, the Wolfman etching looming above his head.

"If I've learned anything," he says, "in all my years of practice, it's what my own training analyst, V. D. Nadel, told me when I started out— that the best interpretations, like the best equations in physics, are always the simplest, most aesthetic, most direct.

"I disagreed with your father's interpretation. I found it tortuously complex. For me, the dream of the broken horses was not about a girl being sexually touched by her father but was simply about sexual guilt.

"The elusive man on the horse ahead is Barbara's father, whom she lusts after and adores. The pursuing posse behind, horsemen of the apocalypse if you will, personified by the lone horsewoman with the red-lined hood, is her mother hounding her, threatening to punish her for her sexual feelings toward her father and by extension toward all men.

"The horse she rides is a generic lover, a stand-in for all the lovers she rode hard and crushed with her sex. The excitement-pain she feels as she rides is the pain of sex her mother warned her about when she explained menstruation and which her riding instructor so memorably referred to as her 'wound.'

"As for the end, the breaking of the horses—that's the crack-up, the destruction she brings to all her relationships, with parents, lovers, even her own children. In short, the broken horses are the wreckage she's made of her life."

He stops, looks at me as if to say: *Well, there it is!* But I'm not impressed. There's something stolid about his interpretation that compares poorly with what I believe Dad was grasping for. Anyway, it's time for me to leave. I'm to meet Pam in half an hour.

At the door, I hesitate. "Dr. Mendoza, I can't leave without asking you this. Did Dad and Mrs. Fulraine have an affair?"

Izzy looks away. "She was a complex and highly sexed woman. Beside her Tom was relatively naive. So—did they make love? Tom never said they did, so I honestly don't know. Do I *think* they did? That's another question. Sadly my answer is—I do."

*   *   *

I FEEL THE ENCROACHING darkness as I drive through the silent tree-lined streets of Van Buren Heights, streets with British-sounding names: Woodmere, Tawsingham, Clarence, Exeter, Greenwich, Oak Hollow, Somerset, Dorset Lane.

With the dusk, the oaks and maples cast heavy shadows upon the lawns, while the houses behind show well-made false fronts: Tudor, Georgian, Spanish colonial; there're even several little Norman chateaux with turret staircases and mansard roofs. Only occasionally do I pass pedestrians: a middle-aged man walking a tired dog; a girl on a bicycle, ponytail whipping behind, pedaling one-handed down a dark, tree-lined street.

Our old house on Demington is just blocks away. It won't take but a few extra minutes to stop by. I turn the corner at Winslow, drive a block, make a left on Stuart, a right on Oxford, then take the right fork where it intersects with Demington. The street curves gently here, winds its way between park land and the Pembroke Country Club golf course. After Talbot, it becomes residential again. This first block is where we lived. I used to know it cold, every bump in the street, every break in the sidewalks. "*Step on a crack, your mother gets a broken back,*" we kids on Demington would chant.

The windows in our old house are dark tonight, except for a flickering in what used to be my parents' bedroom on the second floor. It's a TV set, probably placed where my parents kept theirs, on a bureau facing their bed.

I pull over to the curb, cut my engine and lights. No sounds outside except the whisper of the hot August night wind. In the darkness I catch the trails of fireflies dancing in the sticky air above the front lawn. Then I hear crickets chirping in the hedges. Somewhere in the distance a dog howls sorrow.

We were happy here, I think. *Or was that our family myth?* Remembering Izzy's last words to me minutes ago, I think: *Perhaps that summer we were the unhappiest family in all of Calista.*

A light comes on across the street. I turn, spot a man poised upon his stoop, silhouetted against the interior of his house. He's staring at me, doubtless wondering what a stranger is doing at this hour sitting silent in a darkened car. Burglar scouting the neighborhood? Private detective collecting evidence? Or a kidnapper perhaps, an abductor of prepubescent girls? Best, I decide, to be on my way.

WHEN I STEP INTO Waldo's, Tony tells me Pam called minutes before to say she was running late.

"She's in a meeting with Mr. Starret. Says she'll be down soon as she's finished," Tony says, planting a perfect margarita before me on the bar.

I pull out my sketchbook and start to draw. I'm halfway finished with a sketch of Dad sitting in his car in the Flamingo parking lot, when a shadow crosses the page and a hand descends upon my shoulder.

"How's it going, old boy?"

I look up to confront the cloying grin of Waldo's successor, Spencer Deval, flaunting his trademark open collar and silk ascot.

"Mind if I join you?" he asks.

"Actually I'm waiting for someone," I tell him, covering my drawing while easing my shoulder from his grasp.

"Oh, I know. She'll be down in a bit. Meantime, I thought we might chat." He perches uninvited on the bar stool to my right. Though he's short and stout, I notice he sits erect, angling up his chin to assert dominance.

"What about?" I ask him. "We don't really know one another."

"I'd rather like to get to know you," he says, voice warm, unctuous. "I'm a great admirer of your work."

I make a point of not returning his compliment. His raspy pseudo-British accent amuses me, but his transparent attempt at flattery annoys. Having long disdained him from a distance, I find I'm not yet ready to join his following.

"Rumor has it you're looking into one of our old unsolved murder cases. Fascinating city, Calista, from the unsolved crime point of view. That old Flamingo Motel case, for instance. Lot more interesting than Foster-Meadows. Or maybe you just feel that way because you're bored."

How would he know how I feel? "Who told you I was looking into it?" I ask, wondering if Deval was the man who'd asked Johnny whether I'd been around the Flamingo Court.

"Oh . . . a little birdie told me." He lisps out the words in a musical birdlike voice, then adds a silent tweet-tweet with his lips.

A *little birdie*: the same phrase Waldo used to source the blind item he ran about Dad and Barbara in his column.

"Tell me something—when you say a little birdie, are you referring to a female source? Because if it was a guy who told you, you'd say 'a little bird,' right?"

"Would I? Never actually thought of it that way."

"You still haven't answered my question."

His voice hardens. "A good newsman doesn't reveal sources."

"Way I hear it you deal in gossip."

" 'Gossip *is* news, old boy'—that's what dear old Waldo used to say whenever some scamp challenged the honor of his profession. Then he'd instruct by naming several of the great gossip-mongers: Oscar Wilde, George Bernard Shaw, Madame de Sévigné . . . even Shakespeare, if you know how to read him. The list is long, a rollcall of greats. So let there be no mistake—what I write *is* news. What people say and do and think at social gatherings—that's the very essence of news. And now—would you believe it?—they study Waldo's old 'About the Town' columns in a course on local social history at Calista State. He was not only this town's anecdotist, he was its chronicler, its Boswell." Deval squints, makes an I'm-a-modest-fellow face. "I like to think my own raconteuring, if there is such a word, meets the high standard he set."

Taking in this little oration, I begin to understand why some of my media colleagues are so bedazzled. It's a style that either seduces you or totally turns you off. I put myself in the latter category.

"When you're ready to identify your little birdie, Deval, I'll consider having a chat. Until then, please leave me alone."

He stares at me astonished. Watching his throat contract beneath his ascot, I know he's thinking up a rejoinder to save face. Finally, he comes out with it:

" 'Have you no decency, suh?' " he asks, switching to a Southern accent. " 'At long last. Have you no decency?' " Then, resuming the phony British intonation: "Those were Army Counsel Welch's words to Senator McCarthy back in the Fifties, days when class still reigned and a gentleman didn't behave rudely toward his betters."

He displays a steely little grin, picks up his drink, and, with studied dignity, withdraws.

PAM ARRIVES, PANTING and apologetic. Seems some CNN honchos flew in unexpectedly this afternoon. She pecks my cheek, says she hopes I'm not annoyed.

"Not at all," I tell her. "By the way, have you been talking to Deval?" She shakes her head. I recount our conversation. "Do you think he was the guy who talked to Johnny at the motel?"

"Probably not. I doubt he'd strike anyone as a cop type. But let's face it, he's a pro. He's got his antennae out. You've been asking a lot of people a lot of questions."

"I wonder why he's interested?"

"Probably because the Foster case is a dog and he's always on the lookout for a juicy item. Look at it from his point of view—this weird guy, David Weiss, turns up in town asking questions about an old murder case. When he finds out you're Dr. Thomas Rubin's son, then he *will* have something juicy, won't he?"

"I hate the way he calls me 'old boy.' "

"He calls everyone that. And I got news for you, darling—I can't stand him either."

I DRIVE HER OUT to Covington, show her the Gold Coast, then turn onto Indiana where I park. Walking past the coffeehouses and boutiques, Pam responds to the neighborhood.

"Gays with poodles. Dykes with German shepherds. Kind of a mini Greenwich Village." Outside Spezia, she sniffs the air. "Um! smells good! Is this the place?"

Jürgen Hoff's greeting is smooth and warm.

"Mr. Weiss, how nice to see you again."

He leads us to a small table in back. "This is absolutely our best table . . . from the romantic point of view," he adds.

Almost immediately we receive two complimentary kirs, apparently standard treatment for friends of the house.

Pam lets me know she's impressed. "He's handsome and oh-so suave," she says, gesturing at Jürgen, now chatting with a middle-aged couple at the bar.

"He served in the French Foreign Legion. They say he killed a man in Mexico."

"I get it, a Bogart type. He looks like a womanizer, too."

"He likes black call girls. Doesn't get it on with white chicks."

"Hmm, kinky Bogie. Interesting. . . ."

I've got to hand it to Pam, the way she takes in everything I say without asking where I heard it. This, I realize with admiration, is her trademark technique—getting people to talk by *not* asking questions.

Near the end of our meal, Jürgen stops by to ask if everything's been all right. As Pam assures him it has, I start a quick sketch of his face.

"You know Tony the bartender over at The Townsend?" I ask.

"Sure, known him for years."

"Please, Jürgen, hold it like that. I want to get the line of your nose."

Jürgen, suave as always, indulges me with an ironic grin.

"Good." I draw his eyebrows, then his chin. "I gather you and Tony worked together out at The Elms?"

Jürgen nods. "Tony did a stint there. Most of the better old-time barmen did."

"I like his mouth," I tell Pam as I sketch. "You've got a sensual mouth, Jürgen." I glance at Pam. "Don't you think?"

"Oh, very sensual," she agrees.

"The other night, after I left here, I dropped in at Waldo's to ask Tony about Rakoubian. Tony said Max was kind of a sleazeball, that he did 'bust-in stuff.' Said he was close to Waldo Channing too."

"That sounds about right," Jürgen says. He appears unfazed by my questions.

"The other night you described Max as 'one of the best.' "

"He was an excellent photographer, Mr. Weiss—one of the best in town." Jürgen raises an eyebrow. "Oh, I see, you thought I meant he was the best in—what? Human values?" Jürgen chuckles. "Max was a good guy, but ethics weren't his strong suit. One time he showed me some private stuff he'd shot. Not nice pictures." Jürgen winks at Pam. "Okay now if I move?"

I release him. Jürgen lets his arms hang loose. "Tough work, modeling. I had no idea."

"I'd like to come back one day and do a serious portrait, sit you down, get you into a comfortable position. It wouldn't take more than half an hour."

Again he looks at Pam. "Sounds like fun."

"I'll call you."

"Please." He moves away.

Pam leans forward. "God, what was *that* about?"

"Just one of the curious contradictions surrounding the cast of characters."

"Characters in the Flamingo thing?"

"Uh huh."

"And am I going to be privy to these contradictions?"

"You'll be privy soon enough," I assure her.

"YOU KNOW, YOU'RE QUITE the bad cat in bed," Pam tells me, a couple hours later. "Tomcatty, frisky." I start to laugh. "What's so funny?" she demands.

"The first time I slept with you I thought: 'Making love with her's like driving a Lamborghini, so smooth and elegant.' "

She pouts. "I'll have to consider whether I like that."

I kiss her to let her know I never thought of her as a machine. Then, changing the subject, I remind her of what she said about Barbara being too stylish a woman to enjoy spending much time at the seedy Flamingo.

"I thought it was too tacky for more than a couple of nights," she says, "There must have been something else made her want to keep going there."

"Something dangerous, you said. Well, try this. The woman drove a Jag, a fairly flashy car. She and Jessup arrived separately. She parked her Jag in the motel lot. Not exactly secretive behavior."

Pam, alert, props her head up on her elbow. "Not at all," she says. "And that's interesting."

"Now try this: She met Tom Jessup the same day she engaged my father as her analyst. In the paper he was writing about her case—"

"He wrote about her?"

"Just a draft. In it—"

"David, you didn't tell me!"

"I'm telling you now. In his paper, Dad calls Jessup 'my double' and 'my love-proxy.' He found it significant they both had the same first name. He had some suspicions she might be fantasizing the affair, so he followed her out to the motel."

"Your father *stalked* her!"

"He was very attracted to her. This old shrink, Dr. Mendoza, Dad's mentor—I met with him this afternoon—he thinks they may have had sex. He's not sure, but one thing that's certain is Barbara masturbated in Dad's office right on his analytic couch. He mentions it in his paper. In fact, that's where the paper breaks off."

"Jerked off in front of him! I think that's the kinkiest thing I've ever heard!"

"Suppose they *did* have sex—but not in his office? Suppose she lured him out to the Flamingo, the same room where she and Jessup shacked up? How's that for 'dangerous'?"

"Oh, *that's* dangerous, David! Creepy, too. So you're saying there was a second love triangle—between Barbara, Jessup, and your dad?"

"Maybe."

She winces. "That means your father could have . . . you know. Do you think it's possible?"

I tell her about my sketching session with Kate Evans and the drawing that came out of it, also how closely I resemble Dad and the phenomena of eyewitness transference and screen memories.

"There're pros and cons," I tell her. "The biggest con being I knew the man. He was totally nonviolent. He never raised his hand to me, rarely raised his voice. Not the type to commit a premeditated murder. Still, I'd have to put him on my list."

"Who else is on it?"

"Cody, of course. He stays suspect Number One. Andrew Fulraine's up there, too. Both had motives and both could've paid a hitman to do the job. There's also Jürgen, who could've acted as Cody's henchman or done it on his own. He refuses to talk about it even to this day, which I find odd. Then there's Max Rakoubian, the 'bust-in' guy. He'd been known to bust into love nests with his camera, so why not, if he were obsessed enough, bust into this love nest with a gun? Then there's the woman Tom Jessup befriended, the one Hilda Tucker told me about who lived next door in his rooming house. Suppose she was a stalker? She found out he'd been lying to her, not only that he wasn't gay but was having a secret affair with a haughty socialite. If she was nutty enough, she might have killed them, dressed up in a man's raincoat and fedora. So she's a possible though not a likely. Even, I hate to say it, less of a likely than Dad."

"How will you narrow the list?"

"Talk to more people, reinterview a few. There're still lots of loose ends. If Dad had something to do with Flamingo, I have to know. If he didn't, I need to know that, too."

She nods. "This is why you're doing all this . . . this is why you've come home. Now I understand."

PAM, UP AT DAWN, asks if I'd like to accompany her to the penthouse gym. Feeling lazy, I decline. After she leaves, I go back down to my room, shower, then finish the drawing I was working on when Deval interrupted me at the bar. It's a moody sketch full of long late-afternoon shadows, with Dad nearly lost in the dark interior of his car and, in the background, the half-closed blinds of room 201 reflecting back brilliant light.

As I work on Dad's features, seeking an appropriate expression, I darken his face more and more. What was he feeling that day? Anger?

Bafflement? Frustrated lust? Or did a look of cunning enter his eyes and turn the corner of his upper lip?

Unable to decide, I finally render him in silhouette, then finish up with some detail work on his car, a dark blue Volvo, so appropriate for a shrink, so sensible and well-engineered yet so unrevealing of its owner, an analysts's classic "empty vessel" beckoning his analysands to fill as their transference fantasies would permit.

The Foster trial won't begin for another hour, giving me time to draw the scene in Dad's office, the one described at the end of his truncated paper: Barbara on the couch, one hand thrust beneath her skirt, mouth twisted as she spills out her fantasies, while Dad sits listening with weary patience behind.

Except, of course, that I only have his word as to how he listened to her.

I try another version, this time depicting Barbara with her skirt raised to her waist, labia visible as she manipulates herself with her hand. In this sketch, her expression's lascivious, the Great Seductress at work. And Dad: I draw him as a poor schmuck seducee tormented by her ravings.

These images, each contradicting the other, fill me with despair. Better, I think, to concentrate on setting the scene, rendering Dad's office as best I can recall it—his oriental carpet, reproduction English desk, china vase lamp, dark-stained shelves groaning beneath psychiatric texts, quartet of diplomas clustered in a neat rectangle on the wall. I even work in the collection of primitive masks he displayed opposite his recliner, to which his analysands, in search of self-knowledge, could conveniently free-associate.

The room phone rings. It's Pam asking if I'd like to walk her over to the courthouse.

"I'm in the elevator. I'll pick you up," she says.

A few moments later, she knocks on my door. I open it, prepared to slip out, but then she asks if she can come inside.

"Just for a minute," she says. "I haven't been in here since the day I bribed the maid."

She goes straight to the wall where I've posted my Flamingo drawings.

"David, these are wild!"

I show her the sketches I made this morning. Her first reaction is amazement that I've mounted my head on Dad's body.

I show her the photo of him taped to my bureau mirror beside my Kate Evans eyewitness sketch.

"Yeah, you're definitely spitting images of one another." She turns to me. "These drawings, David—they're so bleak and full of shadows. That's how you see all this, isn't it?"

"Well, it's a pretty dark story, don't you think?"

Outside the hotel, it's blistering hot. The short walk to the courthouse raises a gloss of sweat upon our brows.

"The honchos who flew in yesterday want to pull me out." Although Pam speaks with studied carelessness, I pick up on her stress.

"Why? You're doing a great job. According to Harriet, you're blowing us away."

"Your drawings are stronger than Wash's."

"Big deal! That evens things out."

"It's not that they don't like my reporting, David. They like it too much. They think I'm wasted here. They want to try me in an anchor position. I've got mixed feelings about that."

"You'd make a great anchor," I tell her. "Probably triple your income, too."

"Double's more like it. But that'll mean moving back to New York. And I love reporting. I'm not ready yet to give it up." She stops on the corner. "I told them I have to think it over. They didn't look happy. They're not used to being turned down. My agent says if I refuse, they'll regard me with contempt. Like who turns down a big raise and regular national exposure? I'd have to be a jerk to do that, right?"

She turns to me, hugs me tight. Hugging her back, I feel her small, hard body tremble against my chest.

"I'm so sorry," she says, breaking from our embrace. "I didn't mean to go squishy on you. Now I've got to get my hair and makeup done."

"Let's have lunch, talk it through."

"Sure, lunch!" she says cheerily, striding off toward the CNN trailer in the alley.

TODAY'S COURT SESSION is typically dull until Kit Foster's lawyer, launching into his cross-examination of Caleb Meadows's manager, introduces the notion of a stalker. I find myself electrified. Dad, in Pam's words, "stalked" Barbara, and several anonymous letters implicit with threat, including one containing a condom, were received by her in the weeks before she was killed.

Suddenly everything is cutting too close.

I quickly finish my drawings and hand them off to Harriet, then find Pam on a bench in the corridor finishing up a call. As we walk to Plato's, a lawyers hangout two blocks from the courthouse, she tells me that after we parted this morning she spoke again with her agent.

"He wants me to come to New York, says it's time to put me into play. I'll do my afternoon stand-up, then take the early evening flight. Starret's got a temp reporter flying in. I'll be gone through the weekend at least."

"So your agent's going to shop you around. Reporter or anchor?"

"Either or both. High bidder gets the girl."

"You'll go with the money?"

"In this business that's the only way to go."

Pam's not squishy now; she's tough and on a roll. I think she's right, and I tell her so.

She reaches for my hand, leans over her plate of spanakopita, and plants a kiss upon my palm.

"I'm really glad I hooked up with you."

"We have a lot of fun."

"Will continue to, I hope."

"Let's see how things play out."

She winces. "I'm not a location-affair-type person, David. I'm a relationship girl." She grins. "Anyway, no matter what happens in New York,

I'll be back to finish out this gig. And, if you let me, to stay here with you until you finish yours."

WITH JUDGE WINTERSON'S decision to devote the afternoon to an evidentiary hearing, I find myself with nothing to draw. Fine with me; my hand's tired. Already today I've executed three dramatic courtroom sketches plus three fantasy drawings based on Dad's case study.

As I'm making my way on foot down Spencer Avenue toward Harp, the sky darkens, then suddenly lets loose. Within seconds the street gutter becomes a stream. I run the final block to the Doubleton Building then dash into the lobby soaked and out of breath.

The black elevator attendant with jaundiced eyes sadly shakes his head.

"You're one wet doggy," he tells me. "You got a minute, I'll fetch you a towel."

Nice man. The towel he brings me isn't all that clean, but I use it anyway then tip him a couple bucks. On the ride up to the seventh floor, I use my fingers to smooth down my hair.

I'm making my way along the corridor toward PHOTOS BY MAX, when suddenly I halt, caught by the words MARITZ INVESTIGATIONS neatly painted at chest level on a pebbled glass door.

Walter M. Maritz: That was the name of the former-cop-turned-private-investigator hired by Andrew Fulrainc to build a dossier on the promiscuity of his ex-wife, the same Maritz who confessed to Mace Bartel that he'd gone straight to Barbara to warn her and sell his client out.

Calista, a city of over half a million people, must have at least two hundred office buildings downtown. Isn't it a neat coincidence, I think, that private investigator Maritz and bust-in photographer Rakoubian not only worked from the same building but also from the same floor?

Though undergroomed for an office visit, I knock on the door. A short, dumpy, middle-aged Asian woman opens up. She peers at me through half-moon spectacles.

"Is this Walter Maritz's agency?" I ask.

"This is Maritz Investigations," she says. "Mr. Maritz is retired."

"But this was his firm?"

"Were you acquainted with Mr. Maritz?"

"I'd like to talk to him. Can you tell me where he is?"

"He moved to Florida. I'm afraid I can't tell you more than that."

I show her my courthouse press pass and my Society of Forensic Scientists ID. She studies them a moment, introduces herself as Karen Lee and invites me in.

No seedy private eye's clutter here, rather a minimalist decor—stark filing cabinets, steels desks, Singapore Airlines calendar on the wall, and a large white formica conference table where three young Asian males, each facing a computer screen, continue whatever they're doing without looking up.

Karen copies Maritz's Sarasota retirement address on the back of a business card.

"I bought the agency from him two years ago for the lease and the goodwill," she tells me. "The lease was okay. The goodwill didn't exist." She pauses. "We don't do the same kind of work as Mr. Maritz."

"What kind was that?"

"Gumshoe." She snickers.

"And you?"

She gestures toward the young men at the consoles. "We locate people using electronic resources."

"Interesting."

"Are you looking for someone, Mr. Weiss?"

"Suppose a woman worked at Merrill Lynch in New York twenty-six years ago. She might be married now, she might not. Could you find her from her maiden name?"

"If she's alive, we can find her. That's what we do. A search like that will run you two to four hundred dollars, depending on how long it takes."

I give her Susan Pettibone's name, then write out a check for two hundred as a deposit.

Karen Lee escorts me to the door. I turn to her as I'm about to leave.

"Walter Maritz had an associate."

"Yes, a Mr. O'Neill. He didn't fit in with our concept so we let him go. The business has changed. We don't use any of Mr. Maritz's people. When we find Ms. Pettibone, I'll give you a call."

THIS TIME THE DOOR to the reception room of PHOTOS BY MAX is open. I figure Chip hears me, because a moment after I enter I hear the blowtorch in the inner studio shut off.

"Someone out there?"

"It's David Weiss, Chip. Gotta minute?"

"Sure, come in. Watch the pigeon shit."

Chip, welder visor up, wearing a grungy, gray tanktop, picks up a broom and makes menacing motions toward a trio of pigeons perched on his windowsill.

"Shoo! Shoo!" he yells, waving the broom. "Fuckin' rats with wings," he calls after them.

Though I took in his sculpture during my first visit, this time, I find, I'm unable to pull my eyes away.

"What do you think?" Chip asks.

"Strong work," I tell him.

He smiles; he likes that. "Couple more weeks of welding before it's finished."

"Then what?"

"Out to the synagogue for the installation. She'll weather nicely, I think. I'll leave her a little ragged here and there. I'm working for a sense of timelessness."

"Your old man's why I'm here, Chip. I'm hearing stories that don't match up. You told me he was a fine photographer. No one disputes that. But they're some who say he did bust-in work, in flagrante photographs."

"I don't know what that means."

"It's Latin for 'in the act.' Say a couple of lovers are making it in a motel room, then suddenly Max busts in. *Flash-zap!* He's got proof that can be used against them in, say, a custody battle, or used to make them pay blackmail so the pictures *won't* be shown around."

Chip scratches his head. "I heard the old man did stuff like that."

"Sort of a far cry from gorgeous still lifes of shiny objects."

He shrugs. "What can I tell you? Dad was an all-around photographer. He did what he had to do to support his family."

"Did he know Walter Maritz?"

"The PI down the hall? Sure, he and Walt were old friends."

"Did they work together on the bust-in stuff?"

"You know, David, I think you ought to talk to my mom about this. She may be able to help you."

"I would definitely like to talk to your mom. I'd also like to see your father's *Fessé* album."

Chip is fine with both requests. He'll speak to his mother, set up a meeting, and leave word for me at the hotel.

THERE ARE MESSAGES FROM Mace and Kate Evans at the desk. From my room, I call Mace first.

"That case study—quite a document," he says. "Puts your dad in a whole different light."

"Does it put him on your suspect list?"

"Does it put him on yours?"

"You know as much as I do, Mace."

"Yeah. Too bad he didn't finish writing up his case. Too bad he killed himself just at the pivotal point."

I know what he's thinking—that Dad took his life because he couldn't cope with writing down what finally occurred between him and Mrs. F.

"What strikes me," Mace continues, "is he wrote this after she was dead. He mentions that she was killed at the start. Obviously he was a very troubled man. It's like he was trying to make sense of everything that happened, but hard as he tried, he couldn't manage it. That makes me feel sorry for the guy."

Hearing that, I'm gratified. Mace is showing himself to be a lot more sensitive than he lets on.

"Those footnotes are amazing," he says.

"Dad's old training analyst says that's where his madness shows."

"I don't know about madness, but I don't think he killed her."

"You're not saying that to make me feel better?"

"I'm saying it because it's what I think. What happened between them may have been crazy, but it wasn't murderous-crazy. Call it a cop's hunch."

"Well, thank you . . . because that does make me feel better."

And I continue to feel good after I put down the phone.

I pull a vodka out of the room minibar, pour it over some ice, then call Kate Evans.

"The man who was asking about you, he's been around again," she tells me. "Johnny didn't tell him anything of course."

She says Johnny will be on duty tomorrow one to five. I ask her to tell him I'll be dropping by.

"David, about that sketch we did—I wasn't that helpful, was I?"

"That remains to be seen."

"He looked a lot like you. I realized that after you left."

"That happens sometimes, Kate. People get faces mixed up. Or else they forget what someone looked like and end up describing the artist."

"I don't think I did that—describe you, I mean. But the other thing—"

"What?"

"Getting faces mixed up."

"Yes?"

"I think that could've been what happened—I got two people confused."

ELEVEN

I t's a little past one-thirty when I reach the Flamingo. The area seems quieter than usual. There's some late lunch action in Moe's but the drapes at the Shanghai Sapphire are tightly drawn, suggesting one of those cheerless Chinese places where the cook overuses MSG and the cornstarch-thickened sauces are way too sweet.

I check the pool area. A couple of teenage girls are splashing about in the deep end. I find Johnny in the office behind the reception desk staring at the lounge TV.

"Howdy," Johnny says. "Kate told me you'd be around. Said you want me to describe the fella came in asking 'bout you again. Can't tell you much. Like I said before, he had a cop's way about him. You know—a stache and a cheap suit." Johnny scratches his head. "Come to think of it, he didn't have a stache. Just seemed like the type."

Johnny's eager to have me start on a drawing, but as soon as he begins talking, I realize nothing's going to come of it. Everything he says is too general and ambiguous, much like his statement that the man had a mustache and then that he didn't.

"I don't know, Mr. Weiss. He was kinda average. No distinguishing marks or features. I'd put his age between forty and fifty, maybe fifty-five. He was medium built, medium high give or take an inch, two, or three. Eye color?" Johnny shrugs. "Didn't catch any color in them. Mouth?

Man's mouth. You wouldn't mistake it for a woman's. Skin kinda rough and there were pouches beneath his eyes. Clean-shaven, I know that. Don't know why I thought he had a stache." He pauses. "One thing for sure, though. The guy smokes. His clothes stank of it."

Johnny looks away. He's embarrassed. As much as he'd like to help, he can't describe the man. It's as if there was nothing memorable about him. I've dealt with witnesses who've had the same trouble, and often it turned out it wasn't their fault. The subject's appearance was so neutral there really wasn't anything to describe. In such cases, however closely I'd follow the witness's description, I'd always end up with the same useless drawing, a nothing blah sketch of a nothing blah face I've come to call "Mr. Potato Head."

Driving back downtown, I find myself checking my rearview mirror. And even though I don't notice anyone following, I have the distinct feeling someone is.

3:30 P.M. I REACH COVINGTON and luck into a parking spot in front of Spezia. The restaurant's closed, but I spot Jürgen sitting alone at a little table in the rear, bottle and a glass in front of him.

I grab my sketchpad and go to the door. Jürgen appears to be brooding. When I knock he looks up annoyed, then recognizes me and comes to the door to let me in.

"Mr. Weiss! What a surprise. I didn't expect you so soon."

"I happened to be in the neighborhood so I took a chance."

The way he raises his right eyebrow tells me he doesn't believe that for a second.

"I'm always here. As Jack Cody used to put it: 'A restaurant is a harsh mistress, me boy.' "

He offers me a glass of Ricard. I watch as he adds water, transforming the liquid from clear to milky white.

"Not quite absinthe," he says, "but still makes a good *louche*. I acquired a taste for it in the Legion. You know about my military career?"

"You're a legend, Jürgen."

He grins.

"Actually, all I know is what Mace told me."

"Inspector Bartel's an okay guy for a cop. And you, Mr. Weiss—are you a cop, too?"

I explain that though my drawings are used in law enforcement, I'm a civilian in town to cover the Foster trial.

"And now you want to draw me?" He smiles, strikes a pose.

"I'd prefer you a little more relaxed."

He slumps over. " 'The Absinthe Drinker' by Degas, no?"

"A little less stagey, if you don't mind."

"Sure." He assumes a normal posture, then lets his features fall into repose. In those few seconds, his face seems to age a dozen years.

"That's good. It works better for me when you're comfortable."

We chat casually as I start to sketch.

"This drawing—will you be showing it to witnesses?" he asks.

"If I wanted to show your picture, Jürgen, I'd make things easy for myself and take a photograph."

He nods. "I've heard photographs lie, that only art can tell the truth."

"Photographs can also be art."

"And drawings can also lie, no? Forgive me for asking, Mr. Weiss, but what's the point of this exercise?"

"I like your face, I'm having fun drawing it. And I was hoping a portrait session would give us a chance to talk."

"About the Flamingo killings?"

I start work on his eyes. "Something you want to tell me about that?"

"I'm curious why people are still interested after all these years."

"People?"

"Inspector Bartel and you."

"I was a kid here when the murders happened. I knew the teacher, so I've always been interested."

Jürgen raises his right eyebrow at the same time, making his smile go sweet. It's a characteristic expression, one I want to catch. I set to work on his eyebrows, then his mouth.

"I think there's more to it than that, Mr. Weiss."

"You're right, there is. And please call me David."

"Yes, thank you. Please forgive my formality. It's my European background. Jack Cody always said he liked that about me, the way I made his clients feel so 'well-served.' "

He tells me he returned to Germany this past winter, his first visit since he ran away from home at age sixteen. His kid sister was dying after fighting breast cancer for two years. It would be his last chance to see her, so he closed his restaurant for two weeks and flew over.

"My niece met me at the Frankfurt airport. She had crisscross tribal marks cut into her cheeks, a ring in her nose, a tack on her tongue, and a baby perched on her back in a papoose. 'Yoo-hoo, Uncle Jürgen—it's me, Gisela!' One look at her and I wanted to get back on the plane. My brother-in-law Hans is a podiatrist. He keeps a scabby pink oversize model of a foot on his desk. My sister, Eva, looked bad. I remembered her as a stout girl. Now she weighed less than a hundred pounds. The three of them tried to be brave. They said they wanted me to have a good time, see the 'new Germany.' After a couple days sightseeing, I told them I thought it was pretty much the same as when I left—crappy food, crummy little houses, petty middle-class concerns. 'Oh, Uncle Jürgen you're so funny—isn't he, *Mutter? Vater?*' But Eva knew I wasn't kidding, that I was thrilled to discover I'd made the correct decision when I left." He pauses, clicks his glass against the bottle of pastis. "She died in April, poor darling! I didn't go back for the funeral. Wired over a big wreath." Jürgen bottom-ups his drink, sets down his glass, and wipes his eyes.

I've got him down pretty well on paper, I think: the suave ability to appraise others that shows in his eyes, the bittersweet irony in the set of his mouth. Taking a cue from Pam's perception of him as a "kinky Bogie," I idealize him a little, working to instill the proper degree of cynicism and rue.

"Nice watch," I tell him, indicating the heavy gold Vaucheron-Constantin dangling from his wrist.

"Jack Cody left it to me."

"Do you think Jack had the lovers killed?"

Jürgen shakes his head. "Not Jack's style. If he'd wanted them dead he would have killed them himself. Anyway, Barbara was the love of his life."

"She was cheating on him."

Jürgen shrugs. "They weren't married. He cheated on her, too. They had an arrangement."

"Tell me about Walter Maritz."

"He was a crooked cop who became a crooked private eye. Jack punished him hard for what he did to Barbara. He deserved everything he got."

"What did he do to her?"

"You don't know?"

"Tell me."

Jürgen smiles. I start work on a second drawing. This time I want to catch him in storytelling mode.

He tells me that after Barbara's au pair washed up headless from Delamere Lake, she and her husband hired a slew of private detectives to find their abducted kid. About two years later, after the Fulraines were divorced, Maritz approached Barbara out of the blue saying he'd heard rumors there was a little white girl with blond hair living in Gunktown with blacks. Barbara, grasping at the offered straw, hired Maritz and gave him money to spread around the ghetto. Every few weeks Maritz came back, reported what his informants said, and asked for more money to further loosen tongues. This went on for three or four months until Barbara met Jack through a mutual friend.

"Jack, of course, knew who she was and was taken with her right away. When she told him about Maritz, that she'd given him nearly twenty grand to develop leads, Jack knew right away she was being scammed. He offered to handle it for her. She was relieved. She didn't much like dealing with Maritz. So Jack called in Maritz for a little talk. After ten minutes, he knew for sure Maritz was a liar.

"That's when he brought me in and a couple of muscle guys who used to handle security around The Elms. We took Maritz to a garage out back. Jack told the muscle guys to beat the truth out of the fuck. Maritz didn't hold out long. About a minute in he was on his knees confessing the scam. Jack told him he had to give the money back. Maritz said he couldn't, he'd gambled it all away. Jack, cold as ice, told him if he couldn't pay in money he'd have to pay in broken bones. Maritz, terrified, begged for mercy. Jack, sick of listening to the fuck, told the muscle guys to give it to him good. They broke both his kneecaps and half his ribs, then I drove him to the hospital. I warned him not to say anything. 'You're a lucky guy,' I told him. 'Mr. Cody could have had you killed.' Maritz, still whimpering, got the point. I dumped him at the E.R. entrance. Takes a year to recover from a beating like that. He recovered, went on with his life. 'Live and let live,' as they say.

"Next day Jack met with Barbara, explained the swindle, and told her he got all her money back. Then he paid her every cent out of his own funds. That's what brought them together. Soon afterwards they became lovers, and after that their bond was what they did with each other in bed."

It's a good story and clearly Jürgen relishes telling it. He laughs when I tell him Maritz told the cops he received money from Barbara after Andrew Fulraine hired him to follow her.

"After what Jack did to him he wouldn't dare go near her. And she would never have met with him. A woman like that doesn't get taken twice. She'd have told Jack and by the next morning Maritz's body would've been rotting in a Dumpster."

"Fulraine hired him to follow her. That was confirmed."

"Then Maritz scammed Fulraine, took his money, and made up reports. He couldn't have followed her. She'd have spotted him right away."

"What about his operative?"

"O'Neill? Another crooked cop. He was good, I'll give him that. He was like a shadow, you never noticed he was there." Jürgen smiles. "Still, bottom line on Maritz, you can't believe a word he says. Inspector Bartel should have known that. But you know what cops are like—they stick together especially when they lie. Now if Maritz had done the Flamingo job, that would've been something else. But like I said, he wouldn't have dared. He knew if Jack found out, Jack would've buried him alive."

Jürgen prefers my second drawing. He thinks my first makes him look too old. I offer it to him. He accepts on condition I let him comp me next time I come in. He says he'll post it among the signed photos of entertainers, ball players, and politicians that crowd the wall behind the bar.

As I'm about to leave, he asks if I'd be willing to make a drawing of his girlfriend.

"She's beautiful. You'll like sketching her. Thing is," he winces a little, "I'd like you to draw her in the nude. She's got a great body. I'll pay you well."

I tell him I'll accept the commission, but it's not money I want in exchange.

"What do you want?"

"Information."

He raises his right eyebrow, showing the same sweet, suave smile. "I'll mention it to the lady," he says.

I FLEX MY FINGERS as I drive back to the Townsend. Five drawings since this morning. I'm done sketching for the day.

I check out Waldo's on my way through the lobby. The bar's barely half full. I stop by Reception to pick up my messages. There's just one, from Karen Lee.

Returning her call, I learn she's located Susan Pettibone.

"Easy search, Mr. Weiss. Your deposit will cover it. Once we got hold of her social security number, tracking her was a breeze."

I don't ask by what manner of hacking her operative got hold of the number.

Susan Pettibone, she tells me, now calls herself Susan Ryan, is divorced, has two grown children, is an executive at Pitney-Bowes, and lives in Danbury, Connecticut. Karen gives me her home phone number and street address, then asks me not to reveal where I got them.

"We deal with our clients in confidence," she says.

I WATCH TV FOR A WHILE, then go down to Waldo's for a sandwich and beer. Then, missing Pam, I decide to take a walk following the same route we took the first night we went out together to Irontown to eat.

Approaching the Calista River, I pause to take in the tranquility of the city. It's after nine, a moonless night, and there's hardly anyone around, just an occasional night jogger fleeting along the embankment and sparse traffic heading for the Irontown clubs and cafes.

The river's glassy tonight, without a wave or visible current, slick like polished black marble reflecting the black, moonless sky. A row of well-spaced streetlamps, shaped like enormous candelabra, cast yellow light upon Riverwalk. In the distance, Eric Lindstrom's amazing twin towers, lit from within, soar like beacons from the cluster of old, granite-faced office buildings downtown.

I continue along Riverwalk with the Calista flowing silently below me beside abandoned railway tracks. Here finished steel and the components used to make it were once hauled by barges day and night to and from the mills.

A sudden screech startles me. A high-speed train emerges from a tunnel on the other side of the river, then races along a trestle. In the distance I hear sirens, whether police or fire I can't tell. I look ahead. A single jogger's coming toward me. Otherwise the area's deserted.

As I reach the center of Riverwalk, I hear a car approaching from behind. Then the squeal of brakes. I turn just as a van pulls to the curb. Two men jump out wearing ski masks and black sweats. They grab my arms and drag me back. The jogger is coming abreast. When I call out to him for help, he pushes me roughly from behind. A moment later, I'm pushed and pulled toward an opening in the wall that bounds Riverwalk, entrance to one of the stairways that lead down to the river. I struggle frantically, but the three of them are too much for me. They drag me down a flight, throw some sort of sack over my head, pull it tight at my neck, then spin me around.

"Take my money," I mumble through the sack.

No answer. The sack blindfolds me, it smells bad inside, and makes it hard for me to breathe. As I try to twist free, they suddenly let go of me. Then one of them shoves me forward, another shoves me toward the third, and he in turn pushes me back. I can hear their light laughter as they toss me around, spinning me each time until finally in a fit of dizziness I fall to the concrete, landing on my face.

But that's not enough for them. They pull me roughly to my feet and start the roundelay again. I'm terrified. What do they want? Why are they doing this? Are they just having sport with me, or is there some underlying purpose?

Suddenly two of them grab my arms, while the third punches me hard in the stomach. I feel a sharp pain, double over, fall to my knees. I can feel the vomit rising. I choke on it, try to spit it out.

One of them, the hitter I think, kneels beside me. I can feel his breath as he brings his mouth to my covered ear.

"Stop nosing around," he says, his harsh whisper cutting to me through the sack. "This is a warning. Next time we'll break your hands. Then you won't be drawing any more pictures."

He knows who I am! I've been targeted! This isn't a random attack! Then, as a set of memories floods in, I finally understand what this is about.

He pulls away. I sense the three of them standing above me, looking down. One of them kicks me in the side, then I hear their van take off. I lie still on the pavement until I'm sure they're gone, then pull the sack from my head.

When I get it off, I gulp for air . . . except the air around me isn't all that fresh, tainted by the smell of the river and the old iron smell of Calista streets. I sit up slowly, check myself. My side's sore but I'm sure nothing's broken. That final kick in the ribs was half-hearted at best. I taste a little blood, most likely the result of a split lip when I fell. Though grateful to find myself undamaged, I know I won't look pretty in the morning.

I grope about, get to my feet, make my way carefully up the concrete stairs. Back on Riverwalk, I go to the nearest lamppost and inspect the sack. It's tight yellow mesh, the kind used to hold grain. Two words are printed on it in block capitals: BELSONS FLOUR.

BACK IN MY ROOM, I clean myself up. The cut on my lip isn't as bad as I thought. What the whisperer said was true—what I got tonight was a warning, not a beating, a warning to "stop nosing around." I know what that means: Keep my nose out of Flamingo. It's been twenty-six years. I ask myself: *Who besides me and Mace still cares?*

MY PHONE RINGS EARLY. It's Harriet informing me I have the day off. This morning the jury will visit the crime scene at the Museum of Natural History, no press allowed, and this afternoon Judge Winterson will rule on a defense proffer of new evidence.

I call Mace, tell him what happened.

"Can you ID the people?" he asks.

"No. Two of them were masked. It happened too fast. But I think I know who they are . . . or represent."

"Who?"

"I'll tell you when I'm sure. Meantime, I'm not intimidated. Anyway, I'm calling you about something else."

I pass on what Hilda Tucker told me about the obsessed grad student girl who lived in Tom Jessup's rooming house.

"I didn't see anything about her in the file," I tell him. "Do you remember her?"

"We talked to a lot of people. I don't recall anyone like that."

"Well, it's occurred to me—if she had such a big crush on Tom, maybe she stalked him, found out he wasn't gay. Then she snapped when she discovered he was seeing Barbara."

"Sounds like a long shot, but I'll look into it." A pause. "Listen, David, if you think you know who jumped you, you should tell me. There're laws against that. With you being in law enforcement, it could even be felonious assault."

"Hey, I'm just a freelancer," I remind him. "But thanks for your concern."

AFTER BREAKFAST, I head over to where I probably should have gone my first week in town: the austere ten-story triangular steel and terrazzo fortress at the corner of Toland and LaButte, which the discreet letters, FSI, incised in steel beside the main door identify as headquarters of Fulraine Steel Industries.

Why, I ask myself, did it take an ambush on the street to finally bring me here? The easy answer is my residual bitterness toward Mark and Robin Fulraine. But I know there's more to it—my old guilt over not having immediately reported what I heard between the au pair and Belle Fulraine the day of Mark's seventh birthday. Even though I know better, I'm still burdened with the belief that if I'd told someone, Belle might still be alive.

Sitting in the waiting room on the executive floor, I study the corporation's annual report. There's a glossy picture of CEO Mark Fulraine, looking as handsome as I remember him at Hayes. The golden locks are gone now. His hair appears darker, thinner, and is combed back, giving him a sleek, well-tended look. But the smile's the same, the charming grin of the star athlete, lower school student council president, scion of one of Hayes's four founding families. *The face of a man born to rule.*

I read an optimistic summary of the company's prospects. A pie graph shows that only seven percent of FSI's revenues now derive from steel. These days the company's into all kinds of other things from manufacturing high-end stereo equipment, operating a chain of retail sporting goods stores, making high-capacity disk drives and assorted Internet ventures. In my admittedly naive view, FSI looks like an incoherent grab bag. I think back to my days at Hayes, trying to recall whether Mark was bright. Jerry Glickman and I were tops in our class in academics. Mark, I remember, fell somewhere in the middle.

I'm scanning the list of his Board of Directors, when an attractive young woman with a shag cut approaches with a smile.

"I'm Jane Bailey, Mr. Fulraine's assistant. He's free to see you now."

As she leads me through the door to the executive suite, she chatters on about how excited Mark was when told I'd stopped by.

"Soon as he heard, he cut short his meeting and had me clear his calendar for lunch. You'll be eating in our executive dining room. Chef wants to know what you'd like. Lobster, steak, or chicken?"

I tell her chicken will be fine.

The floors are plushly carpeted, the furnishings all made of steel, there are abstract designs engraved on steel plates encased in steel frames and abstract steel sculptures scattered about exhibited on steel pedestals.

Mark greets me from behind an oval, matte-finished steel desk.

"Dave Rubin!" He grasps hold of both my hands. "Hey, you're looking great, pal!"

Before I can answer, he's off on a riff about our classmates, some of whom I only vaguely remember.

"Jock Sturgis is FSI general counsel. He and I roomed together at Yale. Norm Carter's doing great. He's exec. v.p. over at Hallowell Paints. Whatever happened to your old buddy—Glickstein?"

"Jerry Glickman."

"Yeah, what's Jerry doing these days?"

"He's professor of orthopedic surgery at Harvard Medical School."

"I'll be damned! Hope he holds his scalpel steadier than he held the old basketball!"

He clasps my shoulder. "Real glad you stopped by, David. You left so suddenly middle of seventh grade. Then your dad . . ." He shakes his head. "Things work out all right for you in California?"

"I still live out there. San Francisco now."

"You went to Stanford, right?"

"Pratt. That's an art school in New York."

"Sure, great place! One of our design guys went there. Got kids?"

I shake my head.

"I'm sending mine to Hayes, but they'll finish up at boarding schools in the East. My older boy's headed off to Groton in the fall. Get him some of that, you know, old Eastern polish."

All this hail-fellow-well-met stuff makes me want to puke. Also I'm angry with myself for allowing him to lay down the field of play. I decide to cut the bullshit short.

"I gave my name at the desk as David Rubin," I tell him, "but now I'm David Weiss. When my mother remarried, I took my stepfather's name."

He stares at me. "I think I heard about that. Can't remember who told me . . . anyway. . . ."

Silence. It's brief, lasts just a couple seconds, but it's deep enough to express the gulf between us, the gulf we could never bridge even when we were kids.

On the way to the FSI executive dining room, I tell him how I happen to be in town.

"Courtroom sketch artist, huh? I remember at school you were always drawing up a storm."

"As I recall you didn't like one of my drawings very much."

He laughs. "Hell of a fight we had. Do any boxing these days?"

It's an absurd question, but I politely shake my head.

"We got a gym downstairs. Occasionally I work out on the light bag. No sparring. Haven't done that since Hayes. Just as soon not get my face messed up. Wife wouldn't like it." He beams.

We study each other over lunch.

"We never liked each other much, did we, Mark?"

He smiles. "I wouldn't put it like that. But, yeah, I know what you mean."

"Why do you suppose?"

"Just one of those things, I guess."

"Still there's a connection, and not just our years at Hayes. We each lost a parent when we were young. You know about the connection between your mother and my dad?"

He looks uneasy.

"Dad was a caregiver. Your mom needed help and my dad tried to give it to her. Later I learned she approached him the same day she met Mr. Jessup."

He shakes his head. "I don't really want to talk about this, Dave."

"David," I correct him. "Okay, I understand. But thing is, Mark, since I got here I've been looking into the Flamingo killings in my spare time. People seem to know about that. Someone's been around the motel asking about me, and last night on Riverwalk I was attacked by three thugs. It was a warning to lay off."

He raises his eyebrows. "Really?"

Studying him, I can't tell a thing. Either he had nothing to do with it, or he's one very cool CEO.

I describe the attack. "Sounds familiar, doesn't it?"

He shrugs, but of course he knows exactly what I'm talking about: the very rough Hayes School version of "Capture the Flag." There was a twenty-acre wood on school property where we played. In the Hayes version, when prisoners were taken they could be worked over for information in accordance with certain highly prescribed school rules. You couldn't beat a prisoner to make him talk, but you could haze him in various ways. One way was to blindfold him, then tie him to a tree, then touch him with something scary like a garden snake. Often just the threat was enough to make a younger boy spill his guts. Another specialty from the list of school-sanctioned tortures was bagging—tying a bag around a prisoner's head, then pushing him around and twirling him till he fell down dizzy and confused. The object was to break your victim, make him cry, then divulge the whereabouts of his team's secreted flag. You couldn't inflict physical injury, but terrorization and humiliation were considered fair. Later, if a student's parents complained, the standard school response was that it was just a form of play, akin to football or murderball, and that such play was essential to instill "manliness" in boys, the highest of all the moral virtues implanted by a "Hayes education."

"So what's your point?" Mark asks when I remind him of "bagging."

"Isn't it obvious?"

He stares into my eyes. "Are you accusing me, David?"

"Do I have reason to?"

"Of course not!"

"Okay, I take you at your word. So, what's Robin up to these days?"

He shakes his head. "That's a sad story. What happened was terrible for us both. Still I managed to get through it. Robin didn't. You wouldn't recognize him. He takes drugs, shaves his head, wears earrings and tattoos, lives in a ratty house on the edge of Gunktown. Never bothered to fix it up . . . and, believe me, he can afford to. He owns two million shares of FSI."

I look at him. "Maybe it was him who ambushed me last night."

"Is this why you're here?"

"I'm here because I thought it was you."

"That's not how I'd have handled it. I wouldn't have pulled my punches."

I laugh. *Sure doesn't take much to skim the gloss off of him,* I think, *'that old Eastern polish,' or whatever the hell he calls it. Apply a little stress and the old money varnish comes right off.*

Maybe he realizes how ridiculous he appears or perhaps he wants to regain his self-respect. Whatever the reason, he meets my stare, then suddenly breaks into a grin.

"Really had me going there, didn't you?"

"I'll tell you, Mark, I don't like being bagged and pushed around, reminds me of days I'd just as soon forget. I particularly don't like being threatened with having my hands broken. I make my living with my hands."

"It won't happen again."

"That's a guarantee?"

He nods.

"Not good enough, Mark. First I want to make sure it was Robin. Second, I want to set him straight. By assuring me it won't happen again, you implicate yourself. So where do I find the little fucker?"

A pause. He looks away. "I'll take you to him," he says.

WE DON'T TALK MUCH in the limo. Even here in his plush car, Mark appears smaller to me than in his office. Perhaps it's the lack of props, the corporate art collection assembled to glorify the divine might of steel, or maybe it's because of all the obscene Fulraine family secrets I learned from Dad's case study.

Gunktown's an ugly name for a district that was once one of the glories of Calista, the place you'd automatically think to go if you needed something built by hand. Say you invented a device and needed a prototype to show people how it worked, you'd take your drawings to one of the machine shops in Gunktown and they'd make it up for you fast and for a fair price. Machinists there could make anything, people said.

They called it Gunktown because of the oil and grease that coated everything and stank up the air. The name stuck even when the machine shop days were past. Then, when blacks moved in, the word took on a cruel twist. Gunktown came to mean the people who lived there, "gunks," people of color, and though it seemed shameful for white folks to even say the word, black leaders flung it about with pride: "Down in Gunktown we don't think much of your honky justice!" Or: "Don't come around Gunktown with your phony liberal bullshit!"

Our limo pulls up in front of a decaying Victorian house set forty or so feet back behind a grill fence. It looks strange beside its neighbors, which are all built flush to the street. The wood siding was once bright gray; now the peeling paint's the color of dirty steel. And what was once a small front yard is now a patch of brown strewn with discarded rusty machinery and weeds. There's a BEWARE FEROCIOUS DOG sign on the gate beside a profile of a dog's head displaying gnashing jaws. The main part of the house is two stories high surmounted by an off-center turret. The effect is lugubrious, like one of those weird old houses in Charles Addams cartoons.

Mark turns to me. "Let me talk to him first."

I watch him as he makes his way through the labyrinth of junk to the front stoop. He pauses at the door, then enters. Unwilling to sit still in the car, I start a drawing of the house. Ten minutes later, as I'm finishing work on the turret, Mark steps back into the car.

"Yeah, it was Robin with a couple of his buddies. This is by way of apology." He hands me a check.

I look at it. It's signed by Robin, made out to me for five thousand dollars. I hand it back.

"I don't want this. I want a real apology."

He seems surprised. "He's very ashamed, David."

"So now he's trying to buy his way out. Is that how he thinks the world works?"

"He's not the most stable individual—"

"He sounded pretty stable when he threatened me last night. I want to see him. With you or without you, I'm going in."

Mark studies me. He's embarrassed. I meet his eyes to show him I'm serious. Then, to clinch the matter, I tell him that no matter how well meant, Robin's check could be construed as a bribe.

"To do what?"

"Stop me from filing an assault charge. Maybe get me to stop looking into the Flamingo killings, too."

"Just can't leave that alone, can you?"

"No, sorry, Mark—I can't."

Together we enter the gate. There are piles of dried dog crap scattered about, and the way the old machinery is cast makes it look like someone emptied one of the old Gunktown shops in the middle of the yard.

Ascending to the stoop, I'm hit by an odor of uncollected garbage. Mark doesn't ring or knock, just walks straight in. Standing in the center of the front hall, he calls upstairs.

"David's here, Robin. He wants to talk to you. Come on down, okay?"

After a few moments, I hear the scurrying of animals and then the clump of human feet on the second floor.

"What's the deal?" Robin yells. "I told you I didn't want to see him."

"He won't take your check. He wants to talk. He's pretty offended by what you did."

"Offended, huh!" Robin appears at the head of the stairs along with a pair of mangy black mongrels. He's barefoot, wears baggy sweatpants and a soiled gray T-shirt. He sports earrings on his left ear and his hair's shaved down to his scalp.

"Hey, Dave!" He speaks shyly.

"Hey Robin! I'd say 'long time no see,' but last night wasn't that long ago."

"Real sorry about that, Dave. Something weird got into me."

"David, not Dave."

"Sorry."

"Seemed pretty well planned to me, Robin. Also like you wanted me to know you or Mark was doing it."

"That wasn't my intention."

"I think it was."

"He doesn't know what he's doing half the time," Mark whispers.

"Come down, Robin. Let's talk."

"I'd rather talk from up here, okay?"

"Okay. Who told you I was 'nosing around'?"

Robin's eyes move to Mark. "Just something we heard."

I look over at Mark. "*We?*"

Mark looks away. "A friend mentioned it at a dinner party. He heard it from Spencer Deval."

Him again!

I gaze into Mark's eyes. "So last night Robin wasn't acting on his own. You were both involved."

"That's about it," Robin confirms.

"You guys must think I'm pretty stupid."

"Look," Mark says, "we've been through a lot. First our baby sister, then our mom. We don't need all that dredged up again."

"Don't you want to know who killed your mom?"

"Cody did it. Everyone knows that."

"Nobody who knew Cody thinks he did it. There are other suspects. Don't you care?"

"I do," Robin says.

I turn to him. "Then help me, Robin. You're not going to feel good about yourself till you clear this thing up."

Robin, enticed by my plea, clumps down the stairs followed by his mutts.

"Hey, David!" He offers me his hand. "I'm real sorry, man. Mark said call you, warn you off. The ambush was my idea. I thought it'd be fun, like those games we used to play in the woods."

Up close he looks cadaverous. There are big circles under his eyes, multiple piercings in his eyebrows, and I notice what could be track marks amidst the crude tattoos on his scrawny arms. Like his brother, he has his father's squared-off jaw and powerful brow, but unlike Mark his features are softened by his mother's seductive eyes and sensitively mod-eled lips. His skin, too, is darker than Mark's. *Like Blackjack's*, I think.

"Forget about it," I tell him. "No serious damage. I've got a slightly cut lip and a sore set of ribs which I could've gotten playing football. Remember what Coach Lafferty used to tell us. 'Just ignore the pain, boys—it's part of the game.'"

Robin laughs. "What an asshole he was!" After a moment, Mark starts laughing too.

We adjourn to the living room—if you can call it that. It's a mess: a ratty old dorm-style couch with exposed stuffing and easy chairs with broken springs; piles of discarded newspapers strewn about; clusters of crusted Styrofoam coffee cups; unwashed glasses with strangely colored residues adhering to their bottoms.

When we're seated, I turn to Robin. "What're you trying to cover up?"

Mark leans forward. "There's nothing to cover," he says.

"Shut up, Mark! I'm talking to your brother."

To my surprise he obeys.

"Mark's right. There's nothing." Robin speaks softly.

Listening to him, I realize that despite his unkempt appearance and the grubby way he lives, he's a much more interesting person than Mark, more vulnerable, likeable too.

I look over at Mark. He meets my stare.

"Even if there was, it wouldn't be any of your business," he says.

"David's dad tried to help Mom," Robin reminds him.

"Not all that well, considering what happened."

I turn back to Robin. Mark, I understand, cannot be reached. He's the same cold WASPy son of a bitch who hit me a low blow back in lower school. But Robin's accessible. Sure, he's screwed up, but he's also got some heart. I like his face, the hurt I see in it, would like to draw it if I get the chance. Mark's smooth, American aristocrat's face doesn't interest me at all.

Deciding there's nothing more to be gained by sitting around, I suggest it's time for me to leave. Mark springs to his feet. It's obvious he hates this house and can barely stand his brother. Robin and I shake hands, then he spontaneously grasps me in a hug.

"You're a good guy, David," he says, holding me tight. "I'm sorry. I really am."

As I hug him back, I catch a smirk on Mark's face. Then just before Robin and I disengage, Robin speaks into my ear in the same raw whisper he used last night: "Mom left a diary and I've got it. Call me."

An awkward moment as the three of us stand silent beside the door. Then Mark and I leave, the brothers not touching or even bothering to say good-bye.

MARK DROPS ME AT the Townsend. From the lobby, I step into Waldo's for a beer.

At the bar, Sylvie Browne, the black reporter, catches my eye.

"How they hangin', David?" She picks up her glass, moves to the stool next to mine. "Deval's telling everyone you're a rude boy."

"I probably am."

"At the risk of inciting more rudeness, would you be willing to do some drawings for my book? Portraits of the principal media types sitting around in here. You know, different cliques at different tables. Also couples like you and Pam who met and paired off during the trial. Might be fun for you, chance to do a job on certain folks."

I know just the kind of portraits she has in mind. Listening to her, I can see the finished drawings in my head. She's right, they would be fun to do, and Waldo's would make the perfect setting.

"Intriguing notion," I tell her. "I'll see what I can work up."

ON MY WAY UPSTAIRS, I pick up my messages. After a quick shower in my room, I start returning calls.

Jürgen Hoff tells me his lady friend is game to pose.

"She's excited about it. The way I imagine it, she'll be sprawled out on her bed."

"Then the bed should be unmade," I tell him. "Think of Manet's *Olympia*. I see rumpled sheets."

We arrange to meet at the lady's apartment Sunday evening when Jürgen's restaurant is closed.

Next I return a call from Chip Rakoubian. He tells me he's spoken with his mother and she's agreed to talk to me. Since she's crippled, confined to home, he suggests I meet him at the Rathskeller at five tomorrow afternoon. He'll drive me over to the house, introduce us, then leave us alone.

"She's got a little quirk," he tells me. "I think I mentioned she used to be a professional dominatrix. Thing is she still enjoys the role. . . so it'd be nice if you'd be extra respectful and address her as 'Ma'am.' "

I tell him, *Sure, anything for the cause. . . .*

I'm trying to relax, thinking about what I've set up—tomorrow evening questioning 'Ma'am'; Sunday evening questioning Jürgen while drawing his naked girlfriend sprawled on her bed—when my thoughts turn to Robin Fulraine. I'm about to call him, when my phone rings. It's Pam, excited. Things are going gangbusters for her in New York.

"Two networks want me. The money being offered is huge! Meantime CNN's upping their offer. My agent says Monday'll be The Day."

She tells me she could fly back to Calista tonight, but she's decided to sweat things out in New York.

"If I'm going to leave CNN, they'll keep me off the air till my contract runs out. The idea being, 'If she's going to work for a rival network, why give her more exposure?' "

When she gets around to asking how things are going with me, I tell her I've located Susan Pettibone in Connecticut.

"Would you be willing to interview her?" I ask. "You're barely an hour now from where she lives."

Pam goes for it. I fill her in, tell her about Susan's report of what Tom said when, awakened by her call, he thought for a moment that she was Barbara.

"According to Susan he said: 'God! Did you really do it?' or 'Did he really do it?' The cop who questioned her didn't follow up. Maybe there's something else she'd have remembered if he'd pushed. Also what hints Tom might have given her when he asked her to come out to Calista. Also whether he ever mentioned the girl who lived next door in the roominghouse."

"Gee, David, how is she going to remember any of that?"

"People often remember their last conversations with someone who died."

"If she remembers, I'll get it out of her," Pam promises.

I SET UP A SATURDAY afternoon portrait session with Robin. He seems pleased by the prospect.

"I've always wanted to be drawn by a real artist," he says. "Also it'll give us a chance to talk."

Relieved that he's willing to see me again, I go back down to Waldo's to consider the postures I'll be assuming over the next several days:

The Respectful Supplicant with Chip's mother.

The Empathetic Portraitist-Therapist with Robin.

The Master Draftsman-Interrogator with Jürgen.

So many roles, subterfuges, hidden agendas. Will I be able to stage-manage these performances, keep them straight? Most important, will I be able to achieve my goal . . . and do I even know what my goal is? Solve the Flamingo killings? Absolve Dad? Discover what it was that tore my family apart? Or is it something deeper, such as understanding the strange woman at the center of the web of conflicting motives and warring loyalties, and, by so doing, perhaps come to better understand myself?

WALDO'S IS HUMMING TONIGHT, every table filled. I find a stool at the bar, nod to Tony, my signal I'd like a margarita, then whip out my sketchpad and start making studies for Sylvie's book.

I notice Deval observing me, then turning back to his tablemates, probably to deliver a clever putdown at my expense. I consider trying to make things up with him, then reject the idea. Whatever damage he can do to me has doubtless already been inflicted. Instead I start a caricature of him as Grand Pontificator and Buffoon.

In this respect my pencil has always served me well, sometimes gotten me into trouble, too. It was a caricature, after all, that earned me the enmity of Mark Fulraine . . . and many others since. Call it my equalizer, for a clever drawing can cut most anyone down to size. Others may brawl with their fists or, like the Flamingo shooter, settle accounts with a gun. I look across the room at the portrait of Waldo Channing. He jousted with his typewriter and cruel wit. The media folks now drinking and laughing in the bar wage war with their dispatches. And I, like artists through history, going back to the days when men first drew with ends of burnt sticks upon the interior walls of caves, know that with a line here, a line there, I can puncture any man's pomposity, wither any man's ego with my scorn.

T W E L V E

F riday, 5:00 P.M. The Rathskeller's humming with end-of-the-work-week bliss. Business types sip martinis, working stiffs guzzle beer, and the waitresses in their dirndls pirouette from booth to booth blithely balancing refills on their trays.

Chip looks at me, raises his mug, licks head foam off his brew.

"I brought along Dad's *fessé* proof book," he says, handing it across the table. It's a thick, heavy, black leatherette album with the words *Studio Fessé* embossed diagonally in silver across its front.

I turn the cover. The first picture shows a handsome woman, imperious in manner, dressed in tight-fitting black leather bustier, sitting on a richly carved wooden chair flexing a riding crop. From the way she presents herself, one would think she was seated on a throne. The shooting angle's low, as if the photo were taken from the level of her knees. She's stout, her features are strong, and her expression's filled with disdain.

"That's Ma," Chip says.

I flip through the pages, transparent envelopes, each containing an 8x10 proof sheet of a woman in a dominant pose. There are quite a few of Chip's mom, clearly Max Rakoubian's favorite subject, but there are also other women wearing boots or shoes with exaggerated high heels. Some look silly, others stilted as if the required poses make them uncomfortable. But there are several in which the subjects appear to relish their roles.

About two-thirds of the way through, I find the sequence on Barbara Fulraine. One proof sheet is identical to my photo, but there are others, not so perfect, including several in which Barbara appears greatly amused.

No flexed riding crops in these pictures. Rather Barbara grins at Max's lens in the manner of an actress breaking up after failing to deliver an absurdly serious line.

This is a different Barbara from the woman I've been imagining, far different from the Barbara I read about in Dad's paper. This is Barbara enjoying herself, Barbara having fun.

"I'm trying to imagine their photo session, Chip—what it was like."

Chip smiles. "I'm sure Dad was pleased. His pictures of Mrs. Fulraine were the most elegantly photographed in the series."

I know what he means, but of course it's not the elegance of Max's artistry that interests me, it's the spirit of his sitter, the enigma of her many moods.

MILLFIELD, A PARTICULARLY nondescript suburb west of the city, doesn't seem like a place a dominatrix would choose for her retirement. When Chip turns down a curving street called Tidy Lane, rounds a circle at its end, and stops in front of an ordinary ranch house with a basketball hoop attached to the garage, I wonder if he's putting me on. I'm not sure what I've been expecting—urban warehouse district loft, dark apartment in seedy neighborhood—but surely not an ordinary split-level on a middle-class suburban cul-de-sac.

From the front hall, Chip calls upstairs: "Me, Ma! I'm home."

"You brought the young man?" a deep, cigarettes-and-whiskey voice calls back down.

"He's with me, Ma."

A woman in a wheelchair appears in dim light at the top of the stairs, swings herself into a staircase chair elevator, flicks a switch, and the device begins a slow descent.

As she floats down into view, I recognize the woman depicted throughout Max's *Fessé* album. She looks a good twenty years older now, makeup thick, lipstick heavily applied, hair dyed a too-vibrant red. But what's most striking about her is the ruination of her face: a fallen eyebrow on the right, a drooping lower eyelid on the left, creating a disconcerting lopsidedness that, along with deep furrows in her brow, tells me I'm facing a person suffering from severe arthritic pain.

"So this is the young man interested in Max?" she says, looking me up and down.

"His name's David, Ma."

She squints at me. "Hello, David."

"Hello, Ma'am."

She smiles. "Polite too! I like that in a young man! Wheel me into the parlor, Chip, fetch us drinks, then go about your chores."

Chip winks at me, lifts her into a second wheelchair, then wheels her, me trailing, into a front room that amazes me even more than the conventional exterior of the house.

The little room has been done up with great style in ever-so-fancy reproduction Louis Seize—tapestry upholstered gilded chairs and couch, mirrors in gilded frames, faux Aubusson carpet, even a gilded reproduction bombeé commode. Such *nouveau riche élégance* would be laughable, especially in a little tract house like this, but Ma'am so clearly revels in the theatricality of the room that she brings it off as a kind of ironic statement about her former profession.

"So you want to know about Max?" she asks, after Chip, serving us cocktails, retreats to the kitchen to perform his duties. "He was a gent, fine companion, good father. I take it Chip's filled you in on my lifestyle?"

I nod.

"There wasn't anything Max wouldn't do for me, nothing I wouldn't ask him to if I had a mind. He'd clean my garage on hands and knees if I wanted him to. But I don't take advantage of people's kinks, never have. His devotion was enough."

As she continues in this vein, extolling Max for his support and loyal service, I study her face and also the room, committing both to memory. I want later to draw this woman in all her spectacular peculiarity, and though I would love to begin such a drawing now, I'm afraid to broach the idea lest she start posing for me the way she did for Max. For it's not the dominatrix in her that interests me, it's the wounded look of one who once inflicted pain and upon whom now pain has circled back.

" 'Bust-in guy!' What a hoot!" As the mirth bubbles out of her, I begin to understand her attractiveness. There's a vibrancy in her gestures, an aliveness that shows itself even now that she's crippled and old.

"Max Rakoubian never busted in anywhere. He was much too shy and meek. Which isn't to say he didn't take naughty pictures to hold over peoples' heads. But he would never bust in, especially not on lovers. He got his candids the old-fashioned way—by drilling holes in walls. He had a bunch of little spy cameras and he built equipment so he could operate them by remote. That's how he got the pictures he took for Walt Maritz. And for all the work he did for Walt and Waldo Channing, he never received more than his day rate. They're the ones who cleaned up on it. Max just did it for the challenge."

I'm having trouble believing what she's just said. "*Waldo Channing* hired Max to sneak pictures?"

Ma'am laughs. "Waldo and Walt had a neat racket going. Two peas in a pod. Not many knew about that business. They were so different, Waldo so high and mighty, Walt so sleazy and low. They could barely stand one another, but, as they say, 'beezeness eze beezeness.' Max was just the go-between. Such was his lot. Some folks are destined to get rich, others just to work and sweat and plow the fields. . . ."

There's something odd about the way she speaks, a strange combination of fancy language and down-and-dirty whore talk. Listening to her, my impressions of several of the players begin rapidly to change: Waldo, whom I've hitherto regarded as a snob gossip columnist, is now revealed to be a blackmailer in league with scummy Walter Maritz; and Max Rakoubian, whom I've been thinking of as guy who kicked in doors, is now revealed as a photographer-sneak poking little spy-camera lenses through tiny holes drilled into bedroom walls.

"Max never cared much for Walt, but he did odd jobs for him. As for Waldo, Max was in awe of the guy. Waldo would throw him a bone from time to time, recommend Max to cover a society wedding or introduce him to one of his rich women friends who needed a portrait done. It was Waldo, by the way, who introduced him to the one you're interested in—everyone's favorite murder victim, Barbara Fulraine.

"Max, sad to say, was taken in by the bitch. Chip tells me you have his portrait of her, the one of her flaunting her titties. Pretty, I admit, but nothing to get *that* excited about. Still, according to Max, she was a natural dominant. I'm sure he jerked off over her picture. Men are such fools! Except my sons. I brought them up to respect women. Still they're boys, so heaven knows what they do behind my back. . . ."

She's tiring now. Perhaps all this passionate discourse has worn her out.

"Chip says you're interested in those old murders. Wish I could help you, but I can't. Max knew a secret about them, something he wouldn't tell me no matter how many times I asked. I could have tortured it out of him, but I never did stuff like that. It was just a game, you see, our mistress-slave routines. If there was something Max didn't want to share, fine, it stayed outside our game. I always respected boundaries. Without them SM's just assault. Max and I had fun. That's what I miss now, all the fun we used to have. . . ."

Just as she goes silent, Chip reappears. I have a feeling he's been listening through the kitchen door.

"Time for David to go now, Ma. Time for you to rest."

He tenderly extends her legs so she can lie full length on the couch.

"In half an hour, I'll bring you dinner. Lamb chop, salad, baked potato."

"You're a good boy, Chip," she says, closing her eyes. Then to me: "Good-bye, young man. I've enjoyed our chat. Come again if you want to hear more, though I doubt I've got more to tell. . . ."

SATURDAY, 3:00 P.M. I pull up in front of Robin Fulraine's house in Gunktown. The dried dog turds decorating the browned-out yard give off a particularly pungent aroma this summer afternoon, while the old machinery scattered about exudes the stink of gunk.

Robin, wearing just a pair of baggy jeans, greets me at the door. His skin is dark like Blackjack's, his chest is sunken, and his ribs show prominently through his nearly hairless flesh. There's a piercing in his navel and an elaborate tattoo of abstract Celtic design that mounts his right shoulder then descends down his shoulder blade to the center of his spine.

"Since you're going to draw me, I figured I should show some skin," he says.

I set him half-reclining on his decrepit couch, one dog curled at his feet, the other stretched out parallel on the floor. I'll have no trouble sketching his mutts, I tell him, so they're free to come and go. But I ask him to please lie still a while, at least until I've roughed him in.

He's looser today than when I visited him with Mark. Perhaps our exchange of hugs assuaged his guilt over threatening to pulverize my hands. We converse easily. He seems to appreciate my attention.

"I liked you for what you did the other day," he says.

"What was that?" I ask, outlining his shaven skull.

"Turned down my check."

"Oh, yeah, the reparations check. I told you, I didn't suffer serious damage. A little psychological and spiritual pain, that's all."

"That really shook Mark up." Robin grins. "He's not used to people refusing money."

"He should get used to it."

"He thinks we can buy off anyone."

"Isn't that kind of immature?"

"My father was like that too."

"Tell me about your father." I start work on his eyes. I want to get the hollows right.

"He didn't have Mom killed if that's what you're asking. I know that was a theory going around. Sure, he wanted custody, but he would never resort to violence. His method of getting his way was to bring a lawsuit then fight it out in court."

"How did he die?"

"Heart attack. I shouldn't say this, but I don't miss him much. He was an okay dad, I guess. Not his fault he was the way he was. Mom, on the other hand—I *do* miss her. Not a day goes by I don't think of her."

"What about your father's second wife?"

"Margaret—she's okay. Their kid, my half-sister Cassie, she's finishing up med school next year. Wants to be an obstetrician. More power to her. About time a Fulraine did something useful in the world."

"I gather you're not all that keen on your family."

His eyes, I'm finding, are uncannily bright today. Perhaps he's high on something, heroin or coke.

"My paternal grandparents were rich snobs. Dad's uptight crap was hard to take. Look, I'm not complaining. Thanks to the Fulraines I've got plenty of money, more than I'll ever need. And I'm grateful to Margaret and Dad for all their efforts. Mark and I were in pretty bad shape. Funny how things worked out. Mark did everything to please them, while I upset them every chance I got. Like flunking out of school—except hard as I tried Hayes wouldn't flunk me. After graduation, instead of going to college, I signed up with the Marines. Got discharged for drug abuse. That's a dishonorable discharge. Sent Dad up the wall. All part of the rebellion, as is living here in Gunktown. That really drives Mark nuts. He shits in his pants every time he stops by. He despises my choices, but he's afraid to confront me, scared that if I pisses me off I'll sell my FSI shares. He knows if I do, he'll last about fifteen seconds. He's a lousy CEO. If anyone else gets control, they'll bounce him out in a Calista minute. . . ."

Listening I get the impression that his choices have been determined more by contempt for his brother than anything else.

"Mark's like Mom in one respect. He enjoys hurting people sometimes."

I tell him I'm surprised to hear that since everyone I've spoken to has praised his mother for her kindness.

"She *was* kind, but on her own terms, nice with servants, especially gentle with horses. She was a great hostess. Had incredible charm. But she had a mean streak, too. Not that I suffered from it. I was too small, too cute, her darling little second son. Mark bore some of the brunt of it, I guess, and, of course, Dad took it from her full force."

He pauses, glances at me, grins.

"I'll tell you a little secret." *Is he finally going to broach the diary?* "Concerns you, David. Want to hear?"

"Sure."

"But you won't ask me straight out?"

"I won't grovel for it if that's what you mean."

He smiles. "That's another thing I like about you. You don't kiss ass. Anyhow, here's the secret. I don't think you'll like it much. But you earned the right to hear it the day you fought Mark at Hayes. Remember that mean cartoon you drew of him?"

"Sure."

"It not only infuriated him, which is the side you saw, but when he brought it home and showed it to Mom, he wept."

Even back then my pencil hit its mark!

"He sobbed over it, couldn't take your mockery. Mom tried to comfort him, told him he didn't have to take it. 'Why don't you march into school tomorrow,' she told him, 'and poke that little Jewboy in the nose!' "

"She called me *that?*" *I'm outraged.*

"Yeah." Robin grins. "See, it was Mom who put Mark up to provoking you. It was like she wanted him to fight you, bloody you up. That Friday night when we came home and told her how the fight had gone, there was this lewd gleam in her eye, especially when she heard Mark won. She followed him upstairs, hugged and kissed him. It was too much. I think even he was embarrassed."

This *is* too much. I call for a break. When Robin goes into the kitchen to fetch beers, I sit there reeling with anger.

Barbara Fulraine wanted Mark to provoke me! Was thrilled to hear he'd bloodied me up, that her beautiful brave blond boy had beaten her Jew-shrink's son!

By the time Robin returns, I'm calm again, realizing I was but a sacrificial-pawn in the complicated game she was playing with Dad—a realization, however, that does not warm the cockles of my heart.

Robin, beer in hand, examines my drawing.

"You caught me all right."

"Not much more to do."

"Can I have it when you're finished?"

"Of course. I'm making it for you."

"You're a nice guy, David. Hope what I said didn't upset you too much. It happened so long ago."

"It's okay," I tell him, as he resumes his position on the couch. I start shading his face and upper body, working to give the drawing a proper finish.

"I feel we share something," he says, "on account of how we both lost a parent at an early age. Not to mention that our parents were involved."

"When I pointed that out to Mark, he didn't seem to like it much."

Robin nods. "Of course not."

Drawing his torso, I note the scrawniness of his build, the thinness of his arms. No wonder his belly punch didn't hurt me. He's really in lousy shape.

"I think my father was dazzled by your mother," I tell him. "She came to him in pain. He tried to help her. I know Mark doesn't like hearing that because he thinks my dad failed her. But that isn't how those shrink things work."

"Mark's an asshole," he says.

He goes quiet then, meets my eyes. I take the opportunity to finish drawing his.

"The other day I told you I have Mom's diary." He speaks shyly.

Finally! Maybe now we'll get somewhere.

I apply some accent strokes, then put my pencil down. The drawing's finished.

"Why'd you tell me that?" I ask.

"I don't know," he says. "Mark doesn't even know it exists."

"Does it?"

Robin nods. "Mom kept it hidden inside one of her equestrian trophies. After she died, all her stuff went into storage. About ten years ago, Mark and I went to the warehouse to look it over and divide it up. When we got to the trophies, we each took half. I found it in one of mine, a lit-tle notebook held closed by a rubber band.

"Of course I immediately started to read it. Then I found I couldn't. Who wants to read about his mother's intimate affairs? I sure as hell didn't, so I put it aside." He shrugs. "I guess I've brought it out a couple times over the years, tried reading it, never got very far. Just too painful. Not the kind of stuff I want to know. But still I could never bring myself to destroy it. That would be like . . . burying her again. Anyway, there's stuff about your dad in there, David, and a lot of other stuff besides. Surprisingly little about Mark and me. I guess in her busy life we didn't count for much."

He shrugs again. "I wish I could give it to you . . . but I can't. Like I said, it's too intimate. It'd be like showing you pictures of my mom hav-ing sex."

"I understand," I tell him, "but if you ever change your mind. . . ."

I detach the drawing from my pad, present it to him, watch him as he studies it.

"This is better than just nice, David. It's excellent. I'm grateful. Thank you."

As we get up I notice a piece of furniture in the corner, a beaten-up Windsor-style chair. It's missing half an arm, with several radiating spokes broken on the back. What catches my eye is a fading Latin slogan and crest on the rear support.

"Is that a Hayes chair?" I ask.

Robin smiles. "Wondering when you'd notice. It's from the Trustees Room. When Dad died they offered it to Mark and me, a memento of the years he served on the board. I call it 'the hot seat' because it's where I usually sit when I shoot up."

I glance at him, note the gloat in his eyes, the pleasure he takes in his desecration of the precious heirloom. Perhaps the chair reminds him too of happier days back at Hayes—days of bullying, making other boys cry, and all the wicked satisfaction derived from such as that, the schoolboy schadenfreude we all used to feel.

He walks me out to my car.

"Do you really like living like this?" I ask.

"It's not so bad. I'm comfortable. I wish I had a girlfriend sometimes."

"Why don't you clean this place up, get rid of the dog crap, lay off the drugs, and get yourself in shape?"

"Think that would help?"

"I think you'd feel better."

"I'd probably look a little better but I doubt I'd feel better." He speaks sadly now. "You see, David, the crappy way I live—it pretty much sums up the way I feel."

I FRET ABOUT THAT diary on my way back to the hotel, wondering if there's some way I can convince Robin to let me read it. Then, when I walk into my room, other thoughts intrude.

The moment I enter I sense something wrong, that someone's been inside and my things have been touched.

I make a quick inventory. My drawings posted on the walls are as I left them, but those piled on my desk are ordered differently. My drawing of Dad in his car surveilling the Flamingo, previously at the bottom of the pile, is now on top.

I check the closet to see if my briefcase, containing Dad's paper, is still in the bottom of my garment bag. It is, and, thankfully, still locked.

I walk back to the center of the room, then turn slowly, looking carefully at everything. Beside the disorder of my drawings, what makes me think someone beside the room maid has been in here? It's the air, I decide. There's a scent. Trying to define it, I come up with the aroma of stale cigarette smoke permeating the fabric of a cheap suit.

I call down to the desk. Five minutes later, two guys from hotel security show up. Soon all three of us are sniffing around the room. To me the scent's obvious, but the security guys aren't sure. They agree there's a trace of something and that's odd since my room is on a nonsmoking floor. Then they point out that sometimes smoke from other units gets circulated to nonsmoking areas through the ventilation ducts.

They examine my door lock, declare it hasn't been touched, but change the code anyway and issue me a new key card. Finally, apologizing for any inconvenience, they advise me to store my valuables in the hotel safe downstairs.

After they leave, I open the room minibar, pull out a beer, sit in my easy chair, and sip.

Yes, Robin ambushed me, but this isn't his work, which can only mean one thing: Mr. Potato Head, the guy who was asking about me at the Flamingo, must be working for someone else.

THIRTEEN

Sunday morning: I had hoped to sleep in, but so many things nag at me, so many loose ends. I wake up at 6:00 A.M., and, unable to get back to sleep, do the unthinkable and go up to the rooftop gym.

There's no one around. At this hour all my jock media colleagues are in their or their lovers' beds below sleeping off another drunken Saturday night.

I mount the Stairmaster, work out hard for twenty minutes, until, panting and sweating, I'm too exhausted to go on. Then I go back down to my room, shower, order breakfast, and look over the Sunday papers, which the hotel has kindly left by my door.

Finally, nurtured, rested and well informed, I take up Dad's old agenda book, lay it on my hotel room desk, and see what I can make of the entries.

It's one of those one-day-per-page leatherette bound datebooks with a separate line for each hour increment. In it he lists all his appointments with patients: Mr. L; Dr. K; Mrs. M; Mrs. F; etc.

Mrs. F, I note, was scheduled, starting in late April, every Monday, Wednesday, and Friday at 10:30 A.M. After the Flamingo killings on August 27, Dad drew a line through her name whenever it appeared, this being his way to designate cancelled appointments. In fact, I discover, he had scheduled her at her usual hour through to the end of the year.

There are other appointments noted: medical conferences; Psycho-analytic Institute meetings; lunches with colleagues including a regular Tuesday lunch with Izzy Mendoza; various social engagements includ-ing the April 17 Parents Day at Hayes where he encountered Mrs. F; the April 22 Parents Day at Ashley-Burnett, attended by my sister; and June 6, the day of my graduation from Hayes Lower School.

Yes, it's all fairly straightforward. This is a doctor's appointment date-book, not a personal diary. Still, looking at the pages pertaining to the summer months, I find several intriguing entries:

On July 11, a Friday, he writes: **Difficult session. Headache. Cancel tennis/?**

On July 14, the following Monday: **Very difficult day. No sympathy from I** (which initial, I reason, must stand for Izzy).

On Friday, July 18: **Another tough week. See L about headaches/?**

On Thursday, July 24: **Call MHHC re show/G/?**

And on Sunday, July 27, one of very few weekend notations in the book: **Attend show MHHC 2-5.**

Monday, July 28: **Very difficult session with F. Worried. Consulted I at 6:00 P.M.**

Friday, August 1: **Idea for new approach. Consulted I. Negative!**

Monday, August 4: **Implemented idea. Backfired. Will try again.**

On the afternoon of Wednesday, August 14, all his regular sessions with clients are marked cancelled. A week later on August 20, he does the same thing, again freeing up his afternoon. At the end of the day, there's a cryptic notation: **F/F.**

On August 27, the day of the Flamingo killings, he sees all his regu-lar Wednesday patients including Mrs. F at 10:30 A.M. At the end of the day, he notes the calamity with a single word: **FLAMINGO!**

I sit back, reflect. The killings, I know, took place between at 3:40 and 3:50 that afternoon. Dad had successive appointments with patients at 2:30, 3:30, and 4:30 P.M. If he kept those appointments, he couldn't possibly have been at the Flamingo at the time Kate Evans thinks she saw him there.

Did he keep them? No way to know; his billing records were thrown out years ago. And though I have never really believed Dad was the Flamingo shooter, who *did* Kate see that afternoon?

I try to decipher his other entries. I'm pretty sure I know what he meant by **MHHC**: the Maple Hills Hunt Club, which, mid-summer every year, held a Sunday afternoon horse show. But why would Dad, who didn't much care for horses, be interested in attending such an event? Because it was at a dance there that Barbara Lyman met Andrew Fulraine? Perhaps . . . but I think his notation **Call MHHC re show/G/?** gives the reason. G was the letter Dad used in his paper to designate Barbara's old instructor in dressage, the man who asked her to slap him and with whom she had her first experience of oral sex. But why would Dad want to see G? To validate Barbara's story? Or, God help him, did he view G as a rival, and like many a man pining after his beloved, feel a need to see his imagined rival in the flesh?

August 1, it's clear, was the day he decided to "enter into" Barbara's seduction fantasy. He consulted Izzy about it, Izzy counseled against it, but the following Monday, August 4, he went ahead. It seemed to backfire when Barbara masturbated during the session, but despite that setback, he resolved not to give up his plan.

The two Wednesday afternoons he cancelled all his appointments suggest that on one or both days he followed Barbara to the Flamingo. But why *twice*? One reconnaissance would have been sufficient to verify her affair with Jessup. Why go back again? Could he have been so obsessed he took to stalking her? Or was there some other reason? Could **F/F** stand for Fulraine/Flamingo? If so, did she lure him there or did they meet there by prearrangement? Did they actually go to bed together there, and if so, was that the day Kate Evans saw him, an encounter Kate later mistakenly transposed to the day of the killings?

10:00 A.M. MY ROOM phone rings. It's Mace.

"Good news. I found Jessup's neighbor in the rooming house. Her name back then was Shoshana Bach. Now she's *Dr.* Shoshana Bach, Associate Professor and Chairperson of the Women's Studies Department at Calista State."

"You're sure she's the girl?"

"Positive. She was the only young woman living in the house at the time. I checked with the university. Her campus office hours are Wednesday and Friday, 3 to 5 P.M. I'm going to drop in on her Wednesday afternoon. Thought you'd like to tag along."

"I'd love to."

"I'll pick you up at the courthouse quarter of three."

"Thanks, Mace. I appreciate your including me in this."

"My pleasure." He pauses. "So who was it jumped you the other night?"

"Robin Fulraine and a couple of his buddies."

"Barbara's son — Jesus!"

"Yeah, he and his brother heard I was sniffing around, they didn't like it, so they tried to scare me off."

"Going to bring charges?"

"No. I confronted them and they confessed. At least Robin did. Apologized, too. There's still a core of decency there."

"I think you're the decent one to let them off," he says.

MIDDLE OF THE AFTERNOON the phone rings again. It's the long-awaited call from Pam.

"I'm in my car on Route 684," she says. "Just left Susan Pettibone. She really opened up. We talked four hours straight. It was like she'd been wanting to talk about all this for years."

She tells me Susan has vivid memories of her phone conversations with Tom Jessup those final weeks, far more detailed than the summary I found in the police file.

"I got the impression," Pam tells me, "that in some way Tom was the love of her life. He was the first man she ever lived with, her first real long-term lover. She's led a full life since, been married, divorced, raised kids, and developed a high-powered career, but I think in her mind Tom's almost mythical, the handsome long-lost lover of her youth.

"In their long phone conversations those last weeks, Tom told her he'd become involved with an older woman who was beautiful, wealthy, and socially prominent. He told Susan he was crazy about her, but that she had problems, was involving him in them, and this involvement had begun to frighten him.

"He wasn't specific, but Susan got the impression that the deeper his involvement, the more frightened he became. By the time he called her and virtually begged her to come out to Calista, she thought he sounded desperate.

"Tom also told her about the girl in his rooming house. When I asked if Tom ever characterized her as a stalker, Susan said no, Tom found her intelligent and sweet. He was only troubled because she made it clear she was attracted to him and he wasn't attracted to her at all. In fact, Susan said, Tom considered this girl and Hilda Tucker his only real friends in Calista, at least until he fell in love with Barbara Fulraine."

"What about that last conversation when she called Tom and he thought she was someone else?"

"That was the most interesting part. You told me that in the police report Tom's quoted as saying: 'Hi, did you really do it?' Susan says that's not right, that Tom said, 'Did he do it yet?' When I asked her how she could be positive after twenty-six years, she said she's never forgotten his words, that she can still hear them in her head as if he spoke them yesterday."

"There's definitely a difference between 'Did *you* do it?' and 'Did *he* do it?' "

"Right! And later in that same conversation, Susan asked Tom what he'd meant. She says he mumbled something about 'putting an end to some really bad business,' and that he was expecting a call that night that would tell him it was 'finally done with.' Then he said something like 'I think there's going to be a fire.' "

"*Fire?*"

"Yeah."

"I don't get it. Why didn't she tell any of this to the cops?"

"I asked her that. She said that at the time she didn't think it was connected to the murders. Also that the detective who called her told her their interview was pro forma, that the Sheriff's Department already knew who'd ordered the killings, that it was Barbara's gangster boyfriend and that very soon he'd be arrested."

"You did great," I tell her. "How're things going with the job offers?"

"I'm sticking around tomorrow morning for the finish. I'll fly into Calista tomorrow afternoon. Let's meet in Waldo's at seven, hoist a margarita or two, celebrate my deal however it turns out."

DOWNSTAIRS, discovering it's raining, I step into Waldo's for a quick lunch and a beer. While I'm eating, I ask Tony if he knew that Waldo Channing may have done a little blackmailing on the side.

"There're rumors about everyone," Tony says. "It's a regular wasp's nest, this town. But I'll tell you one thing, Mr. C had more class in his little finger than the whole bunch of 'em put together."

"And Spencer Deval—does he have class?"

"Now that's another story," Tony says. "Let's put it this way—he'd like you to *think* he does. He and Mr. C were always afraid someone would find out they met." Tony smiles, brings his mouth close to my ear. "Spence used to work the DaVinci strip."

He's referring to the strip of porn shops and cheap whores' hotels on DaVinci Road where it runs along the edge of Gunktown.

"Deval was a hustler?"

Tony nods. "For years Mr. C kept it quiet. In his set, it was okay to be gay. You sowed your wild oats in Europe or New York, then met someone from your own class and settled down. But if people found out Mr. C'd picked up his boyfriend on DaVinci—well, that would've been something else. Now, of course, everything's different. A thing like that can even be a plus. After Waldo died, Spence told a couple of his friends and they spread it around. Now people are fascinated he has that in his past."

Which leaves me with no clear answer to my original question, whether Waldo, with his arch manner, malicious wit, and flaunted superficiality, was, beneath it all, a bit of a cheap crook. And though my first impression, upon hearing this from Chip's mother, was that if it were true it made Waldo scum, I now take a gentler view. In fact, I decide, it's

the first thing I've heard about Waldo that makes him truly interesting . . . as does the fact that his boyfriend was a hustler. And perhaps, I
think, since Waldo obviously didn't need to blackmail people for money,
perhaps he did it as a kind of social service, his way of ripping the masks
off the people he wrote about, a confirmation also of his world view —
that everyone was some kind of hypocrite.

8:00 P.M. THE RAIN'S stopped so I decide to walk to Jürgen's girlfriend's place. The address seems odd for a residence, a 1930s-era office
building ten blocks from Calista Center. A uniformed doorman admits
me to a restored art deco lobby embellished by contrasting slabs of marble and alabaster.

When I express surprise that people live here, the doorman tells me
several upper floors have been converted to apartments.

"Very private, one residence to a floor," he says. "Ms. Hanks is
expecting you. You're to go right up."

A high-speed elevator whisks me to the penthouse. Stepping off into
a small foyer, I hear the wonderful old Ella Fitzgerald/ Cole Porter
album playing behind the facing door.

When Jürgen lets me in, the vision before me is so stunning I
pause to draw my breath. We're on a balcony overlooking a double-
story living room with a gracefully curving staircase leading down.
The room below has been done up with a studied absence of color —
black leather upholstery, black and white rug, black and white framed
photographs on the walls. The wall opposite is a broad expanse of
glass revealing a spectacular view: the entire Calista Valley from
Irontown to Delamere Lake caressed by the light of the setting sun.
The Calista River, a soft buff red, snakes its way through the ruins of
the mills, while Lindstrom's twin glass towers catch and reflect the
pink mackerel sky.

It's a drop-dead view from a drop-dead room in a drop-dead apartment. I'm amazed. If this is how a high-class call girl can live in Calista,
I wonder why any girl in 'the life' would stick around L.A. or New York.

"What a fabulous place!"

Jürgen nods. "Dove inherited it from a client. He liked her, set her up here, then he died here, heart attack 'in the saddle,' as they say. His wife and children were pissed when they discovered Dove was in his will. Tried to buy her off cheap. I got her a good lawyer. Now she owns it free and clear."

As if on cue, Dove Hanks appears. Jürgen introduces us and we formally shake hands.

I smile and Dove giggles—we both know why I'm here. She's a lovely, tall, willowy black woman, mid-twenties, with rich, dark skin so silken smooth I'm tempted to reach out and touch it just to see how nice it must feel. Her features are cover-girl gorgeous and there's nothing at all call girl avaricious in her eyes. On the contrary, they convey a tender dreaminess. She's wearing strappy sandals and a simple white dress looped over her bare shoulders by spaghetti straps. Glossy, precision-cut black hair surrounds her face like a helmet.

"Been looking forward to meeting you, David. I've posed for plenty of photographers. You'll be my first real artist."

"I'm more an illustrator than an artist actually."

She smiles again. "I saw your drawing of Jurgy. Caught him just right, I thought."

She's well-spoken and knows how to flatter. I find her immensely likeable.

"I brought along some large sheets of paper," I tell her. "I thought we'd work on a bigger scale tonight."

"Speaking of sheets," she giggles, "I hear you want me to pose on mine."

"Only if it makes you comfortable."

"I'm always comfortable in my skin." She beams at Jürgen. "Ain't I, sweetpea?"

"Dove's always comfortable," Jürgen affirms.

He pours us each a flute of champagne, then the three of us sit on the glove-black leather couch, chatting and listening to Ella while watching the sun set and all color drain from the view. Finally we go silent, awed by the noir vision before us—Calista as night city, towers twinkling, river black as oil, traffic in the streets becoming ribbons of flowing amber light.

A half hour later, we're in the bedroom—Dove sprawled naked on her rumpled sheets, Jürgen seated in an easy chair beside the bed, I perched on a stool facing her and my portable easel, outlining her sprawled nude form in the manner of Matisse, trying to depict her as a twenty-first-century odalisque.

Dove does a line of coke, while Jürgen and I continue to sip champagne. Occasionally we nibble from a platter of cold hors d'oeuvres he's brought over from his restaurant cooler.

I enjoy drawing Dove. She makes for a gorgeous subject, and the wrinkled, white bedding surrounding her chocolate body sets up delicious contrasts between furrowed and smooth, light and dark.

"The other day I heard a surprising thing about Waldo Channing," I tell Jürgen, as I draw the undulating curve of Dove's back. "I heard Waldo and Maritz had a blackmail racket going. Did you know about that?"

"I think Jack mentioned it a couple of times. Like I told you before, he had no use for Maritz. He liked Waldo well enough since Waldo always mentioned The Elms in his column."

"Why would Waldo, with so much going for him, have to stoop so low?"

Jürgen smiles. "That he *didn't* have to was probably why he did. He wrote all that gossip about the Happy Few, but I think he really hated them. Jack, on the other hand, truly liked those people. They were fun and spent a lot of money at his club. But what do I know? I was just maitre d'."

"Maitre d' at The Elms—that would've been a good position to observe."

"Yeah," Dove drawls, "don't put yourself down, sweetpea. Maitre d's and whores, we know folks' secrets like servants always do. We know all about them, but they don't know batshit about us."

Jürgen blows her a kiss.

"So tell me, Jürgen, from the maitre d's point of view, what was it between Cody and Barbara Fulraine besides sex?"

Jürgen raises an eyebrow. "Isn't it always sex?"

"For me it always is," Dove says.

I draw the sweet crevice between her buttocks.

"There must have been more to it. People say Cody was stringing her along about her daughter the same way you told me Maritz did."

"Not true!"

Jürgen's annoyed. I've discovered something interesting about him: that he's still such a loyal acolyte of Jack's that the slightest hint that Jack was less than admirable spurs him to tell me things he'd probably prefer to keep to himself.

"That's what the cops say."

"They don't know anything. Mrs. Fulraine believed her daughter was still alive. Jack knew better. Still he wanted to find out who took her. If he could find one of those people, he'd beat the truth out of him, then track down the rest of them and administer his own kind of justice."

"Kill them?"

"In the Legion we called it *exécution préjudicielle*."

"So in the end what did Jack find out?"

"He developed some leads. He was sure it was a child porno ring. The nanny had performed in porn so she knew those kinds of fucks. Jack figured they put her up to the snatch, then something went wrong, the kid died on them, they got scared, killed the au pair, cut her up, and tossed her torso in Delamere Lake."

Now that I've got Dove's body down, I start on a more elaborate rendering of her face.

"I've heard that theory," I tell him. "It's also the police theory. But the cops never got anywhere with it."

"They didn't have Jack's connections. He had ways of finding out who made those kinds of films."

"You're saying that for the two and a half years of the affair, Cody was trying to track those people down?"

"He was financing it. It was an expensive project, not an easy one either. People who do that stuff operate undercover. 'I'm finally getting close to the fucks, Jurg,' he told me that summer. He hated people who'd kill a kid. He couldn't wait to get his hands on them, make them wish they'd never been born."

"Okay if we take a break?" Dove asks.

We break, she gathers herself into a soft white robe, and withdraws to her bathroom for a while. When she comes out, her eyes flash brilliantly and there's sassiness in her gait.

"Kitten's gettin' hungry," she says, reassuming her position on the bed. "Daddy Cat want to feed his bitch?"

I smile at the mixed metaphors while Jürgen fetches the platter of hors d'oeuvres, brings it to the bed, dangles food above her mouth, then feigns fear when she grins, snaps her jaws, lasciviously chews and swallows.

"She snaps like an alligator," he says.

"Alley cat," she corrects.

Hunger assuaged, she resumes posing. I'm pleased with my drawing, think it's going to be one of my best. I also think Jürgen owes me more for it than he's given. I decide to provoke him by making another slighting remark about Jack.

"Cody knew a lot of gossip, I suspect from time to time he tipped Waldo off."

"So what? They liked to gab."

"Was Cody in on Waldo's blackmail deals? Did he get a cut?"

"You got him all wrong!" Jürgen's angry again. "Jack was a stand-up guy. Compared with him, Waldo was a creep and Maritz was just something you piss on."

"How did Rakoubian fit in?"

"Max took the pictures, Maritz squeezed the people."

"So it was a three-way deal?"

Jürgen nods. "Say Waldo found out a couple, both married to other people, were having an affair. He'd tell Maritz, Maritz would follow them, get the goods, then bring in Max to take pictures. Then Maritz would sell the pictures to the lovers and split his take with Waldo."

"Did Mrs. Fulraine know about this?"

"She might have. Jack might have told her."

"Or Max?"

"Yeah, Max might have mentioned it to her. They were pretty tight there for a while."

"When Waldo spoke to the police after the killings, he said some pretty mean things about Mrs. Fulraine. Did you hear anything about them having a fight?"

"Can't remember, but that sounds about right."

I'm rapidly finishing up the drawing, sketching the sheeting, going for a classic drapery effect.

"Something I forgot to mention the other day," Jürgen says. "Another reason I know Jack didn't order those killings."

"What?"

"I think Jack knew Mrs. Fulraine was having an affair with the teacher. I think he even approved. Don't know why." Jürgen shakes his head. "There was something going on there I didn't get."

Interesting.

I finish the drawing. Dove relaxes, slips again into her white robe, and joins Jürgen at my easel to take a look.

"Oh, real good!" she coos. She slips her arm around Jürgen. "Think so, sweetpea?"

"It's excellent," Jürgen agrees.

Dove slips her hand inside the waistband of Jürgen's pants.

"I'm all cramped from lying so still."

She leans against him, whispers something into his ear while probing her hand deeper.

"Dove wonders if you'd like to party with us," Jürgen says.

I look at her. She's grinning at me, sassy and kittenish.

"That's very sweet," I tell her. "I'm flattered, but I think I'd better pass. Time for the lonely artist to be on his way."

Dove shrugs slightly to show disappointment. Jürgen looks relieved.

Dove offers me her hand. "Thank you, David. You made a beautiful picture."

"Easy," I tell her, "when the sitter's so beautiful."

We embrace, all awkwardness past, everyone happy now.

*   *   *

OUTSIDE THE BUILDING. I decide against walking back to the hotel. The streets are too empty, the night too ominous. I slip the doorman a couple of bucks, ask him to call me a cab. When it comes and we take off for the Townsend, I notice headlights come on in a car parked across the street. The same car does a U-turn, then follows us back to the hotel. It slows when I get out, then, before I have a chance to see who's driving, picks up speed and rounds the corner.

I pause in the lobby. Am I imagining things? Investigating a twenty-six-year-old murder could hardly be a threat, especially as all my prime suspects—Jack Cody, Andrew Fulraine, Max Rakoubian, and Dad—are dead.

I open the door to Waldo's, check the room, survey the Monday night media crowd. Conversation seems more active than usual, perhaps because with the start of the defense presentation, the Foster trial is finally picking up.

I spot Foster's attorney sitting with Spencer Deval and an aggressive female reporter from *The Star*. Judge Winterson has forbidden the lawyers to talk about the case, but there's nothing to prevent them from socializing with journalists, then leaking information with little eyebrow moves and nods.

I take a seat at the bar, order a beer, ask Tony where Sylvie is tonight.

"She was here, then got bored. I think she went out to a jazz club with the guy from *Rolling Stone*."

I ask him about Waldo Channing's demise, whether he was working the bar the day Waldo dropped.

Tony nods. "It was ten years ago. I remember like it was yesterday. I was standing right where I'm standing now. He was sitting in his usual spot, the table beneath the painting. 'Course the painting wasn't up there then. Anyhow, it was a little after 5 P.M. Mr. C was sitting there alone like he often did afternoons, finishing up his column on a yellow legal pad. That's how he wrote it, longhand right here in the hotel lounge, then he'd call *The Times-Dispatch* and they'd send over a runner to pick it up. Mr. C was nursing his usual, a dry vodka martini with a twist. Suddenly he calls out to me: 'Tony!' I look over at him, see him rise up out of his chair, then he drops there on the carpet. Died instantly. Heart attack. None of us could believe it. The man was so alive. You'd feel his energy whenever he walked into the room. I was the first one who got to him. Was me who closed his eyes. A sad day, one I'll never forget. 'Course a month later we had a big party here like he said we should in his will. That's when management decided to rename the lounge to honor the memory of the man."

Tony squeezes shut his eyes. When he opens them, I detect a little moisture.

"You know, he left his entire estate to Spencer Deval, the house, cars, all his art and furniture, but he also left mementoes to all the people he liked—pens, watches, cuff links, stuff like that. And not just to important people, to the little people, too, folks he loved and wrote about—copy boys, shoeshine boys, cabbies, ushers, doormen, even the restroom attendants here at the hotel. Me, I got what he used to call his lucky piece. I'll show it to you."

Tony reaches into his pocket, pulls out a gold coin about the size of a fifty-cent piece, and places it gently on the bar.

"That's a 1918 Double Eagle, year of Mr. C's birth."

I make a quick calculation. If Waldo was born in 1918, he was seventy-two when he died, fifty-six when Flamingo took place. It seems a stretch to imagine a man that age, no matter how angry or threatened, coldly executing Barbara and Tom.

Tony flips the coin in the air, calls out "heads," catches it, smacks it down on the back of his hand.

"Heads it is," he says. "Yeah, Mr. C's lucky piece." As Tony repockets it, he nods at the glowing portrait across the room. "Mr. C always had good luck. He lived a charmed life, he truly did."

TOM TOLD SUSAN: *I think there's going to be a fire.*

I put in a full day's work at the Foster trial, produce four drawings, hand them off to Harriet, then walk swiftly to the Calista Public Library across from Danzig Park, arriving just an hour before closing.

In the periodicals room, I pull microfilm of issues of *The Times-Dispatch* from the week of the Flamingo shootings, take the spools to a microfilm reader, and start searching for news of fires.

In Tuesday's paper, I find two house fires—one in Covington, another on Thistle Ridge in Van Buren Heights—plus a three-alarm brewery fire in Iron City.

On Wednesday, there's mention of an explosion in a machine-tool factory on Danvers and 18th and a grease-trap fire that started in a neighborhood Italian restaurant on Torrance Hill.

Discouraged, I unroll down to the Thursday morning edition to read once again the first accounts of the Flamingo murders. Then it occurs to me that if a fire took place Monday night, it might not have been reported for several days, and even if it was the sort of fire that would have been significant on a normal news day, on that particular Thursday it would have been eclipsed by the huge scandal of Flamingo.

Fifteen minutes before closing, I start searching the single-paragraph stories that appear in vertical columns in the Metro section of Thursday's *Times-Dispatch*.

A hit and run on Thorn Street; a man found dead in a parked car near the corner of Wales and Lucinda; a house fire on Tarkington near Tremont Park; another fire on Indiana; a street holdup on Gale and, a few minutes later, a similar holdup on Pear. None of these stories is promising, but then, just as the librarian flashes the ten-minute warning, I come across a follow-up on the Thistle Ridge fire:

> Arson inspectors, examining the remnants of the house at 1160 Thistle Ridge Road that erupted in flames Tuesday night, told reporters that the charred bodies of two persons, a male and a female, were found bound to iron beds in the basement.
>
> "There's clear evidence of arson," Fire Inspector James Halloran said. "And with the discovery of these bodies, a strong inference of murder."
>
> Halloran said that the County Sheriff's

Department had been brought into the case and that the Calista County Coroner's Office will autopsy the bodies.

"We're not in a position to say yet who these people are or what they were doing," Halloran said. "The faces of both victims were burned away."

The house, according to county records, is owned by Mr. Vincent Callistro of 1492 Laverne. When called for comment, Mr. Callistro stated that the house has been rented for the last four years through the Lee-Hopkins Agency in Van Buren Heights.

A person answering the phone at Lee-Hopkins said the agency, due to privacy concerns, would provide no information on the names of tenants, however, he did confirm that the house was rented and that it was fully insured.

A source close to the County Sheriff's Department, told *The Times-Dispatch* that there is preliminary evidence that the victims may have been tortured prior to the fire. This same source affirmed that the cause of the fire was arson, that empty gasoline cans were found behind the house, and also that there were items of a "sordid nature" found at the site. The source refused to describe these items or speculate further about the fire and apparent homicides.

The librarian approaches to tell me I must leave. I insert a dime into the built-in photocopier, print out the article, then walk back to the Townsend to wait for Pam, due in on the late afternoon flight from New York.

ENTERING WALDO'S, I spot her right away deep in conversation with Tony. She looks good tonight, blond hair gleaming, eyes and face aglow, the confident flush of a winner.

"There he is!" She beckons. "Please, Tony, a margarita for the gentleman."

Tony grins, starts making me a drink. I kiss Pam on the lips, then perch on the bar stool to her right.

"I get the feeling, don't ask me why, that things worked out well for you today."

She shows me her warmest smile. "Oh, they *did*." She lowers her voice. "CNN's tripling my salary, I'll be based in L.A., and, best part, I'm going to have my own show, an afternoon interview show, *The L.A. Report with Pam Wells*."

"Congratulations! We should order champagne."

Tony's delighted to make us a pair of champagne cocktails.

Pam fills me in. Monday morning Fox offered her great money for a political reporting job in the Washington bureau. She was tempted until this morning when CNN counteroffered with an even better package plus the concept for the new show.

"It'll be soft content mostly—celebrity interviews, West Coast lifestyle pieces. But I don't mind. A talking heads show's how you make your name."

She tells me she'll stay in Calista till there's a verdict, then relocate to L.A. It'll take her a couple of months to set the show up. She hopes to be on the air by Thanksgiving.

As we click glasses, I notice Deval, sitting beneath Waldo's portrait, speaking into a cell phone. I turn to Tony.

"Isn't that where Waldo used to sit?"

Tony raises an eyebrow. "He thinks he's Waldo reincarnated."

"How did he come to inherit the column?" Pam asks.

"He was Waldo's gofer, so it was a natural promotion."

"He's definitely got that gofer look," she says.

Tony grins. "Waldo used to call him 'lickspittle' behind his back. When he wanted Spence to feel good about himself, he'd call him 'my Man Friday.' "

"How 'bout that phony British accent?"

"Is that what it's supposed to be?" Tony conjures an ultra-haughty expression. " 'How you doin' old boy, old boy, old boy?' "

We laugh. "Very good, Tony!" Pam tells him. "Excellent imperson-
ation."

"He's not that hard to imitate," Tony says, moving away.

"Listen," Pam says, draining her glass, "I'm starved. Can we go to that
Sicilian place? I feel like pasta. I think I need a carbohydrate fix."

AS WE DRIVE OVER to Torrance Hill, I check my rearview mirror. In
night traffic, I can't tell whether anyone's following or not.

En route I tell Pam about the extraordinary experiences I've had over
the few days she's been away—the ambush on Riverwalk, my encounters
with the Fulraine brothers, my meeting with a retired dominatrix, and
last night's drawing session with Jürgen Hoff and Dove Hanks.

"I've got a new suspect, too," I tell her. "A sleazy ex-cop named
Walter Maritz. Seems he and Waldo Channing had a little blackmail
business going. Also, at the time of Flamingo, he was working as a private
investigator for Andrew Fulraine, tracking Barbara to find evidence
Andrew could use against her in their custody battle. But according to
Jürgen, the story Maritz told the cops about not informing on Barbara
because he liked her was a pack of lies. Seems a couple years before
Flamingo, Maritz, playing on Barbara's obsession about her daughter,
conned her out of a lot of money. When Barbara took up with Cody, the
first thing Cody did was have Maritz beaten up. I'm talking multiple broken bones. So it's occurred to me that Maritz, on Barbara's trail, despis-
ing both her and Cody, could have decided to kill her to avenge the beating. He'd know Cody would suffer, too, when he found out his girlfriend
was killed in a motel room with another lover. Maritz might even have
counted on Cody becoming the prime suspect . . . which, in fact, he
was."

Pam shakes her head. "Jesus, what a maze!"

TORRANCE HILL is the oldest Italian section of the city, also geograph-
ically one of the city's highest points. Southern Italians, who came to
Calista with the great waves of immigrants early in the twentieth century,
clustered here, built houses, churches, stores, and restaurants. And as in

other "Little Italys," along with the carpenters, masons, culinary, and construction artisans, there arrived a small number of underworld characters.

Calistians loved hearing tales about these men, soon dubbed "The Torrance Hill Mob," tales that romanticized their influence and power. When I was a kid, I was excited to dine at restaurants where mobsters allegedly hung out, characters with monikers like Tony "Machete" deCapo, Johnny "The Priest" Romano, and Jimmy "Big Lips" Franchetti.

Enrico's, the restaurant Pam likes, was one of those hangouts. And though the ambiance here is the same as when my parents took me, the food's now a good deal more sophisticated. Instead of gross platters of veal parmigiana accompanied by meatballs and spaghetti, Enrico's now serves genuine Sicilian specialties, Pasta alla Norma and Pasta col Nero delle Seppie.

After we order, Pam turns to me with a question.

"You said Waldo and this ex-cop Maritz had a blackmail racket. Why would Waldo get involved in a thing like that? I thought he had lots of money."

"Jürgen thinks Waldo went into it for sport. He liked to play games, mess with peoples' heads."

I tell her all I know about Waldo, his career and also his decline, how he lost most of his influence near the end.

"How do you know all this?" Pam asks.

"For years I've been an out-of-town subscriber to *The Times-Dispatch*."

She shakes her head. "Just couldn't let go, could you?"

"I guess not. Also I kept hoping I'd open the paper one day and read that they'd solved Flamingo. It was years before I realized that if that's what I wanted, I'd have to come back and make it happen myself."

AS WE DRIVE BACK downtown from Torrance Hill, I again check my rearview mirror. There are a lot of cars, it's difficult to tell, but one set of headlights seems to be sticking with us.

"Hold on tight," I tell Pam. "I'm going to make some moves."

"What's going on?"

"I think we're being followed."

I swerve into the right lane of Thurston, do a hard turn onto Lester, make another right onto Fairlane, then do a quick U-turn, pull in front of a paint store, stop, and cut my headlights.

"Hey! Is this a joke?"

"The guy who was asking about me over at the Flamingo—I'm pretty sure he's been in my room poking through my drawings."

"I can't believe—"

"Shhhh. Here he comes. Slide down in your seat."

As the car, a dark, nondescript sedan, sails toward us, I can't decide whether its headlights show the same signature. As it passes, I try to get a look at the driver, but I can't make out anything except the silhouette of a hatted figure hunched over the wheel. After he's gone, I try to make out his license plate, but by then he's too far away.

"Shit! I guess I should follow him, get his plate at least."

"Sure, go for it, David! This is fun!"

I make another U-turn, then speed up, hoping to catch him at the next stop sign. But the car, which should be ahead of me, isn't there.

"Where is he? Do you see him?"

Pam twists in her seat. "Could be him," she says, indicating a car parked in the opposite direction across the street.

"Jesus! He did the same maneuver!"

"Well, you got him now. Make another U and pull up behind."

But I keep driving. I don't like the neighborhood, it's dark and lonely, and I don't feel like playing games.

"You're sure that was him?"

"I'm not sure, no."

"Do you think I was cowardly not to double back?"

"I think you played it smart. But if he was following you, now he knows you're onto him."

"I wish I knew how long this has been going on. He could've been tracking me for weeks. If the folks at Flamingo hadn't told me, I never would have noticed."

IT FEELS GOOD to be back in Pam's arms, feel the warmth of her body, inhale her fresh sand-and-sun scent, run my fingers along her silken skin. It does my soul good to make love to this gorgeous woman, whom, I'm certain, is going straight to the top.

"How far is L.A. from San Francisco?" she asks, when we settle back.

"An hour by plane. Six by car."

"So you could visit me anytime."

"And you could visit me."

"But will either of us do it, that's the question?"

She goes silent. When she speaks again, it's in a different voice.

"I'd like this not to be over so soon," she says. "I'd like this *not* to be, you know, my 'Calista affair.' "

"Yeah, that could definitely sour it for you—thinking of me whenever Calista comes to mind."

"You really hate this place, don't you, David?"

"How could I? It's the Athens of the Midwest."

"This is where your early life came apart."

"Please, let's not talk about it. Let's talk about you and your brilliant future."

"I'd like it if you'd be part of it."

"God, that's so sweet—" The ironic pose I've been assuming dissolves in an instant. Tears spring to my eyes.

"I wish I could learn to love," I whisper to her.

"You already know how. It's just a matter of allowing yourself."

"I don't get it. You're supposed to be the hard-assed reporter and I the cool forensic artist. So now here we both are talking about not wanting this to end. Pretty funny, huh?"

"Maybe it is funny," she says, "but the thing I've discovered about out-of-town affairs is that you can't accurately evaluate them till you're back on your home turf. Then, back in the rhythm of your life, you either miss the person or you don't. Truth is I've never missed 'the person' very much, though I've almost always thought fondly of him if he happened to come to mind. But after just a few days in New York, I started missing you. That tells me something. And soon, when this stupid trial's over and you go back to San Francisco, it'll be your turn to discover how much you miss me . . . or not."

EARLY IN THE MORNING, when Pam goes up to the hotel gym, I borrow her tape recorder, take it down to my room, and listen to her full interview with Susan Pettibone.

The content is just as Pam described, as is Susan's emotional investment in memories of Tom. No question she loved the guy. I don't dare hope any of my old girlfriends will speak so kindly of me. What comes through most keenly is her regard for his personal integrity. "He had integrity to *burn*," she says.

Seeing Tom through her eyes, I shiver at the thought of him falling into that nest of Calista vipers—Barbara Fulraine, Jack Cody, Waldo Channing, and God-knows-who-else—a fall that cost him his life.

FOURTEEN

Wednesday, 2:30 P.M., I gesture to Harriet to follow me out of the courtroom, tell her I have an appointment, and ask her to cover for me. If anything extraordinary happens, I tell her, she's to call me on my cell phone. Then I'll execute drawings based on her reporting and get them to her in time for broadcast.

"Where do you go all the time?" she asks, annoyed.

"I'm not a journeyman sketch artist, Harriet. I can't sit here all day on the off chance something's going to happen."

"I understand, but—"

"Listen, am I mopping the floor with the competition?"

"You're definitely mopping the floor with them."

"So what more do you want?"

She waves her hands. "You're right! Go wherever you go, do whatever you have to do."

I MEET MACE in the courthouse lobby and accompany him to his car in the Sheriff's Office parking lot.

"This is going to be interesting," Mace tells me. "Professor Bach has no idea we're coming."

As we drive over to Calista State, I tell him about Mr. Potato Head, the disordered drawings in my room, and my feeling that I've been followed.

He pulls the car over. "Let's have a look."

He smiles when I show him the drawing. "Hmm, you're right, could be anyone. Get me a plate number and I'll get you a name. Except I think your girlfriend's probably right—now he knows you're onto him he'll stay a lot farther back."

CALISTA STATE'S a sprawling urban campus, a jumble of old stonework academic buildings, Victorian houses, modern steel and glass additions, a magnificent granite library, and a fifteen-story tower housing labs, lecture halls, and offices. The dorms, such as they are, are renovated old apartment buildings in the neighborhood. Most students live off-campus, either at home or in roominghouses like the one on Ohio Street where Tom Jessup lived when he taught at Hayes.

We find the Women's Studies Department in a yellow-shingled cottage behind the Toland Engineering Building. There's no one in the reception area, though a half-eaten carry-out container of Asian noddles sits open upon the desk. Across the room, a bulletin board is covered with overlapping notices—meetings, lectures, readings—as well as sheets with tear-off tabs posted by people looking to find a roommate, rent a garage, give away a kitten, or sell a musical instrument.

"May I help you?" A young Asian woman, chopsticks in hand, approaches the noodle container on the desk.

"We're here to see Professor Bach," Mace tells her, handing her his card. "This is a homicide investigation so we'd appreciate it if she'd see us right away."

The woman rushes out of the room, chopsticks still in hand.

A minute later she returns.

"Dr. Bach will see you now."

We follow her through a rabbit-warren of cubicles occupied by busy young women, then up a flight of stairs to the doorway of an office where a thin woman in her fifties, gray hair cut short in the manner of a Roman senator, greets us with cool reserve.

"Shoshana Bach," she says extending her hand. Dr. Bach, I note, is all business and doesn't like to get too close.

"Now, gentlemen," she asks, "what is this about?"

"The Flamingo murders," Mace says. "Okay if we sit down?"

She waves us to chairs. As soon as I sit, I bring out my small sketch-pad and start to draw.

"I don't understand," she says. "It's been years."

"The case is still open. The homicides were never solved."

Mace asks if she's the same Shoshana Bach who lived next door to Tom Jessup in a roominghouse on Ohio Street.

"I am. But surely you don't—"

"You weren't properly questioned back then so today we're going to do it right. That is if you're willing to cooperate?"

"Yes, of course." Shoshana stares at me. I smile back. "May I ask why the gentleman is drawing my picture?"

"The gentleman is a forensic sketch artist. Do you object to being sketched, Dr. Bach?"

"No, of course not. This is so unexpected. I really don't under-stand. . . ."

It takes her a while to loosen up, but once Mace gets her going, she seems eager to talk. As I draw her, I'm impressed by her sense of herself, the way she holds her head. This is a very dignified woman, I think.

"Back in those days, my grad school days, I was pretty much a mess," she says, showing us a grim smile. "Then Tom Jessup moved in. I thought he was the most beautiful boy I'd ever seen. As I'm sure you can imagine, I was probably *not* the most beautiful girl *he'd* seen."

It's as if she's speaking of another person with whom she now feels only a tenuous connection.

"We liked each other, clung to one another the way two lost souls will do in a city like this. We were both new here, neither of us knew any-body, and Calista, though a lovely town, can be pretty inhospitable at times."

She says she realized soon enough that Tom wasn't romantically interested in her, but for whatever reason—her neediness, loneliness—she couldn't bring herself to stop trying to attract him. Thinking back on her feeble ploys, she tells us, she still feels a flush of shame.

"I'd press close to him whenever I got the chance, breathe into his ear, lick my lips, make sure he caught me in my underwear, stupid girlish tricks like that." She shakes her head. "I was such a mess! But back then some of us young women didn't understand ourselves very well. We paid lip service to feminism, but beneath the rhetoric all we really wanted was a boyfriend."

Shoshana smiles. "Pretty pathetic. But I'll say this for Tom, he was always a gentleman, never took advantage of me . . . and he could have. God, how I wanted him to!"

She tells us that Tom deflected her come-ons by telling her he was gay. She believed him, had no choice. She decided then that if she couldn't have him as a lover, he would be the loving older male sibling she'd always wished she'd had.

"We had fun together. We'd go out to movies, eat at cheap restaurants, share gripes and confidences, talk about everything—literature, art, politics. On Saturdays we'd pile all our dirty clothes together into a wicker basket, then lug it Hansel-and-Gretel style down to the laundromat at the bottom of Ohio Street. Some evenings I'd wander into his room in my pajamas, sprawl on his bed, and read, while he, in just a pair of gym shorts, would grade his students' papers at his desk. On Sundays he'd drive us out to Hayes, where we'd play tennis on the deserted school courts. Other times we'd pack a picnic lunch, then go hiking in the hills. We'd find a shady spot, spread out a blanket, eat, then move the blanket into the sun, then just lie there side by side soaking up the rays. . . ."

One summer afternoon about a week before the killings, she wandered into his room looking for a notebook she thought she'd left inside. Tom was out on one of his private tutoring jobs, so there she was, looking for her notebook, when something in a half-open bureau drawer caught her eye.

Shoshana blinks. "Actually, that isn't true. The truth is I was still crazy in love with him and sometimes when he wasn't there I'd feed my obsession by going through his stuff."

She dabs at her eyes.

"I knew I had no right. We'd exchanged keys in case one of us was ever locked out, a trust I broke numerous times. I hated myself for being such a sneak. I vowed each time I came out of his room I'd never go in unauthorized again. But still I did. I couldn't seem to help myself.

"Anyhow . . . I was looking through his drawers when I came upon this big manila envelope hidden beneath his shirts. I opened it curious to see what was inside. Then I was shocked." Shoshana grimaces. "It was child porn."

The stuff was crude, she tells us, poorly printed, the photos poorly reproduced, and it was all so blatantly uncompromisingly obscene — lewd, smutty, foul. And then, even as she sat down on his bed to study the material, she felt a terrible pain as if her stomach were suddenly tied in knots.

"I was appalled. Also bowled over by grief. I remember perching there on the side of his bed looking at that stuff, then realizing I was sobbing tears for the children in the pictures and for Tom that he could possess them. The thought that this might be his secret vice hurt me to the quick. 'So *this* is what my friend is into! So *this* is what he is!' "

Shoshana shakes her head. Watching her, I can feel her hurt and outrage. And, too, I gain a glimpse of what this revelation means: that Tom Jessup had been acting as Barbara Fulraine's agent provocateur in her quest to find the people who'd kidnapped and probably killed her daughter, Belle.

". . . I was still sitting there when he came in. He saw me on his bed, saw that horrible stuff in my hands. He came beside me, put his arm around me, begged me not to judge him too quickly, said there were things going on he hadn't been able to speak about. But now that I'd found his stash, he would tell me everything. But first I must promise never to tell anyone, not another living soul."

She promised, of course, and then he confided that he'd undertaken an undercover investigation on behalf of a wealthy woman, a Mrs. Fulraine, who'd hired him to tutor and coach her sons. This woman's daughter had been snatched by her au pair years before and never seen again. Because the au pair had performed in pornographic films, there was reason to believe pornographers had been behind the snatch. Tom told her that basically he was pretending to be a pedophile purchasing pedophiliac material, letting it be known to contacts he made along the way that he was interested in commissioning a home movie of a little blond girl performing sexual acts on adults.

It was a dangerous mission, first because the people he was meeting were extremely suspicious, and second, because, being a teacher, he was putting his career on the line. If the pornographers decided he was a penetration agent, they might kill him to keep him from talking. And if anyone connected with Hayes found out what he was doing, he'd probably be blackballed from teaching for life.

"But how can you do this?" Shoshana demanded. "Why you and not the cops? And who is this woman to you that you'd take such a risk for her?"

He lied to her then, told her the woman was paying him a large sum for his help. Also that the police had failed her and so had the private detectives she'd hired, and that she felt that on account of his manner and looks he had a better chance of getting inside than a pro.

"He told me the people he was meeting with, a couple in their forties, looked like ordinary folks leading conventional suburban lives. It bothered him that they didn't look as he'd expected, weren't the sleazy types you imagine when you think of kiddie porn. When he'd started his search, haunting the porn strip on DaVinci, he'd met his share of the latter—burly, bearded, intimidating guys who wore soiled tanktops and flaunted tattoos. But the couple he'd linked up with, serious purveyors of hardcore child porn, looked and talked like teaching assistants at Calista State.

"In fact they ran a legitimate business making promotional films. Their whole approach was highly professional. They asked him to describe exactly which acts he wished to see performed. Their manner appalled him—sympathetic smiles, soft, inquiring voices conveying their eagerness to create a customized filmed fantasy for his 'viewing pleasure.'

"They inquired whether he'd prefer moody lighting or hard, raw light; whether he wished the little girl's hair to be curly or straight; whether he wanted to see her eyes while she performed or would be content just to see the back of her head; whether the girl should act slutty and wear lipstick, or behave like a schoolgirl, stripping guilelessly out of a jumper or school uniform.

"After he made his initial deposit, ten thousand dollars supplied to him in cash by Mrs. Fulraine, he was shown an album of photos of underage girls from which he was to choose one to play the starring role. Hoping against hope, he asked if he could take the album home to study the pictures before making a decision. 'Sorry,' he was told, 'the casting album is super-sensitive; it never leaves the premises.'

"*Casting album!* The blandness of that phrase made the transaction all the more horrifying. Better, he thought, to deal with the burly porn shop proprietors than this smarmy, cinema-savvy couple. And yet he desperately needed that album, for if it contained a photo of Mrs. Fulraine's stolen child, then everything he was going through would be justified."

He was now at the point, he told Shoshana, where he had to choose a girl from the album and also make a large second payment. The couple was pressuring him. Just the previous week, they'd told him that the moment had passed when he could back out. "It's what we call pay-or-play," they explained.

"Tom told me he'd passed all this on to Mrs. Fulraine, told her he'd gone as far with it as he could. It was now up to her to bring in the police. But if for some reason she didn't or didn't provide the thirty-thousand-dollar balance due on the film, then he would be in terrible trouble, for the couple had let him know that their backers could be pretty unpleasant when collecting an unpaid debt.

"I remember how, after we talked, we went out to the garage behind the house, sat against the back wall, and shared a joint. I don't think we ever felt closer. I was just so relieved he wasn't a pedophile it didn't occur to me to question his story. I remember we got really stoned, hugged one another, and then both of us wept."

I sit back. Tom's mysterious utterances to Susan Pettibone when she called him late at night suddenly start making sense: "Did he do it yet?"; "Putting an end to some really bad business"; "Finally done with"; and "I think there's going to be a fire." All this fits with the *Times-Dispatch* article about the house fire on Thistle Ridge, the two bound-to-the-bed bodies in the basement and "the sordid nature" of unspecified items found at the site. Suddenly various disparate thoughts I've had snap together into a pattern, like iron filings on a piece of paper suddenly arranging themselves when a magnet is passed beneath.

Shoshana continues: "I was in my room studying when I heard about the killings. It was a little after 6 P.M. One of the other kids in the house came rushing up the stairs. 'Tom Jessup's been killed!' he yelled. 'It's on TV. He and some society lady were shot together in a motel!'

"I ran downstairs. Everyone in the house had gathered in the living room. The scene on TV was chaotic. Reporters were shoving microphones into peoples' faces. A detective was being interviewed. He said the two were lovers, that their naked bodies had been found entwined, that they'd been meeting afternoons at the motel for months. Also that the woman was related to the family that owned Fulraine Steel and that the young man had been her sons' teacher at the exclusive Hayes School.

"I think that's when I started to go crazy." Shoshana's voice is level-steady now. "I mean really crazy, not just nutty like before. I remember standing in the back of that room watching that incredible report, suddenly understanding that Tom had lied to me for months—that he *wasn't* gay, *never* had been, that he'd been involved with this woman, that they'd been *fucking* in some sleazy motel. Also that whatever he'd done for her with the child pornographers had been done not for money but for *love*.

"I don't remember much after that . . . except that I didn't stay glued to the TV like everybody else. Instead I went right up to Tom's room, let myself in, went straight to his bureau, pulled out all the kiddie-porn material, gathered it all into a garbage bag, took it downstairs, then stuffed it into the trash pail outside the kitchen door.

"I think I was in some kind of trance state. Instinct took over. I felt this need to protect Tom, make sure no one could ever say that he was bad. Going into his room all those times I'd betrayed his trust, just as he'd betrayed mine with his lies. In some strange way, I felt I'd now squared our accounts. I couldn't hate him for his deception without also hating myself. But what I *could* do was protect him, protect his reputation, his good name."

Two days later, she suffered a complete mental collapse. She wept uncontrollably, refused to eat, screamed in the middle of the night, and in the morning couldn't bring herself to get out of bed. Someone in the house phoned her parents. Her father, an accountant, drove down from Detroit, packed up her stuff, helped her into his car, and drove her home. A week later on the advice of her family doctor, Shoshana Bach was admitted to the Rand-Barloff Clinic, a private mental hospital in Bloomfield Hills.

She spent a year there recovering her sanity and sense of self. She underwent a regime of electroshock treatments and intensive individual and group psychotherapy. She took classes in pottery making and expressive dance, also took up croquet and became clinic champion. She met a young man her age, equally fragile, and embarked upon an affair. The best part of the year were her sessions with Dr. Deborah Barloff, a Jungian analyst, daughter of the clinic director, who helped her work through her feelings of guilt and betrayal while providing her with a feminist perspective, a prism through which she eventually came to view herself as attractive and her alleged "inadequacy" as bogus.

When she left Rand-Barloff, she felt reborn—armed with a strong identity, ready to resume her studies. She returned to Calista State, completed her doctorate, wrote her dissertation on the metaphor of mirror and mirroring in the novels of Jane Austen, the Brontës, George Eliot, and Virginia Woolf. When she was thirty-one, she published her first book, *Dickinson and Plath: Studies In Alienation*, a seminal work of feminist criticism that led to her appointment as a tenured professor at C.S.

Shoshana stops, peers at me, then at Mace. "I know what you're thinking. Why didn't I come forward with what I knew about Tom and child pornography?"

She shrugs. "It didn't seem relevant. My old housemates kept me abreast of the rumors, that Tom had been part of a love-triangle and that it was Mrs. Fulraine's other boyfriend, a gangster, who'd killed them out of jealousy. That seemed as good an explanation as any. I was trying to forget about Tom, put him out of my mind. I told Tom's story to Dr. Barloff, asked her advice on whether I should break my pledge of secrecy. We discussed it in terms of trust and betrayal, how I was possibly setting up an ethical dilemma as a way of holding onto my anger at Tom, not allowing myself to let him go. I came to understand that I'd used Tom just as he'd used me, as a crutch against the bitter melancholy of my loneliness. What good would it have done to bring all that out? And how did I even know he'd told me the truth? He hadn't given me any names or addresses. He'd lied to me about being gay, so maybe he'd also lied to me about this. Finally, I'd have to explain why I'd destroyed all the evidence. It didn't seem worth the trouble, especially when I learned that the alleged killer had been killed himself."

She spreads her hands, a gesture of completion, a signal she's told us everything she knows.

Mace nods. "This Dr. Barloff—is she still in practice?"

"Very much so. I spoke with her just a couple months ago."

"Would you be willing to sign a form releasing her from patient-doctor privilege?"

"Of course I'll sign it. You can ask Dr. Barloff anything you like." Shoshana sighs. "So . . . it wasn't the gangster who killed them, is that what you're saying?"

Mace tells her he'll fax over the release form as soon as he gets back to his office.

"Gentlemen," She rises. "I must get back to work." She gestures at my sketchbook. "May I?"

I show her my sketch.

She peers at it for a moment. "Interesting," she says. "A taut face, a little wan, I'd say . . . but I do like the eyes, sparkling yet full of anguish. . . ."

MACE AND I WALK OVER to Leland Avenue, the main street that bisects the campus, then into a dark coffeehouse appropriately named Café Noir. As soon as we sit down, I show him the Thistle Ridge fire story

I photocopied at the library. As he reads it, I explain how I believe it fits with Susan Pettibone's account of her final call to Tom and now Shoshana's account of Tom's confession.

Mace stares at me quizzically. "You think Cody burned these people out?"

"Jürgen says he thinks Jack knew about Barbara's affair with Tom, that he may even have been all right with it. He also says Jack was working hard on finding out what happened to Belle Fulraine and that around the time of Flamingo he told Jürgen he was finally getting close. Suppose Barbara passed on Tom's information to Cody, who then administered what Jürgen calls 'Jack's own kind of justice.' Make sense?"

Mace shakes his head. "I'll look into this fire story, see what we got on it." He squints at me. "Gotta hand it to you, David, you're quite the investigator . . . even if it turns out you're wrong. But suppose you're right, what then? How does this connect with Flamingo? Were Fulraine and Jessup killed for revenge by the porn couple's backers?" He runs a hand through his hair. "I'll tell you, I'm having trouble with all this. A possible connection to some other horrible crime committed just a couple days before—how the hell did that get by me?"

"Flamingo was so big it obscured everything else that week."

"That month, that year . . . the whole fuckin' decade. Just thinking about it makes me crazy."

"Well, what's making me crazy is that someone's following me."

"Oh, yeah, Mr. Potato Head," Mace says.

HE WAKES ME WITH a call at seven in the morning.

"Shoshana signed the release. I got through to Dr. Barloff last night. She confirmed Shoshana's story, remembers the child porn angle very well. Also that she and Shoshana discussed the pros and cons of coming forward. So Shoshana was telling the truth."

I tell him I'm not surprised.

"Me neither, but I had to be sure. I've been up most of the night going through the file on that old fire/homicides case on Thistle Ridge. The victims' names were George and Doris Steadman. The zinger—

they ran a little industrial film company out of a building on Bailtown Road. After the fire, there wasn't much left up at the house, but our guys found some film cans containing porn in the garage. Not child porn, just the regular kind. No one made too much out of that. As for the fire/homicides, they were never solved. Our guys chalked it up to the mob, the theory being that the Steadmans were producing porn films and the people who controlled the porn market didn't like them infringing on their territory.

"Follow what I'm saying, David? Catch the drift? Suppose Cody, like you said, brings down a torture/hit on the Steadmans, who have special 'friends' who know how to collect a debt. Now let's say those same 'friends' live up on Torrance Hill. Six months later Jack Cody gets whacked. There's been a falling out between him and the Torrance Hill boys. So our guys were wrong, it wasn't the mob who killed the Steadmans, it was Cody, who tortured them first to make them tell what they knew about the Belle Fulraine kidnapping. Later the mob found out and whacked Cody for messing in their business. See how it comes full circle?"

"I see all right . . . but something's missing."

"Yeah, Flamingo. But suppose the Torrance Hill boys ordered the Flamingo murders as retaliation three days after the Steadmans were killed, targeting Tom Jessup because they figured he was responsible for the Steadman massacre?"

"In that case, Tom was the target and Barbara was killed just 'cause she was there."

"Or because the Torrance Hill guys knew Barbara was Cody's mistress. What better way to retaliate than kill her and Tom-the-squealer at the same time?"

"They would have known about Tom since he'd ordered the film, then stalled making the final payment. They could easily have followed him to the motel, seen Barbara and figured out the connection to Cody." I pause. "Is that what you think happened?"

"Could be." Mace laughs. "Maybe so-and-so did such-and-such to whomever, and then what's-his-name did whatever-it-was to you-know-who. It's too complicated. Been too many years. It's a fuckin' ball of snakes. How the hell can I ever unravel it?"

Mace is right, he can't unravel it, there are too many variables, too many supposes, too big a cast of characters, most of whom now are dead. A hitman acting for the Torrance Hill mob—sure, that could be. As good an explanation as any I guess. But in no way conclusive.

So what does this all mean? That the Flamingo killings must forever remain unsolved? That it will become one of those old murder-mystery puzzles like the Black Dahlia case in L.A.; the "Il Mastra" sex killings in Florence, Italy; the Zodiac killings in San Francisco; and a hundred cases more—turning up from time to time as filler in the back pages of newspapers, there to be pored over by obsessives, amateur criminologists, and adolescent boys?

"Interesting idea, maybe a little too complicated, too conspiratorial. But, hey! don't sweat it, Mace."

"Thanks, David, but I'm sure I will. So . . . see you around the court-house," he says.

*M*r. *Potato Head:* Something about him rings a bell. But how could that be since I have no idea what he looks like?

Waiting for Pam in Waldo's, I draw several empty head-shaped ovals. Then, sick of that, I turn on my stool and start sketching faces of people in the room, portrait studies of my colleagues—exuberant, cynical, jabbering, tongues loosened by liquor, faces animated by bonhomie.

"You make it look like fun," says Tony, standing behind me, peering at my heads.

In fact, having negotiated a fee with Sylvie's editor, I'm delighted to have something to keep me busy at the bar.

Pam shows up. "Sorry I'm late. I had a meeting with a source." She leans toward me, whispers into my ear: "Don't tell Harriet, but defense presentation's going to be quick. This whole shooting match should be over in a week."

"Good! Finally we'll be getting out of here."

"Up to the jury, but if I were you, David, I'd stick closer than usual to court."

She scans my sheet of media faces. "What a bunch of clowns. I think you're a cartoonist at heart."

"Cartoonist, courtroom sketch artist, forensic artist, all-around hack. Sometimes I think I'd be happy illustrating children's books."

"Yeah, kiddie noir. How 'bout getting some dinner? I hear there's a good Thai Place out near Indiana Circle."

ON THE WAY, I tell her Mace's ultra-complicated theory about Tom being the Flamingo target. Pam's skeptical, but she likes the way Shoshana's tale fits so perfectly with Susan's.

I tell her Thistle Ridge is only five miles or so out of our way. "Mind if we head over there? I'd like to find the site of that burned-out house."

I find Thistle Ridge Road after a few wrong turns. It's twilight by the time we get there. It's a classic suburban street with mailboxes at the entries to driveways leading up to nice-looking contemporary houses set back on one-acre lots. There aren't any streetlamps, just ambient light from the rapidly darkening sky and light cast out through the windows of the homes.

1160 Thistle is at the crest, last lot on the street. A hedge screens the house and yard. There's a carriage lantern atop a post and a sign on the mailbox, THE HERRONS.

I pull a little past, then back my car into the driveway so we can scan the residence. It's a single-story ranch that looks like a rebuild, not surprising since, according to *The Times-Dispatch*, the original house nearly burned to the ground.

"Lonely up here," Pam says. "End of the street so nobody's likely to drive past, and the house is well set back. Good place to make dirty films. Probably shot them in the rec room."

"Sinister, isn't it?"

"If you're asking do I like being up here, I don't. What did you expect to find?"

"Just wanted to sense the mood."

"So you can draw it?"

"Yeah, something like that."

AT THE THAI RESTAURANT, I tell her that ever since Shoshana Bach's revelations, I've felt empty, disinterested in Flamingo.

"I know what bothers you," she says. "If Mace's retaliation theory is correct, if Flamingo was about the Steadmans and Tom Jessup was the target, then it doesn't cut so close to home."

She's right, of course. The notion that Dad committed suicide out of guilt because he'd murdered his favorite patient cuts a good deal closer than if he jumped out his office window merely because he was depressed.

But Pam challenges me again. "Is it really about which explanation is more meaningful to you, David, or because all your life it's been in your head that Barbara brought your family to ruin? I think you've had a love-hate thing for her for years, turned her into your personal femme fatale. From the way you describe her at that Parents Day, it's clear you've been besotted by her since you were twelve. So you come back here and find out all this stuff, and now that it looks like she might *not* have been the killer's target, you feel empty because that undermines your 'family romance.' "

"Know something? You sound just like a shrink."

"Is that a compliment?"

I smile. "Maybe you're right, maybe a part of me always did hope that Dad played a role in Flamingo. Otherwise I'd feel all the emotion I'd invested in it was a waste."

"Okay, but don't forget—real people were killed. Even if Flamingo isn't the key to your life, it's just as important as your Zigzag murders."

Hearing that makes me feel better. Anyhow, Mace's retaliation theory is just that—a theory. So if I want, I can hold onto my romantic belief that Barbara Fulraine was the key actor in my early life.

BACK AT THE TOWNSEND, after several nightcaps at Waldo's, we adjourn to Pam's room, then go at each other in our customary fashion— panting, grasping, working ourselves up, seeking heart-pounding, shattering release. But then something different starts to happen, our love-making turns sweet. We get romantic, start kissing and whispering endearments. It's more of a slow dance than a quick wheel around the track.

"Well, that was a change," Pam announces when we lie back. "I liked it."

"Are you surprised?"

"Gushy isn't my style. But, then, being with a Calista boy, I guess all bets are off."

"For a Jersey girl, it must be quite the exotic experience."

"Uh huh . . . exotic," she agrees.

I wrap a bath towel around my waist, sit in her easy chair, then start sketching her as she watches me from the bed, chin propped by an elbow.

"Am I allowed to move?"

"Of course."

"You haven't drawn me before."

"There've been so many unpleasant people to draw, I never got around to the good stuff."

She studies me while I continue sketching. To my surprise, I discover I'm executing a serious portrait. I work on her eyebrows, then her eyes. I don't want to idealize her, simply get her down handsomely on the page. I like the way she looks at me, the direct way she engages. She's relaxed, the intensity's still there, but without the overlay of ambition.

"Just can't keep your hands still, can you?"

"My drawing hand—no."

"Why's that?"

"I draw people to understand them."

"You told me that before."

"I also draw a lot because I'm always hoping my hand'll be taken over by the planchette effect."

"Which is—?"

"A planchette's a drawing instrument on casters that slides around like a computer mouse. It can also be a pointing device, the heart-shaped gizmo that zips around a Ouija board spelling out messages from The Dear Departed out in The Great Beyond."

"So what's the 'effect'?"

"That's when an outside force seems to take hold of my hand. Drawing becomes effortless. Of course, it's not an outside force, it's my subconscious guiding the pencil. Psychologists call it 'ideomotor action.'

So, you see, I always keep my drawing hand busy hoping the planchette effect will take hold."

She gazes at me with perhaps a bit of admiration. "That's cool, like an athlete being 'in the zone.' "

"Sure, that's it—being in the 'zone,' the 'groove,' the 'flow.' There's nothing sweeter. It's nearly as good as great sex."

When I finish the drawing, I hand it to her.

"Oh, I like this!" she says. "It looks lovingly drawn."

"It was."

"I like the way you make me look tender . . . not the way I am on TV."

"That's how I see you tonight."

She laughs. "I'm glad, because I wouldn't want you to see me like Mr. Potato Head—just an empty oval."

Early in the morning, when I return to my room to shave, I notice the message light blinking on my phone. I call down to the desk.

"There's a package for you, sir, left here around midnight," the deskman tells me. "I'll have the bellboy bring it up."

The package turns out to be a large envelope enclosing what appears to be manuscript accompanied by the following note:

> Dear David:
>
> I've been doing a lot of thinking since your visit, especially about your comment that maybe it's time to finally put the family nightmare to rest.
>
> Yesterday I pulled out Mom's diary and tried again to read it through. Just as before, I didn't get too far.
>
> Perhaps you'll have better luck. Enclosed please find a photocopy, which is yours to read, study, do with as you like. I believe you'll find it painful to read, but, hopefully, not nearly as painful as it was for me.
>
> Sincerely,
> Robin Fulraine

My heart starts to pound as I glance through the sheets, several hundred pages of photocopy paper upon which are centered smaller handwritten pages. The writing on these is clear, inscribed in a fine hand, feminine, elegant, authoritative. I'm no handwriting expert, but the evenly penned forward-slanting script, the even rounding of the letters, and the nearly total lack of cross-outs suggest a writer in full command, inscribing carefully, perhaps even slowly, as she puts her thoughts to paper.

My visceral reaction—speeded heartbeat, trembling hands —reminds me of how he felt when I first looked at Barbara's bare breasts in Max Rakoubian's *Fessé* photograph. It's as if I've suddenly been transported very close to this woman who has attained a mythical status in my mind.

I take the pages to my bed, lie down, and start to read. Barbara's journal, it's soon clear, is not merely a recording of events, but an extremely personal diary meant for no one's eyes but her own. No entry dates are given, though she always jots down the day of the week. Some entries are terse, while others are long and, sometimes, quite eloquent:

Monday

Bad dream. Went riding two hours then drove out to see J. Lousy time had by all!

Tuesday

Played tennis with Jane. Mopped up court with her! Lunch with W. Left him feeling empty & scornful.

Wednesday

First appointment with Dr. R. He seems a gentle soul. Felt strange to lie on his couch. Felt at a disadvantage. Different than when we met at the school.

Laid everything out for him, all my insecurities. No idea what he thought. Probably hated me for being so troubled in my privilege.

Afterwards rode for an hour, then spent an hour currying and cleaning tack.

Stupid party at L&D's. Dumb conversation. False laughter. We're all so bored with one another.

Hope tonight I don't dream the dream!

Thursday

*W called early, dished L&D's party for half an hour. Couldn't
stand talking to him, couldn't wait to get him off the line. Why do I
put up with him? Basically we can't stand each other, so what inner
emptiness drives us to bother?*

*Afternoon: screwed my brains out with J, then felt lousy. He
picked up on it, said: 'You know, cutie, we're two of a kind.' Hate it
when he calls me that!*

Friday

*Second session with Dr. R. This time more relaxed. He asked for
my 'erotic history.' Gave it to him no holds barred! Told him about J.
No reaction. Then when I said I was afraid of J, I could feel him
tense up.*

*Kids' cute new tennis coach turned up wearing shorts. Nice boy,
nice legs, seemed lonely, also a bit in awe of how we live. Afterwards
I brought down glasses and pitcher of lemonade. Kids worshipful
toward him. What must he think of us? Important not to make him
feel like a servant.*

It's not hard for me to date these entries since I know from Dad's
agenda that Barbara commenced therapy on Wednesday, April 23.

Her entries continue in this vein until Friday, May 9. Then something occurs that alters the scope of her journal, and justifies her hiding
it inside one of her equestrian trophies:

Friday

*Difficult session. Dr. R silent. Turned to him: 'I need you to react!'
R asked why I needed that, what emptiness I hope he can fill.*

*'Emptiness in my wound,' I told him. The word just popped out of
me! I was really surprised. Still no reaction, so I raised the level of
the game. 'I need you inside me, in my—,' and I touched myself
down there. That got his attention!*

Drove straight from medical building to Elms. Found J in office, grabbed his crotch, told him, 'I want you to screw me till bells ring in my ears!' J told me he was busy, I'd have to wait. 'No way! I'm not waiting,' I said, squeezing him hard. 'Okay, okay, mercy, mercy!' But in bed I wasn't merciful at all!

Late afternoon, resting in my bedroom, I heard kids playing tennis with T. 'Love-fifteen!' 'Love-thirty!' 'Love-forty!' 'Game!' Hey, I thought, I could sure use some of that love!

I made up a pitcher of lemonade and took it down to them. Three guys, two of my own flesh, shirtless wonders all. T looked scrumptious. I changed into togs then we played a set. We hit the ball hard and sweated like beasts! Great turn-on. Hope kids didn't pick up on it. They're so innocent. 'Watch out! He's beatin' you, Mom!'

In the end, I took him 7-5. Afterwards we sat around, then I invited him into the house to shower. He was shy at first, then agreed. I showed him the guest room bath, handed him some towels, we looked at one another, and I couldn't resist. Two minutes later, we were all over each other. And all the time through the open window, I could hear the kids splashing around in the pool, their cries echoing ours!

When we were done, just lying there, he got very tender with me, so tender I started to cry. 'Whatsamatter?' he asked. 'Oh, nothing. Just that you're so sweet and I can use some sweetness these days.' He kissed my breasts like they were precious jewels. 'I've dreamed of doing this since I first laid eyes on you,' he said.

God! Till today I never thought of him as lover material, even though I did find him cute. We showered together and I went down on my knees on the tiles and took him in my mouth beneath the spray. 'No one's ever done that with me before,' he said. 'Plenty more where that came from!' I told him.

No wonder Robin couldn't get through his mother's diary and didn't want to show it to Mark! It's hard enough for me to read of Dad's growing obsession with Barbara in his truncated case study and to hear from Izzy Mendoza that he wanted to divorce Mom and run off with her. How much worse for Robin to read this. How could he bear to?

On May 16, my biting, indeed mean-spirited caricature of Mark Fulraine was published in our student newspaper, *The Hayes Eagle*.

On Monday, May 19, Mark, encountering me between classes in a corridor at school, called me "Jewboy" to my face.

On Friday, May 23, before a hundred or so witnesses, we met to settle our differences in a grudge fight in the lower school gym.

Reading Barbara's account of that day brings back a jumble of warring feelings—anger, indignation, fury, pain, outrage over what Robin told me, and also a measure of regret. The latter makes me to want to forgive everyone involved, including myself. This feeling, which I struggle to understand, is based on a conviction that all of us—me, Dad, Mark, Barbara, and Tom Jessup—were caught up in a web of conflicting passions that today, through the prism of twenty-six years, seem but tenderly trivial:

Friday

R arrogant today. Did he know our boys were to fight? If so, he didn't let on. But I had a secret and inwardly I reveled in it. T's been training Mark to box, and there probably wouldn't be a fight anyway if I hadn't pushed Mark to call out R's son!

Unable to wait till Mark got home, I went out to The Elms. Afterwards J put on a robe, lit up a cigar, and said he wanted to watch me prance.

'Prance? Screw you, buster! This lady prances for no man!'

'I could make you, cutie,' he said. 'Just you try it,' I warned. Then we both started laughing. We're so ridiculous! In the end, I agreed to prance for him if he'd promise to jerk off in front of me while I did. 'Deal!' he said. So screaming with laughter, we both did our salacious thing.

Driving home in the rain, I suddenly thought about Belle and started to cry. Why did God take her away from me? Was it because I was bad like old Doris said?

Later: At six the boys arrived home with T. Mark had a black eye and cuts on his cheeks. He went straight up to his room. Robin told

me he got a bloody nose. 'But you should've seen the other guy,
Mom. Mark knocked him out!'

T upset. 'I'm ashamed I was involved,' he told me. 'Was it a fair
fight?' I asked. 'Fair as I could make it.' 'Then you've got nothing to
be ashamed about.' He stayed for dinner, then, after A came by to
pick up the boys for the weekend, we went upstairs and screwed to
oblivion.

Afterwards he told me: 'You know there's nothing I wouldn't do
for you.' I told him I appreciated that and that what I needed
tonight was a warm body with maybe a little lust thrown in.

Prance for him! Reading this, I feel sorry for Barbara for the way she
allows herself to be degraded by Cody. It's not hard for me to feel her
agony over Belle or understand the desperation that drove her to seek
out a new lover. I only wish Dad could have responded to her with more
sympathy . . . though perhaps the coolness she describes is only in her
mind.

Monday

R all too casual this morning. 'You know our sons fought?' I
asked. R acknowledged he knew, wanted to know why this excited
me so much. 'Because we're at war here. Now our gladiators have
fought, fighting's sexy, and I've won the first round.' 'Why's it so
important for you to feel you've won?' 'Well, it's a war, isn't it?'

He wouldn't answer. Then we talked about blood and bleeding
and horses and my dream. 'For you sex is inextricable from blood,'
he said. 'Well, that's nice,' I said. 'Now please tell me how knowing
that does me any good.'

Afterwards, decided not to go see J. Went to club instead, played
furious tennis for two hours, beating Jane and Tracy back to back.
Later both looked at me funny in the locker room. Could tell they
hated my guts. Life's a war, I'm a warrior, and winners are always
envied and despised.

Met W for a drink at the Townsend. He's such a mean little shit!

'Watch out, love. Andy's going to play hardball going after your boys.'
'I can play hardball too, you know.' 'Oh, I know,' he said, fluttering
his eyes like he knew some dirty little secret about me, something
unmentionable. Felt like slapping him right there in the bar.

On June 6, Mark's and my graduation day from Hayes Lower School, the three adults meet up again, a kind of replay of their Parents Day confluence on April 18. Except now everyone's relations have changed, and other parties are also present—my mother; Barbara's mother, Doris Lyman; and Mark's father, Andrew Fulraine, along with his new wife Margaret:

<u>*Friday*</u>

Mark's 6th grade graduation. T all dandied up in his schoolmaster's
best, too shy to make eye contact. R, with his attractive,
Semitic-looking wife, giving me a casual little smile while he put an
arm protectively around his son's shoulders—good-looking kid but I
hate him for bashing mine in the nose. Then there was Mister
Wonderful himself, with his ski-nosed pupsy-baby. Doris, as usual,
was glacial and overdressed, feigning interest in her grandson's
achievement. And W in bow tie, rentboy in tow, spewing
witticisms—his nephew's in the same class.

Speeches, prizes, diplomas, then an awful celebration party on the
school lawn. It was too hot. The kids looked silly stuffed into their
crested blazers sweating in the sun. All they wanted to do was shed
their clothes and jump into the nearest pool. And all I wanted to do
was shed mine and jump into the sack with T. I'd have thought
seeing him in his milieu, underpaid junior faculty member at
phony-tony school, might have diminished my ardor. No such luck!
Every time I snuck a glance at him, I thought of tying him down to
the motel bed like last week and riding him to hell and eternity!

R, I noticed, snuck looks at everyone—Doris, T, even my boys. Did he
think he was going to see something in these characters I hadn't already
told him about? Gain rich insights he could weave into his analysis?

It's probably a good thing he's so curious. Otherwise how could he stand to listen to me ranting on about my creepy dream? Still there's something all-knowing and self-confident about him that makes me want to tie him down to a bed. I bet that would break through his reserve!

Afterwards had to go out to dinner with A and pupsy-baby for the benefit of the boys. Robin cute as ever. Mark very manly now. A his usual stuffed shirt self. Pupsy-baby pleasant enough. Still I'd love to get the bitch out on the tennis court. I'd tear her apart!

Half hour ago, I called T. He said at school he could barely dare to look at me I was so stunningly beautiful. Now there's a guy who knows how to talk to a woman! I told him starting a week from Monday the boys will be away at summer camp, which means we can meet three afternoons a week at the F. Silence, then he said: 'How about four afternoons? Five?' Oh, dear boy!

And so it goes—therapy sessions three mornings a week; two to three noontime or evening visits a week with Jack Cody at The Elms; Monday, Wednesday, and Friday afternoon lovemaking sessions at the Flamingo Court with Tom Jessup; and the rest of the time spent taking lonely rides on her horse, playing win-or-die tennis matches against her girlfriends, partaking of unpleasant phone conversations and occasional lunches with Waldo Channing, and the usual round of summer cocktail and dinner parties that inevitably leave her feeling empty.

On Tuesday, July 3, an entry catches my interest:

Tuesday

J distant this afternoon. After we made love, he stared up at the ceiling. 'Whatsamatter?' I asked. 'I know you've been screwing your sons' tennis coach.' 'How do you know that?' He didn't answer. 'Obviously you get something from him you don't get from me.' 'It's called tenderness,' I told him. 'Oh, yeah, tenderness—that's never been my strong suit.' 'Do you mind, Jack?' 'Not terribly,' he said. 'That's what surprises me. I thought I'd mind a lot, and I don't.'

Didn't know whether to feel insulted or relieved. 'Wow, that's a hell of a thing to say.' 'It cuts both ways,' he said. 'Fact you still come here to see me tells me I give you something he doesn't.' 'I think that's true.' 'So what is it, cutie?' 'You make me feel dirty, Jack.' He smiled. 'You like that, don't you?' 'Oh, I do, Jack. I do!'

He put on his heavy maroon brocade silk robe, poured us drinks, then sat down in his cracked leather easy chair. 'Tell me about tenderness,' he said. 'Tell me what it's like.' So I told him, described T and how he treats me, the sweet things he says to me, the ways he touches me, the total adoration he bestows. When I finished, J swirled his drink and stared into the amber liquid. 'You know, I think there're uses for such a tender young man.' When he told me what he had in mind, I nearly choked.

What *is* she talking about? From what she writes, it's impossible to tell, but I have a pretty good hunch. If, as Tom told Shoshana Bach, Barbara gave him the task of penetrating the local kiddie-porn scene, then, it seems, it was Jack Cody who first implanted the idea. And this dovetails nicely with Jürgen Hoff's notion that Jack knew Barbara had another lover, and that, as Jürgen put it to me, "there was something going on there I didn't get."

With this in mind I read on:

<u>*Friday*</u>

R stubborn. Really hated him today. Told him so in no uncertain terms. 'Even though I'm trained to take hostility,' he responded, 'I'm still a human being, so it hurts.'

After fucking, T told me again: 'I'd do anything for you, you know?' So I asked him: 'Really? Anything?' 'Anything,' he replied as if we were living in olden times when knights pled for ways to prove fidelity to their ladies. 'There is something you can do,' I told him, 'but I'm not ready to ask you yet.' 'Tell me so I can do it.' 'There could be risk.' 'I want to endure risk. I'd gladly suffer pain for you. I want to show you how much I adore you.' 'Please, T, you go too far sometimes. A wicked lady like me isn't used to hearing such talk.' 'I want you to get used to hearing it,' he said ever so tenderly.

R and I are definitely not getting along. 'I'm wondering if I ought to bow out,' I told him. 'I don't think this treatment is helping me anymore.' 'You're too impatient,' he said. 'It's hard, painful work. I never promised you it would be easy.' 'No, and you also never promised me a cure, did you?'

I turned around, stared at him. Then I felt sorry, he looked so crushed. 'Look,' I told him, 'I think you're a brilliant man, but maybe we're not well suited. No crime in that.' Then he annoyed me by asking why I used the word 'crime.' Ugh!

Later with T: he begged me to set him a task, something difficult, he said. 'Well, how 'bout slaying a dragon for me?' 'Oh,' he said, 'I'd do that in a minute!'

Poor boy, poor boy!

Another row with R. I told him when I leave his office I feel like I'm burning up inside, like there's a fire raging in my gut. He said that's a good sign, it tells us something important is going on. 'We've been at one of those painful impasses that always occur in an analysis. The difference between the men and the boys is that the men work the impasses through.' 'But I'm not a man,' I screamed at him. 'Always these gender issues. You knew I was just using an everyday expression.' Sure, I knew, but there's something wacky going on. 'I already have two lovers,' I told him, 'God, I don't think I could manage a third!' 'Do you fantasize about my being your third lover?' he asked. 'Do you fantasize yourself as my third lover?' I snapped back. 'This is something we can use,' he said, 'your fantasy that I'm your lover. Have you any notion of how seductively you act toward me?' I told him: 'Don't flatter yourself, Doctor. I act this way with everyone. It's my nature!'

At the motel, I tied T to the bed, then worked him over with my mouth. 'Today is my day to have fun,' I told him. 'My pleasure will be to pleasure you.' He squirmed and rolled, panted and came. 'And now I'm going to take my pleasure,' I told him, mounting him and galloping home.

Afterwards he said I made him feel like a beast. 'That's my intention,' I told him. 'Start thinking of yourself as my creature.' He seemed to like that, so I told him I'd considered his plea to set him a task, and that I had a quest in mind. Then I told him what it was. He listened carefully, then stared into my eyes to see if I really meant it. I stared straight back so he'd understand I did. Things got very quiet.

'Well?' I said to him as he was about to leave. 'Think it over.' 'I'll meet you here Monday at the usual time,' he said, 'we'll discuss it then.' 'No,' I said, 'if you show up on Monday that'll tell me you've agreed. Otherwise don't bother.'

The poor boy nodded solemnly and slipped out the door. I waited a few minutes, then phoned J and told him what I'd done.

Monday

Good session with R, our best in last three weeks. Less tension, more progress, I felt good when I left, thanked him for his help. 'I know I'm a real bitch sometimes. Please forgive me for that.'

He smiled, nodded sweetly. 'See you Wednesday,' he said.

Felt nervous driving out to the F. Stopped at the house, smoked a joint to calm myself down. When I got there and spotted T's car in the lot, I felt like I do when I beat some hotshot player out on the court: Sweet Victory Mine!

T subdued. 'I'm prepared to do what you ask,' he said. I brought out a second joint, shared it with him. 'A man brave as you,' I told him, 'deserves the best sex anyone's ever had. Guess who's going to give it to you?' 'You've already given it to me many, many times.' 'And today once again. So lie back and let me show you. There're a thousand ways, T, ten-thousand things I dream about every night, dream of doing just with you.'

God! I believe I came six or eight times and he three or four. Poor boy!

Tuesday

*Someone has sent me the newspaper from the day Belle was
taken. No note, no return address, just the whole paper stuffed into
an envelope. And of course today is the fifth anniversary of that
awful day. Today she is eight years two months old!*

*My first thought: it's A who did this. I called him, shrieked at him.
He denied it. 'Barb, how could I do such a thing? For all our differences,
I could never do something so mean.' 'You want to take away my boys!'
'Not take them, you'd still see them.' 'Boys that age should live with
their mother.' 'I don't think you provide a healthy environment, Barb.
We shouldn't be discussing this. Let the judge decide.'*

*I called W, told him about the newspaper. 'Horrible!' he said.
'Beastly! Contemptible!' 'Who hates me so much they'd do such a
cruel thing?' 'They don't hate you, love,' W said. 'They envy you.
They want to see you crawl through broken glass.' 'God, I have
crawled! Don't they know? Don't they realize what it means to lose
a child?' 'Well, love, whoever sent that wants to make you crawl
some more. The only way you win with a person like that is to act
like nothing's happened and carry on with your life.'*

Monday

*Terrible session with R. Told him I'm fed up with his Freudian
claptrap. 'It's like we're going around in circles here and the real key
to it all is hidden in the center.'*

*He said: 'I think if you'd be fair and look at what we've
accomplished, you'd see that the circles we're going around in are
getting tighter and whatever is in the center is starting to come into
view.'*

*It was so hot I went straight home from session. I wanted to swim
and cool off. Found another envelope in the same handwriting.
Again no note, nothing inside but ten one-hundred-dollar bills. A
thousand dollars! What's that supposed to mean? Blood money?*

Ransom money? One thing is clear: whoever's doing this has serious money to throw away. That's scary!

While in the pool, I decided to go and see J. Called T, cancelled our tryst, then drove out to The Elms. When I told J what happened and showed him both envelopes, he turned grave. 'This is serious business,' he said. 'My advice is don't bring it to the cops, not yet. Stay calm until we see how this plays out.'

We discussed T and how that's going and how far we ought to go with it. I told him I care for T and don't want him to do anything riskier than necessary. J said, 'Risk is risk, there's no way to minimize it in a situation like this.' I told him maybe we're making a mistake. He said he's positive we aren't and he'll do everything in his power to protect everyone involved.

When I left, I realized this was one of the few times I've visited him that we didn't end up in the sack. Back at the house, I phoned him and asked how he knew about me and T. 'It's not like it's an atomic secret,' he said. 'You have a very visible car. I'm sure plenty of people have spotted you driving along, and maybe a few decided to follow and see where you were going—out of innocent curiosity, of course.' 'You're a real bastard, Jack,' I told him. 'I didn't say I followed you,' he said. 'Then who did?' 'I don't know,' he said, 'but whoever it was went straight to the person most likely to spread a story like that.' 'Who're we talking about?' I asked. 'Smart cutie-pie like you should be able to figure that out pretty quick.'

Fascinating! I check my watch. It's nearly 8:00. An hour has slipped by without my noticing. I scan through Barbara's notebook. Plenty more entries ahead. Time, I decide, to take a breakfast break. But before I do, I take a few minutes to try to fix dates to the more crucial of Barbara's entries by matching them up with the entries in Dad's agenda.

The difficult sessions she speaks of with R are, of course, her analytic sessions with Dad—Dr. Thomas Rubin, who, unlike the other characters in her journal, doesn't rate use of the first letter of his first name most likely because it's a name he and Tom Jessup share.

Correlating her references to difficult sessions with Dad's notations of similar difficulties and/or headaches, I'm able to date Barbara's entries to Friday, July 11; Monday, July 14; Friday, July 18; and the last session, the one in which she tells Dad she's fed up with his "Freudian claptrap," corresponds to Dad's notation on Monday, July 28: "Very difficult session with F. Worried."

From this I'm able to deduce that Barbara received the envelope containing the newspaper on Tuesday, July 22, and the envelope containing the thousand dollars on Monday, July 28, the same day she made the claptrap remark and but a month from August 27, the day she and Tom Jessup were slain.

AFTER SEEING PAM OFF to the courthouse, I return to my room, too wound up with Flamingo to go to work. Impossible for me now to put the diary down, so I settle back onto my unmade bed and resume reading where I left off:

<u>Monday</u>

This morning R astonished me. 'Consider me seduced,' he said. 'What?' 'Now that you have me in your clutches, tell me what you're going to do with me.'

Was the man mad? Did he want to get off on my fantasies? Fine, I decided, I'll give it to him all right, I'll give it to him in spades!

'I want to suck your dick, Dr. R. I want to tie you to the bed and ride your face. I want to sit on your dick (I'm sure it's big, Dr. R!) and ride your huge, horsehung dick like I ride a horse. How's that, Dr. R? Do it for you yet?'

He sat there still, impassive, the cool all-knowing shrink, while I gushed all this out like a crazed harpy.

'How 'bout this, Dr. R? I want you to crawl over here, stick your head under my skirt, pull down my panties and bury your face in my muff. Then lick-me, lick-me, lick-me till I scream-scream-scream. Suck-me, suck-me, suck-me till I come-come-come all over you, till my juices coat your cheeks.'

The most amazing thing was that even while I yelled all this at him (and I didn't care whether there was anyone listening in his waiting room or not), I felt myself getting hot. Then I realized I was diddling myself, which kind of told me I really did want to do all those delightful things with him.

'You've turned me into Blackjack,' he said when I finally quieted down.

'What kind of bullshit is that? I'm a sexual woman. I have erotic fantasies. That doesn't mean I've got an Oedipus complex. You asked me to fantasize, I did, and now, God, you pull that old Freudian crap!'

He looked stricken, but all I could think was how stupid this whole thing was.

'I've already got two lovers,' I told him. 'I get all I need from them. I don't need you in the mix. Or is it that you want to mix in? If you do, please tell me so I can figure out how I can accommodate you.'

That made him furious. 'You're a very difficult patient. I want to help you, but you constantly reject my help.'

'Do you think asking me to think up sex fantasies about us is really going to help me?'

Silence. We both sulked. Finally I turned to him. 'I think you got hard listening to me.'

'That's an interesting fantasy. What makes you think so?'

'It's not a fantasy, Doctor. I've had lots of experience with men. When they get hard I can tell. Hey! Are you blushing?'

Figuring he'd had enough, I changed the subject, told him about the clipping, then about the thousand dollars. That upset him, proof to me he wasn't the one who sent them.

I told him so. 'My fantasy was that it was you.'

'Why? What made you think that?'

'It's so devious I thought it was maybe part of the treatment.'

'You think my treatment is devious?'

'Sometimes it seems like a two-edged sword.'

He ignored that. 'Who do you really think sent those letters?"

'At first I thought it was my ex, then maybe J. I even thought T

could have done it since we've been having trouble lately. But of course it couldn't have been T, he barely has a dime. Then I figured it out. At least I think so.'

'Who is it?'

'I'm not ready to talk about that yet. What I want you to do is make a date with me, a date for the two of us to screw so we can get it out of our systems.'

'Fantasy time is over.'

'Fantasy time has just begun!'

'Sorry, the hour's up.'

He rose from his chair. As he did, I checked his trousers to see if I could detect a protuberance.

I find this entry mind-boggling. Did she really take control of the session like that? Is this why Dad's paper suddenly stops? Because he lost control?

She really was an impossible patient! How could Dad stand her? On the other hand, in her diary at least, he comes off as something of a dork, relying on the old analyst's scam of answering every question with a question of his own, and employing the classic standby, 'Now what makes you think that.'

The next day, Tuesday, August 5, she receives a sealed condom in the mail. She's appalled, frightened. Based on her reaction, whoever is doing this is achieving his goal:

<u>Tuesday</u>

First the article about the kidnapping, then the money, now a rubber. What's he trying to say? When I opened the envelope and that thing fell out, I nearly threw up. My heart was thumping. My forehead was wet. I called J. He said come over right away. I said no, I need to collect myself, I'm going out to the yard for a swim.

I must have swam a hundred laps, and even that wasn't enough. When I came back into the house, the phone was ringing. J again. He said W's been spreading around a story about my meeting a lover at a crummy motel. 'For some reason he's got it in for you, cutie.'

'Don't call me that, Jack. Not today!' 'Sorry. But listen to me—the little bastard's got it in for you. Think about it. Think about why.'

I know why. Because I didn't tell him about T, didn't share my confidences, cut him off from my secret life. If you keep a secret from W and he finds out, he never forgives you.

'I wonder if he's the one sending that stuff to you,' J said.

W! Little W! Sure, the little turd's fully capable of a stunt like that. It's mean enough, cruel enough, sexually twisted enough, too. But if it is W, then it's not a warning from the kidnappers, it's just a mean, dirty act of a mean, warped, dirty-minded little man who hopes I'll confide in him again about the pain he's causing me, like I stupidly did two weeks ago.

I called up W, told him about the rubber. 'Gawd!' he moaned, 'I didn't know people still used those things.' 'If whoever-it-is wants me to crawl through broken glass, they're succeeding,' I told him. 'I'm tortured, I'm in real pain.'

He wanted to come over and soothe me. I told him I was crying so hard I couldn't face him. Silence, then he snapped: 'I think it's Jack.' 'But why, W? Why would J do a thing like that?' 'Because he's jealous. Because he thinks you're screwing someone else. He can't stand that. It makes him crazy. So now he's sending you all this crazy stuff.' 'But I'm not screwing anyone else.' 'Oh,' he said, 'I heard you were.' 'You know I would have told you.' 'Yes, love, I know. Listen, we'll talk later. Deadline pressure. Gotta run, get my column in.'

I phoned J back. 'W says it's you.' 'That's his game,' J said. 'Stir the pot, then sit back and watch us tear each other apart.'

I told him I want revenge on the little freak. 'I can have him beaten up,' J said. 'Break his legs.' 'No, no violence. I want everyone to turn against him. That'll hurt him most.' 'Well, that's your department,' J said. 'I only know how to strong-arm people, not how to get them disinvited from parties.' 'Well, I do!' I told him. 'And I'm going to do it. I know his weaknesses, where to get him where he hurts.' 'Well, good for you,' he said, 'but be careful, because if you're wrong and it's not him, he'll go to war against you, publish stuff that'll help A with

his case.' 'Well, J, if it comes down to that, you'll have my permission
to break his legs, his stupid neck, too, while you're at it!'

The great revelation for me here is her suspicion that it was Waldo
Channing who sent her the article, money, and condom. It makes sense.
For one thing, he'd have easy access to old newspaper clippings. For
another, he had sufficient malice of heart and financial ability to blow a
thousand bucks on a vicious gesture. But if it was Waldo, what was he trying to convey? Or was Barbara right, was it just his way of pulling her
back into his orbit, coaxing her to confide her latest sexual
escapade,which they could then dish together with complicit smiles?

On Thursday, August 7, she has lunch with Waldo at The Elms. She
reports this encounter and subsequent lovemaking session with Jack
Cody in what I feel is an increasingly alarming cynicism:

Thursday

 Lunch today at The Elms: W his usual bubbly, mean self. On
Elaine: 'She really ought to get some wrinkle cream. She's looking
like an awful prune.' On A's pupsy-baby: 'She's one of those
Bellyboob types. You know—lotsa boob but not much to bet on!'

 After J came over, he whispered: 'He's looking kind of peaked
these days. Must be he's not getting enough sex.'

 Ha!ha!ha!

 'I put the rubber someone sent me on him and J didn't like it one
bit,' I told him. W giggled, but I detected a certain quivering in his
eyeball, the left one, the 'tell' Andy used to say always gave away
W's intentions to their poker group.

 'Look,' I told him, 'whoever's got it in for me had better watch out
because I'm going to find the little creep. I've got detectives working
on it right now, and when I find out who he is, I'm going to expose
him to the world.'

 The old left eyeball started vibrating again. He tightened up so
much I was sure I'd found my man. 'What can detectives do? How
can they tell?' 'All sorts of ways,' I told him. 'Fingerprints on the

paper, saliva on the stamps. Plus some other angles I can't tell you about. Don't worry, I'll find him out.'

More quivering. Great sport!

'I'm surprised you keep saying "him." I just assumed it was a woman,' W said.

'You said you thought it was Jack.'

'I was wrong. Now I sense a feminine hand at work.'

'You mean it's all so catty, is that it, W?'

'Well put, love. Very well put.'

I laughed in a very special way to suggest several layers of private amusement. That unnerved him more. He excused himself before coffee, said he had to get back to town and file his column.

Soon as he left, J and I went upstairs. 'It's definitely W,' I told J. 'And now he's running scared.'

'He's pathetic.'

'Vicious-pathetic.'

'So what're you going to do about it?'

'Wait a while, see how far he goes. I read there's a saying: "Revenge is a dish best eaten cold." '

We made love and J was tender with me, more tender than I can ever remember him being. When I closed my eyes, I imagined he was T. He could have been. It was T's touch, T sensuous grazing on my skin, T's tongue wagging its way into me. For a moment, I thought I was going mad, mixing my lovers up.

On the way home, I pounded the steering wheel. If J can make love as tenderly as T, then what do I need T for? But maybe T can make love as harshly as J. Could I train him to? Could I cross-train these guys, make them interchangeable?

Must ask R about this.

What kind of a slut am I? I wonder. Am I nuts or just perverse?

Fascinating! And I find I'm beginning to respect her for dealing with Waldo with such magnificent sangfroid. Seems to me she beats him at his own game.

But the following day, August 8, she receives another envelope. If Waldo sent it, he probably did so prior to their Thursday lunch.

Friday

A rubber tied in the middle full of—yuk! I immediately threw it in the trash. Then I called W, told him what just arrived. 'If it really is semen,' I told him, 'I'm sure it isn't his.' 'Now why do you say that, love?' 'Cause I'm sure he's impotent, an impotent little toad. He couldn't produce a bag of scum if he wanted to. It's probably diluted mayonnaise.'

Long silence. 'I've been thinking about this since we spoke yesterday, and the more I've thought about it the clearer it is to me it has to be a woman.'

'Now why do you say that?' I asked, taking a page from R.

'It's more than just being catty, love. There's something definitely female-cruel about those letters. Diabolically cruel, I might add. Strikes me this person is some kind of witch.'

'Well, dear, I think it's a man, and he's probably a fruit, too. You know what they're like, W. I mean, a man as worldly as you.'

'Are you trying to tell me something, love?'

'I'm just saying I know it's a man, a pathetic sick excuse for one. Sending me a scumbag filled with yuk! Did he think I'd feel threatened? Me! Barb Fulraine! No, dear, it only makes me laugh!'

'Well, love, go tell your shrink all about it.' Pause. 'I wonder if it's him. Maybe he's got a crush on you. Wouldn't surprise me, you know, since everyone else around seems to.'

On Monday, August 11, more neurotic fissures open up in her already fragile analytic relationship with Dad:

Monday

At session, told R about the second condom, why I think it's W who sent it, what we've said to each other back and forth, and what I think he's trying to do.

'He wants me to confide in him, tell him all my secrets. He can't stand it that I come here. He considers you his rival. That's why he said it wouldn't surprise him if you were the sender.'

'Do you think the man's dangerous?'

'No. What he's doing is cowardly.'

'Now you're trying to infuriate him?'

'That's right. I want to provoke him, make him go too far. Then, if I'm successful, I'll have him cold. I might even be able to file criminal charges against him.'

'I think sometimes in our sessions you've tried to provoke me, make me go too far.'

'Why would I want to do that?'

'I think it's the way you play people. You mentioned that there's been some trouble between T and you. Want to talk about it?'

'No! I want to talk about my dream. Rather, I want you to talk about it. Solve it for me, Dr. R! Release me from it! Do that and I'll be forever in your debt.'

He tried. I was truly touched, even though I didn't buy much of what he said. It all goes back, he believes, to Mom and Blackjack. Pretty good hunch, I guess. When we parted, I saw something caring and sorrowful in his eyes. Touched again, I thanked him for all he's done for me. 'Sometimes I get so mad at you,' I told him, 'but you know it's not personal. It's my rage at my father transposed to you. Anyway, I just want you to know how grateful I am for all the efforts you've made with me and for putting up with all my shit.'

'Thank you for saying that,' he said.

In the car driving home, it suddenly occurred to me that my horsemanship is such an important part of my identity that it's inevitable that anything important to me would be dramatized in my dreams in terms of riding and horses. I also thought that maybe this analysis idea wasn't so smart after all, that I'm going to have to reconsider going on with it after the first of the year and that maybe I'd do just as well going back to card readers and psychics.

This time the little squirt went too far! And gave himself away! He sent a baggie containing tender, long, blond girlish head hairs mixed with short, rough, curly black ones, the latter presumably pubic. By this he's telling me my worst fear has been realized— Belle's being used as a sex slave in a brothel. But what the little stinker doesn't know is that there're only three people on this earth with whom I've shared my fear: J, R, and himself! So that settles it. W deserves to be strung up by his balls, but that would be too good for him. He'd love all the attention he'd get, the martyrdom.

Still I'm relieved. Now that I'm certain it's him, I don't feel menaced anymore. Rather a sense of clarification, that this is how things stand. A feeling of vindication, too, coupled with a feeling that now the power's swung to me, it's all in my hands now.

Later, at the club, I thrashed Greta 6-1 6-0. And she thinks she's my rival for the Woman's Cup! Feeling her hatred out on the court only encouraged me to battle harder!

Doris called from Florida. I told her about the letters. She wasn't too interested till I told her who sent them. Then she got interested. 'What're you going to do about this?' 'Call him on it, call the man to account.' 'Better be careful, Barb,' she said. 'W's powerful. He could do you damage.' 'You don't get it, Mom. It's my turn now, it's me who can do the damage.' 'Listen to me, Barb—don't get high and mighty just because you have the Fulraine name. Since you and Andy split up, it doesn't count for much. You're back to being Barbie Lyman to W's crowd. Don't chew off more than you can swallow.'

She made me so mad I hung up on her.

Great stuff! It's nine o'clock and I still can't put the diary down. In two weeks and a day, Barbara and Tom Jessup will be killed, and there're things in her diary that point toward a suspect I hadn't considered.

What could Waldo have been thinking? If he really was the sender, and it certainly sounds like it was, he had to know Barbara was onto him.

Waldo may have been malicious, but he wasn't stupid. There was no other way to interpret the things Barbara was saying to him.

So, how threatened did he feel? And if he felt badly threatened, to what lengths was he willing to go?

Certainly if it came out that he'd sent Barbara horrible anonymous letters, his position in Calista's upper crust would be severely undermined. At the very least, he'd lose his column, the mainstay of his existence, the excuse for his lifestyle and the only rationale for his superficiality.

But would he really kill to protect himself—get hold of a shotgun, pull a fedora down to his eyes, then march into Barbara's love nest and blast her and Tom four times?

That seems improbable considering how devious he was and the cowardice of an attack by anonymous letter. Still, who can know what a man like that might have done if he believed his reputation, the very currency of his life, was in jeopardy?

It's all very strange and the end game stranger still. For Barbara had more than one game going those final days: her game with Waldo, her game with Dad, and her high-risk game with Tom:

Wednesday

3:00 P.M. at the F. T was waiting when I arrived. He looked upset.
'What's the matter, darling?'
'I can't go on with this. I just can't!'
He told me that last night that awful couple looked at him with scorn. Also how when he paid them, he felt their contempt even more.
'This isn't me, B,' he said. 'I've done my best, but I just can't go on with it.'
'Well, it's a little late to tell me that, T, don't you think? A little late in the game to back out.'
'I never wanted to do this. I only agreed because you asked me.'
'If you didn't want to play, you shouldn't have agreed. If you back out now everything's lost, not to mention the money I've invested.'

'I'll pay you back.'

I laughed. 'You! You can't even afford a decent pair of shoes!'

He was so hurt I was afraid he was going to cry. 'I'm sorry,' I told him. 'I'm being mean. You did enough, delving into that pit of sleaze. I love you all the more because it was so hard for you. Let me show you just how much I love you.'

How could he resist, poor boy?

Afterwards I watched him sleep, then went downstairs where there's a cigarette machine, bought a pack, returned to the room, sat down in the crummy easy chair, and watched him some more while I smoked.

I don't know what got into me. I haven't smoked tobacco in five years, not since Belle was taken. But it felt good to draw the smoke in, feel it fill my lungs. I think because I felt so filthy in my soul I wanted to physically dirty myself inside.

When T woke up, he sniffed the air. 'You've been smoking.'

'Yes, my sweet.'

'I never saw you smoke anything but pot.'

'It's a rare occurrence.'

'Please smoke another so I can watch.'

I lit up again, sat back, inhaled deeply, blew out gusts, a few smoke rings, too.

'I wish this were pot,' I told him.

'I'll bring some next time.'

'I'm shocked, shocked that you, a teacher, a sterling example to children, partake of drugs!'

He laughed. 'There's a girl in my house who smokes all the time.'

'Then bring some.'

'We'll share, get high together.'

'Yes, that'll be fun.'

He paused at the door. 'Because I promised you, B, I'll try to see it through.'

'A man of his word. I appreciate that. Just a couple more weeks and I'll release you from your vows.'

Soon as he left, I called W from the room. It was 5 P.M. I knew
just where to reach him, at the Townsend bar.

'I know it's you,' I told him.

'What're you talking about, love?'

'I bet your left eyelid's twitching as we speak.'

'Are you crazy, Barb, or what?'

'I've got proof. My detectives tracked the letters back to you.'

'That's absurd!'

'I knew you were a snake, W. But I didn't know how poisonous. I
truly didn't.'

Silence. Then: 'When you say things like that to me, you're as
good as declaring war.'

'Let there be war then. So be it.'

'You forget one thing, love. You may be a hell of a fighter on the
tennis court, but the field of battle we're talking about is mine. I was
born to it, you only sucked your way up, and I can push you back
into the gutter any time I please!'

'I'm afraid you're the real guttersnipe, W, as your cozy Happy Few
will soon find out! And I'd watch that left eyeball if I were you.
When it starts to twitch, everyone in town knows you're lying.'

'Meow! Bye, darling!'

'Yeah, darling—meow to you, too.'

Correlating this delicious entry to other dateable ones, I understand
it refers to events that took place on Wednesday, August 13—the same
day Dad cancelled his afternoon appointments and staked out the
Flamingo to determine whether Barbara's affair with Tom Jessup was fact
or fantasy.

The thought of him spying on her there raises the hairs on my neck.
From what vantage point, I wonder, did he observe the arrivals of their
cars, their separate entries to the balcony and room 201, Barbara's post-
lovemaking descent to purchase cigarettes, and finally their separate
exits?

From his car parked in the Flamingo lot? Too dangerous, I think.

From Moe's Burgers across the street? The windows at Moe's were too large, creating danger of exposure if Barbara should suddenly turn and stare. Another possibility is the Shanghai Sapphire, the greasy-spoon Chinese restaurant on the other side of the lot. But the windows there were small and draped, which would have made it hard for him to see. Also, since Barbara reports she phoned Waldo as late as five, it's hard to imagine him sitting there a full three hours.

Then it occurs to me: What if Dad also checked into the Flamingo that afternoon; got himself a room on the second level overlooking the courtyard and pool; pulled a chair up to his window; drew the blinds just the right amount; and thus created a viewing post from which to observe the comings and goings of the respective parties?

This notion's so intriguing I put down the diary and call Kate Evans. When Johnny puts me through, I ask if she still has registry ledgers from that year.

"Sorry," Kate says, "when we switched to computers I threw the old handwritten ones out."

"Kate, about that drawing—"

"Yes?" I feel her grow tense.

"The man you described looked so nice, so kindly, did you think about what I asked you the other day—whether you might have gotten two different people confused?"

A long pause. "Yes, I did think about it. Like I told you, I think that must have been what happened."

"But *who*, Kate? *Who* might you have gotten mixed up?"

"I remember there was another man who came around about that time."

"The day of the shootings?"

"Maybe not that day exactly."

"Well, think more about it, will you, Kate? Try to remember, okay?"

"Yes," she promises, "I'll try."

Putting down the phone, I hope against hope that she decides she saw Dad when he came snooping around the motel, and, so frightened by the shooter, transposed Dad's kindly features upon his.

I pick up the diary again. On Monday, August 18, the proverbial shit hits the fan:

<u>Monday</u>

W's column: This morning he as much as says a certain member of his Happy Few is shagging her shrink on the old analytic couch!

Furious, I phone him up.

'Oh, hi there, love,' he says, all prissy and smug. 'I wonder what's on your cute little mind this lovely sunny Monday morning.'

'How could you write something so vile?'

'Is it, love?'

'You bet it is! Listen, W—'

'No, you listen, bitch! That's just a taste—do you hear me?— the merest whiff of what I can do. So mind your manners and I'll mind mine, and get over this nonsensical notion that I sent you those nasty items in the post. That's not my style. My style of waging war is the same as yours—total! Hear what I'm saying, love?'

'Yeah, I hear you. Sounds like you're making threats.'

'Not threats, darling. Statements of fact. This isn't a big town, at least not our set. We don't have to adore one another, but it's better to live in peace than war. Now the good news—right after Labor Day I'm off to Europe, my usual haunts . . . Venice, Paris, Cap d'Antibes. As I recall, there's a certain Parisian saddlery shop you like. My intention is to stop in at Hermès and pick you up a nice piece of tack, say a saddle and bridle set. Call it a peace offering, my way of saying that for all the harsh words between us, it's my profound hope we can remain friends. So, love, what do you say?'

I ignored his peace offering, changed the subject.

'What am I going to tell my shrink? I'm seeing him in an hour.'

'Tell him "all's fair." He'll understand.'

'Tell me something, W?'

'Anything, love.'

'How many people have you gone after like this? How many have you tried to destroy?'

'What a question!'

'Since you don't care to answer, I'll have to rely on what I know. Since Max and I became friends, he's told me a few things. And then there's the matter of your rentboy, facts your Happy Few may not be fully acquainted with.' I'm sure that chilled him! 'Oh, and one other thing—don't bother getting me any tack.'

'Not even a crop to flog me with?'

'You'd like that too much!'

'Well, next move's yours, love. Of course, I'm hoping there won't be one.'

'You'll just have to wait and see, won't you?'

'I guess I will. Toodleloo, love.'

God, what a fiend!

<u>Later</u>

R in a terrible snit.

'Where does he get an item like that? How dare he publish such a thing!'

'W thinks he's God around here. He publishes whatever he likes.'

'I've got a call in to my lawyer.'

'He'll tell you to ignore it.'

'Tell that to my wife!'

'What he wrote was for my eyes, his way of saying "Don't mess with me." I haven't decided yet whether to heed his warning or take him on.'

'Please listen to me,' R said, sincere and sweet and grave. 'You have serious problems—a kidnapped daughter, a pending custody battle, a terrifying recurring dream. I rarely give advice to patients, that's not an analyst's role, but this feud with Channing's a sideshow compared with what's really important in your life. My suggestion is concentrate on the important stuff and let this sideshow pass.'

*God, he can be such a good fatherly analyst when he wants to be!
It made me feel great that he cared so much.*

*'You're right,' I told him. 'W's not important. This morning's
column is tomorrow's fishwrap. Trash!'*

'Exactly!'

'So let's go back to work on the dream.'

*He was so pleased. He came up with another brilliant spiel
about Mom and Blackjack and breakage and how I must have
seen something traumatic when I was little and froze the moment
like a mental photograph and when it was frozen it became
something that could shatter, and that's what the broken horses
are all about.*

*He was brilliant and I was dazzled. When he was done, I
told him I adored him when he spoke like that, and I wished I
could adore him in body because that's my way of adoring a
man.*

'It always comes back to that, doesn't it?' he said.

'I guess with me it always does.'

*'I told you—assume you've seduced me, assume we've made love,
then move on from there.'*

'How can I believe something like that when I know we haven't?'

'We can't.'

*'Because it would break the rules? Are you so bound by rules you'd
deny yourself what you so clearly want and need?'*

'Listen, Barbara—'

*'Do you know, Tom, that's the first time you've called me by my
first name since I started coming here?'*

*I turned to look at him, caught him mopping his forehead with his
handkerchief.*

'Now that we're on a first-name basis—'

He laughed.

*'See how much you enjoy my company? Thing is, Tom, I just
don't see the difference between "assuming" we've made love and
actually doing it. Because if for therapeutic purposes we're to*

"assume" we have, then seems to me we might just as well do it—
for therapeutic reasons too, of course.'

'That's impossible.'

'I know you want to.'

'If I did, I'd consult a colleague. That's how we handle those
matters.'

'Oh, goody! Bring in a third party! Spread the word around! Play
right into W's hands!'

'Know something? I think you liked his column this morning. I
think now you want to make it all come true.'

Guess what, Dr. R? You're probably right!

<u>Later</u>

As promised, T brought pot to the F. We smoked it together
then made love. I felt I was moving on another level in a
mysterious hazy world where everything was right, every move
slow and perfect and complete. It was as good sex as I've had in
years. When we were done, I started to sob. T couldn't believe it,
kept asking 'What's the matter? What did I do? Did I do
something wrong?'

'No, darling, it's just the beauty of what we did that makes me
cry, this incredible floating feeling I'm left with. Guess I'm crazy,
huh? How do you like being involved with such a crazy lady?'

'I like it just fine,' he said.

When we were dressed, ready to leave, I told him I couldn't meet
him day after tomorrow, but that Friday would be fine.

'How can I bear to wait so long?' he asked.

Driving home, I wondered whether it was just the pot that did it
to me, made me feel so lifted and clear. Is this what I've come to, I
wondered—a slut who requires drugs to feel moved?

At the thought, I started to cry again. I was so red-eyed when I got
home, I put on dark glasses so Marie wouldn't know I'd wept.

'Dinner at seven, Mrs. F?' she asked me at the door.

'No, thank you, Marie. Tonight I'm dining at The Elms.'

'Very good, ma'am. Thank you, ma'am.'
'Yes, thank you, too, Marie.'

After reading this entry, I feel for her again. So many emotional vectors in her life appear, in hindsight, to be heading toward a tragic intersection. But I think even if I weren't aware of the August 27 denouement, I'd feel, reading this material, that some kind of major crisis was in the offing.

She's concluded rightly that her old confidante, Waldo Channing, has not only been a false friend but is pathologically malicious besides. Now she must choose between her natural instinct to try to vanquish him in a social war or deny herself the pleasures of a fight for fear of furthering her former husband's goal of taking away her sons. The reference to Max intrigues me. Could Max have told her about Waldo's and Maritz's blackmail schemes? And is that reference to the "rentboy" the then-scandalous fact that Waldo had originally found Deval on the porn shop-prostitute-hustler DaVinci strip?

Meantime, she's embarked upon her final siege of her shrink, attempting to lure Dad into bed. And then there are the conflicting feelings engendered by her two lovers, Jack Cody and Tom Jessup—a mellowing out, perhaps even a tenderizing of her relations with Cody, while she and Tom appear to have entered a baroque phase in which Tom has rebelled against continuing to play a role in the risky child-porn penetration project to which she and Cody have assigned him.

Finally, there's her existential crisis—her awareness and fear of personal emptiness, her pain as she struggles to decipher her strange recurring dream, and a looming sense that she has lost her bearings in the privileged, rarefied, and terribly lonely world she's created for herself.

I'm also impressed by Dad's various stabs at interpreting her dream. Compared with the sum of all his efforts in this regard, I find Izzy Mendoza's interpretation glib and tepid.

On Tuesday, August 19, she makes a series of remarkable decisions:

Woke up with a sense of mission. No more feeling sorry for myself. Time to take vigorous measures.

Phoned W, told him in no uncertain terms there will be no detente.

'You committed vicious and unpardonable acts. Now you'll pay the piper. And be very careful how you retaliate, W. Go too far and some of Jack's friends might . . . well, you know how they handle things. Also I know what you've been doing on the side, your venomous little schemes. Say one nasty word about me that'll hurt my case with Andy, and, I promise you, all that will come out.'

I hung up before he could reply. The old left eyeball must have been twitching up a storm!

Phoned Jack, thanked him for last night, told him T wants out of the Steadman deal, so if he's going to make a move on them it should be soon. He said he understood and will make arrangements. 'When am I going to see you again?' he asked. I told him I'll be busy the next few days, but maybe Sunday night.

Phoned R, left a message on his machine, said I won't be coming in tomorrow or for that matter ever again unless we can resolve the tensions between us. Told him I'll be in room 201 at the F at three tomorrow afternoon, that I'm inviting him to join me there, that he can come or not as he pleases, but whatever his decision to please not call to discuss the matter as I won't be taking calls.

Phoned Hansen, told him I'm prepared to do whatever it takes to combat A's custody claims. 'Tell his attorney my most vital interests are at stake. Tell him I have knowledge of things that could be ruinous to A, certain sexual episodes and peccadilloes. Tell him that though it isn't my style to stoop so low, the stakes are so high for me that if he doesn't withdraw his claim he can expect a no-holds-barred battle to the death.'

Saying that felt good!

Having completed a good day's work in just half an hour, I treated myself to a two-hour canter through Maple Hills, showered, then drove over to the club, where I played a fierce singles match with Tess.

After I lost the first set, quite a crowd gathered, all the girls eager to see nasty Barb dethroned. Somehow I managed to pull it out 3-6, 6-4, 6-4. Afterwards, Tess and I hugged to great applause. She whispered, 'Will you be my doubles partner if I dump Elaine?' 'Great idea! Give me the weekend to get rid of Jane. Then it's you and me all the way to club finals!' She kissed my sweaty cheek. 'I'm thrilled. I've had a crush on you for years!'

God! Well, I guess that'll be interesting—if we ever get around to consummating it!

Certain sexual episodes and peccadilloes! Does this mean Waldo was telling the truth when he told the cops Barbara had been looking for proof Andrew was fooling around with men?

I hold my breath before reading on, for the next entry concerns Wednesday, August 20, one week to the day before the slaughter and the second Wednesday in a row that Dad cancelled his afternoon appointments:

<u>*Wednesday*</u>

R arrived precisely on time. I opened the door wearing a robe.
'You came.'
'Not for the reason you think.'
'I didn't ask you here for that reason.'
'I find that laughable.'
'Then go ahead—laugh!'
'We're not going to make love.'
'I know that, I'm not a fool.'
'Then why—?'
'Why did I summon you? Because it was necessary that you come. Otherwise all our "assumptions" are just so much garbage.'
'You play a dangerous game, Mrs. F.'
'Now you're back to calling me "Mrs. F"? Isn't professional

formality kind of silly here in this sleazy motel room where I regu-
larly have sex with your namesake?'

Finally, he smiled. I invited him to sit down on the bed.

'Don't worry, I won't attack you. Please make yourself
comfortable so we can talk.'

I told him I didn't think formal analysis was working for me, that
I needed something more warm-blooded, something that will make
me feel as though I'm connecting with a real human being. I told
him how much I've been moved when he's shown concern for me,
and how awful I feel when he coldly applies more formal methods. I
told him that if he can't modify his treatment I'll have to quit
therapy, and that I don't want to do that because I desperately need
his help.

'But real help,' I told him. 'Compassionate help. And no more
games.'

I told him I feel he's played me as much as I've played him,
that his counter-seductions are seductions in themselves, and that
I feel he shares as much of the blame as I for what's gone wrong
between us.

I told him: 'When you tell me I should assume we've made love,
assume my seduction of you has been successful, and that I should
share my sexual fantasies about you, you show me the weakness at
the core of your cool stance. I can't abide that pose. I need a friend,
a brilliant friend who can really help me—because I need help,
tons of it. This is why I invited you to this sordid place, to tell you
all this so we can decide where we go from here. I couldn't tell you
any of this from the couch in your office. Maybe that's part of my
neurosis, that I needed to tell it to you here in this awful room face
to face.'

I started to cry. I sobbed. He moved to me, held me in his arms.
Then I could feel him sobbing, too. We wept together.

'I care for you,' he told me.

'I know you do. Please know I feel the same way.'

'But it's impossible. You understand?'

'Yes. But maybe that's the best part of it somehow.'

We hugged each other, wept upon each other, and I felt so close to him then, so fine and close. It was the most moving experience I've had in a long time. And the strangest part was I hadn't planned it this way. I told him that, too.

'Truth is I don't know what was in my mind when I asked you here. I didn't know myself till I opened the door and saw you standing there so fearful and grave.'

'This is wrong yet it feels so right. That's what I don't understand.'

'Don't try to understand it, Doctor,' I urged. 'Just keep feeling it the way we're doing.'

And at that we hugged and sobbed some more.

When we finally let each other go, our eyes clear and smiles on our lips, he said he owed me an apology. I told him he didn't, but he insisted.

'When you first came to me, I recognized you were an extraordinary woman, but then I got bogged down thinking of you as a fascinating case rather than as a deeply troubled person in need of help. I thought too much about how I was going to write up your case, well-disguised of course, and that led me astray. I forgot that I'm a healer first of all, that feelings and compassion are my most effective tools, not theory and technique. I put personal ambition ahead of my oath to heal. I want you to know I'm not going to write up your case, rather I'm going to put all my efforts into working with you to solve your dream and free you of its tyranny.'

I told him that hearing this from him was more than I could have wished for. I told him I was so glad he held me and allowed me to hold him. 'I needed to touch you,' I said. 'Sex is for pleasure, but I think to hold each other like we just have is deeper and better. Thanks so much for coming today.'

'And you will come to me Friday at the usual time?'

'Oh, yes, Doctor—you can be sure!'

We laughed, stood, embraced again. Then he left, and I lay down

and cried by myself. I felt so moved by what had happened, the
strangeness of it. Perhaps, I thought, there is some hope for me yet.
And now I know the next right thing for me to do is to set T free as
gently as I can.

As I put the diary down, all sorts of feelings flood in. First, pride in
Dad that he didn't give in to his lust, didn't make love to his patient,
rather discovered a truth in his experience with her that seriously altered
his approach to his work. Second, enormous admiration for Barbara, her
vulnerability and also her restraint. When the chips were down, she
stopped playing power games and gave in to the decent impulses that
had always flowed beneath the hard surface she showed the world. Yes, I
feel proud of them both.

In this passage, I see each of them reaching for redemption and
attaining it. And I think: It *must* have been the kind expression on Dad's
face, engendered by his strange meeting with Barbara that afternoon,
that Kate Evans saw when he left the room and came down the stairs and
their eyes met as she viewed him from the pool. The face of a kindly
man, a man who would help you, a man with whom you could share
your troubles.

And now I know too why Dad was never able to complete his paper,
"The Dream of the Broken Horses." How could he? How could he ever
have published a description of his August 20 encounter with Mrs. F at
the motel? Impossible! He'd risk being run out of his profession. He
couldn't even have described it to Izzy at their regular Tuesday lunch.
Izzy would have been appalled.

And yet their encounter rings true to me—two lost souls finding
solace with one another under unlikely circumstances in a terribly
unlikely place. And truly it is the first entry in Barbara's diary that strikes
me as having been written without irony or ire.

But the march goes on. Scanning ahead, I see there are a few more
pages of writing, shorter entries, not as dense as the ones I've just read.
And so I pick up the diary once again, determined now to read uninter-
rupted to its end:

Quiet for once—too quiet perhaps. Decided it was time to call Doris, make up. As expected, she was icy when she heard my voice.

'My only child and she hangs up on me! I tried so hard to bring you up to be a nice, polite girl. What did I do wrong?'

'Spare me the mea culpas, Mom, please.'

'I don't even know what that means. I'm just not as smart and well-educated as you.'

'You're plenty smart and you know it. How're things going at the track?'

That perked her up. She told me she made four grand last month using her new post-position method. 'Doesn't matter who the horse is or who the jockey. Just the post position. Not a very colorful approach, but so far it's working great.'

J called. He's got everything set for Monday night. 'Just make sure you get your boy out of there this weekend at the latest.'

I didn't tell J I'm planning to phase T out of my life altogether. Perhaps I'll tell him Sunday night.

Phoned Jane, told her I've decided to team up with Tess for club doubles. Suggested maybe she should team with Elaine.

'Yeah, the two rejects. Thanks a lot, Barb!'

Bitter, bitter!

Excellent session with R. Worked on the dream. He said it's important we not approach it in a tormented fashion, rather have fun with it, free-associate, try out ideas, think of it as solvable and not as an intractable puzzle.

In the end, I told him how happy I was that we'd finally cleared the air.

He said he was happy too, that he'd learned a great deal from me and hoped he could repay me in kind. He said: 'I'd forgotten that humanist values must be the basis for a successful analysis. Thank you for bringing that home to me again.'

Later with T—told him he's to break off all contact with the Steadmans right away, that someone else will take up the slack and carry the deal through. He looked so relieved, became so sweet, I didn't have the heart to tell him I can't see him anymore after the boys come home from camp.

We made a lazy, dreamy kind of love, and as always I was touched by his tenderness.

'You'll make some girl very happy,' I told him.

'I want to make you happy, not some girl,' he said.

He recited French poetry from memory, beautiful verses by Rimbaud. Afterwards he told me what they meant.

'I've been thinking about what I want to do with my life. I like teaching, but what I really want to do is write.'

I told him that if that's what he wants he should pursue his dream. Which gave me an idea—as a parting gift I could send him off to France for a year. Then I worried he might have too much pride to accept a gift so grand.

Saturday

Hot tempers today at the club. Seems Tess and I have created a crisis. Word is we've ganged up on everybody else and all we care about is taking home club trophies. What the fools don't realize is that if I cared at all about trophies I'd still take part in equestrian competitions, that I already have sufficient trophies to last me a lifetime, and that tennis is only useful to me as a way to blow off steam!

Sunday

Woke up all panicky in a sweat. Bad dream, but it wasn't The Dream this time, was worse somehow, more scary, like I was lying helplessly somewhere in a sea of white while my body was torn apart before my very eyes.

Later—late dinner with J. He had to get up several times to greet people and solve management problems. I loved watching him work. He looked great in his white dinner jacket, by far the most poised, confident man in the club. Everyone makes nice with him, everyone wants his ear. And I like the way he dispenses favors. Watching him, I decided he's the only 'real man' I've ever been involved with.

*   'We're awfully well-suited,' I told him when he sat down again.*

*   'Yeah, the society bitch and the hood.'*

*   'Not too bad a combination.'*

*   'Not bad at all,' he agreed.*

*   He said tomorrow night some people he knows will take care of the Steadmans quick and neat. When I asked him where he finds people like that, he smiled.*

*   'Haven't you heard? I'm what they call "connected." '*

*   'The Torrance Hill Mob?'*

*   'Only the papers call them that.'*

*   'What do they call themselves?'*

*   'Just some guys who have a thing going, what they call "our thing." '*

*   ' "Thing"—hmmm. Well, I guess it is a thing, isn't it?'*

*   'Better you don't know, cutie.' I stared at him. 'Whatsamatter?'*

*   'If you'd stop calling me "cutie" I'd enjoy your company a lot more.'*

*   He laughed. 'That'd be easy if your tits and ass weren't so cute!'*

*   'And your balls and hairy ass—they're just so cute too, you know.'*

*   He guffawed. 'What you need is a good fucking.'*

*   'And you're the cute guy's going to give it to me, right?'*

*   We skipped dessert, gulped our coffee, then hastened upstairs. The usual—lots of tumbling around, biting and scratching, a few well-placed fanny slaps. Then when he slipped into his dressing gown, poured us brandies, put his feet up, and lit a cigar, I asked him why it was so hard for him to be tender. 'I know you can be,' I told him. 'You were incredibly tender with me three weeks ago.'*

*   'Wanted to show you I could do it, too.'*

*   'So it was just an act?'*

*   'That's a side of myself I don't like to expose to many people.'*

'You can expose it to me. I won't tell anyone.'

'Maybe you'll show me your soft side too sometime.'

'I'm hard as nails, J.'

We laughed.

As I was getting ready to leave, he mentioned casually that W hasn't been around for several days. He said he found that odd since W usually comes in on weekends to pick up whatever scuttlebutt's circulating around the club.

'I told W he'd better not try anything nasty with me or some of your friends might have a little talk with him.'

'Well, that accounts for it. You scared the poor man off.'

'I don't think he's dangerous, do you, J?'

'Don't underestimate him, B. If he gets riled enough, no telling what he might do.'

Monday

Got up at dawn, rode for two hours, then changed and drove to session. R very sweet, subdued, mellow, all the hard edges between us gone. Told him I'm starting to miss our battles.

'That's because you think sweetness is boring,' he said. 'You think you need turmoil to feel alive. Your mother taught you that by her strictness and rectitude.'

'She had no rectitude. She was a fake. She had all kinds of affairs, kinky sex, too.'

'Do you know for a fact she had kinky sex?'

I shook my head.

'But you sensed she did?'

'I felt it in my bones,' I told him.

Later—with T. He kissed me over and over, told me how much I meant to him and that if anything ever came between us he didn't know what he'd do.

'You'd go on with your life like everybody else,' I told him.

'But nothing will come between us, will it?'

I told him about W and how he's threatened to feed stuff to A *about our seeing one another. I told him people know, that maybe it's my fault, I haven't been careful enough, my car's too flashy, whatever, but my point was the story's been making the rounds and that isn't good for either of us.*

'We can change where we meet. This place is getting stale anyway.'

'Changing motels won't help if A has people following me.'

T lay back on the bed. 'If this ever comes out, I'll be fired for sure.'

'Don't worry about that.'

'Easy for you to say.'

'Why do you speak to me like that, T?'

'I have so very much to lose,' he said.

'And I don't? Losing my boys is trivial, is that what you think?'

He started to cry, said he was sorry, begged me to forgive him. I hugged him, told him that of course I forgive him, but that with the boys coming back next weekend we're going to have to cool it down this fall. I could feel him wince when I said that, his whole body contract. He knows, poor boy, and now I wonder where I'm going to find the strength to tell him straight.

When we parted, I told him I'd call him late tonight and let him know how everything went with the Steadmans.

He shrugged. 'We'll meet here Wednesday, usual time?' he asked meekly.

Saw tears again in his eyes when he left.

Tuesday

J called in the middle of the night. 'It's done,' he said. 'Burned to the ground.'

'What about the people?'

'Forget them. They don't exist.'

'What are you telling me?'

'Don't think about it, Barb. Just look ahead.'

'You didn't find out anything?'

'I didn't say that.'

'Why are you being so cryptic?'

'It's over, Barb. You're going to have to face the fact that it's all done now for good.'

I couldn't get back to sleep. Phoned T, told him what J said. He said he didn't understand. Told him I didn't either, but that I'll find out and let him know.

Later—early morning, dreamt I was riding through a misty valley. Very bucolic until I noticed another horseman in the distance through the mist. He looked familiar, so I rode up from behind to see who he was. God, it was Goertner! 'Oh, hello, how are you?' he asked. Told him I was fine. 'And your mother—how is she?' 'You fucked her, didn't you, Goertner?' I demanded, furious. 'Oh, yes,' he answered grinning. 'And a mighty sweet fuck she was!'

I kicked my heels into my horse, galloped away, but no matter how far and fast I sped from him, I could hear his laughter ringing through the valley.

What a dream!

Wednesday

Called J, insisted on seeing him, told him I need to know everything, I want the whole truth even if it's bad. He said come out to the club tomorrow night and he'll tell me.

'So is it bad news?'

'It's the truth,' he said.

'Whose truth are we talking about?'

'It's time for both of us to face some facts,' he said.

'What kind of facts?'

'Facts about your problems, facts about mine, and a few facts about the two of us as well.'

Jesus!

Later—told R about my dream, reminded him that Goertner was my old riding instructor, the one I slapped, the first man to go down on me.

R excited. 'I'm sure it's a variation on the broken horses dream.

What we've got to do now is put the dreams together. I think one is the key to the other, but I don't know yet which one is the key and which the lock.'

Whatever that means!

Later—bad feeling as I swam laps, then dressed to go over to the F. Have made up my mind today's the day to tell T we have to end it. Feeling anxious as I'm not expecting a particularly lovely afternoon.

And so it ends.

Within an hour of her writing that final line, she and Tom Jessup will both be dead.

So many things amaze me. Most of all, I think, is the mellowness of these last passages, the feeling that she has started to settle things, put her chaotic life in order. She has straightened out her relationship with Dad, is planning to break off her affair with Tom, is prepared to go to war over custody with Andrew, and seems to have decided that she and Jack, the "society bitch and the hood," properly belong together after all.

As to going to war against Waldo, there's no clear indication what her final decision would have been, but with the crucial custody case coming up, it's hard to imagine that a fight with him would have done her any good. Also it's clear he lied to the police when he feigned shock that she'd been carrying on her affair with Tom Jessup for months.

One other thing stands out: that Cody definitely engineered the fire and other vicious events that took place Monday night on Thistle Ridge, and that Barbara and Tom, the latter perhaps unknowingly, were to some degree party to that as well. "Burned to the ground," "they don't exist," "it's all done now for good" —I interpret all that to mean that whatever specific information Cody may have extracted from the Steadmans, he learned for sure that Belle Fulraine was dead and would have told Barbara the following evening had she not been killed.

Closing Barbara's diary, I feel it has put me in close touch with this extraordinary, complex woman, that I now know things about her that even Dad could not have known. Seeing her through her own eyes as portrayed on these pages, I'm able not only to discern her unattractive qualities—selfishness, manipulativeness, and narcissism—but also the decency, integrity, and brave spirit that so often subsumed them. And what I find most poignant, and which belies any suggestion that these pages were intended for anyone's eyes but her own, is her troubled, torturous, and admirable struggle to know herself.

In the end, it seems to me, that's her vindication.

SIXTEEN

With the diary comes relief: Dad was not the killer and maybe Waldo was. But as relieved as I am, I'm still not satisfied.

As I walk to the courthouse, I ask myself why I still want to pursue Flamingo. *Isn't it enough to know Dad didn't sleep with his patient, was not involved in her death. Why now go on with it?*

The answer, of course, is Barbara. If after months spent studying her image in the *Fessé* photograph and reading and rereading Dad's case study, I became haunted by her bizarre dream, now that I've read her diary, I find myself even more drawn in. Now, like Dad, bewitched by her personality, I yearn to learn everything I possibly can, including who killed her and the precise manner of her death.

During lunch break, I take my copy of the diary to a photocopy shop to have an additional copy made for Mace. While I'm waiting, I dash off sketches that illustrate the end of the Foster trial, various views of each side resting its case. This is, admittedly, a lazy way to earn my keep, but at this point I'm so familiar with the principals I can draw most any possible courtroom scene out of my head.

On my way to the Sheriff's Department to drop off the diary, I once again have the feeling I'm being followed. Deciding to take action, I enter a shoe store, walk to the rear, then suddenly turn and stride back out while staring directly into the eyes of everyone I encounter. No sign of Mr. Potato Head . . . not that I'd even recognize him if he were there. But at least, if he's watching, he'll know I'm on to him. A couple minutes later, entering the Sheriff's Department, I enjoy the thought he may think I'm here to report him.

MR. POTATO HEAD: Sometime in the night, I suddenly open my eyes, turn to Pam snuggled against me, feel her warmth, inhale the aroma of her body, and listen as she breathes deeply in her sleep.

A phrase, ricocheting inside my brain, awakened me:

He was like a shadow, you never noticed he was there.

Jürgen said that the afternoon I drew his portrait.

Who was he talking about? *Who* was it you never noticed was there?

It was O'Neill, Jerry O'Neill, the crooked ex-cop with the alcohol problem who was Walter Maritz's operative. The guy Maritz brought in to track Barbara Fulraine because he couldn't do it himself since she knew him from his having scammed her. The guy Maritz brought in, because, as he told the cops, "I knew O'Neill would fuck up good, and that's just what I wanted." Except, according to Jürgen, most everything Maritz told the cops was a lie.

He was like a shadow, you never noticed he was there.

That could be a perfect description of Mr. Potato Head. You didn't notice O'Neill because he looked like everybody else, a guy with cop training, expert at following people. Johnny Powell figured him for a cop. *"He had a cop's way about him. You know—a stache and a cheap suit."* Except he didn't have a mustache, *"Just seemed like the type. Said your name then showed me a picture."*

The night before I interviewed Kate, she tried to draw the face of the man she saw when she was a girl. Her drawings were childish, schematic. I attributed that to lack of skill. But maybe her drawings were accurate portraits of Mr. Potato Head, a man with a generic face who looked like everybody else.

He was like a shadow, you never noticed he was there.

Mr. Potato Head knows how to get into a hotel room without disturbing the electronic lock. Mr. Potato Head knows how to follow a man on the street without being noticed. Mr. Potato Head can do a U-turn-and-park maneuver when I try to track his car. All skills an old-time cop would have, an ex-cop, an operative.

Jerry O'Neill equals Mr. Potato Head? It adds up, could even be true.

I'm excited. Though it's the middle of the night, I tiptoe into Pam's bathroom to call Mace from my cell phone.

"That diary's really something," he says. "Can't put it out of my mind. And now Waldo . . . it's hard to believe, isn't it?"

"I don't know if it was Waldo or who the hell it was, Mace. I do know that all your Steadman-connected suspects are dead. Cody, the Torrance Hill mob, whoever. But Mr. Potato Head isn't dead and now I think I know who he is."

"Sure, I remember O'Neill," he tells me. "Just barely. He's not the kind of guy you remember all that well. Basically all I can recall about him is his name." He pauses. "Hmmm, that sounds like Mr. Potato Head, doesn't it? Gimme a couple hours. Soon as I get to the office I'll run him through the DMV."

CALISTA COUNTY COURTHOUSE, 11:50 A.M: Kit Foster's defense attorney rests his case. When Judge Winterson asks if the State wants to put on rebuttal evidence, the prosecution team briefly confers, then announces that it rests as well. Excitement in the courtroom. The trial's now basically over. Winterson gavels for quiet, instructs counsel to prepare to make closing arguments in the morning, then dismisses the jury. The moment the judge leaves the courtroom, the media crowd, cell phones in hand, surge into the corridor.

"How long will it take you to get me drawings?" Harriet asks, panting at my side.

"I already have them," I tell her, handing off my sketches.

Her expression is priceless. "*Who* told you, David?" she demands. "How did you know?"

I smile at her, break loose, head for the elevators. Mace is waiting for me downstairs with the DMV photo of Jerry O'Neill.

STANDING BEHIND his counter, Johnny Powell nods. "Sure, that's the guy."

"No question, Johnny?"

"It's him, Mr. Weiss. Just lookin' at him I can smell the suit."

Mace and I thank Johnny, then retreat to the Flamingo courtyard.

"Your geezer's positive, so let's talk to him." Mace laughs. "Be pretty funny if he's tracking you now. He'll end up tracking you back to his own place."

O'NEILL'S PLACE turns out to be an apartment in a crummy building on Tucker Avenue, a tenement with strange, dark, open porches lined two in a row up the facade.

There's an unpleasant pungency to the dark, ground-floor lobby, the smell of over-the-hill fish fried in cheap oil. A NO SOLICITORS sign, defaced by graffiti, is taped to the wall. A coin-operated laundry machine chugs away in a corner, a puddle of soapy water, leaking from beneath, spreading across the floor. No elevator, just a staircase brashly lit by buzzing fluorescent tubes attracting flies.

"2-B." Mace points to the left. The walls are dark brown and so is the woodwork. I can barely make out the number on the door.

Mace pushes the buzzer. No response. He motions me to stand out of sight, then knocks.

The sound of footsteps padding across the floor on the other side. "Yeah-yeah-yeah," a weary voice intones.

A little flash of light in the peephole. The sound of laborious breathing. "Whaduyuwant?"

"Sheriff's Department. Open up, O'Neill."

O'Neill coughs, a smoker's dry, hacking cough. The door opens a crack. A stream of cigarette smoke snakes out. "What's going on?"

Mace motions me to show myself. I step into O'Neill's sight line. He looks at me with little terrier eyes, then exhales and coughs again. Even through the haze of smoke, I see more character in his face than I expected.

"Mr. Weiss here's made a complaint," Mace tells him. "Want to talk about it?"

"Hello there, Weiss. Sure, we can talk about it. Place is a mess. Wasn't expecting guests."

He gestures us into a large, dark, dusty room furnished with battered Salvation Army junk. An oversize refrigerator, door yellowing with age, occupies a corner. Several cheap aluminum ashtrays are overflowing with butts. The stench of exhaled tobacco is nearly overwhelming. When O'Neill steps back, he seems to disappear into the shadows.

He was like a shadow, you never noticed he was there.

"Wanna beer?" We shake our heads. O'Neill shrugs, then makes his way to the refrigerator. "Take a seat . . . if you can find one."

Mace perches on a torn, lopsided hassock. I sit on an old army footlocker covered with a fraying gray towel.

O'Neill's a pear-shaped guy with iron-gray hair and a big ass shown off by a pair of brown trousers held up by suspenders. White chest hairs peek through his shirt. His jowls are unshaven, and he's wearing a raggedy pair of brown slippers. He's got the kind of square-bottom face that reminds me of the bottom of a paper bag.

I wouldn't have trouble drawing this guy. What's the big deal, why's he so hard to describe?

"How'd you guys find me?" he asks, sitting down on his unmade bed, faint smile playing on his lips.

"I'll be asking the questions," Mace says. "To start, why're you following Mr. Weiss?"

"Following a guy's a crime?"

"Yeah, if you're doing it to cover up a crime."

"I ain't covering nothin'. I was following him for a client."

"Who?"

"You know I don't have to tell you that."

"Yeah, but you will."

I like Mace's classical technique. It's as if, figuring O'Neill a certain way, he instinctively uses language he knows will reach the guy.

O'Neill stubs out his cigarette, lights another. "Okay, a guy named Maritz asked me to find out what Weiss is up to."

"Walter M. Maritz who lives down in Sarasota?"

O'Neill exhales toward me. "You seem to know a lot, Mr. Weiss. I'll pass that on to Walt. See, finding out what you know is what he wants to know . . . if you follow my meaning. He heard you were nosing around, pokin' your face into offices in the Doubleton Building, talking to Rakoubian's nutty widow, hangin' out with Cody's old maitre d'. So he asked me to check you out. That's the whole story."

"No, it isn't." Mace rises, walks up to O'Neill, stares at him with disdain. "Right now your client Maritz is looking at serious charges. He lied to us about Flamingo. From what I can tell, damn near everything he told us was a lie. Doesn't matter it was twenty-six years ago. No statute of limitations on murder. The investigation's still open. That means no limitations on hindering the investigation. So start talking, because the one who talks first, you or Maritz, is the one who's going to get credit for helping me out."

There's something almost old ladyish about O'Neill, and it's not his personal hygiene. It's his prissiness, I decide, the prim way he holds his hands together in his lap and the sickly smile that coats his face like a veneer. He's got wide hips, a plump ass, and smoking must have nearly rotted out his lungs. He looks like a guy with maybe a year or two left to live. The only part of him that appears tough is the squirrelly look of cunning in his eyes.

He gazes at Mace, then at me, stubs out his cigarette, then goes into a coughing fit. When finally he brings the cough under control, he looks again at Mace and shrugs.

"Sure," he says, "I'll tell you. Walt hasn't paid me, so he hasn't earned client privilege yet. Anyhow," he shows that sickly smile again, "my private investigator's license already expired."

"Was Maritz involved with the Flamingo killings?"

"No way!"

"So why does he care what I know?" I ask.

"Because like the inspector here said, Walt lied. He told the inspector he didn't know what happened, didn't know about Mrs. Fulraine's affair with the teach. But he *did* know. I told him. I was full time on her butt. I was there in my car in the motel lot the day of the shootings. I even caught a glimpse of the shooter when he ran out."

As he starts talking, I start sketching him. He preens for me a little, blows a couple of smoke rings in my direction, smiles to himself, but never asks what I'm doing or why. Maybe because he knows he's difficult to describe, he thinks I won't be able to portray him. But I have my own motive, and it's not just to see if I can make a decent drawing of his generically ugly face. I want him to get used to me sketching as he speaks, because, though he doesn't know it yet, if he really did see the shooter, he's going to help me make an eyewitness drawing as soon as he finishes telling his story to Mace.

"This rich guy Fulraine hired Walt to follow his ex, catch her doing something untoward he could use against her to get back his kids."

" '*Untoward*'?" Mace winces. "Give us a break, O'Neill."

Jerry blows a perfect smoke ring, then another, which passes through the first. " 'Sinful'—how's that?"

"Go on."

"The pay was good so Walt took the assignment even though he knew he couldn't handle it on his own. Also seems he had a grudge. Couple years before, he and Mrs. Fulraine had a major falling out and Cody had him beaten up. Merciless beating. Put Walt out of commission nearly a year. So Walt hired me. I was just off the force. Maybe I wasn't the greatest cop this town ever had, but I was one helluva tracker. Walt knew that. So he tells me: 'Follow the bitch, get everything you can on her. Nothin' could be sweeter for me than seeing her lose her brats.'

"So I start following her. Two, three days into the job she leads me to a motel across from Tremont Park. One look and I go, 'Whoa! This doesn't fit, she's up to something dirty in there.' "

"Something 'untoward'?"

Jerry blows another perfect smoke ring. "She goes up to this room.

Couple hours later she and this guy come out and get into separate cars. I jot down his plate number, then follow her home.

"When I report this to Walt, he gets excited. 'Tasty!' he says. So he runs the plate on the stud and it turns out he's a teacher at her kids' school. 'Got her by her short hairs now,' Walt says.

"I keep following her and every couple days it's the same routine. She drives over to the motel, she and the teach spend a couple hours, then each takes off in his own car. They're so sure of themselves they don't even try to cover up. I mean she drives a Jag for Christ's sake! Anyone could've followed her.

"One night Walt and I have a couple drinks and he tells me what's on his mind. 'I can pass all this on to Fulraine like I'm supposed to,' he says. 'Then what? He nails her in court and throws us a little bonus for good work.' Walt doesn't think much of that. A little bonus isn't going to cut it. 'I'm gonna blackmail the bitch. She'll pay big time to keep this quiet. Trouble is she knows me so I can't approach her direct. That's where you come in. She doesn't know you, Jerry, so you'll be the cut-out, then you and me'll split the take.' Sounds good to me. I tell him I'm in. 'Okay,' Walt says, 'but we can't do blackmail without something to sell. We gotta get pictures.' So we talk to Max. Max is game and Max is cheap. He even knows the broad, once took pictures of her holding a whip."

I'm shocked; Barbara thought Max was her friend.

"What about Waldo Channing?" I ask, contemplating Max's betrayal. "Did Maritz bring him in too?"

O'Neill shows his old lady's sickly smile. "Why split with Channing when Walt and I developed this on our own?"

"So then what?" Mace asks.

"Max stakes out the motel, sets up his telephoto, gets shots of them coming and going, snaps a kiss or two. But that's not good enough for Walt. 'I want fucking,' he says. 'I want them bare-assed naked on the bed.' So Max comes up with a plan. Since I'm used to her routine, I know when she and the teach take a day off. We book their favorite room on one of the off-days, I sneak in a ladder, then help Max mount one of his remote-control miniature cameras and a transmitter mike behind the ventilation screen above the bed. . . ."

Max knew a secret about those killings, Chip's mother told me, *something he wouldn't tell no matter how many times I asked.* But the worst part of this, I think, is Max's betrayal.

"That fuckin' Max. What a wizard! Couple days later we take a room a few doors down. The lady and the teach check in as usual, we listen till we hear them going at it, 'oohs' and 'ahs.' Then Max starts shooting blind. Every couple of minutes he uses this little radio device to take a picture. We're worried they'll hear the clicks, but we get lucky, there's a thunderstorm. Anyhow, to find the camera they'd have to unscrew the vent register. As it happens, they're so wrapped up in each other they don't suspect a thing. Soon as they leave, we go back in the room, Max takes out the film, and, in case he didn't get enough, reloads the camera and puts it back. Good thing too, because even though the pictures come out great, Walt still isn't satisfied. 'I wanna a crotch shot! I wanna see her snatch! I wanna see her suckin' his dick! Get me a suck shot and you get double pay,' he tells Max. I think he had this idea he'd blackmail the lady, then, when he squeezed out all he could, he'd mail the pictures to Cody for spite. Like 'Fuck you, Cody, take a look at your bitch sucking off her new stud!' Far as those two went, Walt had a hair up his ass. . . ."

"Did Max get the suck shot?"

O'Neill laughs. "Max couldn't see 'em, so whatever he got was a matter of luck. Anyhow, after two tries, I finally persuade Walt to calm down. 'Why go on with it? This is business,' I tell him. 'Forget your personal gripe. We got a lock.' Walt gets my point. So now it's my turn. The plan's so devious we laugh ourselves sick figuring it out. . . ."

As O'Neill recounts his role in the scheme, he again shows his sickly smirk. I decide to work it into my drawing. If I can capture that, I think, I'll have him down cold, pinned to my sketchpad like the sleazy cockroach that he is.

"Next time Barbara and the teach check into the motel, I'm in my usual spot in the parking lot. There's another thunderstorm. I give them half an hour, time to have some fun, then when the sky clears I mosey

over to this phone booth inside Moe's, dial the motel, and ring through
to their room. The teach picks up. 'Yeah?' 'Mrs. Fulraine please.' 'Who *is*
this?' he asks, like who the hell would know she's even there. 'This is
about her kids, so put her on.' As he passes her the phone, I hear him say
something like 'I don't know. Something about your kids.' 'Oh, God!' I
hear her say. Then, to me, '*What happened? What?*' At this point, I'm
starting to feel sorry for her. But bcczcncss eze beezeness, so I come on
tough and deliver my spiel. 'See the vent screen above the bed? We put
a camera up there last week, got pictures of you fucking your brains out
with your kids' teach. If you don't pay us a hundred grand, those pictures
are going straight to your ex. Think about that, Mrs. Fulraine. Wanna
lose two more of your kids? You'll get a sample photo in the mail.' I'm
about to tell her I'll be in touch, when she fuckin' explodes. 'Listen who-
ever-the-hell-you-are, I know who you're working for. Tell the little creep
if he *dares* play any more games with me I'll ruin him, so help me God!'
Then she hangs up!"

O'Neill rubs his eyes, lights another cigarette. "Hangs up on me! I
couldn't fuckin' believe it! My hands were shaking so bad I dropped the
phone. She's wasn't broken, wasn't scared, instead she went crazy mad. I
ask myself: What kind of blackmail can we do if the person isn't scared of
what we got? The way she talked, she had far worse on us than we had on
her. I go back to my car, light a cigarette, try to figure the thing out. What
am I going to tell Walt? And what's he going to do when he hears? Send
the pictures to Mr. Fulraine in return for a little bonus? Send them to
Cody, a guy you don't mess with? Send them to both because he hates
the broad? Maybe, I'm thinking, the smart move for me is to get the hell
out of this while I can."

O'Neill takes a deep drag, then exhales in a long stream.

"That's when I heard the shots."

"How many?"

"Four big ones—boom-boom, a break, then two more. Something, I
don't know what, tells me they're coming from that room. First thing I
think is *Shit! Either she's shot him or he's shot her. Maybe my call set
them off!* Then I see this guy come out, guy in a raincoat and hat. No

gun, but later I figure he must have hidden it under his coat. He comes running down the outside stairs, crosses the street, then walks real fast toward my car. I don't want him to see me, so I slide down and stay still. He passes within fifteen feet. I get a look at him, not much, just a glimpse, then I watch him through my side mirror. He goes all the way through the lot, then turns toward Tremont Park. That's when I decide to get the hell out. I start my car and pull out fast. Later that night, when I meet Walt at his pub, news of the killings has been on TV for hours. As we're sitting there looking at the screen above the bar, some news bitch comes on with a guy who says he saw the shooter run into the parking lot, then a dark car come roaring out. Then somebody comes on and IDs the car as an Olds. Walt and I look at each other. We know we're in deep shit. Why? Guess what I drive? A dark blue Olds sedan."

"That's it?" Mace asks.

"That's it. We couldn't tell you guys. We were implicated; we hadn't told Fulraine what she was doing. The lady was dead so we couldn't blackmail her. We just figured if we kept quiet and nobody saw nothin', you guys would think Cody ordered the hit . . . which was peachy fine with Walt."

"What happened to the pictures?" Mace asks.

"Max burned them, negatives, too. He was scared. I think he thought maybe Walt or I offed those people. I know he and Walt never worked together again."

"Will Maritz confirm your story?"

O'Neill shrugs. "It's true even if he doesn't."

"No special shadings or extra touches, Jerry, to make you look better than you were?"

"I don't think I look good at all in what I told you."

"Unless you or Maritz killed them."

Jerry shakes his head. He's tired now, out of juice. "Why the hell would we do that, Inspector? Mrs. Fulraine was going to be our meal ticket. If I'd seen this guy go in there with a gun, I'd have shot him myself to protect, you know, our investment."

"So what'd he look like, Jerry?" I ask.

"Just some guy. I barely caught a glimpse of him."

"How long a glimpse?" I glance over at Mace. He nods, sits back, his signal it's my turn now to grill O'Neill.

"How long? How the hell should I know? Ten, fifteen seconds."

"That's a pretty long glimpse."

"What're you driving at?"

"You're going to describe him and I'm going to draw him. That's how the inspector's going to know whether you're telling the truth."

O'Neill laughs. "You gotta be kidding. This was twenty-six years ago. I can barely remember stuff from yesterday."

"That's what you think now," I tell him in as warm a tone as I can summon. "I'm going to help you remember. You're going to be surprised at how much comes back."

I start in on him, helpful, empathetic, treating him as if he's a totally reliable witness. I get him to tell me what it felt like sitting in his car through that thunderstorm. Also what it felt like to spy on people then try to scare them into submission by acting tough with them on the phone. I get him talking about his smoking, how he always lit up when he felt stressed, and the stress he felt that afternoon, and the guilt and remorse and second thoughts too, what it felt like trying to be a blackmailer when blackmailing wasn't really his gig. How he was a cop at heart, a hunter-tracker, master of the urban forest, and now Walt Maritz had dragged him into this squalid Peeping-Tom blackmailer role that hurt him in his pride.

He remembers more: the stink of the inside of his car from all the packs of Pall Malls he'd smoked in it through the years. Also the smell of old pizza boxes that littered the floor in back. The way the rain puddled on the tar surface of the motel lot and the red VACANCY/NO VACANCY sign on the Flamingo roof going all purple and weird when the sky darkened during the storm.

Memories flood in: the jolts he felt as the sounds of the shots reached him inside his car and the thoughts that then went racing through his brain. The way he leaned forward as he raised his binoculars to his eyes just in time to make out the shooter rushing out of room 201.

At first he thought it was the teach, but a second later knew it wasn't. The teach was tall, moved like an athlete; this man was smaller and thin. Both his hat and raincoat were dark gray or black, and he had his hat pulled down to just the level of his eyes.

He looked kinda funny too, absurd almost, like a figure in an old-fashioned gangster film, one of those furtive Peter Lorre or Elisha Cook, Jr. types acting as though if they slink around no one'll notice or remember them.

What does he remember about the guy? The posture first, the stiff-back way he held himself. He picked up on that even before the guy crossed the street. Then the way he hesitated a second on the motel side. Then the way he ran—no, not ran but loped across and into the parking lot.

He remembers the feel of the vinyl seat against his sweaty back as he slipped down a little so as not to be seen. He remembers how he worried the guy might spot him. He remembers noticing a vertical bulge in the guy's raincoat as if he were hiding a gun there, not a sidearm but a shotgun maybe, because that's what the shots sounded like they were from.

There was a moment when the guy stopped cold in the lot, actually froze for a second between a Chevy and a Buick, and Jerry wondered which car he'd get into. That's when he saw the guy's eyes. They weren't the cold eyes of a pro killer or the cool eyes of a veteran who'd seen combat in Korea or 'Nam, rather they were wild, frightened, the eyes of an amateur, a guy who'd never shot anyone before, and now he'd done it and now the only thing on his mind was to get away, hide, not get caught.

Jerry approves of the set of eyes I've drawn. He recognizes them, he says. Now, he says, all we gotta do is fill in the rest of the face.

I like the sound of that. Jerry thinks he's the one making the drawing and I'm just there to lend a trained artistic hand. In fact he's right, my drawing hand's now connected to his brain. The planchette effect has taken hold. With each stroke of my pencil, the shooter's face comes more clearly into view.

Jerry remembers how the guy's eyebrows were arched, that his eye-lashes were long, that his chin and lips were delicately modeled. Yeah, there was something sensitive and boyish, even pretty about the guy . . . if you can use a word like that. Kinda funny, since, as it turned out, he'd just blasted two people, spattered their brains and guts all over the motel room walls.

Jerry remembers more: The guy had a narrow nose. You couldn't see the top of his eyebrows on account of his hat, couldn't see the tops of his ears either. The ear bottoms were small, evenly rounded. But the eyes and chin are what stick most in Jerry's mind. And the mouth—yeah, that's coming more clearly now. A longer mouth than most peoples', and the lips thin and delicate. And when the guy opened his mouth—'cause he was breathing hard, breathing from his mouth when he paused there between the cars like a scared deer looking for a place to hide—you could see his teeth weren't in good shape. Surprising for a guy that young. Yeah, he was young, twenty-five, twenty-six at most. The skin under his eyes was smooth like a kid's.

I draw, refine, fill in. Jerry watches amazed as a face slowly comes clear on the paper the way a photographic image will slowly emerge in a tray of developer.

"Yeah!" he says when I set down my pencil. "Yeah, that's him! I can't believe it! That's the guy I saw!"

"Do you know him?"

Jerry shakes his head. "I don't think I've seen him in all the years since. But he's the shooter, I'm sure of it."

Mace comes over, stands behind me.

"Interesting . . . I think I may have seen this man."

"We've all seen him," I tell him. "He was young back then. He's changed a lot since. Back then he was lean, wiry, had a full head of hair—not that Jerry could see his hair what with that stupid, slouchy hat he wore. There was a hunger in his eyes back then, a wildness like Jerry says. But I don't think it was fear, more like a lust for power and success. He looks different now, but if you look carefully, you can see the under-lying structure, the set of the bones beneath the flab. Now he's sleek, bald, middle-aged, plump, content. But every once in a while, his eyes flash and you can see that old hunger in them still."

Mace is getting annoyed. "Quit stalling, David. What's his name."

"You know him, Mace. You too, Jerry. Everyone in Calista knows who he is. He's Waldo Channing's old flunky . . . toady . . . lap dog . . . lickspittle. His name's Spencer Deval, and this is how he looked twenty-six years ago."

SEVENTEEN

H e must have done it for Waldo," I tell Mace. "You read Barbara's diary. That's the only explanation."

We're heading back downtown. The sun beats harshly on the streets. A group of children, clustered around an open fire hydrant, play in the stream of water. Mace, driving, stares straight ahead. After a burst of exuberance back at O'Neill's, he's gone morose and silent.

"I know what you're thinking," I tell him. "A sketch based on a fifteen-second glimpse recollected after twenty-six years—any defense attorney could tear that to shreds. And even if Kate Evans looks at my sketch and says, 'Yeah, that's the guy!' it won't do you any good. She already worked with me, so she's contaminated."

Mace grins. "So what am I left with, David? An uncorroborated ID by a sleazy ex-cop who only happened to be there because he was trying to blackmail one of the victims. Two unrelated crimes taking place at the same time. *Three* if you count what Cody did to the Steadmans. Not to mention that Jessup and Barbara were up to their ears in that, too. I tell you, I could really puke. But I'd still like to nail Deval."

He takes me to a dark, working-class pub in Irontown that smells strongly of ale. A Forgers-White Sox game is playing on the TV. A small group of out-of-work laborers sit in gloom at the bar gazing up at the screen. We order beers, carry them to a booth, then stare past one another trying to figure out what to do.

I'm the one who breaks the silence.

"Waldo must have thought he was in an impossible position—*his* threat to expose Barbara's new affair to Andrew balanced by *her* threat to expose his blackmail schemes. A stalemate based on the prospect of mutually assured destruction. But a stalemate wasn't good enough for Waldo."

Mace scratches his goatee. "So he turns to his flunky, Deval, gets him to be his triggerman. How? What did he have to offer Deval to get him to do a thing like that?"

"Only Deval knows and he won't be telling." I try to cheer Mace up. "The way I feel about it, even if there's never an indictment, there're other ways to bring a guy like that down. Like a wrongful death suit by the Fulraine boys. Rumors, disgrace, all the stuff Waldo was afraid of."

"Yeah, that'd be nice, I guess . . . but me, I'd prefer an indictment."

When he goes to the bar to fetch us two more beers, I turn toward the window. The strong light outside is nearly blinding. Suddenly I flash on a possible motive. When Mace comes back, I try it out on him:

"According to the rumors, when Waldo met Deval he was a hustler on DaVinci. Waldo cleaned him up, then sent him to England for a year to learn how to talk. They lived together, Deval acting as Waldo's errand boy. Then there came a time when Deval started getting co-writer credit on Waldo's column. In smaller letters, of course, but still a byline. So I'm wondering—could that be what Waldo had to offer?"

"Kill two people for a byline?"

"Not a bad deal if you're hungry enough. Think about it: Tough Street Kid gets his hooks into Toney Society Columnist. Columnist picks up tab while Kid learns social graces. Then when Columnist feels threatened, Kid exacts his price: He'll do dirty job Columnist doesn't have the stomach for, in exchange for an assured future. He'll receive co-byline on future columns, inherit column when Columnist retires, plus house and fortune when Columnist dies. That's a deal a guy without too many scruples could go for."

Mace nods. "I'll check when Deval started getting the byline. But even if it was right after Flamingo, it won't make for any kind of evidence." He stares at the TV above the bar. "Still, it's nice finally to know, I guess."

TO FINALLY KNOW may be nice for him, but it's far from enough for me. I want Deval to *know* I *know*, want nothing less than to see him wriggle and flinch.

I drop into Waldo's at 4:00 P.M. No sign of him, but Tony assures me he'll be in soon.

"He stops by every afternoon to drink and finish up his column." Tony sniffs. "Just like Waldo always did."

I hang around the bar working on sketches for Sylvie's book. At 4:30 Deval shows up—slack mouth, shiny pate, crested navy blazer, yellow polka-dot silk ascot draped around his neck.

I watch him as he makes his way across the room, stopping at various tables to pat an important back or whisper into a receptive ear. Finally, with territorial confidence, he sits down at the table beneath Waldo's portrait, orders a drink, places a black leatherbound notebook on the table, whips out his cell phone, leans back, and starts making calls

I turn on my bar stool to face him, expose a fresh page, and begin to draw.

It doesn't take long for him to notice me. When he figures out what I'm doing, he reacts with a mild look of surprise. Then he summons the waiter, whispers something, and the waiter approaches me.

"Mr. Deval asks if you'd like to join him?" I look at Deval, shrug, pick up my drink, and move to his table.

"If you must draw me, old boy, at least do it up close," he says, showing me his best ironic eyebrow-twitching grin. "To what nefarious purpose do I owe this exquisite honor? For, to be frank, old boy, I've had the impression you've been studiously avoiding me."

I hide my revulsion at the highfalutin way he talks.

"Why Spencer! How could you think such a thing when all this time I've been in awe?"

He grins a little more to show me he's amused.

"What fascinates me is your role as arbiter here," I continue, wanting to puff him up with flattery so he'll be all ripe and juicy for a fall.

"But why draw *me*, old boy? What're you up to?"

Continuing to sketch, I tell him I'm doing drawings for Sylvie's book, and that he, being the local media guru, will be among the more prominently featured personalities.

A skeptical smile curls his lip.

"You wouldn't be intending to do me in, would you? Making me out to be the barroom buffoon?"

Since that's precisely what I'm intending, I show him my sketch. "See for yourself."

"Pretty mean," he says, studying my cartoon. "Got a real chip on your shoulder, don't you, old boy? Truly I don't mind being caricatured, but you needn't deny me my good looks." He grins again.

This is the moment.

"You *were* a lot prettier in the old days," I say, laying down the sketch I made with Jerry O'Neill.

He gapes at my drawing. "What the hell is that?"

"That's how you looked just after you killed the lovers at Flamingo. That's the expression on your face when you paused like a frozen deer in the parking lot across the street."

He stares at me. I can see he's shaken. "You're even nuttier than I thought. What're you trying to pull, Weiss? Going to let me in on the game?"

"It's not a game," I assure him. "I have this from an eye witness. Barbara was going to spread it around you'd been a hustler, Waldo didn't want that, so he had you kill her."

He feigns amusement. "Go on with your fantasy. I'm dying to hear it all."

"You marched in there and shot them. You thought no one saw you, but someone did. What I'm wondering is what Waldo gave you in return. Was it the byline? Did he promise you his column?"

Now he glares at me, pure fury in his eyes. "Don't know what you're up to, old boy. But if it's nasty you want, nasty's what you'll get."

I laugh. "Oh, gosh—the wicked columnist! What are you going to do? Slay me with your pen? Maybe a threat like that worked back in Waldo's time, but no more, Deval. Now it just sounds silly."

"How 'bout I sue you for every cent you've got?"

"I'd welcome a lawsuit. It'd be a pleasure to put you on the stand and watch you lie."

He snaps his cell phone shut, notebook too, sits back and studies me, weighing his options. Then, suddenly, he regains his composure. His fury abates, replaced by a crafty smile.

Watching the change, I find myself admiring his cool, wondering too what's going on in his mind. I see him clearly now. He's a totally self-invented creature who plays others as if they're instruments. When you don't respond to one tune, he adjusts, tries another.

"We have a lot to talk about," he says. "But this isn't the time or place. Suppose we get together later in the evening? Eight o'clock all right?"

"Sure."

"I'll pick you up in front of the hotel. Then we'll go someplace quiet and have it out."

"Should I bring a weapon?"

He smiles. "You've nothing to fear. But by all means bring one if it'll make you feel more comfortable, old boy."

PAM THINKS I'M MAD to go out alone with him.

"I know you think he's a coward," she says, "but if he killed those people he's dangerous."

"He *did* kill them. But he won't harm me. If he does you can tell Mace who did it."

"Is that supposed to comfort me?"

I pat her cheek. "Just think of yourself as my insurance policy. I promise I'll check in with you when I get back."

SPENCER PULLS UP on time in front of the Townsend in a big, black vintage Jag, the grand old kind with beautifully curved panels, finely restored chrome work, whitewall tires, and acres of nice-smelling interior wood and leather. The car, I think, perfectly suits his self-image—rich, luxurious, quintessentially British. A gentleman's car . . . except, of course, we both know Spencer's no kind of gentleman.

"Great Jag," I compliment him, strapping myself in.

"Isn't it? It was Waldo's. He used to call it 'Black Beauty.' "

"Part of your inheritance?"

"You know a lot about me."

"I've been studying you for weeks."

"Well, I'm flattered, old boy. I truly am."

He grins, then pulls into traffic. We drive through Irontown, then he turns into an unlit alley and stops.

"Nothing to fear. I'm just going to pat you down. Must make sure you're not wired, you know."

He asks me to open my jacket. When I oblige, he pats me carefully, running his fingers down my chest, belly, then along my sides and back to make sure I don't have a transmitter taped to my body.

"So far so good," he says. "Now comes the unpleasant part. Or perhaps quite pleasant, depending on your point of view. Be so good as to loosen your belt and slip down your jeans."

I balk. "Are you out of your mind?"

"Up to you. I can drive you straight back to the hotel if you like."

Reluctantly I do as he says, trying not to flinch while he pats me down below. But when his hand grazes my balls, I can't help myself, I recoil.

He laughs. "I wonder—does the gentleman protest too much?" He pats me on the knee. "You're clean. Zipper up, old boy. And thanks much for assuaging my suspicions."

As we cross the Calista River via the Stanhope Bridge, I ask him why his vocabulary is so pretentious and his accent so transparently phony.

"People think I picked that up in England," he says, "that I'm some kind of Gatsby type. But truth be known, I'm, well—just a bit affected, old boy."

He steers the big car along River Street, chuckling over the many layers of irony he's laid on. There's something exhausting about him, something in his manner that draws you in then leaves you feeling drained. It's the emptiness, I decide, the hollow core of the man. When you peel away the layers, there's nothing there but the raw hunger.

We follow the twists and turns of the Calista River, covered tonight with mist, then descend to the flat riverbank area where day and night the mills used to roar, belching thunder and eye-stinging cinders which gave the air a sulphurous cast and covered Calista, the would-be Athenian metropolis, with soot.

There's fog down here. The air, I think, has a special aroma tonight, the smell of summer air just before a storm. Spencer drives up to the gates of Fulraine Steel, then stops, waiting for the night watchman to show himself.

"Evening, Mr. Deval," the watchman says, emerging from his shack.

"Evening, Paul. All right if we go in for a while?"

"You're always welcome here, you know that, Mr. Deval. Just give me a minute to open up."

The watchman, a thin, crusty, unshaven old coot, hobbles toward the gate.

"You're known here."

He smiles. "Oh, I am, old boy. I come here regularly to ponder my past."

He gestures toward the watchman now clumsily working the locks.

"Paul was a steelworker. Worked for the Fulraines since he was a boy. Seventy-six now, long past retirement age, but he can't tear himself away. You don't often find such loyalty these days."

"Tell me something, Deval—why are we going in here?"

He grins. "Because it's dark and spooky, a perfect place to dump a body." He pauses, turns serious. "Actually, can you think of a more appropriate venue for what we have to talk about?"

When Paul pulls the gates open, we drive through, then make our way through night fog into the ruins of the steelworks. The broken buildings loom above us like the skeletons of dinosaurs. Spencer drives directly into an old smelting furnace area, roof now reduced to a girder frame open to the sky.

He parks, we get out of the car, then wander on foot deeper into the ruins. Indeed, I think, this venue couldn't be better chosen. What better stage for recounting terrifying acts? The deserted ruins of Fulraine Steel—crumbling brick smokestacks, shattered ceilings, blasted concrete floors, a virtual theater of ravagement and perdition. What better place for one man to open his heart to another, confess terrible past deeds. But will Spencer confess? Or is this all part of a game? Here amidst fog-bound ruined furnaces and broken Bessemer converters, old brick walls blackened by accretions of fire and smoke, does he intend to reveal himself or does he have something else, something unexpected in mind?

"As we were saying—"

"As *you* were saying, old boy. It was you, remember, who broached the subject back in the hotel bar."

He stops, inserts a cigarette into a holder, lights it, draws in the smoke, exhales, then crooks his elbow against his side, archly holding out the holder—his signal that he's now in play.

"Now let's suppose," he says smoothly, "that a certain Gentleman did something similar to what you describe . . . killed a couple in a motel, something ever-so-bad such as that? Someone hearing that story might conclude: 'Oh, he did the awful deed for his Lover . . . who was having a bit of a tiff with the Lady at the time.' This same someone might think that he, the Lover, I mean, hated the Lady sufficiently to wish her dead. And perhaps that would be true, perhaps the Lover *did* wish that. But he, the Lover, would never have had the cajones to realize such a wish. Wasn't his style, as they say. No, not the style of the type of man we're talking about, the Lover, I mean. His style would be far more devious. He might, for instance, send vicious letters containing old clippings, used condoms, pubic hairs, that sort of thing. So when you say—and, remember, we're spinning a tale here—when you say, 'Oh, the Gentleman did it in return for a promise of a gossip column from his Lover,' well then, old boy, I'm afraid you'd be way off the mark."

"Why did he do it then?" I ask, entering into the game, intrigued that he's opening up to me, repelled too by his arrogance, his apparent belief he can spin his tale harmlessly by concealing it within a stylized fiction. Still, I know, I must appear to believe him.

"Well, old boy—for money, of course!" Spencer chuckles. "Helluva lot of money, too!"

"His Lover paid him?"

"*No, damnit! Not* his Lover! You're still missing the point."

"Set me straight."

"Oh, I shall, old boy, I shall! Suppose someone else paid him, someone who truly had a lot to lose if the Lady actually did as she had threatened."

"I'd think the Lover would've had a lot to lose."

"You mean a besmirching of his reputation? You're right, that wouldn't have been pleasant, but the Lover could have finessed it well enough. Couple months vacation on the Riviera, then home to resume his column with a vengeance. No, *not* the Lover, decidedly *not*. You see, vicious as he was, the only way he knew how to hurt was with *words*."

"Then who?"

"Clever whippersnapper like you should be able to figure that one out."

And then it comes to me, and I feel like a fool for not having seen it. "Andrew Fulraine." Spencer smiles. "But how? I mean—I didn't even know you knew him."

"Knew him? I *fucked* him! And, believe me, it wasn't all that exciting either. He picked me up on DaVinci, gave me my start, introduced me to what one might laughingly call 'some of the finer things in life.' On that subject, by the way, Waldo could be most amusing. 'Yes,' he'd say, 'it's true, the best things in life *are* free, but I prefer the second best things . . . and they are *very* expensive.' Andrew introduced me to Waldo. Waldo specialized in Andy's 'leavings.' But, remember, we're not talking about me here. We're talking about the Gentleman. We're weaving a hypothetical yarn about—what do you call them?—archetypes, I think."

Yes, archetypes. . . .

"So Fulraine wanted Barbara dead because of the custody case?"

"I believe it cut a good deal deeper than that. But first let's get our characters straight. So far we have: the Gentleman, the Lover, and the Lady. Now we introduce: the Husband. Which brings us to the matter of the Husband's peccadilloes, as they used, so charmingly, to call them. Now the Husband, as you can imagine, did not wish his private habits known. He wanted custody of his kids, but even more he wanted his secret kept."

"The secret of his peccadilloes?"

"Yes! Those irresistible desires that sent him regularly to the most sordid sections of our fair city. He most decidedly did not want that exposed. He was, after all, a family man."

"And he knew someone who would take care of the matter."

"Let's say he knew someone willing to take care of the matter if he were paid handsomely enough."

"The Gentleman?"

"Good! Now we're back into our story. And yes, indeed, the Gentleman did do the nefarious deed. A whore, after all, is accustomed to performing special personal services for pay."

"Without remorse?"

"Not much really. A year on DaVinci has a way of toughening a boy up. Live that life for a while, you learn to do what you have to to survive. Of one thing the Gentleman was certain: He wasn't going back where he came from . . . no matter what."

"Did the Lover know?"

"The Lover did *not* know! In fact, he found the Lady's demise quite inconvenient. It spoiled all the delicious plans he had in mind, all the ingenious ways he was going to torment her. But, if truth be told, the Lover was a bit of a horse's ass. And the Gentleman was smart enough not to trust him. Not that his untrustworthiness was any kind of secret. The Lover was often heard to say: 'Never tell me anything you don't want the whole world to know.' Silly people who didn't take the Lover at his word nearly always came to regret it."

Spencer would like, he tells me, there to be no misunderstanding—

personally the Gentleman had nothing against the Lady or her Friend. It was simply a dirty job that had to be done. And the payment was commensurate with the difficulty.

Suddenly a bolt of lightning tears the night sky. For a moment, it casts a sharp, crisscross pattern on the concrete floor, shadow of the network of rusted girders above. A moment later the shadow fades, then the sky lets loose.

It's a summer thunderstorm much like the one that broke the afternoon of the Flamingo killings. As the rain crashes down, Deval and I exchange a look. Then, drenched, we seek out shelter, finding it in the alcove of a furnace where, crouching to escape the rain, we find ourselves but inches apart.

More brilliant zigzag tears against the night, cracks of thunder following ever more swiftly. But Deval doesn't stop, he continues to declaim, spewing out his story against the storm.

"You see, it wasn't the money per se, old boy. It was what so much money could *do!* What you've got to understand is that what the Husband offered the Gentleman was far more than a mere bundle of cash. He offered him a magnificent living. He offered him *a life!*"

Spencer extracts the wet cigarette from his holder. He turns boastful as he tosses it away.

"Earlier you proposed the notion that the Gentleman received his Lover's column in payment for the deed. To set you straight, the Gentleman *did not* receive the column as a gift. Rather he *bought* it. That's right, *bought* the column, first receiving a byline in smaller print beneath the Lover's, then little by little making the column his own. Through study and emulation, he learned which knobs to turn, levers to pull, in order to enter society. And, over time, his tongue became tarter, more sharply honed than the Lover's. People found his bon mots more amusing. By the last year of the Lover's life, the old man wore a look of defeat. His sources dried up. People considered him passé. Now they looked to the Gentleman for approval, turned to him for counsel, confided secrets into *his* ear."

The rain slacks off, the lightning passes, the storm quells as quickly as it came. Deval's voice falls too. We crawl out of our shelter. Now his tone turns brittle.

The Gentleman, he tells me, before agreeing to do the deed, pondered what to do if he were caught. He knew one thing: *He* would not fall upon his sword. If it became clear he was going down, he'd bring the Husband down with him. And so, clever boy that he was, he took steps to ensure proof of the Husband's complicity. It wasn't just the possibility that the Husband would disavow their bargain that drove him; rather something far more serious. For if the Husband was so evil as to employ the Gentleman to slaughter the mother of his children, what insurance did the Gentleman have that the Husband wouldn't later employ another to slaughter *him?*

Thus certain steps were taken, and a good thing, for over the years the Husband tried several times to renege. Whenever this happened, the Gentleman would remind the Husband of the hold he had, the means to send him to prison. Then as punishment, he'd require even larger payments.

As expected, the Husband would always relent, in the end making the huge final payment as demanded. So in that sense, at least, their pact was not Faustian, not one in which the Gentleman sold his soul to the Devil and then one day the Devil came by to collect his note. Rather it was a case in which the Gentleman performed a service for the Devil (i.e., the Husband), then used proof of their bargain to extract ever larger sums.

"You're wondering what that proof was, aren't you?" Spencer's eyes gleam in the night, "Remember how I patted you down? If the Husband had patted the Gentleman down, there would have been no proof. Perhaps even, for that matter, no crime. But in the story I'm telling, the scheme between them was recorded."

"Why're you telling me this?"

He shrugs. "It's just a story after all."

He stops speaking then as suddenly as he began. Storytelling time, it seems, is over. He turns, starts back toward his car. I watch him as he gets inside, then beckons me to the driver's window.

"Well, that's it, old boy." He smiles. "Time now for me to bow out." He starts the engine. "I'm sure you'll manage to find your way home." And then, feigning an afterthought, he hands me an envelope. "A souvenir. I know you'll make good use of it. Well . . . so long, old boy. . . ." And, with that, he raises his window, switches on his headlights, then drives off slowly into the fog.

I stand there staring after him, amazed at what he's told me, the cool manner in which he's told it, his strange, cool departure too. What is he up to? Why has he left me here? Why has he told me so much? Is this all some kind of complicated taunt?

When he's out of sight, I tear open the envelope, find a tape cassette inside.

If this is the recording he made of his deal with Andrew, why give it to me now? Why go to all the trouble of patting me down, telling me what happened in the guise of a story, then hand me what appears to be hard evidence of his guilt?

In the post-storm silence, I can hear the throbbing engine of his car as it makes its way through the ruins, then a short, sharp honk when it reaches the steelworks gate. I move out of the furnace area toward the river, hoping to catch sight of the Jag as it crosses the flatlands then mounts the road to the bluffs above.

I make it out finally, its perfect profile, as, headlights gleaming, it ascends River Street toward the Stanhope Bridge. A fine black shape moving smoothly upward through the night. Then, at the crest above the riverbank, it stops.

Good! Maybe he'll come back for me.

Hearing the roar of the engine revving up across the water, I get a feeling that's not what's going to happen. Then with mounting terror, I watch as the big car suddenly leaps forward toward the railing, crashes through, soars out into space, hangs in the air for a moment like a great falcon poised before attack, then plunges down-down-down toward the Calista River, finally splashing in the water, then sinking slowly into the iron-red muck.

*   *   *

CALISTA COUNTY COURTHOUSE, 12:30 P.M. Closing arguments in the Foster trial are done, the prosecution having methodically summed up its case, the defense having emotionally cast "reasonable doubt."

I've spent the morning distracting myself from last night's trauma by producing a dozen drawings, half of defense counsel ridiculing the evidence, half of the prosecutor pounding home his points. As soon as Judge Winterson completes instructions and sends the jury off to deliberate, all of us in the media circus troupe our way back to the Townsend to wait in Waldo's for the verdict.

Lots of rumors circulate around the barroom as to possible dispositions of the case. But as the afternoon wears on, another rumor snakes its way in, not about the Foster trial but about local society columnist Spencer Deval.

3:00 P.M. The first glimmer reaching Pam and me as we sit with Sylvie at the bar is that Deval's car was fished out of the Calista River at dawn.

A few minutes later, Starret stops by to tell Pam he hears Deval was involved in an old local murder case.

A half hour after that, Tony whispers that he's heard Deval was drowned.

"The cops were in his house this morning going through his stuff," Tony tells us. "Course to me it'll always be Mr. C's house. And that car! What a shame! It was Mr. C's pride and joy."

"What were they looking for?" Pam asks.

Tony gives us a "search-me" shrug. "Whatever it was, they found it or they didn't. I hear they stopped early this afternoon."

7:00 P.M. Just as everyone is chowing down on hotel sandwiches, a new rumor hits the room: the Foster jury has been escorted to Plato's for dinner, all jurors looking relaxed and relieved. This, coupled with courthouse rumors, suggests they've reached a verdict.

8:30 P.M. MACE APPEARS at the barroom door, spots us, gestures for us to join him outside. We depart Waldo's casually, search him out, discover him on a couch behind a potted palm in a quiet, rear corner of the lobby.

"It's all over," he tells us. "The voices on the tape check out. It's Fulraine and Deval making a murder deal, cold and vile, utterly vile." He strokes his goatee. "What I don't get is why he patted you down, then handed you that tape."

I've been thinking about that all day myself. "I don't think he made up his mind what he was going to do till the very end," I tell Mace. "Then, by giving me the tape, he forced himself to take the leap."

"But surely he knew he didn't have to do anything. He didn't have to talk with you. He could have gotten away with it."

"Of course you're right. But there was an instant yesterday in Waldo's when I saw him crack. One moment he was going to sue me, the next he wanted to talk. At the time I thought he was just playing me, trying out a different tune. Now I think he was making a choice he'd been considering for years. I think he'd gotten whatever it was he wanted out of life. He had wealth and power, but he knew he was a fraud. Then I came along with my accusations, giving him the excuse he needed to self-destruct. But being Spencer, he had to do it the arch-mannered way he'd learned from Waldo, turn it all into 'a story,' then make a big flamboyant gesture to certify its truth. Driving his vintage Jag off a cliff— that's so consistent with what he thought of as 'high style.' I think for him going to prison would've been worse than going back to DaVinci. Once he handed me that tape he had no choice, he'd passed the point of no return."

Mace raises his eyebrows. "What gets me is this was a murder-for-hire case and the real killer got home free. Fulraine hires this guy to kill his wife, gets custody of his kids, keeps his secret, lives a respectable life, then dies a respectable natural death."

"Remember what you told me about Fulraine, that he wouldn't have known how to hire a hitman?"

Mace shrugs. "I was wrong about a lot of stuff. And you know what? Now that this is solved, I hope I never have to think about it again."

✻   ✻   ✻

I OPEN MY ROOM DOOR at 6:00 A.M. and pick up the early edition of the *Times-Dispatch*. Most of the front page is devoted to the Foster trial, but at the bottom there's a two-column-wide headline:

TIMES-DISPATCH COLUMNIST COMMITS SUICIDE
WAS INVOLVED IN OLD FLAMINGO MURDER CASE

I quickly scan the story, pausing at the eighth paragraph:

> FSI Corp., formerly known as Fulraine Steel Industries, last night released the following statement by CEO Mark Fulraine, son of the more prominent of the two Flamingo Court Motel victims:
>
> "Speaking for the Fulraine family, we do not accept the notion that our father plotted our beloved mother's death. This latest attempt to foist the killings upon a man no longer here to defend himself is one more painful chapter in an awful family tragedy."

Near the end, on the follow-up page, I come upon this:

> Sheriff's Department Chief Inspector Mace Bartel mentioned the important contribution of freelance forensic sketch artist David Weiss, currently in Calista covering the Foster trial for ABC News.
>
> Weiss, a Calista native, is the son of the late Dr. Thomas Rubin, a local psychoanalyst who was treating Mrs. Fulraine at the time of the Flamingo shootings.
>
> According to Bartel, Weiss has been obsessed with the case since he was a child. It was one of Weiss' sketches, Bartel said, that persuaded investigators that Spencer Deval was the actual triggerman at the Flamingo Court Motel.
>
> Weiss, Bartel added, is well-known for his work in a number of high-profile mur-

der cases, including drawings that led
to the arrest of the Zigzag Killer in San
Francisco and the Saturn Killer in
Omaha.

Obsessed since he was a child. Yeah, I think, *they got that right. . . .*

CALISTA COUNTY COURTHOUSE, 10:07 A.M. We in the courtroom hold our collective breath as Judge Winterson asks defendant
Foster to rise and face the jury.

"We find the defendant not guilty."

My eyes, of course, are fastened onto Kit. The low-key demeanor,
sadly hung head, and glazed eyes all suddenly disappear. In a flash, her
body straightens, her head cocks up, her eyes bug out, and a wide haw-
haw grin stretches her mouth. The meek, soulful waif-defendant
becomes the gleeful scam artist. She throws her arms about her lawyer
and whirls him around.

At last I have something to draw! I sketch furiously, trying to catch
the scene in all its horrible splendor, knowing that if I can get it down
right, create a three frame series of close-ups of Kit's transformation, I'll
be able to tell the story of a murder trial gone terribly wrong.

Except for Wash, Starret, Harriet, and me, the courtroom empties
fast. Harriet waits respectfully until I finish up my drawing, takes one
look, purrs with delight, then rushes out. A moment later, Wash finishes
his and hands it off to Starret.

Wash and I glance at one another, then smile.

"It's over," I tell him. "Let's have a drink?"

EVEN THOUGH Waldo's is full this afternoon, people standing two and
three deep at the bar, the mood in the barroom is subdued. Harriet and
I, Pam, Wash, and Starret sit together at a corner table.

The buzz surrounding us is uniform:

Foster got away with murder; not only is she free, she'll end up with
Caleb Meadows's fortune. The only astonishing turn, everyone agrees,
was the way she revealed herself at the end.

"I've covered murder trials for twenty years and I never saw a move like that," Wash tells us.

Most surprising to me, nobody in the room appears to be talking about Deval.

I'M SITTING on Pam's bed watching her pack, waiting for the evening news. She's flying to D.C. tonight on the eight o'clock, then on to L.A. over the weekend. Since I'm booked on a morning flight to San Francisco, it seems we won't be spending a final night together. Or, viewing it another way, we already did that last night.

Her movements are rapid as she pulls clothing out of drawers and stows it in her bags.

"I wonder if I'll ever get back here," she says. "What about you?"

"I doubt it."

"Make you sad?"

"Not really. I don't have family here anymore."

She stuffs a sports bra into a side pocket of her overnight.

"Anyway, you accomplished what you came here for."

"Yeah, I did."

"And now you're feeling let down."

"Pretty much," I agree.

She finishes packing, sits beside me on the bed, gently takes my hand.

"So a rich, screwy young woman and a rich, decadent old man both got away with murder. So it's an imperfect world. Nothing new about that."

AFTER WE WATCH our respective news shows back to back, we descend to Waldo's for a farewell drink.

Tony's strangely cool when we take our stools at the bar. He refuses to make eye contact, barely nods when Pam requests our usual, a pair of margaritas.

"Something bothering you, Tony?" she asks.

"You better believe it," he mutters without looking up.

"Why don't you tell us?" She speaks gently. "We like you. Be a shame to end things on a sour note."

"I got no problem with you, Miss," Tony says, his eyes sallow, face pale as snow. "It's Mr. Weiss here's got me peeved."

"Because of what I told the papers about Waldo doing blackmail?"

Tony doesn't bother to nod or even to look at me, simply faces Waldo's portrait as he speaks his mind:

"Mr. C was a great man. You and some others here would like to tear him down, but the people who really knew him know he could never have done what you say. He was a great man and he will always be great. And now please excuse me, this is my busy time. Lots of clients waiting for drinks. . . ."

Pam and I exchange a look, I leave a hundred dollars on the bar, then we move to a table. A few minutes later, a waiter returns the money on a tray along with a brief explanation: "No gratuity necessary, Tony says."

Pam shrugs. "He still loves the guy. What can you do?"

EVEN IN THE MORNING I can still taste her final salty kiss upon my lips, the kiss she bestowed when I dropped her at the airport, along with her parting words: "I hope you call."

I check out of the Townsend early. There's a place I want to revisit before I return my car. I drive out to Van Buren Heights, pass the Pembroke Club, then stop in front of 2558 Demington, the house where I was brought up.

The place looks different than on the night I drove here from Izzy Mendoza's. It appeared moody then, spooky even, hulking and only vaguely outlined in the darkness. This morning the sun is out full force, sharpening the edges and brickwork, polishing the dark timbers recessed in the facade.

I look more closely. The front door has a dark reddish hue . . . just as it did the morning my mother, sister, and I left twenty-five years ago. It was winter then, a blizzard was raging through the Calista Valley, but there came a moment when we were seated inside our taxi, I in the front seat, Mom and Rachel in back, that I turned to look at the house a final time and sunlight suddenly broke through the slate gray sky and glinted off the cordovan panels of the open door.

Tears spring to my eyes as I recall the image of my father in his shirt-sleeves shivering in the icy wind, standing lean and tall and lonely in the doorway, a stricken look upon his face.

Peering at him through the passenger window, I wondered when I would see him again. Then he moved a little, the sun caught the water glistening in his eyes, and suddenly I felt hollow and turned away to face the windshield. A few moments later we were on our way to the airport, to our new life in Southern California, leaving Dad to face the winter alone and the demons raging in his heart.

SAN FRANCISCO: I've been back here a week, sleeping poorly, trying to impose order on everything I discovered in Calista, wondering too how the end of my quest will now affect my life.

Thinking has never been my best route to understanding. For me drawing works better, mapping my discoveries and insights on human faces. And so I have been drawing since seven o'clock last night, working at my drafting table surrounded by windows overlooking the city and the bay.

The sun was shining when I set to work. I paused at twilight to watch as darkness began to coat the buildings, bridges, and surrounding waters, draining away the colors, turning my view into a nightscape of grays and blacks. Then I set to work again, and, without my willing it, the planchette effect took hold. Once that happened, time had no meaning. With a good thirty or more Calista faces stored in my memory, I drew and drew, covering sheet after sheet, depicting scenes between the actors in the overlapping dramas nearly as rapidly as I could imagine them being played:

My shocked expression, as, seven years old, I stand outside a bathroom door hearing the sound as Becky Hallworth slaps little Belle Fulraine across the face;

Max Rakoubian's jolly smile while photographing Barbara Fulraine in his Doubleton Building studio, counterpoised with the crafty expression on his face as he betrays her by installing a camera behind the grate above her love-nest bed;

Barbara's grimace of ecstasy while making love with Jack Cody in his bedroom above the gaming room at The Elms;

Waldo Channing, left eyeball twitching, telling police investigators that Barbara Fulraine was some kind of slut;

Andrew Fulraine, cold as ice, promising Spencer Deval a fortune if he will but do him the kindness of committing murder;

My father, Dr. Thomas Rubin, pausing outside the door to room 201 at the Flamingo, hesitating, then discovering he has no choice but to knock;

Tom Jessup, possessed by passion and lust, daydreaming of his beloved Barbara when he should have been fairly refereeing my boxing match with Mark in the Hayes School gym;

Scuzzy Walter Maritz mercilessly beaten in a garage by Cody's henchmen while Cody watches from the shadows, a cruel half smile playing on his lip;

Me sitting hunched over my bedroom desk drawing cartoon after cartoon of happy smiling families, trying to blot out the shouting coming from down the hall as my mother accuses my father of having loved my classmate's murdered mom;

Tom Jessup sitting with the Steadmans in the basement recreation room of their house on Thistle Ridge Road, gazing at photos of little blond girls in their casting book, wondering how his life has come to such a turn;

On and on, encounter after encounter, scene after scene, all encapsulated in images . . . until, at last, I reach the double ending, the twin finale of suffering and blood:

A man and woman in a motel room have finished making love. Now they lie naked on the bed, bodies striped by light cast by venetian blinds, the woman explaining to the man why they cannot meet again, the man listening, feeling a crushing in his chest. . . .

A middle-aged man stares out the open window of his office as late afternoon snow drifts slowly by. He thinks about a woman he has loved who now is dead, and then how he can barely bring himself to return to the empty house where he and his family once lived in happiness. As the snow settles upon the ledge outside, clings to the bare limbs of trees, carpets the tops of cars below, he considers how he has brought all this grief and sadness upon himself. . . .

A *telephone rings in the motel room.* The young man hands the receiver to the woman, watches as she listens, speaks angry words, then hangs up. She points up at the ceiling above the bed. *They put a camera up there!* Her face is panicked. *They have pictures of us! Oh, God!* As he moves toward her, there's a sound outside. Both turn as the room door bursts open. A thin man wearing a dark hat and coat is silhouetted against the blazing light. He raises a gun. Feeling his intent, the lovers cling to one another while squirming back against the headboard. . . .

The man steps out the open office window onto a narrow parapet. It's dark outside. The cold night wind batters his face. The falling snow is so thick he cannot see the ground. He shivers in the cold, feeling powerless to resist the mysterious force he has studied professionally for many years, the force he knows as the death instinct, *Thanatos.* Balancing on the ledge like a gymnast on a balance bar, he pauses, spreads his arms, then swan dives ever so gently into the murk of softly falling flakes. . . .

The woman, seeing the gunman's finger tighten on the trigger, understands she is going to die. With that her consciousness blurs and she retreats into a dream state. She barely hears the first explosion, so deep has she withdrawn within herself. When the second shot comes, riddling her body, causing it to spasm against her lover, she involuntarily rises and falls, twists and turns, as the hot steel balls perforate her flesh. Then this woman, who has loved so intensely and unwisely, imagines herself astride a horse, riding, riding . . . and then she feels the horse breaking, breaking, breaking beneath her, until she and the horse are all broken-broken-broken into pieces strewn like shards upon the dark-shadowed ground. . . .

The man, soaring downward through the mist of perfect hexagons of snow, feels close to the woman in her death throes. He smiles slightly as he falls, imagining himself galloping beside her. He knows this sweet sensation must soon end . . . yet it seems to go on and on. And then he feels himself start to break, and he thinks: *The horses broke . . . and broke . . . and broke . . .* and then he knows that he too is broken . . . that the broken horses mean death . . . and then he feels himself falling into a dreamless state as he lies broken and dying in the soft, soft, cold Calista snow. . . .

THE DRAMA IS OVER. I put my pencil down. The planchette effect deserts my hand.

It's dawn. My bay window faces east, and the sun, like a great airship catching fire, rises out of the dark foothills of the sierra, projecting scarlet slashes across the morning sky.

AN HOUR LATER. my fax machine spews out a letter. It's from the FBI field office in San Jose. A twelve-year-old girl is missing, last seen hiking in the hills above Los Gatos. A man in a pickup was observed cruising the area. The witness, another child, seems shaky. Will I come down, interview her, try to produce a sketch of the driver?

I'll come right away, of course . . . prepared, too, to believe everything the "shaky" witness has to tell me.

7:00 A.M. Driving south, I pick up my cell phone, punch out a number in L.A.

Pam answers, voice groggy.

I know it's early. Sorry I woke you, I tell her. *To say I've been missing you is why I called. You said it yourself—that I wouldn't know how much till I got back home. Well, this is my eighth day back, and now I think I know.*

AUTHOR'S AFTERWORD

Calista, of course, does not exist . . . though a side of me wishes it did. It's an amalgam of various Midwestern rust-belt towns of my acquaintance: Pittsburgh, Cincinnati, Cleveland, with bits of Youngstown, Akron, Buffalo, and Erie sprinkled in. All these towns have wonderful cultural institutions, and most, after decades of decline, have made strong comebacks in recent years. In a sense Calista (state not specified) is my best fantasy Midwestern "Athenian" metropolis—with a terrific mahogany-paneled hotel bar ("Waldo's") presided over by a great media-savvy, fund-of-information barman ("Tony"), which, if it existed, would definitely be my hangout.

The fictional gambling club, The Elms, does not exist, but the holdup described in the novel is roughly based on the still-unsolved 1947 holdup of the Mounds Club in Lake County, Ohio, as described to me by relatives present that unforgettable night.

Finally, a word about society murders. Just as there is no Calista, there were no Flamingo Court killings, but in several of the real cities mentioned above there were homicides involving members of the "upper crust" that became great local scandals. I have tried to make David Weiss's and Mace Bartel's obsession with the fictional double love-nest murder of Tom Jessup and Barbara Fulraine a distillation of the real obsessions of local cops, journalists, members of the victims' social set, and, especially, of kids whose playmates' parents were involved in these awful crimes.

William Bayer is the author of the Edgar award–winning novel *Peregrine*, which introduced NYPD detective Frank Janek, the central character of four subsequent thrillers, among them the *New York Times* bestseller *Switch*. *Pattern Crimes* was also a *New York Times* bestseller. More recently, under the pen name David Hunt, Bayer wrote two thrillers featuring the color-blind photographer Kay Farrow: *The Magician's Tale*, which was a *New York Times* Notable Book of the Year and won the Lambda Literary Award for Best Mystery, and *Trick of Light*. Bayer lives in San Francisco with his wife, the cookbook author Paula Wolfert. Visit his Web site at www.williambayer.com